SO
GREAT
THE
PRETENDER

Paige Cotton

SO
GREAT
THE
PRETENDER

by
Paige Cothren

OTHER TITLES BY PAIGE COTHREN

Let None Deal Treacherously
Seeking to Know Her
Walk Carefully Around the Dead
An Academy Called Pain

Oh yes,

I'm the great pretender
pretending that I'm doing well
My need is such
I pretend too much
I'm lonely -- but no one can tell.

Oh yes, I'm the great pretender
Alone in a world all my own
I seem to be
What I'm not, you see
I'm wearing my heart like a crown
Pretending that you're still around

~ Hit pop song of the 1950s

PROLOGUE

The two cars drove up at almost exactly the same time. The drivers both stopped on the dirt road, cut their motors, and for a few seconds glared at each other intently. Then the older man slowly opened the door of his aqua Chevrolet Cavalier, stood erect beside it and scanned the area, his eyes squinting against the blazing South Mississippi noonday sun. A small white convertible sat two hundred yards away, across a plush field of grass, a continuous green velvet covering, interrupted by a dozen or so picnic tables and a few large live oaks covered with Spanish moss. A man, a woman, and two small children sat at a table beside the white automobile. From this distance the bearded, gray-haired slender Caucasian recognized neither the four people nor their car, easing a sudden surge of apprehension. What looked to be food spread upon the picnic

7

table guaranteed his peace of mind. Relieved, he redirected his attention to the car parked next to him and waited for the driver to lower the window.

The driver of the black Lexus 400, a well-built, athletic Chinese man, continued to sit in his vehicle, watching with some disgust the abnormally cautious behavior of the American. A small half-Chinese, half-Caucasian middle-aged male sat restlessly beside him, his nervousness evident to the larger man. "Settle down", the Chinaman demanded, turning toward him, his broken English, worsened by pressure from his government, identifying his foreign birth. "American blood make you scare."

"Not scared, just careful," his little companion retorted. "You ought to be, too."

"Why me to be scare? Your police scare—weak, too. I not scare of them. If they come, give to them money, then they go away, keep mouth shut."

"I'm not worried about the local police, I'm worried about the FBI—and the military police," the dwarfish man countered, his eyes widening, his voice elevating, reflecting deep concern. He wished his anxiety might impute a little wisdom into his large indifferent friend. "We both need to be concerned about the FBI."

"No difference from police", the non-responsive driver angrily declared. Reaching across his diminutive counterpart, he jerked open the pocket of the car, extracted a .45 caliber pistol and waved it back and forth in front of his friend's frowning face. "Show to them this and they all run—fast."

"Please, Mr. Chun, stop. Someone could see the

gun and call the police and we'd have problems we don't need and can't afford. What would your people say— and do—if we foul this up?"

Before Chun could answer, the slim American, who had been patiently but excitedly waiting for the Lexus' window to be lowered, knocked gently upon it. The Chinaman, facing his passenger at the time, jerked his head around as though the intrusion bothered him, and lowered the window. Saying nothing, he gazed intently at the gray-haired visitor who, upon noticing the pistol, quickly stepped backward, stumbling, almost falling. The muscular Chinaman looked again at his apprehensive passenger, smiled and scowled. "See, he gets scare, like all Americans. He scare to die too." Placing the weapon back into the car pocket, Chun turned back toward the recovering Caucasian, who now seeing the gun returned to its hiding place, cautiously moved back toward the Lexus.

Chun snapped with contempt, "I not hurt you, Mister American, you friend, you have what I want."

"I'm afraid I don't have it, Mr. Chun, not all of it, not yet."

The foreigner looked disgustedly into the laconic face of the man who had suddenly become even more of a despised adversary. Mild rage shook his beefy body, quickening his quivering voice and he challenged, "Why not you have it, Mr. American? When you call and say meet you here at Buccaneer State Park instead of hotel room, you say you have it! You say bring rest of money. Why not you have it? I want answer now!"

"I'm going to give you an answer, Mr. Chun. I

think you'll understand why I don't have it now. Can I get into the car?"

"Get in."

The nervous bearer of bad news quickly opened the rear door of the Lexus and collapsed into the back of the vehicle. The two men in the front seat swiveled around and looked questioningly at him as he took a deep breath and tried to relax, the picture of the .45 and consequential thought still pulsating in his demurring brain. He was a scientist not a soldier, and what he had decided to do, by its very nature proposed some danger. He knew that! But he was not prepared psychologically for sight of the pistol. That made him doubt—himself, Chun, whether or not he could pull the thing off—and even if he could, whether or not the risk was worth it. The quick expulsion of breath when he crumpled onto the seat of the Lexus screamed out all these things to a man trained to recognize the weaknesses and vacillations of other men, a red flag before a Mexican bull, a fifth of Old Charter in front of a fundamentalist Baptist preacher, two eighteen wheelers creeping side by side up an interstate hill, slowing all the vehicles behind them to a thirty mph crawl. Chun's loathing of the nervous American sitting reluctantly on the seat behind him deepened, and quickly deepened again, the contempt disfiguring his darkening face.

"Mr. Claiborne," whispered the communist spy, "I come not here to t'reaten you. The money I have for you, but you say that which you were to have for me, you do not. I 'tink you try to stop business deal." Holding a thick envelope up in his left hand, he continued, "Those

I represent not allow it—my country not allow it—I not allow it. You take part money before and I have rest of money for you now, fifty t'ousand dollar bills cash. You will do deal."

"I am not trying to back out on our deal, Mr. Chun. I want the money—I need the money, but I'm not the head of the Oceanographic Department, only a scientist who—"

"Now you say you ONLY scientist. When you contact us about discovery, you say you have, how you say, ah, ah"

"Access", the slight passenger in the front seat offered.

"Yes, access—you say you have access to all info'mation in Oceanographic Department at NASA about cancer cure discovery. Which true? You have info'mation or you lie—which true?"

"Mr. Chun, we believe we have discovered the cure for cancer, a chemical from a plant in the ocean, Bryostatin. But I am not the head of the department. Washington insists upon a few more tests. The tests were supposed to have been run by now, but for some reason they have been delayed—not for long—"

"How long delay?"

"Not long," immediately answered the scientist. "Probably no more than a month—maybe two. Neither I nor the other experimenting scientists have been given the final components nor ratios necessary to complete the formula. But we WILL be given them, and all of us at the lab have been assured Bryostatin will be the cure for most, if not all, types of cancer. As soon as I get the information, I will call you and set up a final meeting."

The old spy, torn now between accepting that which the scared American scientist declared or rejecting it, instantly assessed the situation. The man was a scientist, an intellectual, a brain. Though he possessed little courage, he had all the necessary information, or he would have, if what he now said was true. Chun's government wanted the formula, wanted to own the cure for cancer and the power and wealth certain to accompany it. China knew buying the formula through a spy would not prevent America from merchandising the product too, but America would be forced to do it through capitalist merchants, pharmaceutical companies which would be compelled to create large profits for the stockholders. China would extract the raw materials from the ocean, manufacture the product, and merchandise it—all with national labor, at prices which American drug companies could not come close to touching. He would wait—for another two months—or for six months if necessary—his country would allow it. But if the American betrayed him, then there would be a solution to that problem too.

"You say two months, Mr. American, then I give you two months. You not betray me, Mr. American—and not to call until you have info'mation."

The Chinaman's voice was slow, deliberate, forceful, but the American felt the "prayed-for" relief from the Asian's acquiescence. He got his two months. He did not understand the cause of the delay, why the work had been halted, but he believed his superior's promises. The interruption would be brief, then the experiment would continue—surely in two months—

"Mr. American."

—the tests would be—

"Mr. American."

The scientist heard Chun that time. "Yes."

"Mr. American, do not betray me."

"I won't betray you Mr. Chun. I'll get you the formula. I won't betray you. I know better than to betray you."

Before he got out of the car, the traitor looked in every direction. Seeing no one but the four picnickers, he slowly opened the door, conscious of Chun's eyes and the eyes of the passenger fixed upon him. Immediately after the American stepped outside the vehicle, the agitated Chinaman accelerated the car down the dirt lane, executed a U-turn onto the grass and sped out onto Beach Boulevard toward The Bay. The gray-haired, bearded deceiver glanced around again and saw nothing suspicious. Ten seconds later he turned his Cavalier in the opposite direction and moved slowly away. He did not want to attract attention.

CHAPTER ONE

There IS a parking lot on this beach, observed Patie, as he slowed his navy-blue Chrysler Town-and-Country van to a crawl and looked to his left. But he had not seen it in time to turn into it. Noticing several cars bunched up behind him, he sped up, saw a street leading off Beach Boulevard to his right, slowed down again and darted into it, conscious of the fact that a driver performing the same maneuver in front of him would have irritated, if not incensed him.

"Sorry," he yelled toward the scornful face of the man behind, who gunned his engine, whipped sharply around the van and glared, knowing the angry motorist couldn't hear but satisfied that a measure of retribution had been paid.

"St. Charles Street, huh?" Patie murmured out

14

loud as he waited for five more cars to pass. "Sounds like a replica in microcosm of New Orleans."

Glancing to his right, nothing was coming, so Patie pressed his accelerator, accomplishing a quick, illegal U-turn in the middle of Beach Boulevard. He drove the 300 yards back toward Old Town, turned into the almost vacant parking lot and stopped in the first parking space. One other car was parked there, an old Chevy on the far end of the lot. Its owners, apparently, sat bundled up in lawn chairs, on the edge of the water, an old man and woman, looking southwest out into the Gulf of Mexico, each holding a Coors beer can. Against the roar of the sea, or perhaps their own thoughts, neither indicated an awareness of the invader's presence.

Patie rolled up both windows, cut his motor, and stepped out into the cool, crisp, salty ocean breeze of a late, early-March afternoon. He punched the button on the door which opened his tailgate, revealing a set of golf clubs, a pair of well-used golf shoes, an old pair of Nikes and a knee brace with metal hinges on both sides. Sitting on the dusty rear bumper, he removed his nice Nikes, pulled the knee brace hard upon his enlarged, warped left knee and fastened it snugly with the four straps encircling his muscular leg. Then the newcomer to Bay St. Louis put his old Nikes on, sat facing the water, and like a needle stuck in a groove of a long-playing album, he repeated within the inner sanctum of his own mind the reason he had moved to the coast. Doubt, normally a stranger, tried to nudge its unwelcome way into his thought processes. "Maybe the possibility of danger causes that," the astute observer murmured to himself.

A flock of sea gulls circled overhead a hundred yards away and in chorus, dived like a squadron of fighter planes trying to land at one time, settling softly upon the sand. Farther down the beach, two large dozer-like pieces of equipment moved from the water's edge and stopped near Beach Boulevard, where late afternoon traffic still crept along slowly.

The reticent walker pushed himself into the van, and with his legs still dangling off the bumper, flopped backward onto the floor and lay there. The cool air blew across his bare legs and the sounds of the sea tantalized his eardrums in consort with the waves sloshing against the sand. He closed his eyes for a moment, breathed deeply and reflectively and murmured, "What th' hell am I doin' here?"

* * * * *

Reginald Patrick Corbin stood passively and silently in the kitchen of his 6200 square-foot Germantown home, which nestled in the middle of seventeen prime, tree-studded acres. His head drooped. Tears glistening in his sad eyes hung for a minute, then dropped to the yellow tile floor. He walked over to the counter, pulled a paper towel from the holder, and daubed his oft-broken nose. "I'll never hurt you again, Mattie," he whispered to the attractive, matronly woman standing in front of him.

"I know you won't! Patie, do you realize what you are doing?—AGAIN? This is the THIRD TIME," she retorted, jerking the paper towel from his hand and wiping her tears. "I will never go through this again. Something is really, really wrong with you."

"I won't argue with you, Mattie," answered her husband. "I came back to you this time because I believed we could make it in spite of the other two divorces. I was wrong. I'm sorry."

"You're sorry? You're always sorry! I've spent thirty years of my life hearing 'you're sorry.' Who is she this time?"

"There's no other woman, Mattie. I've told you that."

"No, probably not. You've been too depressed to chase another woman, sitting on the front porch, day and night gazing out into space. What's wrong with you? Why can't you be happy, or at least have the courage and class to act happy?"

"It's not you, Mattie. It's me—and the lifestyle we're living," with a soft and sympathetic voice the husband assured his wife. By now tears ran unimpeded down his face and hers.

The hurt wife took her husband's hand. "Sit down for a minute, Patie, there are some things I've never said and I need to get them off my chest." Still holding his hand, Mattie led him over to the round breakfast table in the corner of the kitchen, windows on two sides affording a view of the beautifully manicured front and side lawns. Vacillating looks of anger and frustration enveloped her face and Patie knew the amassed agony created by more than thirty years of marital failure, the half-of-a-lifetime effort at trying to homogenize water and oil, was about to explode from Mattie's heart.

He wasn't looking forward to it but she had a right!

"Patie, my entire relationship with you has been nothing but a series of bad choices, and that's my fault, not yours!"

Her voice rose in indignation and anger as she positioned herself to catheterize all the emotional poison of years of pain from her system. It was her hour, and nothing could stop her, short of the condemned husband walking out of the house. Patie knew it. She was an infantryman charging the beach at Normandy, oblivious of death; a mind elevated beyond the realm of fear; a football team which had decided to win the game no matter the cost—!

A team that won't be beat, can't be beat!

Patie leaned back in the chair, dropped his slightly graying head, and closed his damp eyes. Oh God—why can't I love Mattie? he silently asked. My life would be so much better and so simple. The sinner knew he deserved no answer. He had squandered many chances to love her, allowed selfishness and whiskey and women to rip from his heart any possibility of being happy with her, in his search for happiness. Whatever she said, he deserved and then some.

"The first mistake I made, Patie, was ever dating you. I knew better! Mister All-American Halfback!!" The strained tone of her voice reflected the deep contempt in her soul, a woman walking barefoot on the shattered glass of a broken heart, of travail.

18

"Bull!! Mister All-American!! I shouldn't have dated you. I did it on a DARE. I knew your reputation but I listened to all the girls in the dorm, rather than my own common sense. But no—I had to listen to them when they dared me to do it."

"Mattie, I—."

"Patie, just shut up, please, and listen, for once in your life—just shut up and listen. Give to me just once, the right to tell you what's in MY heart—please."

Patie raised his sorrowful eyes toward Mattie's distraught face and opened his mouth to answer.

"No," she screamed. "Would you please afford me the dignity JUST ONCE, of listening to me?"

He dropped his reluctant chin back to his chest, closed his moist eyes again and nodded. Lord, give me the grace and strength to do this for her.

"But the two biggest mistakes I ever made were going to bed with you and then marrying you. I KNEW BETTER! I knew it wouldn't work from the beginning but I denied my own intelligence," she sobbed deeply, the tears literally exploding from her already reddened eyes. "I KNEW BETTER—I KNEW BETTER—and I did it anyway—I did it anyway—Oh, God, I did it anyway." The traumatized wife's voice trailed down into silence, like a woman slipping into a coma, her body heaving as though the movement might dislodge the pain.

Patie could bear it no longer. He sprang to his feet, darted to her chair and tried to wrap his still-strong arms around his wife's quivering neck.

"Don't touch me, Patie—No—don't touch me—I

19

mean it." She pushed him away with the strength of a determined weightlifter. "I mean it—don't touch me."

"I was only trying to—"

"I know what you are trying to do. Don't touch me." Mattie started to stand and Patie knew he had to help her continue the conversation, as distasteful as it might be. Decency demanded it.

"Okay, okay—I won't—I promise." He quickly sat back down.

Mattie slowly stood, walked over to the paper towel rack and then to the kitchen sink. She leaned over, turned the cold water on, splashed water on her face and dried it with the paper towels. Then she very deliberately moved back to her chair. Standing beside it, she looked down at her dejected husband and gently declared, "I have to do this Patie, and you have to listen. You owe me that much."

"Yes, I do," he quietly responded, admitting that, even to himself.

"I knew our marriage wouldn't work but I made another bad choice. I was the only child of a wealthy man, you came from a poor family. I had no family and you had brothers and sisters and aunts and uncles and cousins. I was a quiet, reserved girl who had really dated only one boy, a boy who loved me and wanted to marry me. You were Mr. Football_"

The contempt surfaced in her voice again.

"—a hell-raiser who had broken a thousand hearts. You were an athlete and I had never played a sport—never! In my ignorance, you fascinated me, you and your football-playing relatives. I couldn't believe

Patie Corbin would be interested in me. I must have been sick."

"No, Mattie, you weren't sick, you were—"

"Just shut up, Patie. Let me finish. I didn't want to go to New York, I didn't want to be the wife of a pro football player. I just wanted to be a simple wife and mother, and live a quiet life, and own our own home. You were ashamed of me in New York. I wasn't glamorous enough—"

"That's not true, Mattie, I was never ashamed of you!"

"A woman can tell, Patie! A woman can tell if her husband is proud of her. You weren't proud of me."

"I didn't know how to show it, Mat."

"No, Patie, you didn't know how to DO it."

"You evened it up, you divorced me."

"I divorced you because you were having an affair with Amanda—my best friend, Patie—my best friend. What was I supposed to do—?"

"You did right, Mattie. I deserved it."

"Yes, you deserved it. I had to protect Emily and little Corb. Both of them loved Amanda. But then I went stupid again and remarried you. That was another bad choice—my second big mistake. And then there was Kimberly. How many women were there between Amanda and Kimberly, Patie?" the distress in the hurt wife's voice intensifying. "You never have told me. Did you tell Kimberly before you married her?"

"There were no other—!

"Oh, hell, don't give me that. I know there were. But the single, most idiotic mistake I ever made was marrying you for the THIRD TIME—the THIRD TIME, PATIE—the third time. Why in Heaven's name did you divorce Kimberly?" The anguished wife pleaded, tears flooding her cheeks. "Why didn't you just stay married to her? She was beautiful—she has as much money as I have—why, why didn't you just stay with her?"

"Mattie, you made the phone call to—"

"I KNOW—I CALLED—YOU—damn it," she loudly sobbed, her body heaving in rhythm with the vibration of her soul. "I know I called you, Patie," she whispered, lifting her deeply reddened eyes to meet his. "I loved you so much—so much. I kept believing you would change but you can't change. You'll never change. Go on back to your parties and your trips and ballgames and find somebody you can love; please before you die, and who loves you, and leave me alone—PLEASE— leave me alone." Her voice had quieted to a soft whimper, a pleading. She folded her arms on the table and rested her head, now covered with silver hair, upon them. Her aging body softly shook with laments and tears covered her crossed forearms.

Patie slowly rose to his feet. He walked to her chair, and slid his hand down the back of his wife's grieving head. Tears from his eyes splattered on her back and he sighed, "Mattie, I'll never push myself back into your life again—I promise. You'll never have to look at me again. Have Greg draw up the papers and mail them to me at Mother's in Laurel. She'll know where I am. I'll sign everything back over to you. Don't forget to take my name off the condo."

The old football player lifted his tormented head

and with the back of his large hand wiped the remaining moisture from his cheeks. He moved his hand down his wife's back and squeezed her right shoulder. Mattie's head still rested upon her arms, the deep sobs now reduced to slight ones. "Take care of yourself, mother of my children and grandmother of my grandchildren, you hear? You take care of yourself now." Then the fifty-six-year-old man quickly turned and started toward the door leading to the garage. His right hand rested upon the doorknob when Mattie called to him. "Patie?"

"Yes?"

"Patie, are you going to finish the football book?" Mattie's silver-covered head still rested upon her folded arms, her eyes closed, soft sobs moving her shoulders.

"Yes."

"Your children and grandchildren love you. Will you stay in touch with them?"

"Of course."

"Take care of yourself, Patie, and please, please don't ever call me again." Mattie's crying had stopped. Patie looked to see if she had raised her head, and she hadn't.

"I won't, Mat, I swear."

"You're not supposed to swear, Patie."

"Then I promise."

Patie hastily turned the doorknob, stepped into the garage, and walked to his van. He wanted to run, disciplined himself, and refused. With compassionate, or perhaps sentimental tears filling his eyes, he cranked the vehicle, backed out of the three-car garage and rapidly drove the one-quarter mile down his driveway to the street. There he stopped, threw the gear into park with the tears bursting from his puffy eyes again, thrust his head backward and at the top of his lungs screamed, "Oh my Lord, what have I done?'

* * * * *

"Kimberly?"

"Yes."

"Betcha' know who this is."

"Who wouldn't know that weird voice? Where are you, Patie, and why are you calling me?" The shock of hearing his voice cast ominous waves of nervousness into her response. She wondered if he had noticed, figured he had, and grew angry with herself because of it.

"Well, now let's see. Which part of that compound question do you want me to answer first?" Patie had heard the uncertainty in Kimberly's voice. "You've kinda' missed me, haven't you, Gorgeous?"

"Just answer the question. Why are you calling me? Does Mattie know?"

"Well, I've missed YOU too!"

"Yeah, right, you Bastard, I'll bet you have," she retorted, firming her voice, hoping THAT, —and calling him Bastard had reclaimed some of the ground which the shock had caused her to lose. "I can bang this damn phone down just as quickly as I picked it up, Patie."

"Gorgeous, have I ever shown you the best way to slam a phone down? No, I don't think I have. Now the first thing you want to do is put the receiver in the palm of your hand and—my mother—"

24

"Patie!"

"Make certain your fingers aren't wrapped around it because—and my dad—"

"Patie!"

"—if you slam the phone down with your fingers under it, it will—were married—so I can't be a bas----"

"PATIE!! PATIE!!"

"You calling me, Gorgeous?"

"Damn you, Patie, shut up. I know how to hang up a damn telephone. Answer my questions."

"At a pay phone in Germantown, 'cause I love you and you asked me to call you if I ever left Mattie and I have left Mattie and no, she doesn't know but it really doesn't matter because I have left her," he replied, speaking as rapidly as he could, deliberately running the words together.

Silence! "Gorgeous?"

Silence! "Gorgeous, you still there?"

"I'm still here, Patie. Just in shock."

"Gorgeous, was that sound I heard, you hit'n the floor? Now, Gorgeous, you get up off that floor, you hear?"

"I'm not on the floor and I'm not going to be on this phone much longer if you don't get serious. Tell me what happened."

"I'm serious, Gorgeous, I'm serious about you, always have been since that first date—you remember our first—"

"Patie, please." Kimberly's voice softened, she desperately wanted to know what had happened. Exhibiting anger hadn't extracted answers from him,

25

maybe gentleness would. She learned several years earlier not to challenge the man intellectually, having known no one faster with the spoken word. And she had never discovered a verbal wedge with which she could pry answers from him against his will, nor a device certain to move him from his basic prankish and sportive nature to one of a more solemn bent.

"I left her, Gorgeous, today. Just packed up and left."

"Why?"

"You know why. I never got over you. For a year and a half, I've been miserable as hell and I made Mattie miserable and everyone else. I just couldn't re-adjust to that lifestyle, Gorgeous. I missed ours too much." Patie softened his voice and slowed his words.

"Our what, Patie?"

"Our life-style."

"Our life-style. Is that all you missed? Our life-style?"

"Well, I missed you too, Gorgeous—one time I did—I really did—one time. I can't remember when—"

"Patie, stay serious."

"You WERE my life-style, Gorgeous. You weren't in addition to—or a part of—you were all of my life, you WERE my life-style."

"I've heard that before. I think the last time was the day before you divorced me," Kimberly replied, trying to retain the sternness in her voice, and her dignity.

"Now, you can't totally blame me for the divorce, Gorgeous."

"I don't know why not. You were the one who left

and filed," she dryly retorted, the tone of anger real this time.

"I know that, Kim," he explained, "but you have to understand something. My education was incomplete. I had never experienced the emotions of leaving the most beautiful forty-five year old woman in the country, who still looks eighteen, and rich too. Would you have me ignorant for the rest of my life?"

"Patie, where's the rest of your stuff? I know you couldn't get it all in your van!"

"I rented another storage bin."

"Where?"

"Germantown."

"You still have junk in your storage bin here, don't you?" Damn, she whispered under her breath, frustrated that she'd let that slip. He's going to know that I've been checking.

"Yeah. I love storage bins, I mean you don't have to clean'em, or cool'em, or heat'em. Just lock'em up and let the rats hav'em. And thank Billy for me for keeping you informed. Aren't storage bin owners sworn to secrecy like lawyers?"

Kimberly quickly changed the subject. "Where are you going, Patie, do you know?"

"You mean right now? Or when I die?"

"I think I know where you're going when you die—I mean right now."

"That's good," the ex-athlete laughed, "I'm proud of you, Gorgeous. Long term, the Coast. Short-term, I hope to come down there."

"You mean here—to this house?" she exclaimed.

"Aren't you excited?"

"You verbose meathead, what makes you think you can just bounce right back into my life again? I'm not a yo-yo for you to yank up and down. How do you know I haven't gotten involved with someone else? You can't just call me up and invite yourself back into this house, you arrogant goat."

"I can't be both! You're gonna' have to decide," he demanded, his artificial seriousness concealing the lightness of his heart.

"Both what?" she asked, wondering how he arrived at that demand from her declaration.

"Verbose meathead and arrogant goat. Now, I can be one or the other or I can even be a verbose goat or an arrogant meathead, but—"

God, why did I stay on the phone this long? she questioned silently, secretly in her heart knowing the answer. She just hoped the idiot on the other end of the phone line didn't but she knew he did.

"I don't know about you coming down here, Patie. Everybody in Vicksburg knows you and most everyone knows your van, if you still have the same one."

"I couldn't sell my van, Gorgeous. I'd have to sell the seat where you sat along with it. I just couldn't do that—unh, unh, —no way. Anyway, I'm separated now. It won't matter if I'm seen driving up to your house."

"It won't to you, maybe, but it will to me. You're not divorced," she argued, determined to display some resistance. "And I still have a LITTLE pride left."

"I'll wait 'til dark. Leave the garage door up and

let it down right behind me. No one will see."

The deserted ex-wife hesitated—for a full thirty seconds, her mind racing to extract sense from all that had been said. She wanted to see him but she didn't want to reactivate all the emotions and desires. She wanted to hear his explanation but she didn't want to be swayed against her common sense. He had left her and she was trying desperately to recover from it but a year and a half later, she hadn't recovered, hadn't made much progress in getting him out of her mind. She didn't want to trust him again, to be hurt by him again, but she wanted so badly to talk to him, to look into those wide gray eyes, those spaced eyebrows which curved upward on the ends, a family characteristic, she had learned. Her heart said, "Yes," her mind said "No." Why in hell, she thought, can't I ever get my heart to move over to where my mind is, why does my mind always move to my heart?

"Gorgeous? You still there?"

"Why do you want to come down here, Patie? Why can't you just let it alone?" The struggling female couldn't say "Yes," wasn't ready to say "No."

"Because I want to see you and I believe you want to see me. Besides, we need to talk about everything, eyeball to puss-, oh_, er, eyeball."

"You'll never change, you horse's ass," she blurted out, "you CAN'T change."

"Not when it comes to you, Gorgeous. You gonna' leave the garage door up?"

"Come on, Patie," with mimicked dismay she conceded, "but don't get here before seven o'clock. It should be dark by then—and please, if you see a neighbor looking, don't turn in, okay?"

"Want me to cut two holes in a paper bag and put it over my head?"

"Just be careful, okay? Promise?"

"I promise. See you at seven o'clock, Gorgeous."

* * * * *

The ex-football player pushed himself lazily off the van floor and gazed thoughtfully over the heads of the old man and woman, toward the sea. Two small sailboats moved east, heading to the bay—probably. Small white clouds seemed to be racing, as they dashed inland and another group of sea gulls searched for crumbs thrown from compassionate human hands. The salty wind had grown cooler, and the recognizable smell of decaying fish which had washed upon the shore infected the air.

"Well, hell, guess I'd getter get this over with," Patie murmured to himself as he stood erect behind his vehicle. "Sure hope the tide is out." He checked the car key in his pocket, reached into the van and grabbed a blue golf wind-breaker, yanked it over his bare head and slammed the tail-gate, making certain it, and the four doors, were locked.

Five minutes later the walker finished his stretching exercises, felt in his pocket again for the car key, and walked briskly toward the water-line and the old couple, some fifty yards away. The beautiful white sand lay loose under Patie's feet, increasing immensely the difficulty of walking. The breeze chilled his legs, bare except for the brace encompassing his left knee and he rejoiced that he had worn the jacket. One smart thing I've done today, he thought critically. If the tide is out, that'll be two smart things. Sure as hell don't want to walk five miles on this, as he pulled his two Nike-clad reluctant appendages through the soft obstruction. Why is this sand so loose? he disgustedly wondered, looking down with dismay. Noticing large tire tracks every four or five yards running parallel into the distance, he realized that the sand seemed to have been disked, loosened, probably by the two large pieces of equipment visible far down the beach over by the boulevard. Why would they screw up the beach? he silently asked. Sure hope the tide is out.

"Damn! The tide is in. I'm gonna' have to walk in this mess," Patie grumbled out loud. "Why in hell did they do that?

"How y'all doing?" the irritated walker asked, as he bogged by the old couple, neither, until he spoke, aware of his presence.

Jerking his balding head around, the man answered, "Fine, how are you?"

"Okay, except for this sand." Yankees, the Southerner thought.

The old man looked back toward the rhythmic sea. He didn't answer.

CHAPTER TWO

The sun had dropped to less than 45 degrees above the horizon, Patie reasoned, when he turned into it, straight down the beach where he would walk, or try to, in the ankle deep sand. "Forgot my sunglasses," he complained out loud, wondering if the old seagazers could hear him. "And I forgot to check my distance!!" He questioned why, after all these years of exercising, he couldn't remember to wear his sunglasses and check the distance before he walked. "Oh, well," he murmured, "I'll check it later. I ought to be able to eyeball two and a half miles pretty closely."

On days he walked, the retired football player walked five miles. But he couldn't walk every day; his knee wouldn't allow it. Wasn't supposed to walk on it at all, according to several doctors, one of them an old teammate from Ole Miss. "What the hell," he grinned, "I jogged on it twenty years after they tried to convince me I needed a knee replacement. Doctors don't know a hell of a lot more than anyone else." But when he challenged another friend's thirteen year old son to a hundred yard dash three years ago, he blew the knee out totally and had to wear the brace to power walk. Then he could only do it two days a week, no more than three. He was married to Kimberly at the time and his mad dash back toward childhood made her as angry as an old pit bulldog. "Don't know why you're so mad, Gorgeous, it's my knee. Besides, I outran him."

That little burst of immature explanation did little to assuage her anger. She looked at him with disgust, shook her head and exclaimed, "You're an idiot, you know that?"

"Unh Huh, I sho' is," he mockingly replied. "Would you show me how to do that?"

"Do what?"

"Look so teed off when you really aren't. I can look teed off when I am and I can not look teed off when I'm not, but I can't look—."

Before Patie could finish the sentence, his second wife, the wife of his third marriage exited the room, disgustingly. Her ire was genuine.

No sense of humor, the husband whispered under his breath. She doesn't have one drop—! How could I have married two women, neither with a sense of humor?

Patie was never able to answer his own question, and as time passed the differences between the man and his second wife increased until finally both came to believe they were insurmountable.

But the blown-out knee forced him to accomplish one wise act which the doctors had for years encouraged. He bought a Health Rider and an old treadmill, with a burned out motor. Gorgeous already owned a stationary bicycle. He elevated the tread-mill as high as it would go, shoving against the handle bars like a bricklayer pushing a wheelbarrow full of bricks up a hill, an exercise which, surprisingly, produced no pain in his knee. Five days a week, he worked out, either on the Health Rider or the treadmill. The other two days he walked. Rarely did he miss a day, and it paid off. His body was as hard as when he played, or at least he indulged himself in so thinking. He still weighed the same, he proudly boasted to his friends. The hand-weights and a hundred sit-ups a day helped, too.

Walking on a beach rather than the sidewalk or track somehow lifted the old football player into a festive mood. He didn't know why exactly, unless it was because he and Mattie had inherited a condo on the beach in Destin. Actually, her parents had left it to her when they died. The two of them kept it several years, spending at least two weeks each summer there, with the children or other couples. Mattie disliked the water, the heat, and the bikini-clad girls. She accused Patie of walking the beach to look at them, which he aggressively denied, but in a jocular way, which encouraged her to believe her suspicions were true. The beach produced a light-heartedness in Patie, and the girls, well, he had to admit the presence of certain excitement when he saw them. He spoke to all of them, especially those who were walking or jogging. But he spoke to everyone, once admitting to a male friend that he did so to camouflage his interest in the ladies. Occasionally he engaged one in a conversation and twice, or was it three times, a girl invited him into her condo, invitations which he readily accepted. Of course that was in his younger days, nothing like that would likely happen now, not at age fifty-six, although admittedly he looked much younger. Everyone told him that. "Good genes," they said. His stomach was still flat and his muscles firm and distinguishable, outlined clearly. When he wore shorts he deliberately walked on his toes, in order for his calf muscles to flex. Tried to remember to do it all the time, but never forgot when he was in shorts.

He remembered Kimberly, and he wondered what the power, the force, the urging inside of him was—that it could turn his mind away from her so easily. The promiscuous yearning had always been there, bubbling, fermenting inside of him, even when he was in junior high, the eighth grade, no less. It had increased in high school and controlled almost every aspect of his college life. Marriage was supposed to contain it, but it hadn't and now at age fifty-six the battle continued to rage.

Patie heard a Baptist preacher, a friend, preach a few years ago and the man of the cloth identified the urge as lust. The dictionary, though, had not distinguished lust from desire, not clearly at least, so the ministerial proclamation failed to help much. After all, desires are good things. One must desire to play football well if he's to succeed at it. Take away desire, and you eliminate effort and weaken performance. Besides, he didn't just desire sex. The older he grew, the less he desired it and the more he wanted companionship, a buddy. When he and Kimberly were dating, after his second divorce from Mattie, they seemed to have it. They laughed, and joked and kidded around with each other, but when they married, she expected him to become more serious. That wasn't in itself wrong, he supposed, but it meant a complete dismantling and reconstruction of his personality, something he found himself unable, or unwilling to do. A leopard cannot change his spots nor an Ethiopian his skin. Six months into the yearlong marriage, he stopped trying.

Patie had walked, he figured, about half a mile, and it was difficult, like walking in Mississippi mud, without the mess. And it hurt his knee, not badly but some—worse than walking on hard ground. The March sun was setting quickly and he would need to hurry to get his five miles before it set, although he probably wouldn't. The high tide washed all the way up to the soft sand, leaving him no packed area upon which to walk, slowing his pace considerably.

Small creatures darted across the sand in front of him, some kind of crab, he supposed. Dead fish lay still upon the water's edge every two hundred or three hundred yards, placed there by the power of the sea, their heads pointing toward land as though they swam fearfully away from violent pursuers, some half-eaten by carnivorous birds, which took flight in front of the human intruder.

The traffic still flowed upon Beach Boulevard

fifty yards to his right, and beautiful homes, all different colors, and shapes and sizes, with immaculate yards, lined the far side of the street. They continued as far as his eyes could see and he wondered which one belonged to Stephen Ambrose, the author of many of Patie's favorite books. He hoped he would get to meet the writer before leaving the Bay.

A large black pipe, perhaps three feet in diameter, surfaced from its white sand tomb at the water's edge, jutting out into the swollen bay, a shunt draining unwanted water from the body of ocean residents, the walker speculated. Stepping onto it and then over it, he continued slogging for another half-mile or so, where he approached a concrete drainage ditch, an open wound, which ran from Beach Boulevard out into the sea. It looked to be about eight feet across, too far for a braced-knee to jump, and full of water from the high tide, forcing Patie to walk around it—all the way to the street and back. The two large dozer-like machines sat at the intersection of the ditch and the boulevard. Attached to the back of them were the harrow-like prongs, which had loosened the sand.

Except for the small creatures scuttling across the sand, the birds, and the struggling athlete, the beach remained deserted. Probably the loose sand, Patie surmised, and the cold. He was again glad that he had worn his windbreaker.

Before him, from the drainage ditch as far as he could see, wooden piers extended out into the water, dozens of them, in every conceivable state of destruction, broken ribs of a giant, wooden sea monster. Some consisted only of round poles rising like grave markers out of the silt tomb. Several were separated, cut completely in two. A few still held onto the boathouses at the end of the piers, though all the structures seemed to be powerfully violated, boards ripped away by the breath of a mighty adversary. A number of them still retained their floors and those, Patie discovered painfully, because of the high water, required bending over in order to pass under them.

The sun rested considerably lower in the western sky before him, when Patie guessed he had traveled at least two miles. He looked to his right across Beach Boulevard and identified the house, which would serve as his distance marker. It was a large two-story, red brick home with square, white pillars. As soon as he arrived back at his van, he would measure the length of his walk.

He turned around, heading northeast and into a cold wind, estimating he would, in fact, get back well before dark.

The antagonized athlete, still fuming over the difficult walking condition of the beach, had just passed the drainage ditch, about a mile from the parking lot, when he spotted the figure jogging toward him, a good half-mile away, too far to tell whether "it" was male or female. Either way, he thought, It's as stupid as I am, maybe even more. Whoever it is, it's running in this mess, or trying too. Even at the distance he could tell the runner was struggling in the six inches of impediment, but showed no signs of stopping or even slowing down.

At three hundred yards, Patie decided the jogger

looked a little like a woman but it could be his hopeful imagination, not good eyesight. At two hundred yards his hopes intensified. At one hundred yards, he grew excited. And at fifty yards yards, he smiled—a real live girl.

At twenty-five yards he examined her. She had dark hair, not long but not short, curly and hanging down to her shoulders. She wore a gray vest-like halter, which melted into her upper body, revealing the clear out-line of her breasts, which were average like her hair, not big, maybe even small. Anyway, anything more than a mouthful is wasted. Her tiny uncovered waist looked to be twenty-four inches or less and like her arms, shoulders, and legs, was tan, even for early March. Her legs marked her as an athlete, small knees, larger calves and thighs. She wore black shorts and under them, yellow tights extending almost to her shapely knees. At twenty-five yards though, he still couldn't see her face clearly, partly because she looked down as she struggled through the sand.

At ten yards, the welcome female comrade looked up and into the admiring eyes of her male counterpart, who kept his locked into hers. A wide smile invaded her attractive face, as she focused large brown eyes onto his, revealing two rows of perfect teeth. It was "her", or at least she fit the partial description.

"Hi!"

"How are you?" she gasped with shortness of breath, still smiling broadly as she jogged past.

"Damn!" he exclaimed, hoping she heard, believing she had, no more than five yards behind him.

Don't turn around, Dunce, Patie warned himself. She's too close-wait-wait-wait—! He wanted to give the jogger time to look back, like the old Forties song declared—I was looking back to see if she was looking back to see if I was looking back to see if she was looking back at me--. Turning his head slightly toward the Boulevard, with the peripheral vision which had enabled him to evade tacklers years ago, he thought she slowed down and twisted her upper body around.

Now!

He was right, their eyes met again, she smiled again, turned back around and continued jogging, seemingly unembarrassed by the stolen glance, neither her own, nor his.

A hundred yards farther down the beach, the energized exerciser pilfered one more glimpse at the laboring lady jogger. She continued to move, still, away from him.

She has it, Patie smiled to himself. Cutest little rear end I've seen lately. Even at his age, when companionship meant at least as much as intimacy, he had to admit that legs and tails still appealed to him more than any other part of the female anatomy, always had. First thing he saw in Mattie, first thing about Kimberly who appealed to him and first thing he looked for in the girls in between. He had no idea why. Nice strong legs and well-proportioned rear-ends made faces more beautiful and personalities more desirable. Regardless of how pretty a girl might be, skinny, ill-shaped legs and a flat butt mitigated her appeal to him. A beautiful face lost its beauty to the old athlete when carried by thin, unshapely legs. I think I may be able to handle this, he thought.

Twenty minutes later, the exhausted walker reached into his pocket, pulled out his car key and punched the automatic unlock button. The old man and woman had left, probably in the Chevrolet, and the parking lot lay vacant around him except for his car. He flipped the tail-gate up, sat down on the bumper, quickly released the four straps on the brace, pulled his left shoe off and slid the brace off his throbbing knee, breathing a deep sigh of relief. Taking his right walking shoe off, he suddenly realized, she isn't in a car. She must have jogged from her home.

The encouraged man put on his nicer Nikes, took his windbreaker off, and hung it up behind the front seat. His t-shirt was wet and the cool, moist breeze gently forcing its way inland above the quiescent sea chilled him. He quickly sat down in his vehicle and turned the key. "Should have brought a dry t-shirt," he fumed as he cranked the engine. Then he backed up, pulled out of the parking lot onto Beach Boulevard where the traffic had gotten back to normal, set his odometer at 0, and turned his car into the red glare of the setting sun. A mile down the street, the retired athlete turned writer spotted the lone figure traipsing through the sand back toward the parking lot. Estimating her arrival in ten or twelve minutes, sooner if she turned out toward hard ground, he continued south-westwardly. The large house with the white columns suddenly appeared on his right and he looked at his mileage marker—2.2 miles-farther than he had thought. He pulled his van onto a side street a quarter of a mile past the large house, put it in park and reached for his moist wind-breaker and slipped it back on. Then he backed out into the Boulevard and drove slowly back in the direction from which he had come. The observant driver passed the straining runner less than a quarter of a mile from the parking lot where he once again stopped. He punched the tail-gate button, got out of the van, sat down on the bumper—and waited, his eyes fixed on the lovely, distant object slowly approaching him with her head lowered, searching for a firm place upon which to place her feet. He needed a point of contact, a conversational piece through which he might initiate a dialog and he had no more than three or four minutes to find one.

So far as the relaxed onlooker could tell, she still had not seen him.

CHAPTER THREE

The beach ended temporarily at the broad dirt pier, which extended from the boulevard three hundred yards into the bay. It continued on the other side, past St. Stanislaus Catholic School where Doc Blanchard played football in the early forties, past Old Town where several restaurants and gift shops balance on wooden poles above it, and stopped at the Highway 90 bridge.

The boulevard lay adjacent to one side of the parking lot, the pier ran down another side, and the beach bordered the other two sides. The comely jogger stopped where the beach ends, put her hands on her shapely hips and bent over, drawing breath like a victorious sprinter ten yards past the tape, thirty yards from where the lone spectator rested on the bumper of his van, watching intently. A minute later she stood erect, turned toward the parking lot, the only exit from that part of the beach, and saw Patie. The effervescent smile returned to her attractive, sweaty face and she strode through the loose sand directly toward him.

Patie stood, returned her smile, and walked to the edge of the asphalt. "Tough run, huh?"

"Pretty tough," she panted, not having fully regained her breath.

"You live here?"

"Yes—right down the street." She pointed back toward Old Town.

"Can I ask you a question?"

"I suppose so. You seem to talk well. You certainly MAY ask me a question." The smile remained on her face.

"What? Oh!! Ohh-kay! MAY I ask you a question?"

"Of course, but first I need to sit down and pull these shoes off. They're full of sand and they're killing my feet."

"Sit on my bumper," he invited.

"I think I'll sit on the bumper of the van if it's alright," Marti quickly retorted, limping toward the vehicle, not waiting for Patie's permission. She quickly sat down, removed one shoe and then the other, dumping a half cup of sand from each. "Boy, that feels better!" she exclaimed.

"Would have to—! I'm gonna' have to spread the sand to back my van out of here." He was standing three feet from her, leaning on the side of the vehicle.

44

She laughed and looked up at him. "It wasn't quite THAT much, although it did feel like it."

Perspiration had darkened her shirt and continued to flow down her face. Patie noticed she seemed oblivious of it. Unusual for a pretty woman, he thought.

"By the way, my name is Patie—Patie Corbin."

"I THOUGHT you looked familiar when we met on the beach," she blurted, looking up at him inquiringly. She had taken her socks off, revealing strong athletic feet, red polish covering her toenails. "You spoke at my high school athletic banquet when I was a senior."

"Last year?" he teased.

"No, year before last—I wish," she laughed a deep laugh, emanating farther down than her vocal cords—a genuine laugh from a face whose eyes were sparkling, two dark, almost black pearls, on a white velvet cloth. "Actually it was 1971."

"Let's see. If it was 1971 and you were eighteen or close to it, and it's now 1998, that means you are—."

"DON'T DO IT—DON'T DO IT," she squealed.

"I'll do it later when you're not around."

"I'll always be around—if not here, somewhere, I'll always be around. Course, after I die I don't guess I will, but that oughta' be a while yet, I hope."

That sounds familiar, the old jokester thought, like something I might have said.

"Around ME!" he corrected.

"Around you? Oh, Patie, I don't know about that! I can't be around you—not all the time. I'm married."

Patie laughed, profoundly, loudly. "Well, that

answered my second question—you're married. You never did give me your name."

"I don't think I can!"

"Why not?"

"Well, I don't know how I can GIVE it to you. 'Course if I could figure out how to wrap it in a box and—."

"TELL it to me then!" he corrected.

"Which one?" she grinned.

"Which one what?"

"Which name? You want my first name, my maiden name, or my married name?"

"I want the one you go by now," he pleaded, trying to control the amusement and amazement suddenly forming inside him.

"I never have gone by a name." Mock seriousness enveloped her face as she assumed a reflective expression. "Now, I've gone by many a shopping center I wanted to stop at, and a few dress shops—but a name? Naw, I have never gone by a—."

"Oh, hell," the old jester laughed, "Who's on first?"

"No, Who's on second—!" she responded immediately, almost before the words cleared his mouth.

By that time Patie was smiling broadly. Marti still exhibited a studious expression as though lost in deep, serious philosophical thought, part of a new, yet delightful challenge to the experienced jokester.

"I'm Marti Claiborne," she smiled, still resting on the bumper of the van, thrusting out her hand, which the grinning male quickly grasped.

"Humh—strong hand!" he mused.

"Milk a lot of cows," she quickly retorted.

"Yeah, I'll bet."

"You haven't asked me your question."

Patie had forgotten about the question. In the midst of the intellectual skirmish, the verbal encounter, more didactic than confrontational, he had completely forgotten about the question. "Move over, my sides are hurting, I need to sit down," he laughed.

"Please!" she softly requested, still smiling.

"What? Oh, sorry! Please move over. Wait a minute, it's MY van!"

Marti scooted over to one side of the bumper, pushed herself inside of the van a little, leaned back against the side and drew her right knee up to her chest, around which she locked her two hands. Then looking directly at Patie, who had just sat down on the other side of the van, she asked, "What was your question?"

Patie tried to keep his eyes directly on Marti's engaging face but it was difficult. She sat three feet away, one knee against her chest, the other leg still dangling outside the van and in shorts, notwithstanding she wore knee-length tights under them. As he twisted around to face her, his eyes deliberately swept across the lower part of her body and then moved to her face. He figured she had seen him look—women do, of course. They seem to notice every man who looks at them, even from behind. He hoped she had seen. If she stayed there, and continued to display a congenial attitude it would mean he hadn't offended her. Plus, it would indicate she had no fear of him. Yeah, he thought, I hope she did notice.

She did, and was surprised that it hadn't offended her. After all, he was a man, a well-known man with a charming reputation—no, she thought, he's a charming, well-known man with a questionable reputation. In a state no bigger than Mississippi, where almost everyone claims kinship, reputations spread. She had for years listened to friends talk about him.

Swinging his right arm toward the beach, he asked, "Why in hell do they disk the beach up?—Makes walking and jogging almost impossible, especially when the tide is in. The soft sand goes right down to the water's edge."

Marti looked the critic directly in the eye, holding her gaze there for a full ten seconds, the corners of her wide mouth turned up into a modified smile, a twinkle in her large dark brown eyes. "From what I have heard about you, you are a conservative Ole Miss Republican. Well, I want you to know you're sitting in the back of a van with a liberal Mississippi State Democrat."

"God, two people can't be farther apart than that," Patie exclaimed, "not even a capitalist and a communist. But how does you being screwed up three different ways affect the answer to my question?"

"Could you use two other words? I don't like to talk about that with a stranger."

"About what?—What two other words?" he quizzed, acting indignant, fully expecting, by now, a mischievous response.

"Being screwed."

He laughed. He didn't mean to—he wasn't trying

not to—it was completely unexpected, an unconscious reflex, a compulsive reaction. It emanated from an appreciative attitude, impressed more with her quickness of mind than by her turning the conversation to sex.

Her expression didn't change, the slight, confident smile still graced her face, her eyes fastened onto his, as though she were declaring, "Okay, Big Boy, what are you gonna' do with THAT?" She need not have wondered, his mind had conceived the response by the time she sounded the word "screwed."

Patie had employed that method of breaking the social ice many times, suggestive sentences, double-meaning words. It carried a danger, though. Once understood to have a second, or sexual meaning, the statement angered some women. Some it amused. He learned eons ago to walk away from the hostile ones, toward the others. Could that be her technique? Could she be applying that system to him?—For the same reason as he? If so, it would be only the second time in fifty-six years a woman ever did it to him, the first time for one so desirable. And the other one was twenty-five years ago while he was playing football. She could be enjoying the mental gymnastics only, however, and interested in nothing beyond that. Might as well find out, he thought.

"Yours or mine?"

"Yours or mine—what?" she asked.

"Place," he quickly retorted. "I'm already tired of being a stranger."

"Mine!"

That was easier than the old Rebel had figured.

He had, for years, insisted to his Mississippi State friends that four years of school with red-necks pushed the State girls toward Ole Miss guys. Of course, the future farmers usually responded in kind with statements like "Well, they sure as hell don't want to fool around with Mama's boys out of a liberal, liberal, liberal, liberal-arts school." But the 'necks must be wrong. This particular, attractive liberal Mississippi State Democrat does—fifteen minutes after meeting her, she had already invited him to her house.

"Where is it?"

"Maybe you ought to ask, 'What is it?'," she grinned.

"WHAT is it? A house?"

"Well, no, it's not a house. It's my favorite restaurant, the Bay City Grill. I'm offering to take you out to dinner tonight if you would like—and, oh, yes, if you have no other plans."

"You and your husband?" He smiled at her but he knew his voice probably sounded a little caustic, his disappointment a little obvious, though true to his elastic nature, he quickly recovered. Anyway, he hadn't failed—not yet. Being invited out to dinner so quickly after meeting a pretty woman was a good day's work, actually, even if the husband accompanied them, especially since it was her.

Marti's big brown eyes sparkled at him teasing, taunting, engaging, bewitching. She put her socks and shoes back on, swung her right leg out of the back of the van, stood, and stretched. "Got a little stiff sitting there," she confessed.

"So did I," standing in front of her he joked.

She ignored his suggestive remark, but retained her pleasant expression. There was no evidence of shock or anger. "No," she explained, "Just me. My husband is out of town visiting relatives in Maine."

"You sure about this, ah, oh, Marti?" Thank the Lord he remembered her name. For just a moment it had left him, floated right out of his mind. He almost got embarrassed, if that in fact were possible for the ex-athlete.

Marti noticed, laughed, and replied, "Of course not, ah, oh Patie," she mocked. "We have an understanding marriage."

"You sure?" Patie frowned. "This is a small town. You must eat there often. Won't everyone know you?" The old football player may have been a playboy in his younger days, but he wasn't an idiot. He wanted no more trouble than necessary, especially with a jealous husband, not at age fifty-six. Officially he had moved to Bay St. Louis to finish writing a book and he certainly decried the distraction of being vilified by an irate husband. Kidding around with another man's wife on the beach was one thing, and even slipping undetected into her house, but going out to dinner with her publicly? Besides, his attorney would throw a fit if he knew about it. Many Ole Miss fans lived in and around Bay St. Louis and the divorce would not be final for another two months, at least. The news about another woman might possibly filter its way back to Germantown, producing any number of unwanted problems, especially with his children and grandchildren. Surprisingly, even to him, a little common sense began to seep, however limited, into his usually imprudent mind. "Think about it a minute, Marti, are you really certain it's okay?"

"As certain as a liberal Mississippi Democrat, married to an indifferent husband can be. Maybe Ole Miss people have no guts!" she ridiculed, laughingly.

"Oh I have guts alright," the old running back argued. "I have LOTS of guts. I'm just not all that anxious to spill them out on a restaurant floor at the hand of an indignant husband."

"He's in Maine!"

"On MY floor then when he gets home!"

"Won't happen, trust me," she invoked. "I promise you it won't happen."

"I don't know that I've ever placed my life into the hands of a Bulldog before," the Rebel responded, "You want to meet me at the restaurant or would you like for me to pick you up?"

"Where do you live?" she inquired.

"North Beach Boulevard, on the other side of Highway 90."

"Pick me up then—that sounds like fun! Been ten years since I've been picked up."

"What time—and where's your house?"

"Oh, about seven thirty, and I'm going to jog home. It's only about a quarter of a mile and you can follow me in your car. It's easier to show you than to tell you." She turned and moved away from him rapidly. After ten yards she looked over her shoulder, smiled her broad, inviting smile again and yelled "Come on, Rebel, I'll race you."

Jerking his windbreaker off, he hollered back at her. "How in hell can I win, I don't even know where I'm going?" Then he thought to himself, that was an interesting comment—the story of my life in microcosm. He jumped into his vehicle, turned the starter, backed out and followed. She was already fifty yards ahead. He quickly caught up.

The muscles in the new female friend's legs tightened as she pushed against the pavement revealing clearly their enticing outline and the black shorts served only to cover her buttocks—they could not extinguish the seductive and magnetizing movements. The rapturous runner turned on Beach Boulevard, headed down a side street, then another and stopped in front of a small but inviting bungalow, perfect for two people, within sight of the ocean. The grass had been cut immaculately. Flowers, all kinds and colors, surrounded the house and filled the corners of the yard. She stopped on the edge of her seashell driveway and when Patie pulled into it, she motioned for him to lower his window. Leaning on the side of the van and breathing deeply, from two feet away, she looked him directly in the eye. "Think you can find your way back here, Ole Miss, or should I draw you a map?"

"Unh-hunh," he retorted, "got you breathing hard didn't I—just knowing I was looking at you from behind."

She smiled again, pushed herself away from the vehicle, and almost whispered, "See you around seven thirty. I'll answer your question then."

Patie smiled, raised his power window and

backed out of the driveway. He watched his new friend dart into the front door of her house as he pointed the van back toward Beach Boulevard. What question was she talking about? Beneath the fascination of her sprinting quick mind he had already forgotten that he asked her two questions, neither of which she answered.

* * * * *

The amused ex-athlete, quickly heading toward his newly rented condo, followed Beach Boulevard across the busy railroad tracks through Old Town of Bay St. Louis, or "The Bay" as natives refer to it. Cars were quickly lining both sides of the street, delivering hungry diners to the five or six highly regarded restaurants, which along with another five or six saloons and bars, gift shops, art galleries, and small attractive stores of all kinds form the quaint little city's historic district.

In front of the Dock-of-the-Bay restaurant, the impatient driver stopped to let another motorist back his large black Lexus into a parallel parking space, an effort which required several attempts.

Patie had eaten at Dock-of-the-Bay several times, once years ago when passing through the Bay on his way to a speaking engagement at a state convention of Mobile-Home dealers in Biloxi, and three or four times recently, when he met the owners, a man and his wife. He had taken Kim there the day she came down to help him furnish his condo, and the gracious couple had given him permission to write on the open deck part of the restaurant. The food had been delicious, the bread pudding "sinful," or as old timers often said, "Make you whup' yore' Mama to git' to it!"

Patie thought of his Mother and how hurt she had been when he told her that his marriage with Mattie had failed again; what a great Mom she had always been, loving and encouraging when few others did, times when he didn't deserve her support. He knew, now, even at his age, how she worried about his move to Bay St. Louis alone, and he was certain that she prayed for him every day. "I hope she does," he murmured out loud, "I damn sure need it."

Finally after three tries, the Lexus found its way into the parking space and Patie defiantly mashed his accelerator slightly harder than necessary, frowning at the other driver, who turned his head toward his companion and away from the impatient motorist, as he opened his door. "Damn foreigner!!" the irritated American exclaimed out loud.

Three hundred yards past Dock-of-the-Bay, the "would-be" writer passed Ulman Street Pier, a concrete and board jetty extending about two hundred yards to his right out into the bay. On either side of the pier, alternately, the city built several gazebos with seats. "A great place to write," Patie thought as he slowed down and glanced at it. Several people dangled fishing lines into the water, a few others, couples mostly, strolled down it.

Less than a minute later, the impetuous driver sped up to make the green light at Highway 90, continued less than a mile on North Beach, and turned into his new temporary residence.

The condo, only a couple of hundred feet from the water's edge, rested upon ten-foot poles, a precaution against high tides caused by hurricanes which occasionally slammed into that part of the Coast. The unit, one of six in that particular building, faced east across the water, toward Pass Christian, on the other side of the bay, two miles away. Close by lay the Bay St. Louis Yacht Club, one of many across the Mississippi Gulf Coast—in every town from Bay St. Louis to Pascagoula. A former Ole Miss teammate, who had grown up in Gulfport told Patie, "You may want to think about joining either the one at The Bay or the one in Pass Christian. They put on some pretty wild parties both places and you can meet some nice looking people there, Ole Miss people—women, Dummy, women. And some of them may even remember you—the older ones, heh, heh, heh."

"Not interested in women, old friend—going there to write. Besides, you old bastard, you and I played together—you're as old as I am!"

"The day you're not interested in women will be the same day I'm asked to be one of your pallbearers—and I damn sure don't look as old!"

Patie pulled into his parking space, opened the tailgate, extracted his knee-brace and windbreaker and climbed the twelve steps up to his elevated front porch. Unlocking the front door, he tossed his windbreaker over to the stairs, which turned once up to the two bedrooms, one of which he did not need, and bathroom. He flopped down on the second stair and pulled his shoes and socks off, placing them by the windbreaker so he would remember to take them up later; stood and walked through the living room, through the kitchen, and through the sliding glass door out onto his covered back deck, leaning the soggy knee-brace up against the wall so it would dry by tomorrow, noticing in disgust its awful smell. Gotta' wash that thing soon, he thought, forgetting momentarily that he had never washed clothes, nor dried them. Then he walked back into the kitchen, pulled a Coors Lite out of the refrigerator, retrieved a jar of dry-roasted peanuts from the kitchen counter, picked up the portable telephone and walked back onto his front porch. Easing down into his rocking chair, he glanced at his Casio Illuminator exercise watch and noticed that he still had an hour and fifteen minutes before he picked Marti up, time enough to drink a couple of cool ones, call Buddy, and bathe.

"Buddy?"

"Yes."

"This is Patie."

"I recognize that strange voice, old friend. How ya' doin'? Got settled in yet?"

"Almost. Haven't unpacked all the boxes."

"What'd you do about furniture, Patie? Your condo furnished?"

"No. Kim and I found a furniture rental place on 603 up near Kiln, you know, Bret Favre's hometown. They delivered it this morning."

"Yeah, I know Kiln. Been through there several times."

"Got bad news for you, Buddy."

"Bad news? What the hell have you done now?"

"Sunk to an all-time low. Taking a liberal Mississippi State Democrat out to dinner tonight—and she's married."

"WHAT? You're taking her OUT?"

"You heard me! I'm taking a liberal Mississippi—"

"Patie!"

"Yeah?"

"You've lost your warped, blood-deprived, vitamin deficient, meathead mind—you know that? If Kimberly doesn't relieve you of your gonads, that woman's husband probably will, and if they don't I know someone else who definitely will!"

"But Buddy," Patie teased, "you don't understand—she's really good-looking!"

"Won't dull that knife any, old friend."

"I know. I'll call you back in a day or two. Take care."

"You, too. Stay in touch—it's important—and you be careful. Oh yes, could you buy a calling card and call me from a pay phone? It'll be safer."

"Humh," Patie, considered, after hanging the phone up, "still have time for another beer."

CHAPTER FOUR

Marti had glanced over her shoulder unbelievingly at Patie pulling away from her house.
Looking out her front window she saw him turn
on the street which led out to Beach Boulevard and then
watched his van disappear around the corner. She
slumped down into an easy chair in her living room,
closed her eyes, smiled and emitted a loud, "Damn, I
can't believe that." Then reflectively and quietly she
whispered, "And I can't believe all the things I said to
him either—and that he said to me!! But wait a minute,"
she pondered, "lots of men say those things to a woman."
Then she threw her head back, looked at the ceiling and
exclaimed, "But nice women don't say those things to a
man—a stranger—whom she just met!! Damn!! What's
he gonna think of me? Oh, well, when he gets back over

here I'll tell him I shouldn't have done it—that will elevate his opinion of me a little—maybe."

The forty-five-year old professor was born in Aliceville, Alabama, the daughter of schoolteachers. Both her mother and dad taught in the local high school, and her father coached the football team. He had played junior college football in Mississippi, graduated from Mississippi Southern, before it became the University of Southern Mississippi, where he met Marti's mom. Soon after graduation, they married, got the teaching jobs in Aliceville and started rearing their family, Marti and her younger brother Ben. They were "church going" people as folks down South refer to them, Christians, and a very close, fun-loving family.

When Marti graduated from high school, she decided to study education at Mississippi State, only fifty-five miles from Aliceville. After graduation, she married her husband, who graduated with a degree in chemistry. She taught high school in Columbus, while her husband earned his master's degree, his doctorate, and was awarded a teaching position at Mississippi Southern in Hattiesburg. From that institution, Marti likewise earned both her master's and doctorate. That, of course, required a move to Hattiesburg.

A minute after the tired jogger collapsed in self-amazement onto the living room chair, she pushed her lithe body up, walked briskly into her tidy kitchen, opened the refrigerator door and extracted a half-full bottle of white Zinfandel wine and a small bottle of water, noticing the dirty breakfast dishes and unwashed coffee pot, two blemishes in an otherwise immaculate room. She set the wine and water on the counter next to the sink, reached into a cabinet and withdrew a wineglass, filled it two-thirds full, took one sip and gently reposed it next to the wine bottle. Then she turned the water bottle up and drank all of it.

"Well, better wash these dishes," she thought out loud. She rinsed them; dumped the coffee grounds into the garbage can beneath the sink; put the dishes and flatware in the dishwasher, and dried the coffeepot, wiping both it and the counter with a dishtowel. Then the housewife and college professor picked up her wineglass in one hand, the wine bottle in the other and walked over to the screened-in side porch. She pushed the door open with her trim hip, took three steps and dropped into a rocking chair, gazing out into the eternity of the sea. A gentle smile spread across her relaxed face as she reflected upon the scintillating events of the last fifteen minutes and she was amazed that she felt no guilt, absolutely no guilt, not even concerning Mac.

Still a little warm from running in spite of the chill in the air, and with her mind still locked upon her intellectual tussle with Patie, she quickly rose to turn the overhead fan on, sat back down and propped her feet upon the stool in front of her, not needing to jiggle her mind away from current events in order to do all that.

She usually noticed beautiful sunsets, but not today. Nor did she exult in the several hummingbirds, which hovered like miniature-feathered helicopters around the three sugar-water feeders, which she had attached to the eaves of the house.

Marti knew she was emotionally vulnerable. She

hadn't flirted with a man in twelve years, not since the affair in Columbus when she and Mac were having trouble—but today? She flirted. She issued suggestive remarks and she received them, without guilt, without regret. Why? she wondered.

She and Mac had, since moving to the Bay, drifted far apart, at least sexually and the thought suddenly exploded into her consciousness, I wonder if he would even care that I flirted! Probably, a little, but only because of the fierceness of the male ego, not because he REALLY cared. She wondered if her assessment was true or if she was only looking for an excuse. It's probably moot, anyway, she thought, Patie Corbin couldn't REALLY be interested in me—not REALLY. She smiled, "But he is taking me out to dinner!"

Her conversation with Patie had seemed so natural, so relaxed, yet very provoking. It had been fun, challenging his thinking, trying to out-flank him intellectually. He had a quick mind and she respected that, a mind unlike the static nature of Mac's—lethargic, indifferent, disinterested, sedate, at least toward her. She admitted to herself that his perceptive and sagacious intellect and rapid expression excited her as much as his ruggedly handsome, though scarred face and firm muscled body. She was a little surprised at the tingle in her lower abdomen, a feeling displaced for many years and suddenly she realized that her breathing rate seemed to have intensified at the thought of him—just slightly.

"How Dad would have loved to have met Patie," she whispered, unaware that in the inordinacy of her musing the words were spoken, rather than simply thought. Many times, as a young girl, she had heard him speak of Patie Corbin, great running back for the Rebels, mostly to other men in small groups before church, or at the country store just outside town where men gathered on Saturday mornings to discuss Friday night's high school football game and debate about Saturday's college games. Sometimes they laughed about his off-field antics, which surfaced from time to time. Mostly, though, they debated his football abilities and argued whether he was the Southeastern Conference's best running back. Never once, in her wildest dreams did she imagine she would experience a private social relationship with this football-playing phantom from her childhood past.

The sun nudging the western horizon cast a pink glow against the puffs of cotton-candy clouds drifting inland from the ocean and the gulf-breeze accelerated by the ceiling fan, had turned cold against Marti's thinly-clad body, jolting her back to self-consciousness. She casually glanced at her watch. "Lordy, it's already six forty-five," she exclaimed, "you gotta' get goin', gal!!" finishing off the remaining wine left in her second glass.

Pushing her chilled body nimbly from the rocking chair, the liberal, Mississippi State democrat flipped the ceiling fan off, and smiled when she realized she had called herself "gal." An unsuspecting man, any man, would quickly face the indignation and wrath of her liberated, feminine nature if HE did it.

Depositing the wine bottle back in the refrigerator, and the wineglass in the dishwasher, she moved down the hall pulling her jogging clothes off as she walked, dropping them there, continuing through her bedroom, into the bathroom. The warm water felt good against her symmetrical body, splashing upon her comely head, dislodging the caked salt from her burnished skin. She usually sat on the stool in the shower stall after her daily five mile run, but tonight she didn't have time. Even if she had time, she didn't want to be ready when Patie arrived—not completely ready, almost ready—ninety-nine percent ready. When he got there she wanted to be able to call, "Come in, Patie." And when he came in, she would declare, "Make yourself at home. The wine is in the refrigerator and a clean glass is on the counter. I'll only be a minute."

The college professor had just finished applying her make-up when she heard the chiming clock announce seven-fifteen. She wore little make-up for her age, a trace of black around the eyes, a touch of red upon her lips, and a slight shade of color upon her cheeks. Pulling her shoulder length auburn hair behind her petite ears, she pinned it up on both sides. Then she reached into her closet and drew out her long black linen dress, slipped it over her head, and buttoned it up the back. Moving to the front of the full-length mirror she observed, and she liked what she saw. The low cut gown fit tightly against her small but shapely breasts, angled down to her tiny waist, and flared slightly over her slim hips. It nudged the carpeted floor, but it wouldn't when she put her shoes on, which she quickly did. Then from her jewelry box she retrieved a set of earrings, silver droplets that hung down one and a half inches. She held them in her hand, glanced at the clock on the table by the bed, continued to stand, and waited. Two minutes later, the doorbell rang. "Everything is right on schedule," she smiled as she started down the hall toward the front door.

"—I'll only be a minute, Patie," holding out her hand for him to see, "I need to put my earrings on." Walking back down the hall toward her bedroom, in clear view of her wide-eyed escort, she bent over and picked her discarded jogging clothes off the floor.

Patie whispered, "Damn,"again just loud enough for her to hear. He couldn't see the smile on her face as she turned into the bedroom, nor could she see the one on his—but she knew it was there.

"Now THAT is a good looking woman!" Patie was still standing where Marti had left him. She had quickly attached her earrings and now stood directly in front of him, six feet away. She extended her arms out to each side and curtsied as his eyes swept over her from head to toe and back again.

"Thank you, Patie. Coming from you I take that as a compliment exceeding the narrow bounds of all Ole Miss expectations."

"Of my expectations that I could recognize beauty in a Mississippi State woman?"

"No—of mine, that you would admit it."

"I have ulterior motives," he quickly retorted.

"A conditional compliment, huh?" she smiled, looking her amused friend directly in the eye and shifting her weight from one foot to the other in mock irritation.

"Aren't they all?"

"Maybe in Oxford! Not in the civilized world!"

Patie tried to keep from laughing but he could not. Again he admired the youthful looking, lower-middle-aged woman's wit, her astute mind, her ability to respond instantly, with a smile. That, reasoned her admirer, indicated not only a lack of malevolence, but the presence of a healthy self-worth. No inferiority complex in her! And he was glad.

The ex-halfback had dated girls infected with an inferiority complex, as it was called then, an image problem. And when he was young, he had even noticed the characteristic in some of his male friends. He hated it. The enveloping emotions characteristically cast a defensiveness into its bearers, rendering them incapable of jesting back and forth with another person, afraid of looking the fool. And the psychological disease always impregnated its mournful carrier with extreme possessiveness, living midst the fear of losing a relationship. Beyond that, women and probably men cursed with the infliction often seemed to "get their feelings hurt easily," as those untrained in psychological behavior labeled it, and when its possessors observed laughter in someone standing apart, they usually assumed it was directed toward them.

Early in Patie's life, he resolved not to suffer that particular malady and when he was older, he determined that he would not fall in love with a woman cursed by it. Earlier in his adult life he had failed—but he wouldn't again. The girlfriend's enslavement to an unhealthy self-worth translated into her disapproval of his extroverted personality, a condition with which he would not live. Hidden beneath his gregarious exterior, the athlete secretly longed to enter old age with a companion of like mind, although his friends had not perceived the social metamorphosis occurring in him. Nor was he yet willing for them to see it. A fifty-year old reputation expires only with considerable difficulty.

"I'm under-dressed," Patie declared, the laughter leaving an ebullient twinkle in his large, gray eyes, made to focus, by her appearance, upon her.

"What do you mean, Reb?'

"Wa'l, look at you—exquisitely and beautifully dressed. And here I stand in plain 'ol khaki slacks, faded blue sports shirt, and a wide, out-dated leather belt."

"You look just fine. Besides I wanted to look nicer than a conservative Ole Miss Republican."

"You succeeded—this once. I'll be ready for you next time though," he challenged.

"Think there'll be one, huh?"

"I'll let you know after tonight."

She laughed, "Touche', Rebel, touche'."

"Finally!" he blurted out.

"It won't last."

"Probably not," Patie admitted as he touched Marti's left arm. "Ready to go?"

"Ready to go!" she affirmed. "Take me to my favorite restaurant." They turned to go out the front door but stopped as she fumbled for her house key in her purse.

"Which one is it?"

"The best one in town!"

"Dock-o-the Bay?"

"No—Bay City Grill."

"Bay City Grill?!? Don't think I've heard of it," Patie admitted, "but then I've only been here two weeks, actually only twelve days."

"It's not on the beach but only about half a mile from here."

"It's gonna have to go some to beat Dock-o-the Bay."

"Why do you say that? Is that your favorite?"

"So far," he replied.

"Marti, you sure about this?" the old warrior asked seriously, as the two of them walked out the door, across the front porch and to his van. "This is a small town and you've been here for awhile. If you and your husband eat at the, ah-ah—where are we going?" Patie opened her door, closed it behind her and walked around to his side of the car.

"Bay City Grill," she yelled through the closed windows.

Sitting beside her he questioned, "Yes, Bay City Grill. Surely you'll be recognized, won't you?"

Patie had moved to the coast for two reasons, two important reasons. He was glad he could live in Mississippi as distant from Germantown as possible. In spite of all his past erratic and irresponsible behavior, he really didn't want to be embroiled in a domestic triangle. He was concerned, too, about someone recognizing him. But Marti's situation presented a far more dangerous predicament to the experienced party-boy and he had been hoping her favorite restaurant lay miles from there.

Marti sensed Patie's concern and was a little surprised, it being inconsistent with what she had heard about him. "Probably."

"Well, then aren't you concerned?"

"No."

"Why not?"

"I told you earlier, that's the kind of marriage I have. Mac and I trust each other."

"You want to go to New Orleans? It's not that far and-"

"No," Marti interrupted, "I have to teach an early class in the morning and I really can't stay out THAT late."

"What if we go to a restaurant over in Pass Christian or Gulfport? Maybe The Chimneys?" Patie had acquired years of experience doing this sort of thing and he knew if Marti's acquaintances saw her with a strange man, they would discover his name—and besides, she would be forced to introduce him to her closer friends. He didn't want that or at least he told himself he didn't.

"Ashamed of being seen in public with me, Reb?" Marti challenged.

"Hell, no," he immediately answered, "but you'll have to introduce me to your friends and they will—"

"Know who you are? Don't flatter yourself, Mr. Ole Miss."

"You did!"

She smiled at the quickness of his retort. "You're right. Why don't I introduce you as Archie Manning?"

"They'll know it's not Archie—I'm too recognizable," he taunted.

"They'll know it's not Archie, but not for THAT reason," she rebutted with a twinkle in her eye. "Besides, as many people know me in Gulfport as here. I teach over there."

Patie had been sitting in the driver's seat, his door still open, illuminating Marti's beautiful face with the dim interior light. "Well, hell," he exclaimed. "Bay City Grill, Bay St. Louis, Mississippi, America, here we come—ready or not." He closed the door, started the engine, backed twenty feet out her driveway, and stopped. Looking directly at her through the gray light, brightened only by the reflection of his headlights off Marti's house and a distant street light, he placed his right hand on Marti's left arm and softened his voice into pretended sensuality. "I do believe it will be worth it."

"Don't you mean it damn well BETTER be worth it, Reb?"

"Well, yeah, maybe, something like that."

Both were still snickering when Patie pulled his van into the only parking space near the Bay City Grill. They opened their doors at the same time and the old Rebel, not quite shouting, exclaimed, "Shut that door, woman." Then he jumped from the van, sprinted around it and looked at Marti's surprised countenance through the window. He slowly opened her door, took her right hand and lifted her from the car seat. Her amazed expression had surrendered to a grin, extracting from him, "Damn, you're pretty when you smile."

"Thank you for opening my door, Patie. I haven't had anyone do that for me in years." Her voice was soft, her expression grateful.

"You are welcome, Ma-Dahm—the Cavalry has arrived."

Bay City Grill occupied an old brick building, part of a small strip of businesses on Blaize Street, a quaint, very interesting-looking establishment, reflecting the heritage of the old port town. It exuded an inviting appearance and several waiting diners stood in a group, stretching from inside the front door to the sidewalk outside and the two assumed their positions at the rear of the line. He turned to her questioningly, "You know, I didn't even think to ask you if I needed to call for reservations. Should I have?"

"I invited you out, Reb. I should have called."

"Marti, how are you?"

Patie and Marti, focused upon the potential wait to be seated, and each other, had not noticed the couple who had joined the line behind them. Marti confidently turned around, facing the other couple, smiled and responded, "Hello, Susan—Harry." Patie, who stood behind Marti and slightly to her right, moved farther right and continued gazing ahead, feigning interest in the movement of the line of people in front of him. His new female companion continued exchanging niceties with Susan and Harry—the children, work, up-coming Bay social events. When the conversation lulled, Marti touched Patie's left arm and the introduction which he knew was bound to come, did. "Ya'll, I want you to meet a new friend, Patie Corbin. Patie, this is Susan and Harry Dedeaux.

Susan smiled and Harry extended his hand, "Good to meet you—oh, ah—Pate, is it?"

"Close," the hesitant man replied, feeling his heart beat a little faster, "Patie! Good to meet you folks, too. Y'all natives of Bay St. Louis?" trying to conceal his concern.

"New Orleans," Susan answered. "Got out of the rat-race three years ago. Moved over here."

Patie heard the relief in his own voice, "Do you like it?"

"Love it," she said. "Of course, Harry still drives to New Orleans every day, but it's not that far."

"Oh, you own a business there, Harry?"

"I'm an attorney. I started a practice in New Orleans twenty-eight years ago and still practice there. Thinking about establishing an office up here, though."

While the four of them talked, the line had moved forward considerably and Patie became conscious of Marti and Susan, engaged in what appeared to be a serious discussion, having shifted slightly away from Harry and him. He heard Susan mention Mac, but he could not hear her comment nor Marti's response. It worried the suddenly concerned man, and he couldn't help but think of the Christian counselor he once heard say women could listen to three or four conversations at one time, an ability which few men possessed. Something about the tissue connecting the two sides of the male brain, the action side and the receiving side, being destroyed by testosterone, disconnecting them at about age twelve or thirteen. Female's brains, still connected, allow them to talk and listen at the same time, and even listen to several conversations at once, an ability which fascinated the old pro. It was one of the female characteristics which attracted him to women and augmented his desire for their companionship. Even now, he secretly wished he could eavesdrop on Marti's and Susan's conversation, but he could not talk to Harry and do so. The counselor was right.

"Ms. Claiborne, your table is ready." Neither Marti nor Patie, both partially facing the other couple, had noticed they were next to be seated.

"Thank you," Marti responded. Then turning back toward her friends she asked, "Susan, would you and Harry like to sit with us?"

Patie felt the blood drain from his face and he hoped the others had not noticed. Damn, Marti, he thought. Don't exacerbate the problem. Even though Marti might be in trouble, he wasn't—and he didn't want to be. At that point, they did not know him—but after two hours of conversation, they would. Please say no, he silently prayed, not knowing to whom he begged.

"Thank you, Marti—but we can't. We're meeting another couple who may be here by now. I'll call you tomorrow," Susan promised.

I bet you will, the anxious escort thought, I'll just bet you will.

The interior of Bay City Grill was as interesting as the exterior, a modern reflection of the historical culture. The cavernous room had walls of brick, unadorned except for the hand-painted silk wall hangings. The unfinished cement floor abetted the noise, which reverberated throughout the room. Young, attractive waitpersons darted about the area like bees around a bed of clover. A large fountain occupied the middle of the room and was surrounded by tables of varying sizes, each with a simple, burning candle and filled with merry diners. Grillwork fashioned of iron, reminiscent of New Orleans' French Quarter traversed the back of the room. The wall-length mahogany bar was occupied by the usual upscale crowd one expects to find in a nice establishment.

The two new acquaintances followed the hostess through the crowded restaurant toward their table, which seemed now to be at the rear of the restaurant, near the grillwork. Patie, not wanting to catch the attention of the other diners, kept his eyes straight ahead, hiding as closely behind Marti as possible. The entourage had moved only a short distance when the apprehensive athlete heard again dreaded words, which both worried him and excited him.

"Patie?? Patie Corbin!"

The mildly anxious man, torn between fear and pride of being recognized, stopped like a test car driven into a concrete wall, in part to open the gap between himself and Marti. He looked down into the face of an older man sitting at a round table with three others. Marti, who had slowed down when she heard Patie's name, glanced over her shoulder, smiled, and moved on behind the hostess toward their table, certain Patie would be uncomfortable having to introduce her.

"Patie, I thought that was you. How are you?"

extending his right hand and standing.

"Fine," the nervous responder answered, "How are you folks doing?"

"Great," the greeter replied. "I'm Brad Jenkins and this is my wife Mary Kay. We have seen you play many times. We're Ole Miss and so are our friends here. Meet Jim and Fran Michaels."

"How are you?" Patie uttered. He made a special effort to maintain his smile and confident demeanor. It was difficult to do and he was irritated at its arduousness.

Glancing in Marti's direction, he saw she had been seated at a table for two in the bar area. She was smiling at him and she waved, as if to say, "Here I am." He wondered what remark she would make when he finally got there.

"Where you folks from?"

"Corinth. Came down for a convention over in Biloxi. Been eating here periodically for many years. Great restaurant.

"Micky Slater is a good friend. He talks about you all the time—when you were playing together at Ole Miss."

"Yeah, he was a good one, a great end. We still talk occasionally."

"That's what he tells me."

"Tell him I said 'hello' when you see him." That ought to prove I'm doing nothing wrong, Patie considered. If I was doing something wrong I wouldn't invite this man to tell Micky he saw me here with a woman.

"I certainly will! That'll be next Saturday. We're

playing golf."

"Great," Patie exclaimed. "Good meeting you folks."

"Good meeting you, Patie," Brad said. The others smiled and nodded in agreement.

Patie turned and moved toward Marti, who was still seated, smiling at him. He knew the four back at the table would be discussing him, maybe wondering why his female companion didn't wait for introductions. What the hell, he thought. She could be my sister, his conscience immediately countering, Yeah, right.

"Sorry about that. Why didn't you let me introduce you?"

The hostess had seated Marti in the bar area at an elevated table for two, on stools. Her discomfited date had made his uneasy way through the back part of the restaurant and was climbing onto his stool. An amused expression governed her lovely face, creating even more of a twinkle in her large brown eyes.

"You got a kick out of that, didn't you?" he asked before she had time to answer the first question.

Marti laughed. "It was kind of funny, watching you squirm, Reb, afraid you WERE going to have to introduce me. I granted you mercy. You owe me."

"Good, I've already decided upon payment!"

"With what, Confederate money?" she grinned, at his answer and his quick retort.

"I'll tell you after a couple of drinks. By the way, would you like something to drink?"

"I've already ordered—a white zinfandel. I would have ordered for you but I didn't know what you wanted."

"White zin sounds good to me." Patie motioned for the waitress and gave her his order. Then he turned back toward the new friend sitting on the stool across the small round table in front of him. "Now," he concluded, "that we've maneuvered through the maze of unwanted recognizings, let's get back to what we were talking about?"

"And what's that?"

"Hell, I don't know. Weren't you paying attention?"

"Yes. I was paying attention to your lack of paying attention."

"That'll be the day," he smiled.

"It preserves the beach, I'm told." The mischievous prof changed verbal directions on purpose. She had already accepted the challenge of his mind and enjoyed hearing his rapid responses. But she also delighted in the quizzical expression on his face the split second before the old debater understood the question and thought of an answer.

"What does?"

"What do you mean, Reb—'what does'? I thought we decided to do all of this in order to talk about the stirring of the sand."

"How does stirring the sand preserve the beach?" quickly questioned Corbin, without admitting that he had temporarily forgotten about the beach, hoping she failed to notice, or at least declined to elaborate upon his momentary amnesia.

But Marti had no intention of deviating from this

intellectual opportunity. "Kinda' lost track there for awhile, didn't you, Reb?"

"Well, hell!" the old ball carrier exclaimed. "I hoped you would overlook that one." Then he laughed deeply.

"What are you laughing at? It wasn't THAT funny."

"It wasn't funny at all, Ms. Bulldog. I was reminded of something I hadn't thought of in years, when 'well hell' came out of my mouth."

"What?"

"An Ole Miss football story. You wouldn't want to hear it!" he declared.

"It couldn't be any worse than being out with an old Ole Miss football player!"

"May not be any better either. Wanna' hear it?"

"Sock it to me, man!"

"Hummm—" the storyteller grunted with raised eyebrows. "Anyway, back in the sixties when I was playing at Ole Miss, by the middle of the season only two major college football teams remained unbeaten, Michigan and us—"

"Us?" Marti interrupted, "us meaning Ole Miss?"

"Yeah, us. Well, one week Ole Miss would be ranked number one in the polls—then the next week Michigan would be. Finally after about the seventh or eighth game, Michigan lost one so the Ole Miss student body sent a telegram to the Michigan student body which simply asked 'Well?' and all the newspapers ran the story. The next week Ole Miss lost the game, so the Michigan student body fired a telegram back to Oxford.

'Well, what?' Ole Miss' telegraphic response was short and sweet but reflected the depth of the Rebels anguish. 'Well, hell!'"

"Well, hell!" the beauty responded.

"What?"

"Well, hell, I don't understand."

"The certain result of having absolutely no experience with being number one—speaking, of course about the school you attended, not your looks. That's number one."

"Great mid-stream recovery, Mr. Corbin."

"Easy to make when my life's at stake."

"All this and a poet too?" she exclaimed.

"Romantic, isn't it?"

"You folks ready to order?" Neither customer, each of whom was completely focused upon the other, had noticed the presence of the waiter who stood patiently a few feet away.

"Sorry," confessed Patie. "I didn't see you. Give us another minute or so?"

"Certainly. I'll be back in a minute or two."

Looking his companion directly in the eye, the old playboy asked, "Since this is your restaurant, Loverly, what do you recommend?"

"I always get the Curried Chicken Pasta, but everything on the menu is good. Whatever you order though, save room for their bread pudding."

"Really good, huh?"

"It'll be the best you ever ate."

"The bread pudding?" he smiled.

The attractive teacher hesitated a moment as her

eyes searched the face of her new friend. She noticed the slight smile on his face and his quickly acquired expression of imitated innocence. "Of course the bread pudding, what else could I—oh, never mind." Looking immediately down at her menu she could not suppress the grin. Neither could she depress her head for long enough to hide it from her examining male escort, who lowered his head in order to look up into her face. It seemed important that she knew he saw her smile.

CHAPTER FIVE

That was a great meal, Marti. Thank you for coming out with me, especially for bringing me to the Grill. It really was good," Patie somberly observed, momentarily forgetting his earlier concern, then conscious of it. Good company does that to you, he figured.

The two had finished their dinners, with coffee and a large bread pudding which they split. Noticing the time, Marti reflected apologetically, "Patie, I need to go home soon. I have an early class tomorrow and I have to prepare a little, else my students will know more than I do."

"Hey, no problem, Loverly, I'm just glad you invited me out. Thank you," he answered with an understanding voice. "I've had those kinds of days." He immediately motioned for the waiter and gave him his Visa wondering if he should. Credit cards leave a wide trail, cash doesn't. But a platinum Visa also transmits a loud monetary message, which he wanted his companion to hear, although he would never admit that—not even to himself.

After signing the ticket, Patie followed Marti through the restaurant, and he discovered he was relieved that his new Corinth friends had already left. Outside the two walked slowly through the cool, moist air to Patie's van parked around the corner and a few minutes later they sat in the Claiborne driveway, quietly enjoying the other's presence, a mood of quiescent ecstasy seeming to encompass them both.

"I had a good time, Patie. Would you like to come in for a little while?"

"Of course! Should I? I mean is it okay? You're married and your neighbors must be aware of a strange car in your driveway, the houses are so close together."

The old experienced Valentino, without even having to think about it, published his concern for Marti's reputation and he did it in such a way she could control the situation. He wanted to go in—he had exclaimed, "Of Course." If a danger did exist, as it well might and she ignored it by inviting him in, it would reveal, at the best, a growing romantic interest, at worst, foolishness. If no danger existed, he would have risked nothing by going in. Besides, the house belonged to her so the decision ought to be hers. Giving her an opportunity to reconsider, though, conveyed his concern for her, but it also illustrated his willingness to deny himself for her welfare. Most importantly, it might indicate an emotional involvement, a desire to continue—although not absolutely. He still might not know if she did so out of curiosity because of football and his reputation, he pondered, or simply as a friend, or because she was considering an amorous relationship with him, perhaps even a sexual one. She'll have to initiate, the romantic veteran resolved to himself, I'm not going to!

Instantly he wondered if his resolution not to initiate a sexual relationship extended from a fear of rejection or from a fear of offending. The latter, he decided with an invisible smile, it's been years since my self-worth was so fragile it couldn't handle rejection. But I don't want to anger her! Best that I should leave that decision to her, too.

The middle-aged charmer's thought surprised him. I must have changed. Even ten years ago I wouldn't have considered a woman's feelings, whether or not I had aggravated or embarrassed her. Fact is, ten years ago he would have proposed a sexual relationship by now, in very explicit language. If she agreed—fine—if not—fine. He would simply move on to the next one. But this liberal Mississippi State Democrat was different, though not so much in appearance. Others had been as beautiful, a few even more beautiful. But he had never confronted a female mind and personality like hers, as sagacious, as ebullient, as self-reliant. Already he had identified an ability in her to "take" as easily as she could "give" and to laugh at herself, characteristics seldom, in his observation coupled with physical beauty. He wondered if those attributes continued when she loved a man, or would they fade into a morass of defensiveness, jealousy, negativism. No, the aspiring writer concluded, she seems to be very real, very settled, very satisfied with who she is—what I see today I believe, for the most part is genuine—but maybe not! Who knows?! Patie, you've been around too long to be fooled and don't be cynical—give her a chance.

As quickly as the invitation passed across her amiable lips, Marti questioned her offering of it. What would he think of her? Would he assume—assume she wanted sex? She did, of course, and she could admit it to herself. After all, Mac had lost all desire for her years ago, four and a half to be exact, although she felt no present inclination to inform Patie of that, a relative stranger—and besides she needed to apologize for her comments on the beach this afternoon. It's just that— Patie is so easy to talk to, so natural, unlike Mac who had never teased much, none in the last four or five years, leaving their relationship polite, formal, serious. Oh well, she resigned to herself, the canary is out of the cage now, flying around in a cloud of joking, laughter, desire and maybe even lust, looking for a place to land, no telling where. The invitation has been given, maybe he won't come in—oh be honest with yourself girl, maybe he will.

"It's okay Reb, you seem harmless."

"What?—oh sorry. Guess my mind wandered a little," Corbin, shaken from deep thought responded.

"It really is okay."

"Vunderbar, and I AM harmless."

"Been to Germany, huh?" Marti had opened her

car door by the time Patie moved around to that side of the van. Fog drifted inland from the gulf mutating the street light into a full moon struggling to reveal itself through thin clouds, and the sweet scent of flowers carried through the air, nudged along by the soft ocean breeze. The confident paramour, sensitized and trained by years of practice, noticed, almost subconsciously that the neighbor's lights were still on. Maybe the chill would keep them inside the houses. If not, then perhaps the fog might choke back their view.

"A couple of times, have you?" the escort asked with a touch of vanity, reaching to help his pretty companion out of the van. Marti swung both legs out simultaneously.

"Damn long dress!" her admirer exclaimed. "And I had good position, too!"

Outwardly disregarding his comment but acutely aware of it, the smiling beauty, standing now outside the van, very close to the ex-athlete who still held her right hand with his left one, reflected, "No, but I've always wanted to see Germany and the rest of Europe. Just never had the chance."

The old enamorer, his eyes locked into hers, stood his ground for ten seconds or so. Trained in the ways of women, her body only twelve inches from his, activated his mental computer, recording her every move and word, no matter how slight or brief. She returned his gaze. She exhibited no discomposure. She left her hand in his. And she smiled—that same exuberant smile which had graced her alluring face on the beach and then at the restaurant.

"And I would bet you will go to Europe someday," he surmised, releasing her hand.

At the door, Corbin hesitated again and when Marti inserted the key he asked "Are you absolutely certain about this?" knowing his delay and his question displayed both discipline and concern, however artificial each might be.

"Only if you want to, Ole Miss. Anyway I thought running backs made a hole whether there was one there or not."

"Marti?"

"Yes" she answered, flipping the light on inside the kitchen door.

"Marti?"

"Yes?!?" turning toward him quizzically.

"I'll give you a chance to rephrase that if you'd like."

"What?" she questioned.

"That comment about me—making a hole."

"That's kind of a stretch, isn't it Reb?"

"Not if my purpose was to bend the conversation in that direction."

"All of which reminds me of an explanation I need to make, maybe an apology."

"To me?" he asked. They were standing in the kitchen. She reached toward the refrigerator and removed a half-filled bottle of white wine and a wine glass from the cabinet.

"Want some more white zin?"

"No thank you, Loverly. But I would like a drink."

"What would you like?"

"Either a Yellow Bird or a Singapore Sling," he teased.

"Never heard of either one of them."

"Probably don't serve them at the Crossroads."

"What would an Ole Miss Rebel know about the Crossroads?"

"Oh, I used to slip off to the Crossroads occasionally when I had a date with a girl from the "W"."

By that time, Marti was standing in the middle of the kitchen, sipping her wine. Patie was leaning against a counter, his arms crossed. Her kitchen was neat and very clean. Decorative wine and bourbon bottles lined the tops of the cabinets. The opposite side of the counter faced the living and dining area and served as a breakfast bar. Several stools lined the counter on the living room side.

"Well since I obviously cannot mix you a yellow—ah, yellow—"

"Bird!"

"Yes, a Yellow Bird or a—a—"

"Singapore Sling!"

"Singapore Sling, can I get you anything else?"

"Well, then I'll take that good old Rebel substitute—bourbon and coke."

"You want to mix it, Reb, or would you like me to—."

"We'll form a team. You hand me a glass of ice, the bourbon, the coke, and a napkin and I'll mix it."

"Deal!" she exclaimed.

A few minutes later the two of them sat in her living room, itself a study in beautiful antiques, she on a small chair. Everything in the room seemed to belong to an earlier time and only when the former athlete sat down upon a settee did he notice the armoire, the desk, the small table in front of the curved back sofa with carved feet like eagle's claws clutching stolen eggs, all beautiful, old, and probably valuable, some perhaps only to her, inheritances from parents and grandparents. Several softly faded patterned rugs partly covered the polished hardwood floor. The small modern television set looked terribly out of place tucked back onto a shelf of the armoire and the small family pictures resting in front of the screen affirmed its insignificance to the residents.

"Can I ask you a question?" the man, anxious, though trying not to be, asked his new hospitable friend.

"Of course," she replied, "but first let me turn on some music." She walked over to the stereo, opened the door and placed a disk into the machine, soft, candle-light dinner music. Taking her place back on the chair, she crossed her legs beneath the floor length gown, positioned her glass of wine with both hands on her knee, looked him directly in the eye, and with mocked sensuality whispered, "Now, ask."

Finding it absolutely impossible to refrain from smiling at Marti's feigned sigh of lasciviousness, Corbin attempted to deliver seriousness into the conversation. "Tell me about your marriage and make me understand why it's okay for you, a married woman, to go out with me in the midst of your friends and then invite me into your home—openly—late at night."

"Please?"

"Yes, sorry! Please!"

"It's really not all that late," she joked.

"That's true but I need to understand. Would you explain it to me—please? Do you have an 'open' marriage?" Patie was cautious of treading upon another man's turf in plain view of other people—especially now. The relaxed expression on his face belied the fragment of anxiety in his mind. The excessive concern momentarily surprised even him.

"Mac and I trust one another," the attractive wife explained softly. "His closest friends are the women with whom he works, and some of my best friends are men. This is a second marriage for both of us and we agreed from the beginning that jealousy would not be a part of it."

"You've been married BEFORE then?"

"Yes. That's what a second marriage means, Ole Miss."

"Are the two of you close?" he quizzed.

"Mac has been my best friend and I believe I am his."

"What would he do and say if he walked into the house right now. Be honest."

"Oh, he would probably smile, give me a hug and introduce himself to you. We're both liberals, remember? He would not assume we were doing anything wrong, which we aren't."

"That's true, but are you saying he would never question my presence here under these conditions and never ask you about it—after I've left."

"NO! Of course not, he had better not," the slightly vexed woman quickly answered, a diminutive frown instantly negating the smile, which just as suddenly returned. "Is that hard for a conservative Ole Miss Republican to understand?"

The woman-wise man raised his eyebrows, smiled and lifted his open-palm hands in amazement and let them fall back to his legs in bafflement. "I don't know—I guess so. It's just that I've never encountered that attitude in people with your, your, well I'll just go ahead and say it—your social status and intelligence. I mean, you're not a bimbo. You're probably smarter than I'll ever hope to—"

"You passing judgment on me?" the smiling female interrupted.

"No, not really. Those attributes are self-evident."

"Thank you, Reb. I take that medley of compliments as—compliments."

This is the right time, the middle-aged romancer thought to himself—NOW!

"What would Mac do if he discovered our friendship had advanced to much more than that?"

"Which again reminds me of something I need to say," ignoring his question. "This afternoon I was pretty aggressive in talking to you, at the time a perfect stranger. I hope you don't think less of me for it."

"You mean our kidding and joking—about sex?"

"Yes."

"Of course not. I was involved just as much as you—anyway, I love it," he forcefully declared. "Don't stop now."

Marti laughed, took a sip of wine, and looked almost admiringly at the old athlete. "Thank you."

"You're welcome. You sure you're as liberal as you say?" he teased. "True liberals, at least social liberals, don't often apologize for liberal behavior."

"I try to be."

"What do you think Mac would do—if he caught us having an affair? I know that's not possible, it's a hypothetical question. Given all that you've said about your trust, etcetera, I just wondered."

The question did not seem to shock, nor embarrass nor offend the forty-two year old wife. She hesitated a moment or two before answering while her visitor examined her face, watched her body language, waited for her reply. It came immediately.

"It would bother him—you know, the male ego— he would be hurt, and he might even cry a little, but he would not resort to violence—he might even understand."

"Understand? What do you mean by that?"

"It's a long story. I don't want to get into it."

"Would he divorce you?"

"No."

"Would he broadcast it, I mean tell others, your mother or brother or his friends or relatives?"

"No. He would suffer in silence, if he suffered at all."

"How do you know that, Loverly?"

"You called me that earlier several times, Loverly."

"You are lovely. Loverly is a personalization of that."

"Not in my grammar book," she contended.

"But in my eyes—it is! How do you know he wouldn't tell others?"

"Because I know him. We've been married a long time."

The smile, so prominent upon Marti's face, had by that time gently acquiesced to a simple, quiet, pleasant expression and the old halfback noticed the change. The discussion seemed to have altered her personality slightly, and he imagined it to be caused either by guilt or indifference, probably. When she lifted her wine glass to her mouth, her eyes met his and neither spoke for a few seconds.

"You were bothered by that conversation, weren't you Good-lookin?—about his feelings?"

Her sudden response surprised him. "NO! I'm not worried about his feelings. I'm really not worried about anything except maybe running out of wine." Holding up her empty glass she complained, "This was the last of it."

"Want me to go to the store?" he offered.

"No, I'll pick some up tomorrow on the way home."

"Well, when you've run out of wine, it's time to recline, I've always heard. Since I can't recline here and you have to get up early, its time for the old man to go home." Picking up his empty glass and the napkin upon which it sat, Corbin moved past his hostess, as she too stood, toward the kitchen. Placing his glass in the sink he turned back toward her, only a few feet behind him. Before he could say anything, she held her arms open and asked, "Give me a hug?" Patie was very conscious of standing in a well-lighted kitchen before a large window which faced the street, but he had no intentions of missing this unexpected opportunity, whether he was seen or not, although he retained a touch of cautiousness.

"Hell yes, damn right, hotty-toddy," the ex-Rebel exclaimed. "But could we move away from this window a little?"

Without answering or moving, the slender woman threw her arms around the amazed man's neck and gushed, "Now put your arms around me and squeeze, Reb, unless you don't know how."

"I know how, Ms. Bulldog," Patie assured, obeying her command. He noticed that she did not press the lower part of her body against his and he could not refrain from commenting, "Notice you are very elastic from your waist down, Loverly."

She smiled but he could not see it. Her face was pressed into the right side of his chest.

Outside the kitchen, a small man dressed in a black chauffeur's uniform peeked over the hedge which surrounded three sides of the house holding a large, expensive camera. He snapped a picture, another one, another one, and a fourth one. Then he crouched down, moved away from the hedge and melted into the darkness.

"Are you going to run tomorrow, Miss Sprinter?"

"I run every day," the athletic lady affirmed, sometimes before I go to school, sometimes after."

"What about tomorrow?"

"After school, probably."

"Then I may see you—on the beach."

"I hope so." She stood at the open door and watched her new friend walk down the driveway, open his van door, back out into the deserted street and she waved as he slowly pulled away from her house. She knew he was still looking, and he was. What she didn't know was what was in his mind—I wonder if her neighbor saw any of that?

The fifty-six year old man, normally so alert and so conscious of his surroundings in this kind of situation but not now, his attentiveness deadened by the night's events, failed to notice the black Lexus which, with lights off, pulled onto Beach Boulevard behind him.

CHAPTER SIX

The light flashing on Corbin's answering machine when he opened his front door cast an intermittent green glow against his dark living room wall. He flipped the light switch on, kicked off his shoes, shed his shirt, unzipped his trousers, letting them fall to the floor and walked out of them, leaving a trail of clothes between the front door and the telephone. Neither ex-wife allowed him to commit such an unforgivable sin, he remembered as he picked up the recorder and sprawled out on the couch in his underwear, balancing it upon his bare, flat stomach. He punched the message button.

"Hi Patie, this is your long lost but beautiful ex-wife, oh, the second one. Call me when you get in from partying, you turd. I love you—though I still don't know why—bye."

"Pate, this is Buddy. Like two teenage girls, I want to hear all about your exciting date, you old fart. Call me back."

The old pro dialed Buddy first. He wanted to talk to Buddy before he called Kim, thinking something his old friend had to say might affect his conversation with her. "Buddy? Patie."

"How was it old friend?"

"So-So."

"So-So? Just So-So? What the hell does that mean?" the old teammate yelled.

"So-So I can't touch it with a powder puff."

"You're still a Meathead, you know that, Pate?" Buddy laughed. "Well if it's 'sore' that means she must have liked you. How DID it go?"

"She seemed to like me but she didn't like me THAT much. It's not really 'sore', but it did go well. We had a good time. She gave me a big hug before I left."

"What did you do?" the friend wanted to know.

"Went out to eat, then to her house for a little while. Her personality changed when I started talking about her husband."

"In what way?"

"From effervescent to solemn and she acted as though his catching us wouldn't really bother her. That may have been an act though, air of independence, women's lib thing, you know! You talked to The Jack lately?"

"I talk to him every day. Can't talk to you about him on the phone, remember? Keep me informed. You know how interested in my old mentally challenged and helpless teammate I am. By the way, I may be heading down there soon—for a meeting at Beau Rivage. Find a golf course and I'll bring my sticks."

"Already found it—the Bridges at Casino Magic. Great course, kind of expensive though. When are you coming?"

"I'll call you," Buddy promised. "Not for a few days yet, if I can work it out. Talk to you later."

"Right."

After disconnecting Buddy, Patie dialed Kimberly. "How are you, Gorgeous?"

"I shouldn't be here—waiting for you to call!!"

"That's a strange answer. You never have curtailed your social life for me, not even when we were married."

"I'm not going to do it any more, either. Tonight was enough. Where have you been?"

"Oh, I met a couple of Ole Miss fans down here, graduates. They took me out to dinner. Ate some great raw oysters. You'd better hurry on down."

"Ugg! You'd have to try to do it without kissing me, not after you've eaten raw oysters, and that wouldn't work."

"Do what, Gorgeous?"

"Oh how quickly he forgets," she retorted, seriousness creeping into her voice in spite of her effort to thwart it. She knew her ex-husband was kidding and she tried to appreciate it, participate, but it simply wasn't her nature. A large part of his personality consisted of teasing and very little of hers, differences which would in all likelihood never be reconciled.

"I haven't forgotten. Can't you come down for a day or two? Bay St. Louis is only four hours from Vicksburg."

"I don't think so. You come up here when you can. You know I don't enjoy the ocean."

"You want to know what I think, Gorgeous?"

"What?"

"I believe you consider Vicksburg your world and Bay St. Louis mine—you want a relationship with me, but only on your turf—for some abnormal reason. Anyway, only three weeks ago you insisted that I wait until after dark to come to your house."

"Patie?"

"Yes?"

"You know what comes out a well-fed bulls' ass?"

"Beautiful women?"

"Good night, Lover Boy. You call me tomorrow during the day. I may not be here tomorrow night."

"You'll be there, but I'll call tomorrow after-noon—late. Love you—bye."

"Lover Boy" sprang up from the couch, replaced the telephone and answering machine on the end table, retraced his steps to the front door picking up his clothes and took them upstairs to his bedroom. He hung his shirt and trousers in the closet, stuck his shoes under-neath them and threw his socks and underwear in the dirty clothes hamper which Kimberly had given him. Then he trudged into his bathroom at the top of the stairs for a late-night warm bath. When he turned the light switch on, the exhaust fan came on automatically, which along with the sound of the shower made so much noise, he could not hear the telephone ring downstairs nor the voice leaving the message. Twenty minutes later the tired would-be author lay on his bed watching the late news on Fox Network. "Thank goodness for Fox News," he murmured to himself. "I guess that liberal Mississippi State Democrat across town's watching CNN, if she even looks at news." A smile enveloped his ruggedly handsome and youthful looking face as he thought about Marti, then yielded to a frown. "I don't know, Jack, I just don't know," he whispered to himself, no more than five minutes before turning the TV off and slipping into a deep sleep. It had been a good day, a long day, but a good one.

* * * * *

The eight o'clock sun hurled its bright rays across the bay, through Corbin's inexpensive drapery which attempted in vain to cover the windows, glanced off the dresser mirror, onto the bed, and into the sleepy eyes of the old halfback. He yawned, stretched, and finally pushed his naked body up into a sitting position. He thought about Mattie and Kimberly. Both had been totally repulsed by his nudity at night. Even before he retired from pro football he had discovered all his injuries made him toss and turn in a futile attempt to get comfortable. He couldn't sleep on his back very long because two operations had left his left knee slightly bent. Unable to straighten out, it throbbed under the weight of itself. After awhile the pain forced him to turn onto his side. But he couldn't sleep long on his right side because of a torn rotator cuff in his right shoulder, which he refused to submit to the doctor's knife. "You will someday," an old teammate, now an orthopedic surgeon once told him, "when the pain gets too great, and it will." Sleeping on his left side made his left nostril clog up, drainage from a broken cheekbone, in a nose which had been broken many times. Sleeping on his stomach stiffened his back so the old warrior found himself sentenced to the agony of a gyrating body all night. Every time he turned, his pajamas crept farther up his legs until they rested between the cheeks of his butt. Finally late one night in total discomfort he sprang from the bed, ripped the pajama bottoms from their hiding place and threw the cursed garment onto the bedroom floor, never to be worn again.

"You'll just have to get used to it," the adamant nudist proclaimed to both wives. In between marriages, the girlfriends hadn't seemed to mind.

"I wonder what Marti sleeps in? I'll probably never know," he muttered as he floundered toward the bathroom to tend to his bodily functions. A few minutes later, with washed face, brushed teeth, and wearing a pair of Bermuda shorts he eased toward the stairs. Halfway down he exclaimed disgustedly "DAMN, I think I forgot to make the coffee AGAIN," a self accusation which proved to be true. "How in hell can I remember the score of every ball game I ever played in but I can't remember to make the coffee at night? You have a real mental problem, Meathead."

Only after making the coffee and starting toward the front door with his car key in one hand and fifty cents for a paper in the other, did he notice the blinking light on his answering machine. "Patie, thank you for a wonderful night. I haven't had that much fun in a long time—honestly. 'Course some of it came from Ole Miss bashing which I thoroughly enjoy. I'm gonna' run the beach again at five tomorrow afternoon. Maybe I'll see you there."

When did she call? he wondered, walking out of his condo in search of a newspaper. I never heard the phone ring.

The walker was sitting in the open rear end of his van pulling his knee brace onto his leg when he spotted Marti jogging up Beach Boulevard toward him. By the time the smiling beauty arrived at his vehicle, he had tightened the brace on his left knee, put his left shoe back on, locked his car, and was waiting on her.

"Hello, Reb," she grinned widely. "See you made it."

"Hey, Loverly! Wouldn't have missed it after getting that warm, heartfelt invitation? By the way, when did you call? I never heard the phone ring."

"I don't know. Last night. I thought I gave you enough time to get home, but apparently I didn't. You must have stopped at the Fire Dog!"

"Not without you, Baby. I went straight home," he adamantly replied, as if to prove he believed without her there could be no party, at the Fire Dog Saloon, or any where else. Patie knew his rebuttal sounded a little counterfeit, maybe a little childish but perhaps not unexpected in the beginning of a new relationship.

"Better check those ears, Reb. Sometimes they are the last things to go before the whole body does."

"Guess I'd better," he affirmed, but he knew he had no hearing problem. He had already decided that she must have called while he was showering. That meant her mind had stayed on him after he left the house. That's good! Telling him the exact moment she would jog and arriving at precisely the announced time meant she had thought about him all day. That's probably a stretch, honesty forced him to admit. But she could have, I hope.

"I see the sand-demons are still fluffing the sand, Loverly." They were walking together toward the water's edge under an absolutely clear sky, the temperature in the mid-fifties. A slight breeze blew from the ocean and the sea gulls seemed to be attacking the entire coast line.

"It won't matter today," the scantily clad jogger observed. "The tide is out."

"I see that." A twenty yard walking trail of hard, packed sand lay before them, left by an ocean which had backed that far away from the beach. "This is great, but I'm surprised those idiots on their machines haven't tried to loosen this sand up, too," the male walker grumbled, as the two of them assumed a power-walking pace. She glanced at him as if to say cool it, chum. This is my beach and I love it.

"Hey, I thought you were gonna' jog, Good Lookin'."

"I think I'll walk today. You mind some company?"

"No, of course not! By the way, when is your husband coming back?" Like yesterday, the two of them were alone on the beach, the crisp air and breeze apparently combining to keep all but the hearty, or perhaps the foolhardy away. The concerned man wanted the security of knowing Marti's husband would not see them walking together without exposing his anxiety. Wasted effort.

"Still worried, huh?"

"Well, not really worried. I'm just not anxious for him to see me walking with you. I don't think I would like my wife doing it—not if I really loved her."

"We're not doing anything wrong, Reb. I promise you, Nooo' problem. But I'll jog on ahead if you want."

"No, No, I didn't mean I wanted you to do that. Do you think any of your neighbors will tell him we walked together?'

"Reb, this is Bay St. Louis, not Oxford. Down here folks don't give a damn about things like that. They don't even give a damn that anyone else gives a damn, nor do they give a damn that others don't give a damn. They just don't give a damn. You'll realize that after you've been here awhile."

"Loverly?"

"Yes!"

"Folks down here don't seem to give a damn."

"I think you're finally getting it, Reb"

"Still a dim hope," he teased.

"Oh Lord, I believe that was Mac," his frightened-sounding companion exclaimed, looking intently toward the boulevard.

"Who?"

"Mac, my husband."

"DAMN!! WHERE?!?"

"Just wanted to see if you were awake, Mr. Football. He's coming in late tonight, after midnight, he said."

"I'm awake now!" he laughed with relief. "If I wasn't before, I am now!"

The two had walked about half a mile during the dialog. The sand was hard and the walking easier then yesterday. The water's edge lay well to their left and the loosened sand well to their right. The drainage pipes, mostly under water yesterday, jutted completely out of the water today, large black tunnels lying upon a gray roadway, obstacles, some of which must be climbed over, rather then stepped over. Marti, walking to Patie's left and a couple of paces in front, sat upon the first one of them facing her co-walker, swung her left leg over the pipe and then the other one. Her loose, extremely brief shorts stretched well beyond the unobtrusive point, and for half a second, the woman's profoundly observant male companion surveyed at least one-half of everything she owned—a suddenly opened and shut window to total ecstasy, an ebullient oasis in the midst of a frozen tundra, a rhapsody in rapture. He felt clearly a quickening of his heart-rate, a draining of blood from his head. And when the moment ended, Patie, standing on the near side of the pipe tore his eyes from the scene and looked up into hers. She looked directly at him and from the far side of the pipe, standing with her hands on her slim hips, she smiled. "What's the matter Reb? You look like you've seen a ghost."

"One half of the most beautiful female Casper this old boy has ever seen. Damn, Loverly don't do that to me—I can't take it!"

What in the world are you talking about, Mr. Corbin?" she quizzed in a hoarse, whispery, deliberately sensual voice.

"You know damn well what I'm talking about, or at least I hope you do—'cause I hope you did it on purpose. How far to the next conduit?"

The lovely smiling lady reached her hand to the spellbound man, yet to climb over the large tube. "Here, let me help you," she offered in obvious jest, "you look a little weak."

"Damn legs are like jello—melted jello," he grinned as he grasped her extended hand, stepped over the pipe, wrapped his muscular arms around her in a big hug. He held onto her hand for at least twenty paces after they had started walking again.

The very moment Patie seized Marti's strong extended hand, a camera with a photo lens swung nimbly out the driver's side window of a black automobile parked along Beach Boulevard, one hundred yards away, a Lexus. It recorded the entire episode—from the time the woman helped the man over the pipe, until he turned her hand loose ten seconds later. The driver then raised the darkened window, cranked the expensive vehicle and drove on down Beach Boulevard toward Waveland. Corbin never knew that his privacy had been compromised on film—a second time.

A minute later her wide eyed escort exclaimed,

"You don't have panties on, do you?" more of a declaration than a question. Before she could answer he asked again, "Do you ever wear them?"

The comely female jogger, slowed to a power-walk by her desire to exercise with her new friend strolled, still, a little ahead and slightly to his left. She glanced over her right shoulder into her companion's face. "No, that bother you?"

"That means you didn't have any on last night under that long black dress? And define 'bother'," he beseeched.

"I didn't think it would—and that's right. I had none on."

"I'm waiting for the next drainage pipe," he grinned. "By the way that picturesque exposure to which you allowed me access reminds me of a joke. Think you can handle it?"

"Is it bad?"

"Not as explicit as the exciting panorama you displayed a few minutes ago," he promised, "but it's pretty earthy."

"Well, then, let me have it."

"Right here?—on the beach?"

"The joke, Reb, the joke!"

"An old man and an old woman sat rocking on the front porch of the senior citizen's home. The old woman liked the old man much more than he seemed to like her and she decided a long time ago that she wanted sex with him. She had tried everything to engender the same desire in him, but nothing had worked. Finally, that particular morning she left her panties off, dressed in a nice loose outfit and took her customary place beside him on the front porch, rocking. After about fifteen minutes of again failing to interest him, she stood up, as quickly as she could, placed herself directly in front of the old man, lifted her dress and exclaimed 'SUP'ER PUS'SY!'"

"The old man looked at it for a second, then raised his eyes to meet hers and with a shaky, aged voice decided, 'I think I'll have the soup'."

If the lovely lady's physical disclosure a few minutes earlier failed to prove her 'raison d'être', her intentions by itself, compiled with her hearty, prolonged chortle at the joke left no doubt in the old romanticist's mind. She was willing, a perception settled but demanding other knowledge: Why?—Certainly with her looks and personality she would have no problem interesting men in her; Why me?—Could she be thinking blackmail? Could her husband be a part of it?; Why SO willing—SO quickly?; Is she pursuing only physical pleasure or is she looking for a long term relationship, maybe even divorce and remarriage?; Does she do this with every new male friend? Maybe she's conducting some kind of a social, academic experiment.

Patie could not suppress the smile when he considered the many questions, nor the surprise at himself. Hell, a few years ago, he thought, I would never have considered the issues, they wouldn't have mattered to me. But he was older now, wiser and the mission upon which he had reluctantly embarked, demanded it. Oh well, he speculated to himself, not to worry. The reason or reasons will surface. They always do.

The walker's companion suddenly shattered his train of thought. "Patie, how far do you walk?"

"About five miles—two and a half in each direction."

"Do you know where your turn around point is?"

"Yes. I checked it yesterday. See that big white house with columns? That's two and a quarter miles from the parking lot. There's a drainage ditch a quarter of a mile past the house, the turn around point, but for the life-of-me I can't understand why the engineers cut a drainage ditch rather than install a large black pipe. I'm kind of partial to them, you know! I think I'll always have a special place in my heart for large drainage pipes."

By the time, the two had reached the turn around point and retraced their steps back down the beach to the initial drainage pipe, each of them knew something, a little, about the other's childhood, high school, college academic, and athletic experiences. The only thing left totally undiscussed dealt with family and marriage.

At the large black tube, Patie grabbed Marti's hand and stopped walking. "Now Loverly," he explored, "this time let's do this right. What I would like for you to do is sit on the pipe, of course, and gradually swing your right leg over it. Take as much time as you'd like, ten minutes or so, and then gradually bring your left leg over it. Think you can do that for me?"

The confronted female playfully hesitated for a second or two, as though in deep contemplative thought. Finally, taking his other hand in hers, holding both now, she stared intently into her questioner's face. "Hell,

Reb, I don't think you can handle it. One second drained the blood out of your head. Ten minutes would probably kill you."

Before he had time to reply, she jerked her hands from his, sat on the large clay tunnel and swung both her long shapely legs simultaneously to the other side of the tube. Before he could climb over the man-made barrier she was ten yards down the beach, but looking back, challenging, "Come on slow poke. Let's hurry and finish. Tonight, I want to take YOU out—unless of course you have other plans!"

"I have no other plans," he admitted, jogging to catch up with her. By the time they reached the parking lot and his van, plans for the evening had been formulated. In an hour she would come to his condo in her car, pick him up, and take him to the restaurant of HIS choice. And, oh yes, tonight she would treat him.

"Sounds great to me," he agreed, sitting on the bumper of his van, tail-gate raised, pulling the sweaty brace from his red and swelling left knee.

Jogging on, in the direction of her house, Marti yelled over her shoulder, "See you in an hour, Reb, try to be ready."

"I'll be ready," he yelled back. "You know where I live?"

"Yes," she confirmed. "You told me."

"Okay" he called loudly after her as she darted quickly across Beach Boulevard. "See you in an hour."

A few minutes later the retired halfback, having ridded himself of the brace and having changed shoes, stood to put those things into the back of the van. A sudden thought echoed through his mind. I haven't told her where I live—how does she know that? When he looked in the direction she had run, to ask her, she had already turned the corner and was out of sight.

CHAPTER SEVEN

Fifty-five minutes after the exercisers parted, a loud knock reverberated into Patie Corbin's rented condo. He stood in his kitchen fully dressed in off-white trousers, a long-sleeved New York Giants blue-colored knit shirt, black loafers, and a stylish black belt—an improvement, he thought, over last night's attire. Holding a frosted glass mug in his left hand, he poured a Coors Light beer into it with his other. At the sound of the knock, he leaned backward in order to look out of the kitchen through the living room to the entrance, and yelled, "Come in, Loverly".

The front door slowly opened and a portrait beautiful eased through it—a full length fire-engine red gown, slit on the left side from the floor to mid-thigh, where it yielded to a row of large white buttons, desisting by the moderately small left breast, made somehow to look larger. The lady's fine-textured auburn hair, pulled to the back of her head and bound by a beautiful barrette, framed itself with informal ringlets tumbling loosely down almost to her shoulders. A smile, familiar now to her exhilarated escort, celebrated her jubilation, published without intent and without shame her love of life, her passion for the man though he did not then know it.

The fifty-six year old suitor, still leaning backward when the vision transmuted into reality before his spellbound eyes, took two steps back, holding his beer mug in one hand, the empty Coors can in the other, and his usually loquacious mouth opened wide in entranced silence. From the middle of the small living room to the middle of the kitchen, the two acquaintances faced each other for fully ten seconds, neither speaking, looking at the other—a lovely, liberal, Mississippi State Democrat married woman—a fascinated, conservative, Ole Miss Republican separated man, both hammered, molded, merged, pressed into one by the mystery of correspondent metamorphosis. Suddenly, to him, his guest evolved from play thing to person, from female to woman, from platonic friend to—to—to what? From somewhere deep inside, his mind and his spirit and his conscience and his body were at it again, warring against one another, a full-fledged battle, no prisoners taken, fight to the death. How, at times like this, they always seemed to assault him independently as though he were a one-room house inhabited by four adversaries, each intent upon annihilating the others, in order to control the affairs of the home!!! How each seemed to hate the others!

"Marti is so beautiful," declared the Mind, "and I want her and I will have her, but listen— it's wrong, wrong, wrong—what you do to her, will do to her, have done to her, it's wrong".

"Yes," warned the Conscience," and she's married, another man's wife. She doesn't belong in this house unless you truly love her—that makes everything right—love—that makes everything right—love does, so do you love her? That would make it right, that would purify it, wouldn't it?—catheterize it? Yes—love—a catharsis, love—that makes it right."

"To whom do you speak, Conscience? To me, the Mind, the seat of the emotions? Are you speaking to me? What makes you the learned one?—the one to control what to do? Who appointed you? Did God appoint you? Did those who sit in the dark, musty halls of academia select you to control me? Have you considered my emotions? Do not they matter? Do you tell me how to disregard them, to imagine they do not exist? How do I do that? What about the pain? Will you assuage the pain for me if I walk away? Yes I know—you say I may stay if I love, but can you tell me when I love? How to love? If I love?"

"I must now speak", cried the Spirit. "I have stood in patience watching, listening, mar-

veling at your words. You say, Mind, because the beauty of woman belongs to her, because the angels of loveliness have dressed her, you desire her, you desire to hold her, to own her, to claim her for your own. What gives to you that right? Who gives to you that right? Certainly not I, the Spirit, that part of you created in the image of God. That life within you. Do you not remember why you know her?—Why you came? Have you forgotten your task? Can you no longer think, oh Mind, can you not project yourself into the times ahead and see the horror of outcome, not years but days from this moment? Are you so weak, so fragile, so incomplete that you allow a function of your being to control you? Can you not control yourself?"

And to the Conscience thus speaks the Spirit. "You say love makes all wrong to be right? Who then determines the meaning of wrong or the meaning of right? Do you define it? Alone? Or does someone help you? And what IS love? You speak of its power to make a wrong into a right simply by its passive presence? I ask you, can love be passively present, and, if so, can you define it? Is there no movement in love, no action? If there is, define love. You speak of love's passive presence moving a wrong and making it into a right, but you offer no defini-tion. If a man can take that which is not his, but he does it with love and it's made right, then can a man kill another for love and that be therefore made right? Can one fail in all that God and man has given him to do, and that failure be made right by the presence of love?

"Do you not know, oh Conscience, that you can be trained, programmed, to accept that which God and man rejects? Do you not remember how you have permitted without guilt man to eat other men as food, cannibals in deep jungles who devour the flesh of others in festival, with joy, and dancing and singing. Can you then be made our immutable judge to judge us in what we do? If the cannibal loves the taste of man's flesh and if he loves those whom he eats, can it be right, Oh Conscience—can you swear it to be right? Should you, which can be altered, programmed, bind us to your absolutes, when you yourself aren't absolute?"

"I, Body, speak to you, Spirit, and to you, Conscience and to you Mind. What if my love for her fails to be the love of angels and God, must I ignore my cravings? Can you satisfy those desires burning within me which only woman may satisfy? If you can, then I will listen to you. If you cannot, must I heed your call? Should I live in the prison of my sensuality forever? Do you have a plan to help me? If you do, please give it to me. If you can dissolve my desires, I will obey you. You, Spirit and you, Conscience, you do not ache with the pain of suppressed passion, but if you possess the power to quieten my lust, then I will obey you. But do not ask me, in

*your impotence, nor command me in your lack of
desire to sentence myself to agony, for I cannot,
I will not do it."*

"My God, last night I thought I saw beauty perfected. Now I face perfect beauty enhanced! I did not
know perfection might be perfected. My entire observation and value systems just came tumbling down."

"Are you talking about me, Reb?"

"I'm talking about you, Loverly!"

"Thank you for the compliment, I think. I was
just about to tell you how handsome you look tonight,
perhaps not quite so eloquently."

"For the first time in my life," the admirer
extolled, "I feel inferior to the woman by my side."

"Now what in hell does THAT mean? You have
never been afflicted with inferiority in your life, you
turkey. Have you?"

"I don't know! Probably. Anyway, I thought it
sounded good."

"It did—thank you—where are you taking me
tonight?"

"You said you were taking me out, Loverly."

"I am, but I want you to choose the place. I chose
it last night."

The two mutually infatuated admirers, moved
toward one another. He took her willing hand and
kissed it. Then looking upward into her wide, mystical
eyes, he gently asked, "Would you like a drink?"

"Do you have wine?"

"Yes, even white zin. I'll pour it into a traveling

cup you can take with you." He emptied the wine and his beer into plastic cups, turned the kitchen light off, led the compliant woman to the front door, and stopped there. Turning, he wrapped his strong arms around her, taking great care not to tilt his cup of beer, and he squeezed, conscious of the position of her body. From her amiable head, which rested on his broad shoulder, to the floor, she pressed her trembling body against his. Seconds later, he nudged her quivering chin upward with his free hand and placed his lips upon hers and they were his, pressed hard, moist, warm, sensual. They parted, yet remained. Her curious tongue moved just slightly against his large front teeth and pushed its way into his receptive mouth, lingering, grasping, moving, examining, fermenting within her a moistness she had not experienced for a long time. When she felt him against her body, growing, struggling, searching, she shivered, pulled her lips from his, and dropped her head back onto his shoulder. "We'd better go, Reb."

"I think we had, Loverly," he retorted with a low, breathless whisper.

"But we'll be back," she smiled as she looked him in the face, longingly.

"I think so, Loverly," the impassioned man, reaching for the door agreed.

Following her through the opening out into the dusk, he locked the door behind them and draped his right arm around the beauty's shoulder. At precisely that moment, a black Lexus on Beach Boulevard some twenty yards away, sped up, accelerated one block, and squealed around the corner. In silence, the two watched.

"What the hell—did you see that?"

"Of course. What about it?" she asked innocently.

"He was sitting in front of this condo. When we came out, he goosed the hell out of his car. Looked like he didn't want us to see him. Didn't you notice?"

"Well yes," she admitted, unimpressed, unconcerned, "but what do you make of it?"

"You came out before me, Loverly. What was he doing?"

"Oh, I don't know," she slowly pondered, remembering. "Nothing—the car was just sitting there. Actually, I don't think it was completely stopped, but it WAS moving SLOWLY."

"Yeah," the concerned chaperone exclaimed, "real slow. If he was moving at all, you would have to line him up with something to tell it."

"Why is it worrying you, Reb? People drive down Beach Boulevard slowly all the time—looking at the bay, the condos, the boats."

"Well, for one thing, I've noticed a car just like that one several other times when we've been together. For another, it's really too dark to look at the scenery. Besides, your car is in my driveway."

"Now THAT'S a ditty! Make a great country song. Oh, her car was in my driveway when the Lexus drove slowly by", she sang, quickly, in jest, creating her own tune.

"Could be serious, Marti, Mac MIGHT be checking on you."

"Serious? You mean like the clouds-cirrus?"

"No, not like the clouds," he smiled, "serious—you know—like a load of buckshot aimed by an angry husband."

"You think Mac owns a Lexus? Hell, Reb, Mac has never been in a Lexus. He doesn't even KNOW anyone who owns one. Besides, I thought we had solved the Mac problem. No wonder State beat the hell out of Ole Miss last year. You Rebels ARE paranoid."

"Come on, Loverly, quit ringing that damn cowbell. Ready to go?"

"Been ready, Pate. Where we goin'?"

"Well, I would like to take you to my favorite place, Dock-o'-the-Bay, but I've already eaten there several times this week. Ever dined at Harbor Lights?"

"In Pass Christian?"

"Yeah. It's sitting over the water and I heard the food is good. Ever eaten there?"

"No. But I've heard the food IS good. Been wanting to go."

The two had been standing on the condo deck sipping their drinks, Corbin still looking in the direction of the Lexus' quick departure around the corner. The concerned man took Marti's hand in his and led her down the ten steps to the driveway below, opened the passenger door to his van and settled his appreciative companion into the seat. A minute later, he turned left onto the two mile bridge extending across the Bay, connecting the town of Bay St. Louis to Pass Christian.

"Wait," she exclaimed. "I was going to take you—."

"Maybe we had better go in my van," Patie declared, thinking the larger vehicle was safer, but not saying it.

Sparse traffic upon the concrete span and a clear night cooperated to magnify both the distant lights of the heavens and those much nearer, of Pass Christian. The large moon hung over them like a spotlight and added mystique to the setting, causing the driver to wish he could pull the van over to the side of the bridge, stop, and more fully absorb the beauty of the night. He could not, of course, there being no place to do so, but he did slow the vehicle down to twenty miles an hour. "Loverly, that's a beautiful scene," nodding his head toward the small town now only a mile away, the lights reflecting off the pulsating bay water below.

"Sure is, Patie. Kind of romantic, too."

"Yeah. You'd be in trouble if I could find a pulling-off-place."

Two minutes later the pair reached land, and a few minutes after that, passed the Pass Christian Yacht Club on their right. Shortly, they turned into the parking lot of the Harbor Light restaurant.

The owner of the Harbor Light had many years before constructed the restaurant in the form of an old lighthouse. It consisted of a square main floor, which housed the food part of the business and a round imitation of a light house on top of that, featuring a revolving harbor light. The upper round part housed the large bar which offered drinks from every part of the world, plus live entertainment. A large wooden deck extended from the first floor out over the water, an elevated appendage resting on creosote poles, covered with vines, pot plants, and twenty or so tables and chairs.

Corbin discovered that Harbor Light offered no valet service, a fact which surprised, but did not disappoint him. An old athlete had just as soon walk. Quickly surveying the building and the brightly lit parking lot, he parked his van directly in front of what seemed to be a large window on the main floor. A few minutes and a short stroll later, the two customers walked up a long ramp to the side entrance into the restaurant. From there they noticed the inviting nature of the outside deck. The maitre d' met them inside the door. The eatery seemed almost full and Patie was glad he had made reservations.

"Good evening, Sir, Ma'm, did you have reservations?"

"Yes. Patie Corbin for two—but we're thirty minutes early. Could we have a drink, on the deck, if possible?"

"I'm sorry, Sir. The deck is full."

"Where's your bar?"

"I think you'll love our bar, Sir. See that spiral staircase? That leads up to it."

Glancing over to his left, Patie saw the narrow, metal staircase circling straight up into the room above. The large open window lay immediately on the other side of the stairs, adjacent to the lounge, the location of the downstairs restrooms.

Reaching the first step of the unusual stairway, the middle-aged jester indicated to his companion by a waving gesture of the hand that he expected her to go first. The beauty, with one hand resting on the rail, stopped, looked him firmly in the eye and threatened, "Since you have goosing on the mind, I don't want you goosing me on these stairs, Reb."

"Wouldn't think of it, Loverly. Biting, maybe."

She looked at him menacingly and with her strong athletic legs almost ran up the steps. He followed.

An attractive hostess in a very short red servers uniform met them at the top of the stairway. "Not many people climb those stairs that quickly without breathing hard," she observed, "you two must be in good shape."

"Pretty good shape," responded Marti, "but I need to ask you a question." Her escort looked at her with suspicion. Speaking in a low voice, she whispered so that only the three of them could hear, "My friend here is an alcoholic. He gets rip-roaring, mud-leveling, belly-scratching drunk every night. How am I going to get him down from here?"

The hostess, expecting a teasing smile from her female customer but not getting it, jerked her head quickly around toward the man. He looked as stern as his companion. Then she looked back at Marti, "Well Ma'm, oh, ah, actually we would hope that—"

"Oh, hell, Loverly," the old drinker gravely considered, "That's not gonna' be a problem. Just get some help and pull me over to the stairs on my belly. Point me head first down the stairs and push. I'll slide down. Fact is, when all the others see how much fun I'm having, they'll probably all slide down that way."

The distracted hostess, apparently considering the worst possible scenario, looked from one face to the other, obviously waiting for a sign of jest. She got none. A second later, Marti, in absolute seriousness declared, "I guess that'd work, Honey, but it's sure gonna' mess up your clothes. I'll go down first and catch you when you get there, though. So you don't bump your head."

For a full five seconds, no one spoke. Finally the "drunkard" asked, "Ma'm, can we have that table over by the window?" The hostess was staring at Marti.

"Sir? Oh, ah, yes sir, of course."

After seating the couple, the hostess walked quickly to the bartender and engaged him in solemn conversation. The bartender smiled, nodded, and said something back to her. He looked a little amused. She seemed to relax slightly.

"Wish I could read lips", Marti whispered.

Quickly, the attractive hostess strode back to the table and smiled. "May I get you something to drink?"

"Yes, thank you." Turning toward his lovely female friend, Patie asked, "Want white zin?"

"Yes."

"She wants a glass of white zin and I'll have a Yellow Bird."

"White zin for the lady and—and—did I understand you to say 'Yellow Bird'?"

"Yes, I would like a Yellow Bird, please."

The hostess, turned server, took the order to the counter. A few seconds later, she returned. "Sir, the bartender says he isn't familiar with a Yellow Bird."

"You gotta' be kidding!"

"No, Sir, but we have a policy here. If we are asked to mix a drink we've never heard of, the first one is on us."

"Great", the pleased customer responded, "Works almost every time. I'll give you the recipe. I hope the bartender has all the parts. Can I borrow a piece of paper?"

"May I," smiled Marti.

"Hell! May I borrow some paper?—and a pen! Serves me right for going out with a schoolteacher."

"Yes of course." The server bounded over to the bar, grabbed a notepad and a pen, hustled back to the table and handed them to the pleased patron.

Speaking as he wrote, Patie scribbled, "One and a half jiggers of Bacardi clear rum; one jigger of crème de banana; one-half jigger of Tia Maria; one and a half jiggers of orange juice; one and a half jiggers of pineapple juice; and one jigger of grapefruit juice. Mix well and serve over ice cubes. There," he finished, "I hope the bartender has all this."

"I expect he does. That's a strong drink. No wonder you have ah, ah, well, kind of a problem—"

"Actually", Corbin quipped, "that's a relatively mild drink. I usually drink bourbon—on the rocks."

The glance and nod of the head which the attendant threw at the liar over her shoulder suggested a better understanding of the reason for his "problem".

Now alone at the table, the two blossoming friends looked at each other, silently. The woman moved her hands slowly across the table until both of them encircled his. Then she looked passionately into his eyes, and with a low throaty voice, whispered, "I'm so proud of you, Reb. I didn't know you could do that."

"What, Loverly?"

"Memorize all that. My, that was a long recipe." The soft admiration of her voice almost seemed real, the expression on her face almost genuine.

"Thank you, Loverly. I DO have wonderful memory genes. Inherited them from both my parents. Why, all three of us could actually recite the Lord's Prayer and the Pledge of Allegiance—both—without cheating— very retentive, we are."

"Could I hear the Lord's Prayer?"

"Certainly", he agreed, suddenly pushing his chair back and standing erect. At the same moment the poised proclaimer raised his right hand to invoke silence, his suddenly reluctant mate quickly repented, "Not now—later," she squealed.

"You sure? We may forget."

"I won't forget", she promised. "Later." Her certainty seemed absolute.

"You need something, Sir?" The waitress stood behind the threatening orator, a glass of wine in one hand and a large yellow drink complete with a red cherry, punctured by a small white plastic sword in the other.

"No thank you. I was getting ready to preach, but I think I'll have my drink instead."

"Preach, Sir?"

"Unh huh", he murmured, "but I decided not to. I'll drink my Yellow Bird instead," taking the drinks from the woman's tray.

The disconcerted server took a couple of steps backward, turned and walked briskly to her bartender boss again. Her arm movement suggested she was conveying the latest information to him, not without some emotion. Patie and his relieved companion sneaked peeks at the two and smiled. Then turning to her, he asked, "Ever drink a Yellow Bird?"

"I don't think so. I may have years ago; I can't remember."

"Want a taste?" He slid the drink over to her.

"Wow!" she exclaimed, "That's good!"

"Good for you, too, lots of vitamin C."

"You sure all that alcohol doesn't neutralize that vitamin C, Reb?"

"Not according to my research!"

"And what research is that?"

"I'm still healthy, of course. I drink lots of Yellow Birds and haven't had a cold in—oh—I'd say—at least a month or so. You drink four or five of them, Loverly, and you'll feel healthier, too."

"Four or five Yellow Birds and I'LL be sliding down that spiral staircase."

By the time the two drinkers finished laughing, they heard Patie's name over the intercom, "Mr. Patie Corbin, your table is ready."

"Uh-oh," clamored the ex-athlete, "I didn't know they were going to do that." He glanced nervously toward the other imbibers, some of whom laced the bar, some at tables. When he and his lovely companion stood, four or five men suddenly turned toward him. One immediately launched himself from his barstool, moved quickly to Patie, thrust out his big right hand, smiled and enthusiastically broadcasted, "Patie, I'm

Frank Holmes,—from Jackson. I've wanted to meet you for a long time."

The old All-American felt familiar emotional stirrings, the battle between a desire not to be recognized, under these conditions, and his ego—which did! He smiled, extended his hand and announced, "Glad to meet you, Frank. This is Marti, a friend." She, by that time, was leaning over the table to retrieve her purse which she had deposited on the floor. Rising up, she smiled and offered her hand to the new acquaintance.

"I know they have called your name downstairs, but do you have time for me to tell you one short story?—about a football game—and what happened between you and me?"

"Well, I—ah—".

"It won't take a minute, I promise."

"Sure. Go ahead. I'd love to hear it." The ex-pro, as he had done many times through the years, patiently listened to ex-high school athletes who remembered playing against him in high school. Sometimes, like now, forbearance came with some difficulty.

"I played at old Central High in Jackson, right halfback. We were on defense and y'all ran a sweep around our right end. You were leading the play and I think a guy by the name of Robertson was carrying the ball. Anyway, I came up to make the tackle. I faked like I was going inside of you, to get you leaning—then I was gonna' slip outside to make the hit, but you didn't take the fake and at the exact time I turned back, you hit me—hardest lick I ever took. My feet went straight up in the air and I crumpled to the ground, out cold. That was it for me the rest of the night. You remember that play, Patie?"

"Seems like your telling about it resurrects a distant memory,—ah—Frank? Yes, Frank, seems like I vaguely remember that play. Thank you for remembering it. That's a real honor after all these years. Thank you. It was great meeting you!"

"Good meeting you, too, Patie. I always loved watching you play. Great meeting you, Ma'm." Marti, who had already moved toward the stairs, turned and with her patented large smile softly echoed, "Good to meet you, too, Frank."

By the time the two diners started down the stairs under the scrutiny of the other bar patrons, Frank was talking to his female companion, "Great guy, Patie Corbin. You know, Marge, after all these years, he remembered playing against me."

The bartender and his attractive employee watched the pair with antipathetic curiosity, she, less than disappointed to see them go.

At the bottom of the stairway, the concerned man glanced to his right toward the large window overlooking the parking lot. At the same time, the host, who had been waiting for them to descend the stairs requested, "Please follow me, Sir."

After being seated and ordering wine, Patie interrupting the quiescent mood, asked, "Excuse me? There's something I need to do." His attentive companion recognized the solemn tone of his voice. "Anything wrong, Reb?"

"No, I just want to check my car. I'll be back in

a minute."

Patie moved as though he were going to the restroom, but when he neared the window he stopped. Leaning toward the glass to reduce the glare of the dim lights from inside the restaurant, he gazed intently toward the direction of his van. Moving slowly through the parking lot, just a few yards from his vehicle, crept a Lexus,—a black one. It stopped and backed up into a parking place, four spaces from the observer's vehicle. The Lexus' passenger door opened and a small man, dressed in dark clothes quickly stepped out, scanned the parking lot, and momentarily stared at the restaurant. The alert spectator stepped sharply back against the plush drapery which outlined the window. When he looked out again, a second later, he saw the man drop to one knee and extend his right arm beneath the Chrysler's rear bumper.

A cold chill joined a sudden flash of anger, both coursing through the old competitor's body. The adrenalin surged within him, doubling and then tripling his energy level, a vicious line-backer seeking to separate him from the ball, if not his head; a hopeful halfback thinking to knock him down in an open field; an angry and suspicious husband flinging open the bedroom door. "Son of a Bit- -" he exclaimed, a vain attempt to whisper.

The irate viewer started toward the door in a quickened walk, almost a controlled run. Remembering Marti, he motioned across the room to her, pointing toward the parking lot, supposing she would understand. She did not, but she assumed something was terribly amiss, both by the suddenness of his move and the expression on his enraged face. Before she could acknowledge his signal, he had disappeared through the door.

Forgetting his damaged knee, the ex-All-American halfback sprinted down the ramp toward the van, some thirty yards away. The man still knelt behind it, still seemed to be feeling its underside. Running down the ten yard ramp was difficult, made more painful for a joint robbed of its cartilage by a surgeon's knife and time, than running on level ground. The furious sprinter tried to ignore the piercing throb, carelessly disregarding any thought of personal danger. He wanted to throw his aging but still solid body into that of his adversary, to render him prostrate upon the ground, to lock his fingers around the man's throat and get answers to some questions: "Who are you?" "Why are you following me?" "What are you doing to my car?" He could not resist the sudden notion that it might be Mac or Mac's friend seeking only to discover the actions of a promiscuous wife, but he knew, too, that it could be much more than that, more serious and much more dangerous. Spinning through his mind like a nightmare, the knowledge did little to slow the raging runner and he felt elation at reaching the bottom of the ramp. The pain would lessen now, and only twenty yards separated him from the man. Suddenly, a car horn sounded, probably the Lexus', and a voice screamed from within it through the open right-side door. "LET'S GET THE HELL OUT OF HERE!"

The kneeling man twisted around to face the sprinter and recognizing him instantly, he wheezed,

"SHIT." Springing to his feet, now only a few yards ahead of his foe, he turned toward the Lexus which had pulled half-way out of its parking space into the drive-way. At precisely the same instant the small man thrust his left leg into the car, Patie locked his strong right hand onto the collar of the invader's dark blue shirt— and pulled. But the Lexus was already moving, turning left away from Corbin, toward Highway 90. The power of the athlete against the small man's shirt forced the cul-prit to reach for something inside the car onto which to hold. He grabbed the steering wheel at the same moment the Lexus' driver pressed the accelerator and tried to turn the car. Prevented from doing so by his compan-ion's grip, the Lexus' right front bumper bounced off the rear of a parked dark green Mercedes. The driver screamed, "Turn the steering wheel loose, you little bas-tard," and the car lurched forward barely missing sever-al other cars parked in the same row as the Mercedes. But the passenger didn't let go, nor did the adamant fol-lower, who held onto the shirt. Patie could hear the shirt's owner choking as the Lexus finally scraped past all the parked cars and began to increase its speed. He knew he could not hold on much longer, and he made one final effort to yank the passenger from the moving vehicle. Throwing his right leg forward in order to stop, the fifty-six year old man jerked with all his strength.

The shirt ripped.

The little rival, freed now from the force against his neck, pulled his head and right leg inside the speed-ing vehicle and turned the steering wheel loose. The auto sped away hastily. Corbin tried to read the tag number, but it had been smeared with something, and he could not.

A second or two after the passenger door slammed shut, the Lexus reached Highway 90, turned east toward Gulfport and lost itself in the dense traffic, which always seemed to move much too fast on that particular stretch of road. The fatigued and hurting sprinter gazed disgustedly toward the disappearing car, then down at the wad of shirt crumpled in his hand.

"Damn it, damn it," he fumed, "I almost had him."

A soft voice filtered over his shoulder from just a few feet away, "Patie, what happened?"

When the perspiring middle-aged warhorse turned toward the gentle voice, he could not help wondering if she knew what was happening. But maybe it was his frustration at losing the contest—or the pain in his left knee which made him wonder.

CHAPTER EIGHT

I 've heard about these things, but I sure as hell don't understand how they work?" admitted the old footballer. "I am an electronics illiterate, still trying to figure out the coal oil lamp."

The small, round, black metal object lay on the table between the two mutual admirers, both of whom were astonished at the events of the last thirty minutes. They had walked slowly back into the Harbor Light following the chase, slowly because of Corbin's pulsating and quickly swelling left knee. After reporting the unfortunate news to the maitre'd that a black Lexus had pounded the rear bumper of a customer's green Mercedes, the sweaty pursuer spent ten minutes in the men's room rearranging his disheveled clothes, drying his perspiring body with paper towels, and combing his disarranged hair. By the time he sat back down at the table his thoughtful colleague had ordered a large glass of "ice" water for him and a glass of white zin for each of them. In between gulps of water and sips of wine, the fifty-six year old competitor explained to his counterpart all that had happened outside. She easily recognized the look of frustration on his face and the strain in his voice, choosing not to joke about it, a prudent decision, and a little surprising to her, if not to Patie.

"I don't know how they work either," she confessed. "Do you really think that's what it is?"

"Oh, it's a bug alright. I'd bet my life on it, but it's the first one I've ever touched—or even seen." And he almost added "but I'll find out for sure." He didn't want to say too much, doubt about her possible involvement lingering still in his suspicious mind.

"Without that flashlight I never would have found it, not until daylight. But what I don't know, Marti, is why? Why did that idiot put a bug under MY van? What's he after? Why does he want to know what I'M doing?"

Patie could hear the anxiety in his own voice as he asked those questions and the presence of it angered him, deep down where no one else could see. His obsessive concern about it refuted his masculinity and attacked his male ego. It belied his jovial spirit and he hated that. He had spent his entire life developing a persona, a nature, personality which took nothing too seriously, which could handle any adversity, declaring as much to many others—and to himself. He hated weakness, especially in men, and excessive worry or inordi-

nate fear indicated infirmity to him. She might be innocent, that adorable, feminine creature who sat across
the table, and if so he could not bear for her to see
imperfection in him, then realized he would not want her
to see his faults even if she were NOT innocent.

"I think I would have caught him before he
reached his car if he'd been wearing a maroon football
jersey!"

"You didn't on the Mississippi State football
field!" Her retort was swift, gentle, and funny. He had
set her up and she didn't even know it, fashioning in the
process his launching pad from which he could propel
the relationship back to where he had left it. Without
realizing it, she had helped him.

"That's true. Those State Boys just kind of got
out of my way, especially when I ran the football. I
couldn't catch up with them. Fear does that to you, I
guess. By the way, I haven't told you this, but I love
Mississippi State. They helped make an All-American
out of me. I'll forever be indebted to them."

"And to me—for listening to this bullshit."

They both laughed.

"How does your knee feel, Reb?" Her question
seemed honest enough, portending concern and care.
He admitted to himself that it hurt, and he could feel it
swelling even as he sat there.

Against the softness and solicitude of her engaging eyes, the aching ex-athlete lied, "It's okay, a little
stiff. It'll be alright. It's not hurting badly enough to
keep me from walking the beach with you.

"Has the waitress come to take our order yet?" the

hungry sprinter inquired, carefully changing the subject.

"No."

Patie looked around the room, caught a server's eye, and motioned that they were ready to order. A few minutes later they had, and he realized that for the next thirty minutes or so they would probably not be interrupted. A good time to talk.

"Loverly, you said Mac's coming home tonight?"

"Yes."

"What time?"

"Late. He's flying in to New Orleans and driving up from there. He can't get here before midnight."

"You know that for a fact?"

"Yes!" she blurted out, a little louder than necessary. "I saw his plane ticket. He's arriving in New Orleans at ten thirty-five tonight."

Mellowing his voice that no provocation might be initiated, the concerned paramour inquired, "Are you absolutely certain that Mac has nothing to do with the black Lexus and the men in it?"

"I'm more than absolutely certain, Reb. Mac has never checked up on me—nor I on him. That's not the kind of marriage we have. I told you that last night. If you're going to see me, you're going to have to trust me. I have no suicidal nor self-destruct tendencies. I DO NOT want to get caught with another man, and besides, he was out of town when we met. He could not know about you."

"That's true, of course! But is it possible that his suspicion might be aimed at you, not me?"

"No, he cannot suspect another man and me for two reasons. There is no other man nor has there been since Mac and I married," she lied. "Plus, he isn't the suspicious type. He has many more friend-girls at NASA than I have friend-boys. Neither of us has ever been jealous of the other one, well, with one exception. Whatever else you believe about me, Patie, you must believe this—I would not get you, nor myself, into that kind of trouble."

The old experienced suitor looked his date directly in the eye throughout her convincing discourse. She returned his gaze, speaking in a slow quiet voice, no stress, no threats, no uncertainty. Patie discovered believing her to be easy. Conscious that he had known her less than forty—no—less than thirty hours, hardly enough time to develop trust in another person! Still, he found himself being gently tugged into trust, recognizing no deception in her. Are you thinking with your heart again, not your head, you Dodo? he silently asked himself. Maybe, maybe, but if I'm going to do what I came here to do I have no choice but to trust her, he thought, and besides I want to continue seeing her.

"Reb, could that Lexus be from YOUR past? You had a pretty active one!"

Corbin knew that dreaded question had to come and he silently admitted that it contained merit. Mattie would not spy on him. Whatever else resided in her heart, one thing remained certain—she had closed the door on her ex-husband. She would not want to hear his name again, ever. Kim? Probably not. Out of curiosity, she would want to know what he was doing, but she wouldn't spend a lot of money finding out. Then, there's her pride! She could never condescend to the lower level of spying on him because to do so, she must surrender her pride—and she needed her pride, created and artificial though it may be. It concealed her severe image problem. A lack of self worth hidden behind pride would not subject itself to common jealousy, at least not publicly, not enough to hire a private detective.

The "thinker" concluded subjectively that neither of his ex-wives would try to discover his activities. If Mattie had spoken the truth the day Patie left, then only one other explanation could be logical, and he didn't want to believe that!

"No, Loverly, I don't believe the Lexus came from my past, but your question does demand some discussion. We probably need to talk about it."

"Do we have to?"

"No, we don't HAVE to, but I think we ought to," he pleaded.

"Will you go first?"

"Yes, but we aren't parachuting out of an airplane. We're learning more about the other person. Under the circumstances, something reason would seem to demand. Don't you agree?"

"Probably, but you talk first."

"Oooh-kay," the verbose extrovert agreed. Careful not to boast, but anxious for his new friend, and possible lover to know more about him than she had heard, he started with his birth, worked through his grammar school years, explained his high school career; discussed his decision to sign with Ole Miss like several relatives before him; discussed his college and pro foot-ball careers, touched upon his marriages and divorces with Mattie and his marriage and divorce with Kimberly. He perforated his monologue with stories about girl-friends, without giving names, of course, as a true Southern Gentleman should refrain from doing, and he concluded by revealing that "I came to the coast to write a book about football and I got as far away from Germantown as I could—and still remain in the state of Mississippi."

"Is that all?" the quiet beauty inquired, jestingly?

"No, I only gave you ten percent—the high places."

"You could write a book about all THAT, Reb."

"Thinking about it, Loverly, I want you to be in it, maybe the last and best chapter."

"Sure you do!! When I tell you my boring story, I may never see you again.

"Oh, here comes the food," she observed.

Thirty minutes later, the two had finished a fab-ulous dinner and two glasses of wine each. The male charmer picked the electronic device up and tucked it into his right front pocket. Then he slid both hands across the table, palms up, an obvious invitation for Marti to place her hands upon his, which she did. Their eyes met and for fully ten seconds neither spoke. He broke the silence. "Like an after-dinner drink?"

"Are you having one?"

"Yes."

"Then I'll have what you have."

Patie motioned to the female server, standing

nearby, who had been watching them with apparent curiosity, her approving smile so indicating. "Two Tia Marias, please." Then, still holding his lovely companion's two strong but remarkably soft hands, still gazing into her large inviting eyes, as she looked quietly back into his, he almost whispered, "When I was a boy growing up in Laurel, my parents took me to Sunday School and church, First Methodist. I remember the story of John Wesley's conversion experience after his mission trip to the Indians in Georgia had been a complete failure. He returned to London and was walking alone, depressed, down Aldersgate Street one night when he heard preaching coming from a small nearby church. Out of curiosity, he went in and listened to the story of Christ, the Messiah, preached by an old pastor, from the Book of Romans. Suddenly, the message of salvation gripped his mind and coursed through his heart, and he fell upon his knees in repentance. Later in relating the story to a friend, he said of that moment, 'I felt my heart strangely warmed'. Marti, a minute ago when I took your hands in mine and we looked so deeply into each other's eyes, I felt my body and my soul—strangely warmed, maybe for the first time in just that way."

Marti said nothing for what to both of them seemed an eternity. A few seconds later, a gentle smile enveloped her responsive face, a woman admired, and she whispered, "Thank you, Patie. That was a beautiful story and a lovely thing for you to say. I felt a strange sensation too, but as you said earlier, 'We do need to talk', and it's my time. Now I should tell you some things about me."

"Could we wait until we get to my apartment?"

"Yes, of course," she sighed.

"Guess you need to be home before twelve?"

"By eleven-thirty."

"It's nine-thirty now. We ought to have time."

"For what?" she unpretentiously smiled, casting forth her own style of suggestive comment.

He didn't answer. Standing, he moved around to her side of the table and slid her chair back, lifting her from it. "Suppose it was the wine?" he teased.

"No, I think it was the Tia Maria. You slip Spanish Fly into it?"

* * * * *

"Well, I don't think they followed us home," mused the alert man. "At least they stayed out of our sight."

After the two had crossed the bridge, at the west end of it, Patie turned left and cruised through the downtown area of the Bay. He swung his van into the same beach parking lot from which he had walked the two days, turned his lights off and waited—a full five minutes, feeling like a fool but determined to exercise wisdom and care none the less. Convinced that they weren't pursued, the driver cranked the vehicle, drove back through town, crossed Highway 90 and proceeded toward his condo—but he didn't stop there. A half-mile past home he affected a quick u-turn in the middle of the street and headed back toward it. He wasn't attempting to lose the Lexus. The two men obviously knew where he lived. He wanted desperately to yank the Lexus' door open and look his despised adversaries in the eye. He wondered, after all the years, if his left-jab and right cross still contained the power he occasionally used when he played football, and the passengers in the black Lexus had pushed him past the point of restraint. The old pro turned his van into his driveway next to Marti's red sport car, shut his engine, took her hand and cautioned. "Let's sit here for a few minutes—just to make certain."

Ten minutes later, the two new but becoming-very-close friends walked up the steps and into the condo. The black Lexus had not appeared, its absence doing little to assuage the concealed anger of the old competitor.

"Would you like another glass of wine, Loverly?"

"No, I don't think so. What I would really like to do is use your bathroom and then look at your condo."

The man and woman were standing in the middle of the living room. The events of the night and the drive to the condo tempered somewhat the voluminous interest each held for the other, at least outwardly, temporarily redirecting their attentions, modifying their emotions, a condition which neither would allow to continue.

Unknown to each of them, both harbored the same concern. While the developing relationship was just that—new—each had already discovered very exciting, very desirable, very—very—addictive attributes in the other, an attitude, an energy, an intellectual astuteness, a love of life. And beyond that, each revered the physical looks of the other. Separately, neither wanted to lose what seemed to be germinating, yet each for dissimilar reasons. She, because no man had ever excited her like Patie. He, because he had never encountered a woman with what seemed to be a selfless but confident ability to exchange verbally with him—like a football teammate—and—oh yes—because he had promised a friend, a former teammate he would accomplish a task, a promise he was beginning to regret.

"I'll go upstairs," Patie pointing toward a closed door in the hallway between the living room and the kitchen, extolled. "You can use the half bath there, Loverly."

"May I use the upstairs bath?"

"Certainly—but why? The downstairs toilet flushes just as good."

"Just as well."

"Oh hell, just as well; I'm a poet and love to show it."

Marti smiled. "It's a woman thing."

"Oh, oh,—I won't ask. Follow me, woman."

Halfway up the stairs, the condo renter stopped, turned around, and looked down into the still smiling face of his follower, who likewise had stopped. "Two things," he declared. "I'm very disappointed that you haven't goosed me. Secondly, what do you teach at that community college?"

"I'm head of the English department."

The man looked intently into the woman's face

for a moment, and exclaimed, "Now why doesn't that surprise me?"

"Probably because you use bad grammar and I'm forced to—"

"Okay, okay. I understand."

At the top of the stairs the two stopped again. "Might as well show you my two beautiful, well furnished and exquisitely decorated bedrooms while you are up here. To the left is the master bedroom as you can tell. It's the one with the bed and chest of drawers. To the right is the guest bedroom, the empty one. Through that door you'll find the bathroom, the dirty bathroom. I would have cleaned it some, not much, but some—If'n I'da knowed youse a'comin—!"

"No, you wouldn't have!"

"You're right! When you get through, I'll meet you either in the master bedroom or downstairs," he grinned.

"Downstairs," she smiled. "I want to get a few things off my chest."

"Uh—oh," mumbled the teasing man. "Gonna get a Dear John before I get off the line of scrimmage."

"Hardly," promised the genial beauty as she stepped into the bathroom, locking the door behind her.

After limping back down the stairs, the amateur bartender extracted all the Yellow Bird ingredients from a kitchen cabinet and refrigerator. "Might as well stay with them," he muttered to himself. Pouring a glassful, he turned the living room light off, slowly opened his front door and stepped out onto the deck. Scanning Beach Boulevard each way as far as the palm trees and the live oaks would allow, he saw nothing. By the time he had re-entered the room and switched the lights back on, he heard the Southern Belle descending the stairs.

"Want one, Loverly?"

"Yellow Bird?" she asked, nodding toward the drink in his hand.

"Yes," he quickly retorted almost defensively, aware that he already had too much to drink. "It makes a great after dinner drink, drink." They were standing in the middle of the small living room floor again, almost the exact spot where they had stood earlier. The expression on her face metamorphosed from smile to solemn. Taking her curious consort's free hand, she turned toward the couch.

"No, thank you—could we sit down and talk for a few minutes now?"

"Of course, Loverly," recalling his suggestion in the restaurant to talk, but not appearing TOO anxious.

A second later, the couple moved to Patie's rented loveseat, still holding hands. They sat turned toward one another, their knees touching, their eyes interlocked. Marti started to speak, stopped, started again, stopped again. Her observant admirer, conscious of what appeared to be apprehension, remained silent but continued to focus upon her eyes, which by now were lowered, fixed upon their gripped hands. Finally, the obviously worried woman lifted her face and with a slightly quivering voice spoke. "Patie, I lied to you and I need to make it right."

"When did you lie to—?"

"I would like to start at the beginning. I know a

lot about you—everyone does, but you know very little about me or my marriage. I need for you to know about me."

"Marti, all I really need to know is that our seeing each other produces inordinate danger for—"

"For each of us, I know. It doesn't, but I want you to know more about me and more about my relationship with Mac before—before—we—well, before we do whatever we're going to do tonight. I'm beginning to feel a, a special—"

"Hey, I'm usually the one who gets accused of taking the romance out of a relationship. Glad to see someone else can do it."

"What do you mean? I'm not trying to take the romance out of, away from our relationship—I don't think."

The old romancer shifted slightly, moving away from Marti a little in order to face her squarely. Enough had occurred already tonight to defuse and destroy many relationships, and this one hadn't kicked off the starting block yet. His companion's serious demeanor and tone of voice suggested a movement away from where he wanted to go. Her last response was the only time in their short companionship that the mentally astute woman seemed to go on defense. Patie knew she liked him a lot but he also knew he was beginning to like her a lot. He could not afford to let that happen. He had to keep their pursuit of each other light, non-binding. The day would come when he would drive out of Bay St. Louis and he reminded himself that on THAT day she might hate him, but neither could he allow their relationship to end now. He ignored her question.

"Wal, now little lady," He joked in an exaggerated southern drawl, "Yew done got serious in yor' tone o'voice. I 'spect you's 'bout t'tell me yew done fell in love with a Rebel. Wal, that thar' is alrite—hit's fer' a Bulldog to'do."

Marti smiled. "You didn't answer my question, but I know what you mean. Can I talk a while, now?"

"MAY I talk a while, now?"

The attractive schoolteacher's laugh was deep and meaningful. "You've been waiting a while for that one, haven't you, Reb?"

"In an excavated and fully camouflaged foxhole."

"She squeezed his hand, which she still held tightly. "I really do need for you to know some things about me and my marriage, Patie. Will you listen to me?"

"Of course. It's your time." After all, he needed to know!

Like with Mattie, what she was about to say would be cathartic for her, a cleansing, a renewing of self-worth, an easing of the conscience. But it would be different, too. Mattie's catharsis ended a marriage forever. Marti's would clean the past slate, polish the foundation upon which a new relationship might be built. The battle within him would probably rage again but he would deal with that later.

"Patie, I know I have come on to you pretty strongly-"

"No stronger than I have you, Loverly," he interrupted. He knew she had—something the older southern culture frowned upon. The man pursued the woman, not the reverse, but Patie could see what was coming, and he did not want her to denigrate herself for becoming attracted to him in such a hurry. It had happened often in his fifty-six years. He preferred to believe it occurred, due more to his charm, which he had unleashed full-throttle upon her, than a weakness in her. He could not, of course, advertise that. The same allurement in him which attracted her prohibited it.

"I know, Reb, and you're responsible for THAT. I'm responsible for ME. May I make a request?"

"Certainly."

"Would you please allow me to finish before you say anything else? I know you're trying to comfort me, but I don't feel badly, either about what I've done, or am about to do—or even how I feel about you. Would you do that for me?"

"You're asking a lot," he teased, smiling. "All I can do is promise I'll try. You know how hard it is—for me to keep my mouth shut, I mean."

Her smile told the debater that she had recognized the suggestive comment. Her verbal silence concerning it revealed the serious notion of her heart. He cast the bait, she acknowledged it and swam away. She walked on—he became still and silent, moving completely out of her pathway. She really needed to say this— and he really needed to listen. Decency—and fairness, like with Mattie, demanded it. That which he had to do depended upon it.

"I know you aren't going to believe what I'm about to say, but I have to say it anyway—because it's true. Patie, I have never flirted with another man the way I have flirted with you, not in my entire life. I wanted to tell you that on the front end so you'll understand everything else I say. But in all honesty I have to admit, if you hadn't come along when you did I WOULD have done it with someone else."

The ego in Patie which wanted to cry "Yes—yes" at the beginning of her statement considered yelling "To hell with you" at the end of it. She would have done it with someone else if I had not come along? With anyone? She was just looking for a man!! She didn't give a damn about the kind of man—just a man. Hell, why should I get involved with someone like her?—Because that's why you came here, you idiot. Remember?

The old suitor looked at the lovely confessor. She had dropped her head, moved her eyes away from his as though she were ashamed of what she had just said. But she really wasn't, or she said she wasn't. Where was she going with this? One thing for sure, his conscience would not bother him nearly so much now. SHE WOULD HAVE DONE IT WITH SOMEONE ELSE?? Why should he regret what he's doing—if she would have done it with someone, no not someone—anyone else. Hell.

"Mac and I haven't had sex in more than four years, not because I haven't wanted to—because HE hasn't wanted to. I wanted to—tried to, but he couldn't, or wouldn't!"

"Do you know why he—"

"Yes! He got involved with his secretary at the time he stopped wanting me. I don't know which came first. He said he was 'in love with her'. When I asked him how he felt about me, he said he 'loved me but he wasn't IN love with me'."

"Can I interrupt—MAY I interrupt you, Marti?" Patie saw the pain of remembering in his friend's face, the agony of a trusted man drifting not only away from her but toward someone else. Corbin had occasionally used that phrase in the past, "I love you but I'm not in love with you". When he used it, it seemed to be real, valid, sincere, but when he heard it used by other men, he realized the shallowness of it, the deception, a coward's way of ending a relationship while protecting his own conscience. "I love you!! Oh, I still love you—yes I do, I certainly do, but for some strange and weird reason I don't crave your body or your presence any more. I don't know why!! I want to want you but I can't! It's not my fault, you see? I WANT to want you."

But the coward cannot tell the hurt woman that he's lost the desire to hold her tightly, to look deeply into her eyes and say "I love you unconditionally, without restraint, and I want to live with you the rest of my life, so he says "I love you but I'm not IN love with you". Knowing Mac excused his adultery with those exact words cheapened them even more. The breaker of a dozen hearts tasted the bitterness, the gall of anger— that a man would utter those words to Marti. Yet, his history contained the same—and anyway—any man?

"Marti, did he explain 'I love you but I'm not in love with you'?"

"I asked him to, but he said no one could explain it—it was something that just happened. But when it did happen you would know it. You just couldn't explain it."

"Of course it can be explained. Would you like for me to do it?"

"Yes, I would, if you can."

Very slowly and very carefully the old womanizer, temporarily turned counselor by the pain in his friend's sorrowful eyes, established the conditions which prompt a man to utter those words and the probable state of his heart and mind when he did. He concluded the discussion by declaring, "Loverly, any one of three situations might exist to make him believe he loves you but he's not in love with you: an unappreciated and unsavory familiarity with your body; taking you for granted, which usually means he trusts with unscrupulous faith your commitment to him and can therefore do what he wants without fear of losing you; and then of course, getting involved sexually with someone else."

"You hit him right between the eyes, Reb. He exhibited all of that."

"What have you done about it?"

"The first thing I did was forgive him for screwing the Bimbo. Then I talked to him until I was blue in the face—for three and a half years. I tried to have sex with him—for the first year or so, then I quit trying. I tried to get him to go with me to see a counselor. He wouldn't."

"Does the woman still work for him?"

"No, not exactly. His boss transferred her to another area, but he still sees her—at work—and probably at her apartment. We don't talk about it any more—and haven't for three years."

"You still love him, don't you?" Patie tried to tone

his question so that it might sound official, antiseptic, formal. He wasn't deceptive, never had to be. He always asked questions forthrightly, directly, but he wanted Marti to think, no, to know, he was trying to help her, to provide answers from a man's perspective. He wondered if the sound of his voice conveyed that message, yet suspected it didn't. His mind wanted to hear the hurt wife say she still loved her husband. That way, what he had come to the Bay to do would be easier. But his heart—his heart!! His heart wasn't even supposed to be involved in all of this. He was Patie Corbin, the woman's man, the breaker of hearts, a modern Casanova in shoulder pads. He learned a long time ago to rein in his heart while at the same time turning his mind—and charm, loose to roam where they would.

Oh, hell, admit it, he wanted to hear her say she had stopped loving the jerk.

Her retort was sudden and much too forceful, contained too much emotion and it did not conform to the evident condition of her heart, "NO!! I don't know, I've tried not to, and I have lost respect for him. To be honest, I don't even WANT sex with him any more. We sleep in the same bed sometimes—he on his side and me, mine. He's civil to me and I am to him. He hugs me like cousins, or brothers and sisters hug one another."

Patie's heart wasn't cooperating. "So you made up your mind to find someone else?"

"Yes, but not just someone. I'm not going to pick up a man—in a bar—or on the beach."

"You and I met on the beach."

"But you're not JUST a man. And besides, I

already knew a lot about you."

"A lot of bad stuff."

"And good stuff," the female countered. "I've heard about your speaking at school assemblies—and civic clubs, athletic banquets—and—Fellowship of Christian Athletes meetings—even churches."

"Some of which made a hypocrite out of me. I discovered I wasn't always able to do what I knew I should do, and what I encouraged others to do, especially concerning alcohol and sex—even drugs."

"You took drugs?"

"I came out of the NFL on drugs."

"You gotta be kidding! What? I thought the NFL was really tough on drugs."

"They are now, but when I played, things were a little looser."

"What did you do?"

"Bennies—Benzedrine, uppers. Our trainer filled a punch bowl with them the day of the game and set it on a table in the training room. The players took a handful of them, enough for the game and to last through practices the following week."

"Did they help your performance on the field?"

"Yep! Many people thought then that it was only psychological but it wasn't. Without question they kept players from getting tired. Now everyone knows it isn't just mental. That's why they're banned now—, why the NFL has banned all drugs."

"Are you still on them?"

"No. I gradually stopped after I retired from football. Haven't taken a Bennie or any other illegal drug in, oh, I guess about twenty years now. Don't even want them any more. Wait a minute, how did we get on this subject, Loverly?"

"You said you were a hypocrite—"

"Yes and you said I wasn't just ANY man—"

"And you aren't Patie. You're special to me and I really want to have a relationship with you. I know it's over between Mac and me. We bought our house together and real estate's very expensive here in Bay St. Louis. It takes both our salaries to make our house payment and live comfortably."

Marti's mind was on a roll now and she spoke rapidly—with emotion. The storm water behind an earthen dam had burst free and was pouring through, unbound, unfettered. She had come to this moment, finally, a woman convinced she should do what she was about to do, wanted to do. She knew Patie Corbin better than he knew her, but she wanted him to know her, to know that she wasn't promiscuous, wasn't a tramp, wasn't loose morally. She was aging and she admitted to herself that she wanted it all—laughing, holding hands, holding each other tightly, respect for one another, trust and faith—and sex—and—all those things. She had been looking, for the past several months—looking—and now she had stopped looking. She knew Patie might eventually hurt her. Hell, he might not even want her right now. He acts like he does but it might be just that—an act. She wouldn't expect much. He's not divorced yet and he might be in love with someone else—he hadn't said—either way. Probably not, though, otherwise he wouldn't want to be seen with me—but—but—

he didn't. That could have been because SHE was married though, not because he was committed to someone else. I'll tell him, she thought, I'll tell him I won't give him a problem. I won't cling, or beg, or cry when he's gone—but for four months, or was it six, that he'll be here—we could give to each other so much, no commitments—no regrets—that's what I'll tell him—no commitments—no regrets. Maybe I can give him, well, companionship while he's here and he can give me attention and—and sex.

"I told Mac I wanted a relationship with a man. That we would continue to live together if he wanted but that I would no longer live without love, and that included sex."

"What did he say?"

"Something stupid as hell and as shallow as his feeling for me—'Well, you gotta' do what you gotta' do'."

"When did this conversation take place, Loverly?"

"About two months ago, maybe three."

"Has it come up again?"

"No, but neither has his d—, his desire for me."

"Go ahead and say it, it's not going to bother me," he taunted. Her eyes had dropped back to their entwined hands. With his right one, he gently lifted her face to the place where their eyes met. She smiled.

"Marti, I need to tell you something, about my marriage—my marriages."

"Everyone in Mississippi knows about your three marriages to Mattie Stein, Patie,"

"I was married to someone else, too."

"Everyone knows about your marriage to Kimberly Burkes, Patie. Besides, you told me about your marriages earlier, remember?"

"But what everyone including you doesn't know, Loverly, is that Kimberly and I are planning to marry again. I want you to know that. I want everything on top of the table, visible, honest. I'm going to be in The Bay four more months finishing the book and then I'm going to leave to marry Kim. I want you to know that. I don't want to hurt anyone else the rest of my life—especially you."

The man, softened by the passing years, or perhaps by hearts which he had shattered, or lives he had wrecked, did not want to sound arrogant to this pretty woman who was in the act of offering herself to him, nor did he want to hurt her. Whatever else should be true, this must be—she must know his plans and his feelings perfectly, but he wanted her to know also that she wasn't the only one who could be hurt.

"—Nor do I want to be hurt. I believe I love Kim—"

He weakened it, damn it, he thought—he weakened it! He didn't say "I LOVE Kim" nor did he assert "I'm absolutely, without question, ten-thousand percent certain that I love Kim. He said "I believe I love Kim." Was he so afraid of Marti's rejection that he modified his declaration, inserted doubt into it? Why is Marti so appealing to him? Did the weak statement manifest a hidden truth within him, a truth which he was unwilling to admit even to himself?

"—And I'll be leaving here in a few weeks. Can

you handle all of that, Marti?"

Marti had dropped her melancholy eyes back to their hands while the old pretender, turned virtuous, talked. Ten seconds passed, then another ten, perhaps a minute. Slowly she lifted her eyes, softened by sensuality—and locked them into his again. Her answer was inexorable, considered, unequivocal. "Yes!"

"You sure?"

"I said 'yes!'"

The ex-pro loosened his hand from hers. He placed each of his hands on the sides of her responsive face and for a moment, from only a few inches away, each gazed deeply into the glowing eyes of the other, as though with human sight they could search each others' minds. Then the man drew the woman's face to his and they kissed deeply, more deeply than they had earlier, with conviction, and intensity released by the commitment they had made to one another, a commitment of freedom and respect, a commitment of no commitment— no regrets. He would provide closeness and sex, she, companionship. Slowly her hand dropped to his stomach, then to the upper part of his leg. The ecstatic sound of a slow-moving zipper filled the vacuum of his brain.

"Let's go upstairs, Loverly."

"No, not tonight. I can't tonight. What I want to do for you, I can do right here."

Their faces moved apart—his backward to the loveseat—hers downward to the towers of exultation.

Thirty minutes later Patie, alone now, Marti having hurried home in order to be there by midnight, could not, for the life of him stop the old fifties song from invading his gratified mind: *Oh, oh, oh, oh, yes I'm the Great Pretender; Pretending that I'm doing well; My need is such, I pretend too much; I'm lonely but no one can tell.*

CHAPTER NINE

The Chinaman Chun and his small companion stood in front of the Delta incoming flights panel in the New Orleans International Airport. They looked intently at the lighted board, searching for the flight number and arrival gate of a flight from Atlanta due to land at ten thirty-five, neither speaking. Finally, the little man, part Chinese and part American, spoke, "There it is, flight 1344. It's coming in at gate 22."

The larger man asked, "It is on time?"

"Yes. Gate 22, on time."

"Then you meet him at gate. I go to car. Bring him there."

"Mr. Chun, it's only ten o'clock. He'll probably have to get some luggage from baggage claim. We may not get to your car until ten forty-five or later. Why

159

don't we go to the bar for--"

"No, you to gate. Plane may be early. I wait in car, understand?"

"I understand, Mr. Chun. We still have time to get a beer."

"No, you go to gate. Do what I tell."

"Okay, I'll meet him at the gate," the diminutive partner complained. Chun watched until the part American disappeared through security and down the wide, well lighted hallway toward gate 22. The terminal, usually very busy, wasn't crowded at ten o'clock at night, although more passengers were there than Chun expected. Satisfied that his companion had indeed gone to gate 22, he turned away, walked slowly to the escalator, riding it the one flight down to street level, past baggage claim and through the tunnel to the parking garage where his black Lexus 400 was parked.

The middle-age Chinese spy was not happy. Research had been delayed again and the American could offer no reasonable explanation. Then too, the NASA worker had left the area without informing him, which worried the muscular man. The American SAID he was in Maine visiting his sick mother but he could have been anywhere, even Washington talking to anyone, the American authorities—the Secret Service, the CIA, the FBI. Or he could have met with representatives from another country, in order to raise the ante— get two or three countries bidding against one another for the prize, which might be one of the most heavily sought after in the history of mankind, certainly in the history of medical science. The American, already two months late in delivering the formula, had left The Bay in a hurry, without a contact. That worried and angered Chun. The call from Maine did little to mitigate the Chinaman's concern. The last meeting with Claiborne at Buccaneer Park had not been satisfactory and Chun had already decided the time had come to finalize the deal. Then too, there was the American—the American—footballer. The Chinaman didn't like it, another man being involved with Claiborne's wife. What did she know? What did she tell the footballer? The situation was becoming far too complex for the spy, too involved.

When the Delta 727 pulled up to the gate, the Chinaman's partner rose from his seat and positioned himself where he could see everyone getting off the plane. He had darted into a nearby lounge, downed a couple of beers and eaten a small bowl of peanuts before assuming his waiting position at gate 22. The plane was a few minutes early, and he had been there only a short time, when the 727 arrived.

Chun was absolutely void of all fear or sense of humor, the small spy thought, reckless at Buccaneer Park, furious at almost getting caught placing the electronic button under the football player, Patie Corbin's van. The large Chinaman's frustration had only increased when they were forced to drive into Gulfport, to replace the shirt which Corbin had torn off the little man. Now at a large international airport near The Bay he sends the reluctant accomplice to meet the scientist, apparently ignoring the fact that someone might easily recognize them. Made no sense but waving the pistol out at Buccaneer didn't either. Oh well, the small colleague thought, I've gotta' do it so might as well not worry about it.

The minute spy positioned himself so that other people who were waiting for passengers stood between himself and those getting off the plane. He wanted to find Claiborne before the passenger spotted him, making certain that the NASA worker was alone—or that no one else came to meet him. He would follow him down the wide hallway for a short distance, catch up to him from behind, tell him that Chun was waiting in the car to talk to him. That way seemed safer than approaching him as soon as he exited the tunnel from the plane.

Two thirds of the passengers had already gotten off when the short man spotted Claiborne. He could see only his head, could not determine if he were alone. No one waiting for the passengers approached the ambling associate, as he moved through the crowd. The little spy maneuvered himself to one side of the waiting area where he could easily spot Claiborne proceeding through the people and to a position which would place him thirty feet or so behind the traitor when he started walking down the hall.

The spy hated this part of his assignment—too much light—too many people. Even though it was in the middle of day, meeting at Buccaneer had been much better, no one else had seen them, well, other than the man and woman and two kids having a noon-day picnic. There were no cops, no joggers, no cyclists. The motel room after dark was much better than either the park or the airport.

What th' hell? Who's that, for Heavens sake?, the illegal scout exclaimed under his breath. A woman— attached to the man's right arm. The spy hadn't seen her until Claiborne moved out of the crowd and started down the hall. She wasn't much taller than the spy himself, that's why he hadn't seen her, a blonde in tight jeans, a blue silk blouse which hung down to her hips, and white walking shoes. The two walked slowly, probably because they knew their luggage would delay them anyway, and seemed completely oblivious of their surroundings, unconcerned about all the people walking down the hallway beside them, in front of them, behind them. Stupid! How stupid can a man be? And he's supposed to be smart, a scientist—! Maybe scientists are as ignorant in illicit affairs as medical doctors are in business.

Walking a short distance behind the two, the impatient man wondered what he should do. If he caught up with them, stopped them, and insisted upon talking to Claiborne alone, it would look suspicious to the woman and probably indicate that the meeting was not accidental. If the lady happened to be Lori, the one with whom he was involved, she would almost certainly question the situation. Then when Claiborne left her to talk to Chun she would realize something serious, if not sinister was occurring. Where would she wait? No question his entrance into their lives right now would present a serious problem for the man.

Maybe at some point between here and baggage claim the two would separate for some reason and he could talk to the scientist alone. She might visit the

ladies room, or he might go to the men's. While he waited for the luggage, she may get a bite to eat or something
to drink. Perhaps at the luggage carousel itself
Claiborne would stand near the belt while the woman
waited for him in another area. They couldn't have
much luggage—they had been gone, what, six, seven
days?

Well, she doesn't need to visit the ladies room,
nor he the men's room, the spy realized as the three of
them passed restrooms, then a Starbucks coffee bar,
where only two people waited in line. They apparently
wanted neither coffee nor a snack. The contact would
be at baggage claim. He would have to talk to him at
baggage claim. He could only hope the two would separate there. He did not want the woman to see him, but
if the man and woman did not separate there, he would
have no choice but to approach Claiborne, ask him for
privacy, and tell him Chun was waiting to see him in the
parking garage. Damn it—damn it to hell, he hated this
kind of business, sloppy, reckless, dangerous. If he got
through this night without the woman seeing him, without her suspecting something unusual, it would be a miracle, a miracle—an unlikely miracle.

What would Chun want him to do? Let him go
back to The Bay and talk to him another time? Or talk
to him in the presence, albeit a removed presence of the
woman? The half-American, half-Chinese spy, already
shaken, became extremely nervous. He wanted to run
down the escalator and sprint through the parking
garage to Chun. What do you want me to do, Mr. Chun,
pull him away from the blonde woman and talk to him or

let him go? Those may be my only two choices—what do you want me to do? I'll do what you say, I want to do what you want. What should I do? He might be able to run to Chun and get back before Claiborne's luggage made it, but what if he didn't? He would lose him. Did the scientist park his car in the garage? Maybe we could wait just outside the toll gate! That wouldn't work, there are several gates out of here, and besides they might catch a cab, or a friend might pick them up. No, that will not work, he must talk to him at baggage claim, even if the woman sees! She could be dealt with later if need be.

The three walkers, two in front, one a few feet behind, moved up the hallway, past security, and to the escalator. The little spy had closed the distance between himself and the pair so that only five people rode the escalator down between himself and them. At the bottom of the moving stairway the couple stepped over to their left and stopped. When the spy reached the bottom, he darted to the right behind Claiborne's back, maneuvered himself behind the escalator, no more than ten feet away, hidden by it and those riding down it. Claiborne spoke to the woman, pointed toward the passageway to the garage and moved through the throng of people to the automated carousel belt which would deliver their bags. By the time he anchored himself close to the belt, the relieved spy, unnoticed by the taller man, stood beside him.

"Mr. Claiborne?"

"Yes. What! Spikes—what the hell—What are you doing here?" the scientist exclaimed, jerking his head around toward the blonde, who stood unnoticing fifty feet away on the distant side of the waiting baggage collectors. Satisfied that she had not seen the dialog between the two, Claiborne turned back toward the spy and whispered again, "Spikes, what the hell are you doing here?"

"Chun wants to see you."

"When?"

"Tonight, as soon as you get your luggage."

"Where is he?"

"Sitting in his car—in the parking garage."

Glancing back over his shoulder toward the attractive blonde, the shaken American breathed, "I have a problem, I have someone—"

"Mr. Claiborne, Mr. Chun wants to see you. You must not let the woman see us talking and you must not tell her about us. She cannot know what you are doing."

Claiborne grew alarmed, obviously alarmed. His face turned red and his eyes squinted. A thin line of perspiration formed on his wrinkled brow and across his twitching upper lip. Caught in an unexpected vise, hemmed in between two powerful opposing forces, his attention was redirected—away from the bags which were beginning to appear on the large moving belt onto Spikes, who stood relentlessly beside him. The frustrated man wanted to reach down onto the carousel, pluck his two hanging bags off it, grab Lori, get to his car and drive to Bay St. Louis. Maybe Chun would let him do that. He could drop Lori off in Waveland and meet Chun and Spikes at the motel—.

"Spikes, this isn't going to work. Ask Mr. Chun if

I can meet him later tonight at his—"

"Mr. Chun wants to see you now—in his car in the parking garage. I cannot allow you out of my sight. Please get your luggage and come with me, Mr. Claiborne. Mr. Chun has been waiting forty-five minutes already."

"What am I going to tell Lori? I can't just walk— I mean, I can't just tell her—What am I going to say to her?"

Spikes held a higher opinion of Americans than Chun. After all, he was half American. His dad had fought in the Korean Conflict, and had met Spikes' mother, who was working at the Chinese embassy, while on R & R in Tokyo. Along with her mother and father, Spikes' mom had escaped the iron curtain, first to Singapore, then to Sidney. A year later his father bought passage on a freighter for the Chinese family to San Francisco. Several months after they arrived in America, Spikes' father, now discharged from the army, returned to the States. He and the Chinese woman were married and three years later little Spikes was born. He grew up closely attached to his mother, especially after his father deserted them for an American waitress, his mother said. Though an American citizen, Spikes' mother continued to love her homeland and when a Chinese diplomat visited her one day, convincing the Chinese woman and her son to spy for China was very easy. The emissary gave them money to move from San Francisco to Picayune, Mississippi where they were to get jobs, or try to, at the large NASA plant which was even then being built. It was there that Spikes' mom heard about the research being conducted seeking a cure for cancer. Shortly after that they focused their attention onto Mac Claiborne, one of the experimenting scientists, a weak man who had been part of the rebellious hippy movement of the nineteen sixties, married to a pretty wife, but who was having an affair with his secretary. He had refused to fight in Viet Nam, and along with others, fled to Canada to avoid the draft. And, Spikes discovered, the scientist was in debt—up to his eyeballs.

Spikes sympathized with Claiborne, in his dilemma, but that changed nothing. Chun wanted to see him, tonight, in the parking garage. Neither he nor the scientist had a choice.

"Tell her to go back upstairs to the restaurant, order you a drink and as soon as you get your two bags, you'll meet her there—that you've gotten hungry."

Shaken, his voice quivering, the uneasy man blurted out, "But we ate on the plane. She knows I'm not hungry—I missed a bag, Spikes—there goes one of my bags, I missed it."

"It'll come back around, Mr. Claiborne. Please collect your bags and talk to the lady. I'll be watching. As soon as you send her away, follow me to Mr. Chun's car." Spikes watched as his NASA connection pulled both of his bags off the carousel and walked toward the woman.

Claiborne's throat was dry as he made his way slowly through the crowd, at least half of whom were still waiting on THEIR luggage. The fine sliver of sweat still moistened his face and his heart thumped against the walls of his chest. He could tell it was beating much harder and faster then usual and it bothered him greatly. He wasn't young anymore and people die from hearts running away like this. He knew why Chun wanted to talk to him and he dreaded it with all of his hesitant being. Chun was mean, maybe evil, and Claiborne feared him for good reason. The Chinaman held the American scientist's entire future in the palm of his hand—no, his entire professional life—in fact he held even his physical life in the palm of his—hell!—he had considered all of that before but tonight it seemed more than just possible, as it had in the past, probable, maybe. The two spies had seen him with Lori, now they thought they could squeeze him into obedience with that knowledge. He loved Lori and he wanted to marry her but he needed Marti right now, needed her status in life, her income which was almost as much as his, especially since NASA had slowed down research on the cancer project. He didn't know why yet, he couldn't find out, but he had grown very concerned about it. Even more so when he asked for a week off and got it. Now he must provide answers to Chun, not tomorrow after returning to work when he might get information about the work-stoppage but tonight, in just a few minutes. By the time the miserable boyfriend reached the blonde waiting for him at the exit to the parking garage, a knot feeling the size of a softball had developed in his stomach and he could not erase the uninvited sick expression off his face, a look which Lori quickly noticed.

"What's wrong, Honey? You look like you've just seen a ghost. Are you ill?"

"Lori, while I was waiting for the bags, I heard a couple of guys talking and their conversation reminded me of something I forgot to do this week involving a lot of money. Now listen carefully. I want you to go back upstairs to the lounge and order yourself a drink. In twenty minutes or so order a White Russian for me. I should be up there by then, I have to make several phone calls to—"

"This late at night?"

"These guys are friends. They won't mind me calling this late."

"You haven't said anything to me about a new business deal with friends."

"I was going to surprise you if and when it went through. Trust me with this. I'll explain it to you later, okay?"

"Are you sure about this, Mac? Are you telling me the truth?"

Mac felt additional frustration easing into his already established despondency. The last thing in the world he wanted to do was to offend or frighten Lori— no, the LAST thing would be to make an incontestable enemy out of Chun—.

"Lori, I need to make the calls before it gets too late. Please go on upstairs. I'll join you in a little while. Don't forget my White Russian."

Claiborne's girlfriend looked disbelievingly at him for a moment and shook her head. "It's hard for me to believe that this can't wait until—"

"Please, Lori"

"Okay, Mac, okay. But could you hurry? It's

already ten-thirty."

"I won't be long—I promise."

The concerned paramour watched Lori turn, walk toward the "up" escalator, catch it and disappear into the main part of the terminal. When he turned back around, Spikes was standing beside him, reaching for one of the folded clothes bags. "Here, let me carry this for you."

"Enter the car, Mr. Claiborne, please." Chun had rolled both front windows down and was looking toward the passageway which led into the baggage area when the two men came through it. After Claiborne closed the car door, the Chinaman asked "Did you make good trip, old friend?" Spikes had settled into the back seat with the two bags.

"Yes, I had a good trip, Mr. Chun. Can't this wait until we get back to The Bay? I have someone with me and I need to get her back—."

"You have with you someone? Who?" He asked Claiborne the question but he turned and faced his small companion in the back seat, the annoyed expression on his face demanding an explanation.

"A woman, Mr. Chun," Spikes answered. "He sent her to the lounge. She doesn't know he's here."

"Who is this woman, Mr. Claiborne?"

"A friend."

"A good friend, Mr. Claiborne?"

"Yes, Mr. Chun, a good friend." Mac could not keep the quiver out of his voice as he faced the man for whom he held great fear. The Chinese mind, he knew, considered life differently, arranged facts intellectually into strange configurations and often drew totally opposite conclusions from the Caucasian, especially the American. How would he view this, his being involved with a woman—other than his wife? He assumed he already knew.

"You sleep with her, have sex with her?"

"I don't know why you should be—"

"If you have sex with her and you married, then woman can—how you say—?"

"Blackmail!" Spikes chimed in.

"Yes, blackmail—woman can blackmail you and that my business."

"She can't blackmail me, Mr. Chun—my wife already knows about her."

"Maybe true, maybe not true but you not to tell woman any'ting, understand? Do you understand, Mr. Claiborne? You not to tell her, not to tell your wife, not to tell anyone about us or what you do, understand, Mr. Claiborne?"

"I understand, Mr. Chun." Claiborne could see the consuming fire in the Chinaman's eyes, hear the obsessive tone in his high pitched voice. There was no doubt that the man meant what he said. He would kill if he had to, without hesitation, without guilt, without remorse. Claiborne knew the spy could not go back to China without the formula—he had nothing to lose. "I haven't told anyone, Mr. Chun, and I will not tell anyone about what I am doing, nor about you nor Mr. Spikes— I swear to you."

"When do you give to me the information, Mr. Claiborne?" Chun failed to acknowledge Claiborne's persuasive promise of secrecy. He ignored it and that lack of a response in itself added to the sovereignty of this foreigner over an American citizen, who, for money, placed himself under the Chinaman's authority and alienated himself from national loyalty. Claiborne dreaded to hear the words which must now come out of his own mouth.

"Mr. Chun, I've been gone for a week to visit—"

"You've been gone for week with woman, American." The contempt in Chun's voice could not be missed, not by a man already fearing for his life.

"It's true, I took Lori with me but I had to go see about—"

"Why you not call to say you were going. Why you slip off in secret?" the Chinaman interrupted again.

"When we last met, Mr. Chun, you told me not to call until I had all the information. Research has been delayed-"

Chun interrupted Claiborne again. "When does research begin? When do I get the info'mation, Mr. Claiborne? How you know research not begun while you gone? How you know?"

"It hasn't begun, can't begin without me. I called last Friday. It hasn't begun again. I go back to work tomorrow, Mr. Chun, and I'll find out more about what's going on then—I'll call you tomorrow night."

"You call tomorrow night, Mr. Claiborne. I give you one more week to get info'mation. Understand, Mr. American. I give you one more week."

"I understand, Mr. Chun, but if research hasn't begun again, I can't—"

Was this it, was this the drawing of the noose, the line in the sand? How could he sell information which hasn't even been developed? Could the Chinaman be that—blind, that ignorant. Could he be bluffing? If so, that meant he believed the scientist was lying, that he already had the formula. If he wasn't bluffing that meant a week from now he must hand the spy the formula, or—or what? Be killed?

"I understand, Mr. Chun—I'll give you everything a week from now, everything I have."

"Do you know your wife has boyfriend, Mr. Claiborne?"

"WHAT!?"

"Your wife has boyfriend."

"What do you mean Marti has a boyfriend? Do you mean she's going out—out--." Claiborne's voice trailed off into excruciating silence and he turned toward Spikes in the back seat for denial, to hear him say that it was a mistake, probably went to lunch with another teacher and was seen by someone. Not a real boyfriend, not the kind you would go to bed with—not Marti. Marti loved him, of that he was certain and he knew, had heard all his life that men and women are different. Men are tempted through their eyes, can't help it, way they are born, part of their nature, like testosterone and mustaches. But women are tempted through other things, like respect, gentleness, personality, discipline, and then after that, touch. She could never let another man actually touch her—not as long as she loves

174

him. She would have to stop loving him and then be confronted with all these other things and he'd only been gone for a week, for Heaven's sake. She hugged him and told him to take care of himself the day he left. She hasn't had time to develop a boyfriend since he has been gone—has she? Has she?

The question haunted Claiborne as he looked from Chun to Spikes to Chun and then to Spikes again. In the past he imagined he wouldn't care if Marti got involved with someone else, she as much as told him she was going to after she found out about Lori. He imagined it would not bother him but just hearing the words, "your wife has a boyfriend" sent waves of nausea into his stomach. He wanted to throw up.

"What do you mean, she has a boyfriend?" he repeated, looking finally at Spikes as though an American could perhaps explain it better, could understand how a woman might eat lunch with a man, a platonic friend, a friend-boy and not actually—not actually—be a —.

"Your wife has a boyfriend, Mr. Claiborne." Spikes' sharp voice contained no more compassion, no more uncertainty than Chun's. It was harsh, critical, unqualified.

Claiborne felt strength ooze from his legs, and he groped for confidence, turning away from Spikes. Then he quickly glanced at Chun and for thirty seconds or so peered spiritlessly through the windshield toward all the other cars parked in front of the Lexus. A moment or two later, he turned weakly back toward Spikes, then Chun, both of whom were looking intently at the adulterer who just learned his wife was more than likely an adulteress. "How can you be so certain?" he meekly asked.

"We have been following her—for two days—and two nights. We have seen your wife and the man together with our own eyes."

"You followed her?" the sickened man inquired. "Why did you follow her?"

"We drive by your house to check on you and we see them, walking on the beach together, at your house together, at his condo together, eating together. We have pictures."

"You have been checking on me?"

"Of course, Mr. Claiborne. We know when you get to work. We know when you get home from work, we watch you jog in the afternoon. We know when you turn your lights off at night. We know where you buy groceries and gas, and we know where you like to eat dinner—with the blonde—and with your wife."

"Then, you already knew about Lori?" meekly he whined.

"Certainly! We have pictures of you with her, too. The stakes are very high, Mr. Claiborne—the cost of failure very great. We leave nothing to chance."

"You say you have pictures of Marti and the man?"

"Yes. You want to see them?" Spikes asked.

"Yes."

The tiny spy reached down and lifted a brown briefcase off the floorboard, placed it on the seat and punched the two buttons which opened it. The sound of the opening container thundered through the Lexus, two 105 howitzers exploding directly behind Mac's head, projectiles of disappointment and travail, ripping through the defenses of his heart. Spikes reached into the case, extracted a stack of photographs and placed them into the strengthless and frightened man's hand. Chun flipped on the Lexus' overhead light.

Mac held the pictures for a moment as if summoning strength from some far off place, perhaps from childhood when he was considered a promising high school basket-ball player, or maybe from the time he avoided the Viet Nam draft by fleeing to Canada. He took a deep breath, held the first picture up and looked.

Marti and a muscular man were walking on the beach and laughing; neither of which she had done with him in months.

Marti and a man were hugging in his kitchen.

Marti and the same man were kissing—and the date and time written across the bottom of the picture said it happened only a few hours ago.

There were other pictures. He refused to look and handed them back to Spikes. Tears, stimulated by the emotions of the evening, especially the troubling news about Marti, moistened his eyes and he wiped them quickly away.

"Do you know the man, Mr. Claiborne?"

"No. Do you?" he feebly asked.

"We know his name. Patie Corbin. And we know he just recently moved to The Bay, a few weeks ago."

Claiborne stunned already by Chun's threat and now by Marti's involvement, whimpered, "Did you say his name is Patie Corbin?"

"Yes. Do you know the name?"

"I've heard it. He's some kind of a professional athlete, either baseball or football—football I think."

Chun, who had been patiently listening to the dialog between Claiborne and Spikes suddenly exclaimed, "What does the man do with your wife? He screw her but what else? Why he come to her when you leave? What he after? If she know nothing, why he want her?"

"Marti is a beautiful woman, Mr. Chun, a lot of men—"

"No. He want something else too. You find out, Mr. Claiborne, you find out what he after."

Mac Claiborne desperately wanted to end the conversation, gather up Lori, get back to The Bay, and he became even more distraught than he had been before, pushed into vulnerability and insecurity by these two vile men, with their threats and their sickening pictures. His problems had multiplied several times since he got off that Delta 727, and then multiplied again. Maybe when he was physically removed from the two spies presence, his afflictions would seem less severe.

"Can I go now, Mr. Chun?"

"Yes, Mr. Claiborne, you go now but you get formula for me in one week—and you find out what this man Corbin want. You understand? You do this, understand?"

"I understand Mr. Chun. I still understand. You'll hear from me, I promise."

"Would you like for us to drop you off at your

car, Mr. Claiborne?" offered Spikes.

Claiborne hesitated, uncertain, doubtful. He had left his car in Quick Park, a remote long-term parking lot, and caught their shuttle to the terminal. He could have Chun drop him off there and drive back to short-term but that would take time, although he would not have to man-handle his bags anymore, or rather have them manhandle him. He wondered about Lori. She might be looking for him even now and he wanted to get away from the two spies. "Thank you, no. I need to go back in for Lori—before she gets worried and maybe suspicious." He opened his door and by the time he pushed his trembling body into a standing position, Spikes had gotten out too, and set both bags on the pavement beside the left rear tire of the Lexus. Mac picked both bags up and walked nervously back toward the terminal, glaring back as the Lexus rolled through the garage, disappearing in the direction of the toll booth.

"Mac, I hope that's you."

"It's me, Marti. Sorry I woke you."

"That's okay. Glad you made it back. How was MeeMaw when you left?" Marti shouted from the bedroom. Mac had turned the kitchen lights on and it sounded like he was moving items around in the refrigerator, probably pouring himself some ice water, which he always did at bed-time.

"She was better. Just a minute, I'm getting some ice water. I'll be there in a second."

Marti turned the bedroom lamp on and glanced

at the bed-side clock. It was twelve-thirty-eight. She reached down to the foot of the king-sized bed for her housecoat. She had discovered, several years ago a total absence of desire to exhibit her naked body to Mac, who revealed absolutely no interest. My pride, or maybe dignity, she thought. She knew Mac would come into her bedroom and give her his big, customary, meaningless, conscience-easing hug and she wanted to be completely covered when he did, so she sat on the side of her bed and waited. A few minutes later he walked slowly into her bedroom, hugged her, and sat on the bed, far enough away so that he could turn slightly toward her and look into her face.

The estranged wife marveled at her wayward husband's appearance, the depressed expression on his face, his slumped shoulders, his tentative tone of voice. Immediately after sitting, he leaned over, resting his elbows upon his knees, his head down, neck twisted slightly to his left gazing obliquely at his curious wife.

"I missed you, Marti," the adulterer whispered.

"Where did that come from, Mac? You haven't missed me in years. You sure your mother is alright?"

"She's alright. Marti, we need to talk. Could we do that tonight. I know it's late, but I really need to—"

"Not tonight, Mac. It's almost one o'clock. Can't it wait until tomorrow?"

"I suppose it can but I would really like to—"

"Not tonight, Mac. We'll do it tomorrow if you still want to," she interrupted.

"You promise you'll talk to me tomorrow?"

"I don't have to promise, Mac, I gave you my

word."

Probably having problems with Lori, the hardened wife thought, as her weak husband walked out of the bedroom. He probably wants me to counsel him, the idiot. I'll do a lot of things for him, she reckoned, but one of them will definitely not be counseling him about Lori.

"Good night, Marti."

"Good night, Mac."

CHAPTER TEN

Patie pushed himself out of bed at 6:59, exactly one minute before the alarm went off. He staggered into the bathroom, taking care of all necessary tasks, including an extended period of brushing his teeth—or rather his gums. A dentist friend had told him years ago that "healthy gums hold on to many teeth". At night he spent even more time on them, brushing, flossing, brushing again with a fluoride mixture, treating the gums with a horrible, soap-tasting liquid called hyber-cleanse or some such name, which was supposed to stop all gum disease, and then swishing Listermint around in his mouth for forty-five seconds. That extended procedure must work because every time he sat down in his dentist friend's chair, the old football teammate grunted several times and then exclaimed, "Not on man nor beast have I ever seen better looking gums than these. Boy, if you had been as diligent practicing football as you are working on your mouth, you would have made all twelve of those All-American teams rather than those measly eight you made." Patie could never respond because by that time his mouth was filled with dentist hands. At parties he accused the dentist of self-adulation—boasting about his advice.

The new coast resident splashed a little water on his face, massaged his scalp which was supposed to make it grip the hair, which he combed. Then he slipped on a pair of loose bermuda shorts, a tee shirt which advertised the Grove on the campus at Ole Miss, some flip flops and walked down the stairs on his daily trek to hunt a Clarion Ledger, the Jackson daily newspaper. He checked his coffee pot on the way out, making certain, first of all that he had fixed it last night and that he had set the automatic timer—so it would be ready when he got out of bed.

"Well, would you look at that," the old writer exclaimed, exhibiting a touch of negativism, "I actually made the coffee and set the timer. Wow—I am arriving."

So far he had not found a place in Bay St. Louis where he could buy a Clarion Ledger. A local paper, yes, and the Times-Picayune out of New Orleans which was everywhere, stacked on Quick-stop counters, filling numerous paper racks, given out freely in coffee shops. "Hell," he had exclaimed in frustration to one Cajun gas station owner, "I thought Bay St. Louis was in Mississippi. This must be a Cajun town. I think it ought to secede from Mississippi and join Louisiana."

Apparently the man saw little humor in Patie's exclamation—he didn't laugh.

The searcher had decided to look for a Clarion Ledger on Highway 90 West all the way to Highway 603 this morning, that part he had not already searched, the last mile or so of it. This morning was no different, the disgusted newspaper reader discovered, and forty minutes later he took his Times-Picayune to the back deck, which faced west, away from the rising sun, with a mug of coffee, sweetened by artificial sweetener, one pink and one blue, no cream. The moment he flopped down into the folding lawn chair and deposited his NFL coffee mug on the top rail surrounding the deck, his phone rang. He made a mad dash back inside.

"Reb, you awake?"

"Mornin', Loverly. Wide awake. I've already been out Clarion Ledger hunting," he fumed as he plopped down onto one of the straight-back rented breakfast-table chairs.

"What?"

"Oh, just a little frustration. I can't find a—by the way, do you take the Clarion Ledger?"

"The newspaper?"

"Yeah, Loverly, the Clarion Ledger, from Jackson.

"No, as a matter of fact, we don't take any newspaper. Liberals don't read newspapers—they just try to do good," she snickered.

"Yeah, right. Do you know anyone who sells it?"

"No, not off-hand but you ought to be able to find one on 90."

"I've looked—I can't find one anywhere in this town."

"Sorry about that. Patie, we have a problem and boy, do I hate to tell you about it." Her voice was soft, solemn and the old Rebel could tell by the tone of it that she indeed seemed worried, or else she was about to pull his leg—again. Suddenly he remembered that Mac was due home at midnight last night and he wondered whether or not the problem concerned him, if Marti wasn't joking.

"Where are you, Loverly?"

"At school"

"Mac make it in last night?"

"Yes, about twelve-thirty. Patie, he knows about us—"

"WHAT!? You ARE kidding aren't you?"

"No. He knows about us."

"How do you know? Did he tell you? Does he have proof—?" Patie had never really been caught red-handed with another man's wife before, he didn't think,—certainly not this quickly! He had always prided himself on being smarter than those who tried to catch him, including girlfriends when he started dating other women, certainly husbands who trusted their wives or who didn't care, like Marti described Mac. But the experienced paramour knew already who had caught him. The men in the black Lexus 400 had followed him for a reason—damn private investigators, stupidly conspicuous in their black Lexus, two Chinamen even.

"Patie, Mac has pictures." Marti spoke softly, slowly, without emotion, causing her lover to wonder if she cared that they had been caught, maybe even glad. Hell, she may have hired the two Asians for all he knew, though that thought certainly struck at the heart of his male ego.

"Start at the beginning, Marti, tell me all of it."

"Well, when he came in last night, he looked a little haggard like something was really bothering him and he told me he had missed me, which would have blown my panties off if I had been wearing any. Then he sat down on the side of the bed next to me and asked me if I would talk to him. That's when he asked to talk to me. I didn't want to talk last night, so I told him I would talk to him this morning. He agreed, reluctantly, so—"

"What was his attitude—was he mad, indifferent, arrogant?" Whatever else the socially experienced man knew, or didn't know, he knew men. In situations like this much of their intentions usually surfaced through their attitudes.

"No, none of those—subdued, humble, almost— actually kind of broken."

"Broken? What do you mean by that?"

"Oh I don't know, he was—different—like I had never seen him, not even when I found out about Lori."

"Lori?" Corbin questioned, "his girlfriend?"

"Yes, even then he was kind of supercilious, pompous, certainly not humble."

"What happened this morning?"

"We both got up around five-thirty. He fixed the coffee and I got dressed for school. Then around six-fifteen he asked me to come into the living room with him, which I did, of course. His little presentation was short and sweet. He told me that he knew about us and that someone had taken pictures—"

"Of what?" The normally disciplined man wondered, the trauma of his worried mind reflected in wrinkles on his forehead.

"Us on the beach, in my kitchen, at your place."

"What were we doing?" he asked.

"Hugging, kissing. He also had a record of all the time we've spent together."

"All the time?"

"Yes."

"Was it accurate?"

"It was accurate down to the minute, Reb. I'm sorry. I guess I was wrong about—"

"My entire old competitive nature cries out to yell 'I told you so, damn it', but I'm not going to do that to you." He heard the guilt in her voice and it was not an appealing thing. Centered in the midst of an impulse to say 'I told you so', he discovered even more of a desire to protect her. Why, he couldn't say—he just didn't want her to sink into depression, to lose her enchanting personality

"I deserve it Reb. I could never have believed Mac would hire an investigator—and he said he didn't."

"You asked him?"

"Of course," she replied instantly, as though she were proclaiming, give me SOME credit—don't think I'm THAT stupid. "He denied it."

The tough halfback, All-American, pro-football star found pity and sympathy, stirring around in his heart for this woman who just hours ago was so certain about her knowledge of her husband. She was eating crow and trying to retain an appearance of confidence at the same time, a tough combination. She accomplished it, and it forced the middle-aged man to respect her for it. "How did he get the information on us then?"

"Mac told me that he and some others are working on a highly-classified project out at NASA. The government had to make certain that the information wasn't compromised, as he phrased it, stolen, and sold."

"So they keep tabs on the scientists AND their wives?" the amazed man asked, unbelievingly. He intended for her to hear the doubt in his voice though had he not known about the experiments, he could have believed it. It made sense.

"Apparently. You're not going to like the next thing he told me, Reb." Doubt filtered back into her voice and she had trouble holding it steady!

"I haven't liked anything I've heard so far, Loverly, so lay it on me." He was getting frustrated and angry but he had also become acutely aware of how badly this mistreated wife must feel, once so certain of her husband's character, now appearing so ignorant of his devices, and so foolish, at least to herself.

"Mac said the authorities, probably the CIA, believes you instituted the relationship with me in order to develop a rapport with him—"

"With whom? Mac?"

"Yes."

"Bullshit! I try to take a man's wife to bed so he and I can become friends? So I can steal scientific secrets from him? So I can sell them to—to—by the way did he say who wanted to buy these—so called secrets."

"Other countries, he said."

"Bullshit magnified!" His patriotic ire now incensed, Patie, who had never been considered a traitor, certainly not accused, exclaimed again "Bullshit."

"I think so, too, Reb. I don't believe Mac. I think his male ego finally surfaced after I told him I was going to find someone else and since he would be gone for a week, he figured it would be then. I believe he hired a private detective and—"

"No more than twelve hours ago," reminded the frustrated man, "you didn't believe it. At least that's what you said. What changed your mind so completely?" Corbin didn't want to trample on Marti's ego, she seemed to feel badly enough, but in this moment of emotional upheaval, he needed to extract information from her. She had been wrong, she knew it and he knew it. He also knew she was apologizing, but he could not desist now— would not. Too much was at stake—personally—socially, with this woman whom he had grown to respect and admire in only a couple of days—and maybe even nationally, as corny and ridiculous as that might sound to anyone else. Patie Corbin involved in international intrigue? That would produce some laughs in the old New York Giants dressing room!

"Reb, it's kind of hard denying the pictures, as much as my pride would like to. I feel very badly about this." The sound of a muffled whimper was evident to the listener, and he felt another surge of sympathy.

"I guess so. He didn't leave you copies, did he?" Patie wanted to see the pictures, to be reassured that everything he had just heard was true, not that he wanted it to be—he didn't. But he DID want to know—to know beyond a shadow of doubt that Marti was telling him the truth. That would probably mean she wasn't a part of the deception, not absolutely—probably. At least the pictures would prove to the athlete that Mac now knows about his and Marti's relationship. He could choose either to believe Marti or he could visit Mac. See the pictures for himself, perhaps. Maybe he would do both.

"No, I didn't even think to ask him for copies. I didn't know there was a reason to. Why do you want to see them, Patie? Don't you trust me? Don't you believe me?"

No, the frustrated but disciplined man didn't trust her. He wanted to—because he had begun to care for her but he wanted to trust her too, because of his ego. He couldn't bear thinking he had been duped by anyone, especially by a woman with whom he had gotten—had gotten—what? Involved? Yes, involved, certainly involved physically. Oral sex IS sex in spite of what HER president, Bill Clinton recently avowed. We HAVE had sex, he thought and sex IS involved. Could she sing, should she be singing Oh, oh, oh, oh, yes I'm the great pretender too? Is she deceiving me? Could she and Mac be planning to blackmail me?—working together to bribe me? So they won't give information to whom? Mattie, to use against me in the divorce? Kimberly, thinking I fear losing her? They couldn't blackmail me by threatening to give the information to Mattie. I asked for nothing in the divorce, nothing which could be lost by having sex with a married woman. Fear of losing the love of the children, therefore the love of the grandchildren? Probably not, there would be no leverage THERE. The children already knew about many of my escapades and they had not separated themselves nor their children from me—besides, if Mattie knew about the events of last night she might, under Mississippi law, have a winnable lawsuit against Marti, so trying to blackmail me to keep Mattie from knowing makes no sense. Kimberly? Perhaps. They might think he would be willing to pay in order to keep Kim from finding out, but they would have to have known about my plans to remarry Kim, and they could not have known that, not before last night. Besides, I came to Bay St. Louis to initiate a relationship with Marti, not the reverse. The "philosopher" reasoned, therefore, that the guilty wife could not be collaborating with her husband to extract anything from him, not money, not information. She must be telling him the truth. That being the case, then, the Asian looking men were probably protecting their interests by making certain Claiborne's wife wasn't a weak link, a risk. To be a risk, though, she would have to know about her husband's clandestine affairs. Does she? That could account for their attention to her activities. If she does not know about Mac's involvement what would be the purpose of their knowing about her relationship with another man? Security? Safety? If she isn't a part of the intrigue, then the Asians could only HOPE she doesn't know, that Mac has told her nothing. But they could not KNOW that for a fact. Therein lies their vulnerability, reasoned the worldly sage. They can only take Mac's word that Marti is ignorant of the arrangement to steal secrets, but to be safe, they investigated her activities, scrutinized her lifestyle when her husband wasn't around and behold they found me, hallelujah, they found old me, lucky me, he exclaimed sarcastically to himself. Well, there are two things I DON'T know: I don't know if that imbecile of a husband hired two poorly-trained Asian private detectives who stand out like two black bears at a salmon convention in order to catch his wife in an illicit relationship, an unlikely scenario, OR if they are two foreign agents protecting their interests—AND their butts. And there are two things I DO know: A husband knows I am having an affair with his wife, AND I need to have a long, deep heart-to-heart with my old friend Buddy—and Jack too!

"Patie?"

"Yes, Loverly."

"Where are you?"

"What do you mean?"

"I asked you a question thirty seconds ago and you haven't answered it yet. Was it that difficult?"

"Sorry. What was it? I was thinking."

"Do you trust me?"

There it is, asked clearly, full of emotion—and fear. He could hear it in the tone of her voice. In her presence, he could gain knowledge from the expressions on her face and the movements of her body, when she was jesting and the few times when she had been serious. But on the telephone he could gather that information from the tone of her voice only, the inflections of the most important word or words. She accentuated the word TRUST—"Do you TRUST me?" You walk with me, you hold me, you laugh with me, you take me out to eat, you want sex with me—but "do you TRUST me?" Not, do YOU trust me, as if to say everyone else in the world trusts me but do you trust me? Not, do you trust ME. You've trusted others, you've trusted Mattie, Kim. But do you trust ME? That wasn't what she asked—she asked "Do you TRUST me?" It was a simple question, due a simple answer—and—it cut to the core of his heart—it magnified the reason he came to The Bay to write his book—not to Natchez, not to Iuka, not Ocean Springs, not Vicksburg, but to Bay St. Louis, the home of Mac and Marti Claiborne.

Yes, of course I trust—no, I can't be stupid enough to render myself vulnerable by trusting a stranger—HELL, I don't know—! "Yes, Loverly, of course I trust you. I can't believe you doubted it enough to ask. Don't you trust me to trust you?"

"Well, you managed to turn that all the way around," the woman accused, sounding perplexed—or was she just acting perplexed?

Patie shrugged. "Of course I did, Loverly, I'm an American male. We come into the world knowing how to do that!"

"Now, that's one thing a liberal and a conservative can agree upon," she laughed somberly, "men know how to redirect negative attention to women, especially wives. But in this case, Reb, I admit it's justified. I deserve it."

"Not really, Loverly. I wasn't accusing, but answer the question if you will. Do you trust me?"

"Yes I do, completely."

"And I do you," he lied "Now let's examine the situation. Mac knows about our relationship and he probably hired those two idiots. Or if he didn't, then the two Asians followed you, us, on their own, for their own reasons? What could they be?"

"I have a problem with each scenario, Patie. I find it very hard to believe that Mac cares enough to spy on me. But if he didn't I don't know the answer. I don't believe you are a spy trying to steal secrets—I don't believe that."

"Is Mac working on top secret stuff, for want of a better word, at NASA?"

"I suppose so. That's what scientists out there do."

"Generally, what does Mac work on?—I'm assuming he doesn't give you specifics." Corbin had two reasons for asking the question. First, he wanted to know if she knew. Secondly, he wanted to hear her confess on the phone that she did not know, if she didn't. Buddy had been concerned that Patie's phone was tapped but the new Bay St. Louis resident had not believed it, of course. That was before the two Chinamen forced their unwelcome way into his life. It might be tapped, could very well be, probably is. From now on, he agreed with Buddy, he would assume it is. The condo was high off the ground and the area beneath it visible and available to anyone who might want to walk under it. All the utilities probably enter the house through the floor. If anyone wanted to tap his phone, it ought to be easy enough to do. Anyway, from this time on, he would use his phone accordingly and later, when he got off the phone with Marti, he would check, although, admittedly, he wouldn't know what to look for, probably some kind of a small box-like apparatus, maybe with an antenna.

"I don't know specifics, Reb. I do know that he works on extracting chemicals from plants found in the ocean."

"He's a chemist, then—a chemical scientist."

"Yes, but he has never talked to me about the intricacies of his work—and I have never asked. I really don't want to know."

"So you have no idea what he's working on right now?" The novice in intelligence gathering regretted asking the question as soon as it left his tongue. It might sound to anyone listening that he was asking in order to discover the secret rather than the real reason, which was to authenticate the innocent wife's ignorance. But he had asked it, now he would have to carefully establish the reason why.

"No." Marti's voice was unsteady as though the possible enormity of the question might in fact have something to do with the events which occurred over the last few hours.

"That's good, Loverly. By the way, I need to run an errand. Could I call you in about an hour, or would you call me back about ten?"

"I'll call you about ten-fifteen. I don't have a class that hour."

"Good. Talk to you then."

One half mile away, the small spy Spikes, sitting in the black Lexus with his large friend, lowered the telephone receiver from his ear, turned the tape player off, pressed a button and waited for the tape to rewind so both of them could listen. "Mr. Chun, they are through talking now but she's to call him back at ten-fifteen. Why don't we go eat breakfast and take the recorder back to my apartment?"

"Is fine. We listen to tape there and record next conversation. Put new tape in and certain to leave on."

Patie placed the telephone back onto the receiver, stood and stretched, due not to indifference, but because he had gotten stiff sitting during the long conversation with Marti. He gazed out the rear window in total disbelief, over the head of the yard-man cutting the grass behind the condo. Then he walked back out on the rear deck, retrieved his mug half-filled with cold coffee, proceeded to the micro-wave and reheated it, performing his calf exercise, lifting his heels off the floor, while waiting for it to get hot. He did five-hundred toe lifts a day and he had set the micro-wave timer for a minute and a half so he should get at least one hundred and fifty. Ninety seconds later, with his coffee mug in his hand, he opened the front door, walked down the steps and looked around for anyone who might be looking at him. Seeing no one, he stepped under his condo which was more than six feet off the ground and casually, a little disbelievingly, examined the sub-floor for anything attached to a telephone line and capable of sending signals. He regretted again being an electronics illiterate and wished for even basic knowledge. It will have to be damned obvious for me to find it, he thought. And it was, a small black box with a three inch antenna protruding from it, clipped into a black line which ran up one of the many large pilings upon which the condo was built. It was attached to the line at the very top of the post, where the floor of the building rested upon it, partially hidden by a floor joists.

"The bastards," the disgruntled resident murmured out loud. His first impulse was to grab the device and rip it from its mooring, but he hesitated long enough to reconsider. When Buddy had cautioned him about talking about Marti or Jack on the phone, he thought his friend was being overly cautious, melodramatic even. But Buddy was right, his counsel was intelligent. Smart guy, he thought, a heck of a lot smarter than I am, though I sure as hell would never tell him that. Better get my rear-end to a payphone. Think I'll leave that thing there until I talk to him.

The normally agile fifty-six year old man shuffled back up the steps, deposited his mug on the counter, grabbed his car key off the living room table and hustled out to his van, cranked it and headed toward Highway 90. He turned west and a half mile later he pulled up next to a pay telephone at a Seven-Eleven, one of the places where he bought diet Cokes, beer, skim milk, and Times-Picayunes. No one else was using the phone and no one seemed to be noticing him. Using a credit card, he dialed Buddy's home phone.

"Hello." The voice sounded sleepy or hung-over.

"Buddy? This is Patie." The jester usually mixed a little humor into the initial contact of a telephone conversation with his old and dear friend, but not today. He felt no exhilaration after all he had learned. The situation had grown much more serious.

"Hey, old friend. You sound a little solemn. Everything alright?"

"Did I wake you, Buddy?"

"Naw—you know how slow I get started in the morning. Also drank one beer too many last night. You ARE calling from a pay phone aren't you?"

"You'd better believe it, after what I found and found out this morning. Buddy, we have a problem. Wait, let me rephrase that. We have major problems. I have a lot to tell you. You ready to hear all of this?"

"Of course, old friend. Is anyone near you?"

"No!" I'm in a Seven-Eleven parking lot, where it meets the street. The nearest human being is getting out of a car, going in the store two first downs away."

"Good," Buddy exclaimed. "Now look around and see if anyone seems to be watching you."

Rotating his body three hundred and sixty degrees, Patie saw no one. "Not that I can see."

"Good. Well let me have the bad news. Start at the beginning."

"First of all, I've been followed. Two Chinese or Asian looking men in a black Lexus 400." Patie then recounted every episode which had occurred, spelling it out in great detail to his old team-mate, including the part that they photographed him with Marti.

"Well, there can be no doubt they are following

you, can there, Old Friend?"

"None whatsoever, not with me standing in the Lighthouse parking lot with a hand full of shirt, and then pulling a bug out from under my car." Patie had not wanted to tell Buddy about taking Marti out again, but he decided he should. Jack needed to know everything including that little tidbit of careless, if not arrogant, behavior on his part. The ladies' man part of the assignment had controlled his behavior, not the clandestine part. He realized just now how he had subconsciously de-emphasized the danger part, almost ignoring it as he focused upon the female-challenge side of the issue. The ease with which he enticed her to respond to him reduced the notion of danger even more. Add then to that his love for her—no not love—his great liking of her—well, maybe love, of a friendship sort, anyway his enjoyment of her, of being with her and he seemed to have thrown all caution to the—! Wait a minute! Buddy knows me, he thought, and so does Jack. Both of them knew I would turn all my abilities loose on her, or as others would say, my charm. Maybe they counted on that and maybe that's why they turned all theirs loose on me when they convinced me to do this. Both of them had to understand I wouldn't sit discreetely in my condo playing cards with her, or having Bible study. May wish I had, especially the Bible study, before this is over with— they knew I would go out to eat with her, take her to night clubs, dance with her. That's what I enjoy doing. They probably WANTED me to do all those things, bring everything to the surface.

"What a break, old friend. I know this creates a

rather large imperilment for you but what a break. This may mean we now know something about the buyers. Two Chinese or Asian looking men in a black Lexus 400, huh? Were you able to get their license number, or any part of it?"

"No, I tried but by the time I recovered my balance, I couldn't make it out. It was an out of state tag though, definitely not Mississippi."

"I'm sure Jack will get right on this. They are probably staying somewhere in the area," Buddy surmised.

"Including New Orleans."

"Yes, including New Orleans, and maybe even Mobile."

"But that's not all, Buddy. Marti's husband, Mac came in from a week long trip supposedly to Maine, after midnight last night and told her everything we've done. Said he has seen pictures of us kissing. Then he showed her a written detailed account of all of it."

"Was it accurate?"

"Down to the last hello and goodbye."

"Patie, I already know the answer to this question but I have to ask it anyway. Jack will ask me if I've asked you and you know I can't lie to our old—"

"Go ahead and ask me Buddy. You can't hurt my feelings except when you think my feelings can be hurt."

"Glad to see you still have your sense of humor. You haven't told Mrs. Claiborne anything have you, I mean about the CIA and why you're there?"

"No. Assure Jack that I haven't—and ask him who made the B and who made the C in logic class, will you?"

"I'm assuming you made the B."

"That would be a logical assumption. You remember the old southern proverbs, I may be stupid but I'm not an idiot? My Mama didn't raise 'no' fool? I didn't just fall off the watermelon truck? Tell Jack THAT for me, too, tell him not to worry about me divulging any information to Marti or to anyone else."

"I'll tell him. Anything else happen?"

"Buddy, I found a small square black box with an antenna under my condo this morning. It was attached to a black electrical cord coming out of the ground and going into the floor."

"What did you do with it, Patie?"

"I left it there—didn't touch it."

"Was it your telephone line?"

"Hell, I don't know. I don't know one line from another but it probably is—unless it's the T.V. cable. For the first time in my sordid life I almost wish I had taken electrical engineering with Harvell. I tell you, when you are standing under your own house looking up at a piece of electrical equipment which is probably sending your telephone conversations out to other people, you would really like to know more about that crap than I do."

"Harvell was a quarterback, old friend, he's smarter than we are. He handed the football off to you, got rid of it, stood back and watched you try to run through a hole that I was supposed to have opened. That's why he's a wealthy electrical engineer today while you and I—."

"Did okay," Patie interrupted.

"Yeah, I guess we did okay."

"What should I do about the device, Buddy?"

"I really need to ask Jack about that, Pate. Just leave it there unless I tell you different. If you don't hear from me, you'll know Jack wants you to leave it."

"How are you going to get in touch with me? We can't talk about it on my phone."

"I mentioned in one last conversation that I had planned on coming down there to a convention. If I call you back to give you the dates, that means leave the thing there. If you don't hear back from me today, take it down—and remember to talk on it naturally—don't tell any Chinese jokes."

"Buddy, there's one other thing Jack ought to know."

"Before we talk about that, Patie, with all that's happened, I need to say one other thing. If you want to bail out of this thing and leave Bay St. Louis, I wouldn't blame you and I know Jack wouldn't!"

Patie had already considered quitting. He did not want to be confronted by a hostile husband, not even a weak one like Mac. He didn't want the conflict, he didn't want the anguish, and he certainly didn't desire the danger. Football had furnished all the risk that he would ever crave, and then some. And now, he faced an exposure to physical harm. A weak husband sometimes equalized the conflict with weapons, pistols, rifles, shotguns, knives. He wasn't worried so much about a knife, as he was about the guns. Mac probably wouldn't want to get close enough to use a knife. Anyway, the old athlete figured he was still in good enough shape, still strong enough, to repel a knife attack by a frightened man. Muscles could not deflect a bullet though. But the idea of quitting soon passed. He would run from CERTAIN danger but he would not run from the possibility of it. Besides running from danger meant running away from the liberal, Mississippi State democrat. He wasn't quite ready to do that yet.

"Thank you Buddy. I really appreciate you saying that. I'm finally aware of the risks, but I'm not going to stop,—not now. I'll stay with it, at least a while longer."

"Okay, my friend. I'll tell Jack. But please be careful. Now, what was the other thing Jack ought to know?"

"When Mac told Marti he knew about us, and showed her the pictures, she confronted him about spying on her—"

"That was to be expected, wasn't it, out of a jealous husband?" Buddy inserted, "that he would face his wife with the facts?"

"Yes, in most cases, but Mac has been openly involved with a co-worker out at NASA, so Marti rejected his assertion that he had the right to spy on her. Anyway, when she challenged him, he told her that security at NASA had followed her—"

"Because Claiborne is working on a top-secret project!"

"Yes, because of that, so Mac told her that NASA had caught us and—get this—that they, the people at NASA, believe I am trying to get information from him, through her. That I am courting her, so to speak, in order to get to him. Can you believe that?"

"Not knowing you, you old Republican patriot. But of course he had to tell her something. I guess even in the midst of selling classified documents to another country, an adulterous man still wants to look righteous to his wife. Anyway, I'm sure Jack and the CIA know what you are doing and NASA is their responsibility, so try not to worry about that. Did Marti believe her husband?"

"No, she believes he hired private detectives. Hopefully she will continue thinking that."

"Yes, hopefully." Buddy grew silent for a second or two and Patie was preparing to hang up when the pulling guard quietly asked, "Patie?"

Speaking his name in the form of a question alerted Corbin, who by that time was ready to get out of the sun. He heard concern in his team-mates voice.

"Yes, Buddy."

"Patie, I'm not fussing at you, understand. I want you to know that. You are performing a great service for your country, risking your—well—at least your safety, and I don't have a right to counsel, or lecture, but I love you, you old turkey and I need—Jack needs to know—you haven't—"

"Fallen in love with Marti, have you?" Patie finished the sentence for the man who once opened holes in the opposing line for him. He knew Buddy almost as well as the lineman knew himself. "No, I haven't fallen in love with her? What made you ask that?"

"I don't want you to get mad at me, Patie, but—"

204

"Buddy, there are four or five men whom I could not get mad at if they were cutting my throat. You're one of them. Now, why do you ask?"

"Well, every time you mentioned her name in this conversation, your voice kinda', well, kinda' softened. It just seemed like I could hear a special—a special—."

"I do like her a lot, Buddy. She's a great gal and I really enjoy being with her but I haven't forgotten why I'm here—and I won't forget."

"Sorry I brought it up, Old Friend. Take care of yourself and call me back soon. Remember if I call you at your condo about the dates of my convention, leave the transmitter there. Rip it out if I don't call back today, okay?"

"Got it—again," Patie laughed. Then the old pro flexed his stiff knee, made that way by standing on it while he talked to Buddy, and glanced around again to insure that no one had been watching. No one was.

The sky seemed to be darkening, as Corbin cranked his van and nudged it up to the four lanes of Highway 90. Checking the traffic to his left, none was coming. Looking quickly to his right, an ominous line of black clouds had already slipped up on him, almost overhead.

"Very appropriate," he muttered out loud, speeding out into the eastbound lane of Highway 90 and heading back to his condo, "Storm clouds OVER me too."

CHAPTER ELEVEN

By the time the "patriot" reached the bottom step of his condo, the line of black clouds, blown in by a hard Southwest wind, had enveloped The Bay, a dark canopy spawning rain in horizontal sheets—and his phone was ringing. His condo faced east, so the building offered a little cover but the weight of the large sacks of groceries, one in each arm, pilfered that advantage. He got soaked, evoking another mystical proclamation—"Just what I needed on the same day I got 'soaked' with all this crap."

Patie hated grocery shopping, something he had never done before moving to The Bay. Maybe the culture in which he was reared taught it, or maybe it was his profession, but grocery shopping seemed so feminine, so mundane. Oh, he would stop by the store to pick up a few items for Mattie and Kim occasionally, the smaller stores, but as the small stores grew into super-markets, then into Mega-foods, his dislike of them increased proportionately which introduced another negative factor— time. The investment of time just didn't justify going to the store. By the time he parked, walked a hundred yards to the entrance, then another two or three hundred yards up and down grocery isles looking for a loaf of bread and a three pound can of coffee, stood in the check-out line for fifteen minutes waiting on the checker to get change or to get a check approved by the manager, and finally arrived back at his car, he figured he had invested at least one hour in the transaction. It just didn't seem worth it to him. He suggested to both his ex-wives at one time or another, very dictatorially, "Think ahead—you know—plan it out. If I had been as uncertain about which hole to hit as you are about your grocery list, I wouldn't have made All-American nor All-Pro, and you wouldn't even want me. Think ahead." Surprisingly the jestful remark drew less criticism from Mattie than from Kim, probably because she knew him better, or at least longer. Kim hated his proclamation and her contemptuous response was always filled with nefarious comment. She considered it a demeaning statement made by an arrogant sexist male pig to a dutiful, loving wife. Patie had never been able to convince her that he was, in his words, "jes't a ' joshing, Georgeous." Admittedly, the fact that she never understood he was joking and always responded negatively never changed his attitude about grocery shopping though, nor his affirmation.

The oft married man proudly confessed to his friends that not only did he find grocery shopping intolerable, but he had never vacuumed the floor, washed nor dried clothes, nor run a dishwasher. Only those friends who knew him well could believe it, but it was true. Living alone in The Bay, however changed all of that. He learned to grocery shop and he had already man-handled the vacuum cleaner once. Hadn't turned the dishwasher on yet though, finding it easier to wash the dishes by hand and use the dishwasher for a drainage rack. He didn't even rent a washer or dryer believing he would eventually find someone to wash his clothes. His grocery shopping consisted of cooked vegetables from the Jitney deli, low-fat dinners from the frozen food section, Fiber One, raisin bran, bananas, low-fat pimento and cheese, Branola bread, fresh red grapes, apples, orange juice, skim milk, diet cokes, wine, and beer. One thing Kim had done for him, for which he would be eternally grateful—put him on a low-fat diet and started him taking an entire battalion of vitamins. "Three vegetables, three fruits, and your vitamins each day, Meathead. You'll stay healthy." She was right.

The shopper dropped his two water-soaked bags of groceries on the front deck, fished for his key in his pocket, found it, unlocked the door and got to his telephone just in time. Breathlessly he wheezed, "Hello."

"Out of breath, huh? Guess I know what I interrupted."

Corbin couldn't help laughing. Kim sounded so—uncertain to him, so insecure, which was unlike her.

She usually managed to appear confident, self-assured to Patie, never giving him an edge, always tried to keep him guessing, wanted him to see no dependence in her. "At ten o'clock in the morning, Gorgeous?" he countered.

"Oh, you'll do it any other time, just not ten o'clock in the morning?"

"Now THAT is a wife's pure response, not polluted with masculine reasoning, not weakened with practicality, not attended by common sense—uncontaminated, undefiled wifely thought process."

"I'm not a wife."

"By uncontaminated, undefiled female thought process, then. By the way, I'm glad you brought that up," he corrected.

"Brought what up?"

"Us getting married," retorted the jesting ex-husband.

"When did I bring up marriage?"

"You said 'I'm not a wife.' You WERE reminding me we needed to get married, weren't you?"

"Patie, you—," she exclaimed, the exasperation and frustration dominating her emotions, regulating the tone of her voice.

"Lover Boy."

"What?"

"Just call me Lover Boy, a name manifesting in no deficient manner my undying, my unrequited, my everlasting, eternal, my all-consuming love for you—your hair, golden brown strands of light streaking across an endless sky; your beautiful eyes, two blue-white diamonds implanted in a perfect setting; your teeth, two immaculate rows of completely flawless pearls cast into the mouth of a Greek goddess, your—"

"Patie!" the ex-wife shouted.

"Lover Boy!" he corrected.

"Patie, have you been reading Song of Solomon again?"

"Wa'l," he exaggerated, "I do thànk I got to that part yesterday—why you ask?"

"Why I ask is obvious. What's not so obvious is where you were last night. You want to tell me THAT?—since you failed to call me at six like you said you would."

The guarded rogue was in trouble and he knew it. He had forgotten to call her. How in hell could he do that? he asked himself, conscious already of the answer. But one thing he knew—in order to look innocent, he had to hold his ground. "Wa'l now, it's obvious to me, Gorgeous 'cause I was there."

For ten seconds dead silence pervaded the phone. The jester decided he would wait his ex-wife out, and although she was two hundred miles away, he figured he could see her clearly. She had probably called from the den, sitting on the large couch which forms the base for the flared U, between the two large matching chairs in front of the giant television screen. Now she was standing, the telephone in her right hand down by her side, trying to decide whether to hang it up or continue the 'stupid' conversation, a look of disgust encompassing her beautiful face, shifting her weight, which was nominal, from one small foot to the other. Patie was wrong, what he was doing to Kim and he knew it. He really didn't feel like joking with her this morning but now he had no

choice. Behavioral alteration indicated romantic confrontation or condemnation, something like that, he had
always heard. Apparently she had tried to call early last
night, and hadn't gotten him. By the time he and
Marti—Marti—what was he going to do about—Well, by
the time he got back to the condo, Kim had probably gotten mad, snatched a book off the library shelf and
curled up in bed to read, determined not to call again.

"Patie?" He heard contempt in her voice.

"Yes, Gorgeous."

"Of all the stupid, idiotic statements you have
ever made to me, that one might be the stupidest."

"Oh, I think so, Gorgeous."

"Can you be serious for one minute?"

"Yes, of course, Gorgeous. Sorry. I guess your
voice just kind of elevates me into a festive mood.
What's on that beautiful mind of yours?"

"Are you getting any writing done?" Patie knew
that wasn't what Kim wanted to talk to him about. The
question was a prelude to her next question or comment,
but her voice was kinder—more gentle so he knew she
was trying to challenge the anger within her.

"Some. I found a great place to write—Ullman
Street pier. It sticks out in the bay about two-hundred
yards, has several covered sitting—."

"I've seen it, remember?"

"That's right. Of course," the would-be author
recalled.

"How would you like to meet me in New Orleans
this weekend? I figure you need a break."

Corbin had not expected it, this invitation.

Seldom was he caught so flat-footedly off balance, especially with someone he knew so well. He needed to leave The Bay for a day or two, just get away from all this mess—! An emotional wrestling began to develop within him, although he already knew what his answer would have to be—yes, of course, I would love to meet you in New Orleans for the weekend. But would he love to do that? Not like he once would have. When he moved to The Bay, he was so certain he loved Kim, so sure that he wanted to live the rest of his life with her. Any day now, or would it be any year, she would grow to understand how much he loves her, and that his teasing really did illustrate that love. He couldn't clown around with someone he didn't care for—. The Bay had changed his heart, no, face it, be honest, Meathead, Marti changed your heart. Patie's mind and Marti's work in unison, their laughter melts together like butter into hot cakes, something the old womanizer had always wanted. He didn't want to go to New Orleans with Kim, not now. He would have to change his personality in order to keep the peace—be serious, reserved, and have a serious, reserved, and formal weekend, else be himself and taste the ire which would surely come. He had been spoiled— in just two days, by a woman he had been asked to deceive.

"I would love to, Gorgeous. What brought this on?"

"Well, I want to see you but if you come up here, we'll have to stay in the house. I'm ready to go out—."

"You can come down here," the ex-husband reminded her. "The Bay is only forty-five minutes from

Bourbon Street and I'm already paying the rent here. Be a lot cheaper."

"I thought about that but a lot of people know you there now. It would be safer in New Orleans. Besides, I've already made reservations at the same hotel where we stayed and restaurant where we ate when Ole Miss played in the Sugar Bowl three years ago. You remember their names?"

Oh-oh, being tested again. What was the name of that hotel?—Oh yes. "Certainly, Gorgeous, the Royal Orleans and the, the—"

"Commodore Palace."

"You're right, the Royal Orleans and Commodore. Great places. When do you want to go?"

"I've made reservations at the hotel for Friday and Saturday nights—Commodore Friday night. Can you be at the hotel by three Friday afternoon?"

"Sure can," Patie agreed, the sinking feeling in his stomach suddenly intensifying, he figured, by deciding upon the time. Definite plans seemed to do that.

"Good. Call me tonight?"

"Can't wait," the reluctant man reaching for a touch of diplomacy answered. "Talk to you about ten. Oh, by the way," quickly changing the subject, he asked, "I bet you can't guess what I just got through doing?"

"Grocery shopping?"

"Now how in hell did you know that?"

"My little secret," she giggled, exhibiting a rare expression of humor—for her.

"Good guess I'd guess! Talk to you at ten."

Hanging up the phone, the dissident shopper

213

rushed outside to get the two bags of soggy groceries. He wanted to deposit the frozen and refrigerated items in their respective places before Marti called. It was almost ten-thirty.

The patient man's mind, normally disciplined, to a degree, was rushing like a mountain stream toward flat land, thoughts popping into and out of it like lightning— the conversation with Buddy and Kim, the phone-tap device and whether or not to tell Marti, how much to tell her. Talking to her on the phone today in vague termi- nology would alert her and his two Chinese listeners. At ten thirty-five the phone rang.

"Hello."

"Hi, Reb. Get your errands run?"

"Yeah, finally. Listen we need to talk—about a lot of things. I thought at first, we might walk the beach but I can't subject this ol' knee to the sand three days in a row especially after that wild sprint last night. I'm going to work out on my treadmill today. You want to come by?"

"Would love to. I don't always run the beach. Some days I jog on the Boulevard, right by your condo. I'll drop in—What time?"

"What if it's still raining?"

"Bulldogs are tough, Reb. I run in the rain all the time."

"I'm going to exercise about five. Six sound alright to you?"

"Six what?"

"Six o'clock—or," he quickly mocked, "six times—take your pick."

"How does six times at six o'clock sound to you?" she asked.

"Six times would obviously refer to you, Loverly, not me, unless I hustle to the pharmacy for Viagra. You a multiple Milly, huh?"

"A what?"

"Multiple Milly. Every woman is either a single Sally or a multiple Milly. Six times would definitely elevate you into the latter group."

"Maybe some day we'll find out," she laughed.

"SOME day—why not TOday?" Weird—being that explicit on a phone which I know is being tapped, Corbin thought. In my wilder days I wouldn't even have done that.

"See you at six, Reb. Don't wear yourself out on that tread-mill."

"I wouldn't dare, Loverly."

Patie knew too well the danger of Marti coming by his condo, knew their adversaries heard the conversation, and would more than likely tell Mac, not that it mattered much now. Everyone already knew everything. It would be interesting to see what that knowledge would do though—how far it would go, what Mac would do with it. The experienced adulterer knew all too well about the male ego. Several times in his life he had sworn to friends, like Buddy, that "she ought to find someone else—she knows I don't love her," and then when, for one reason or another he thought she had, he resented it. Mac may be experiencing that phenomenon right now, an indifferent attitude about Marti becoming involved but then when she did—. Or the chemist might be concerned only about his dishonorable business deal with the Chinese, who were worried about Corbin's affair with Marti. So that might be the source of Mac's concern. Either way, he didn't want Mac knocking on his door while Marti was here, not that Patie feared him, unless the traitor showed up with a gun. Patie would know if he did that, however, simply by locking the door and looking out the window when the doorbell rang. But the uneasy resident loathed even the idea of a screaming confrontation with a jealous husband within hearing distance of neighbors, who certainly would hear. Hell, he didn't want an altercation with Mac whether or not the neighbors could hear. Yet he needed to talk to Marti, and the best place to do that was in his condo—unless— surely not—surely they haven't placed bugs on the inside too. Well, even if they have, he could overcome it. On television and in the movies, the people just turned the radio up real loud and talked low. He and Marti could do that.

The rain was falling straight down by the time Corbin got off the phone, the wind had stopped blowing and the sun seemed to be trying to penetrate the lingering clouds. It was close to eleven o'clock and he had not eaten breakfast, which always consisted of a mixture of Fiber One, raisin bran, artificial sweetener, skim milk and a table spoon of fat-free Cool Whip mixed in, trying to deceive the taste buds into thinking they were eating half-and-half. He decided to wait until about twelve to eat that, so he poured himself another cup of coffee, doctored it, and strolled out onto the back deck, repositioning himself where he sat before Loverly called earlier.

Rain still pounded the roof like a thousand woodpeckers, the water continued to flow furiously off it, and the temperature had dropped ten or fifteen degrees. The waters of the bay were absolutely placid, a smooth sheet of silver steel, pock-marked only by the falling rain. No sailboats were visible to the new Bay resident, docked by smart sailors, he thought. Even the sea gulls seemed to have found a safe harbor somewhere. The rain was still falling so hard from the one large remaining cloud that The Bay bridge disappeared less than half-way across. The coffee drinker couldn't even see the land at Pass Christian, two miles away and no other humans were in sight, except those in the few automobiles which eased back and forth through Beach Boulevard, now flooded.

The old pro, prompted by the sheets of rain which fell earlier, allowed his mind to drift backward until it settled in remembrance upon a football game played in Giants stadium many years ago. New York was playing the Redskins in the NFL championship game and it was the fourth quarter. A blowing rain, like the one which just came through The Bay started falling before halftime and the field drainage system could not handle the voluminous amount of water. Player after player complained they had "NEVER seen a rain like this." Sand, apparently placed on the field to nourish the grass, mixed with the water and became liquid sandpaper, scraping the skin off under the arms, between the legs, even in the crotch, an uncomfortable enemy almost as potent as the opposing team. Three minutes and forty-two seconds remained in the game, and the Redskins were six points ahead, 20 to 14, on two field goals. Neither team had scored since the downfall started. The Giants had the ball on their own forty-three yard line. It was third and a bunch to go. Jared Aldrich, the Giants quarterback, on one knee in the huddle looked up at his all-pro running back, Patie Corbin, and called, "Y left, fake 35 draw, 48 screen right. Patie, make this good, fake a block on the end, or the linebacker if he blitzes, go to the ground. I'll have the ball to you by the time you get up—conceal it, now!"

When the Giants lined up on the ball, it was evident that the linebackers were coming, unwilling or perhaps unable to hide their intentions because of the sloppy field. The snap of the ball brought all three of them and the cornerback on that side, so certain were they that the Giants would pass. The screen pass call was perfect. Aldrich faked a draw to Patton off the left side, wheeled all the way around as though he were going to sprint out right. Patie faked a block on the weak side blitzing backer, fell to the ground, lay there for a count of thousand one, jumped up and immediately saw the football floating over the outstretched hands of the Washington pass rushers. Half the Redskin defense was rushing the passer and the other half went for the fake draw. No defender was within five yards of Patie when he caught the ball and no one had a shot at him except the free safety, who covered the weak-side receiver, Eddie Baker, when the corner blitzed. But Baker ran a fifteen-yard deep post-pattern taking the safety to the middle of the field. The defensive back had seen Patie catch the ball, though, and pursued, however bogged down and slow-motioned the race turned out to be. When Patie reached the fifteen yard line, he was only five yards, or less, from the right sideline. The Redskin safety was on the twelve yard line, five or six yards to the running back's left, but closing the gap rapidly, or as rapidly as one could in ankle deep water, in a driving rain storm. Patie considered racing him to the flag, he thought he could beat him, and the film bore that out, but the former Rebel decided to cut back behind the defender, perhaps thinking that the safety could not possibly retain his footing on the drenched field. When Corbin planted his right foot in the slop, it shot out from under him and all his weight came down on the inside of his left leg. He heard the ligaments tear before the football flew out of his hands and the Giant's back lay there in excruciating pain, his left knee out of place, and the football skittering toward a trailing Redskin who fell upon it.

Every coach and every sports-writer said the same thing. Patie would have scored if he had run for the end zone flag. One writer, a perpetual critic of the Giants' entire organization, even went so far as to accuse Corbin of "show-boating", maintaining that he wanted to cross the goal-line standing up, not sliding in on his belly like a Mississippi hog. Patie's initial anger at the statement had subsided by the time he got out of the hospital. His knee had been a mess, dislocated, torn ligaments and torn cartilage. The doctor, actually doctors, told him that he would be very fortunate to play again, even with intense rehab. They were right! He was not able to run very well, and after two mediocre seasons of trying, he retired.

"Maybe that son of a bitch Cullison was right too," the contemplator murmured out loud. "Maybe I was showing off."

The rain had stopped. Patie looked at his watch and it was eleven-fifty. Time to eat, he thought, so he fixed himself a larger bowl of cereal than usual—he was eating a combined breakfast and lunch, and he wanted to see if he could push his mind past all that had been happening back onto writing. He really needed to work on the book and he could identify almost four hours of what he hoped would be uninterrupted time on the Ullman Street pier. The novice writer had already discovered that he seemed to write best when he set up his writing table within sight of people but away from them—helped him take his mind off his work then back onto it quickly. Sometimes that caused a word or even a concept to pop into his mind, kind of like slipping up on an unsuspecting lizard when he was a boy growing up in Laurel. He had tried writing behind the closed doors of his condo, but that really didn't work for him. He needed outside stimuli with which to suddenly draw his mind away and then suddenly bring it back, like a rubber band—seemed to develop intellectual elasticity. Of course, when he found himself in the "writing mode" or "writing zone" as he once heard a writer refer to it, he could write anywhere, alone in the desert or in the middle of a busy airport. But when he wasn't in the zone, he needed help. Today, he had not yet determined if he were in the mode. Either way, he didn't want to spend the next four hours in the condo.

After finishing lunch the hopeful writer washed his breakfast dishes and stuck them into the dishwasher to drain, common work which allowed his mind to wander. Lately, when left to its own devices, it seemed to rush naturally to Marti, not to Kim, a surprising venture. Even without a sense of humor, Kim still appealed to the ex-husband. She was beautiful, well respected by people in high places, exhibited mutual interests, especially concerning Ole Miss athletics. She and Patie both lived essentially the same lifestyle, so their cultural tastes were similar.

Marti was different-intellectual, tremendous sense of humor, quick mind with a tongue attached to it, pretty, respected. He trusted her but he was still a little uncertain about her role in this—this mess, that's all it is, a great big mess—and, he complained to himself, I don't know what the hell I'm doing, bogged down right in the middle of it. I do not know, I cannot understand how I could have let Jack and Buddy talk—. NO! I can't afford to think about that now. I AM in the middle of it, I'm going to stay in the middle of it, I'm not going anywhere and I have got to keep my mind on writing, at least for the next few hours. But he knew the time would come, and soon, when he would be forced to devise a plan—where Marti would either knowingly or unknowingly, depending upon her innocence or guilt, help him prove that her husband is selling secrets to a foreign government. And it will most likely be without her help. She doesn't love Mac anymore but she certainly hasn't indicated she wants ill for him. Thank goodness they have no children. At least that won't be an issue.

Patie emptied everything off the card table, bills, mail, his writing case, then packed his case, making certain the large synonym finder, his small radio, a notebook and plenty of pens were in it, and took those two items to his van. Limping back up the steps conscious of the painful swelling in his knee, probably intensified by his dash to the phone earlier, he dropped a couple of diet cokes and the half-full jar of dry roasted mixed nuts into an ice cooler, consciously looking at the percentage of peanuts to other nuts. The experienced reveler habitually ate the preferred nuts, like cashews, first, sometimes leaving nothing but peanuts in the jar. The pier had benches upon which to sit, so he took no chair. Five minutes later, the determined scribe pulled his van to the entrance of the pier, a wooden extension of Ullman Street across Beach Boulevard, stopped, and unloaded it. After setting all his material on the end of the pier, he drove onto Ullman, a half block down it, and parked under a large shady live oak tree decorated by hanging moss. A few minutes later, he had positioned himself in the second gazebo, setting up his card table and placing his radio and writing paraphernalia on it, ready now, hopefully for a few hours of uninterrupted writing time.

The pier was deserted and the writer at first wondered why. A few minutes later he knew why. The air was cold out there above the water—at least fifteen degrees colder than at the condo. The wind blew hard from the sea and the roof of the gazebo shielded him from the warm rays of the sun. "What the hell am I gonna' do now?" he grumbled out loud. "I don't want to carry all this junk back to the van in order to go get a coat. And I can't leave it out here!" Then he remembered his golf windbreaker in the van. "Ah yes, I remember well," he muttered again, mimicking two old ex-pro football players whom he had seen recently doing a commercial on television. Neither of the old opponents could remember a damn thing, but dressed in tuxedos at a party, each recalled what the other person had done to him on the playing field. Then alternately each actor would proclaim, "Ah, yes, I remember well." Walking the two hundred yards back to the van, half of it on the pier, Corbin couldn't help but smile. The commercial was his favorite, not only because he knew the two players but also because he had begun to notice a decrease in his own memory. Strange how that happens, he thought. An article which he had read recently in a newspaper attributed it to a loss of brain cells, but he questioned that thesis. It wasn't so much that he couldn't remember anything—he could recall names, dates, places and events which happened to him when he was young, years ago, better than he could that which he had experienced recently, football games and funny athletic stories, for example. Youth had a way, he surmised, of making situations more exciting because so much of that which happens to you when you're young, happens for the first time, making the events more memorable—at least that's how he figured. Age and experience seemed to reduce the number of new things which could happen to you. Anyway, he thought as he ambled toward his van, that's how I figure it.

The contemplating writer reached the end of the

pier at the street before he saw the black car parked at an angle in front of his van. From a distance he couldn't determine whether it was a Lexus, but it resembled one and he wasn't about to be careless. Moving to his left behind other automobiles, parked between Beach Boulevard, where he was just then crossing and his vehicle, he crouched down and moved over to his left between the cars and a fence which meandered down that side of the street. There was no sidewalk on that side of Ullman. Some kind of a retirement home, perhaps a senior citizens home, or nursing facility was located on the other side of the street. Residents had been brought outside, helped by people who appeared to be nurses, positioning themselves in the warmth of the sun. The facility covered at least a city block and Corbin had parked his van exactly opposite the front entrance, which faced Ullman Street.

Patie refused to believe the black car could be the Lexus. Surely the idiots aren't that brazen or stupid, he thought, but deciding to take no chance, he continued to crouch, making certain his head was lower than the five automobiles which were parked between himself and his van. From his position he could see only the hood of the black car, and he quickly calculated that the driver, looking in his rear view mirror, could not see him because the rear of the car pointed toward the retirement home across the street. Unless he gets out of his car and looks back this way, I'm safe, reasoned the amateur detective, who in his suspicious maneuverings suddenly realized that several of the senior citizens across the street were watching him curiously. "Damn," he whispered, "they probably think I'm going to break into one of these cars. They'll probably call the police." So the thinker stopped, raised up, then bent down as though he were picking something off the ground, and walked slowly toward the black car. If it WAS the black Lexus, they were probably going to depart in a hurry when they saw him. If it wasn't, then slipping up on it was foolish. What th' hell, I might as well just walk up to it. He still couldn't tell if it was a Lexus. He could only see the left side of the hood from the windshield to the front bumper, and he could not see the insignia on the front of the car at all, even when he stopped at the rear of his van. Before doing anything else, he had to know whether or not the car was a Lexus, and then, whether or not it was THE Lexus. He hoped it wasn't but feared it was, and he fumed that so many new cars look alike. The only way he could determine if the car was a Lexus, he decided, was to peep around the right, rear side of his vehicle. From that point he could see the back of the black car, then he would be able to tell. When he walked around the back of his van, he was also moving toward the nursing home, and he noticed several of the senior citizens continuing to watch, apparently waiting to see what he would do. The old pro decided reluctantly that their attention could not deter him. He had to know if his adversaries were again following him. Slowly the cautious observer leaned around his van and looked at the rear of the black car, which protruded partially out into the sleepy, low traffic street. The name of the automobile, emblazoned across the rear in clear silver letters, jumped off the trunk of the car.

It was a Lexus.

Patie quickly pulled his head back behind his vehicle, and leaned against the rear of it, trying to think. Should he dart around the front of his van, jerk the Lexus' door open and swing from the ground? No, the curious senior citizens would surely call the police, and he had no evidence with which he could convince the officers that the Chinamen were doing anything wrong. Maybe he could wait for the Lexus to leave and follow it. No, the driver or passenger would certainly spot him, and his van could not stay close to a speeding Lexus. That would accomplish nothing, and besides he couldn't drive off and leave his writing material on the pier. He might just walk slowly up to the driver's door and knock on the window. The Asian might talk to him—might tell him what he's after. Or he might pull out a weapon. Probably not. Lots of older people and a few nurses could see the entire episode, producing many witnesses. What if no one was in the car? What if they had parked at an angle in front of him to irritate him, provoke him into doing something irrational. If he wanted to leave he could not get his van out, not with the Lexus in front and another automobile parked close behind. What were they doing?—what were they up to?. Well, the irritated writer decided, I can't stand here all day looking guilty to the people across the street.

Corbin intended to walk casually up to the driver's door and stand there until the Chinaman either rolled the window down and talked to him or drove off. He wanted to bring the issue to a head, wanted to extract something from the two agitators and he was willing to fight if need be. If a fight did occur, and the police were called, he could at least accuse the men of blocking his van so he couldn't leave. That, in turn, he could argue, proved evil intentions on their part, a reasonable defense. He would let them initiate the provocation and he was glad he wore his good Nikes—good traction— good maneuverability. He didn't really want to fight in the street, but he convinced himself he was ready to do it. Maybe the two Asians would be less aggressive there, in daylight, than in some dark Bay St. Louis parking lot at night.

With a little trepidation Patie stepped around the front of his van. The driver's side door of the Lexus was only four or five feet away. And the window was dark. All the windows were dark. He could not see into the car—but he knew everyone in it could see him, sending a cold chill up his spine. He was totally disadvantaged and he knew it. Impulsively, he bounded the ten feet or so to the front of the Lexus, leaned over the black hood and peered into the car through the front windshield. A middle-aged woman sat behind the wheel and the sud- denness of Patie's moves, his aggressive behavior, caused her to scream, loudly. From across the street a large, young attendant in a white uniform sprinted directly toward the embarrassed writer, yelling as he ran, "What the hell are you doing to her?"

Patie's mistake, the woman's scream, and the man's reaction all combined to shock the old football player into recognition of what he had done. He lifted his hands so the man could see them and slowly backed away from the car, toward the front of his van "I'm sorry, Ma'm, I'm really sorry. I mistook you for a friend and I was trying to scare him. See? That's my van parked right behind you and I was out on the Pier and—"

By that time the attendant had arrived and stood between the embarrassed man and the woman, who wanted no explanation. Patie tried to move to the side so he could see around the white-coated attendant, toward the darkened driver's window, toward the fearful woman. He wanted to explain—she had no reason to fear him. It was a mistake—a joke, but the uniformed worker kept moving in front of Corbin, taking away his line of sight.

"Ma'm, were you leaving?" the attendant asked the woman.

"Yes," came the muffled reply from inside the car.

"Then go ahead. I'll handle this."

"Look," Patie responded, "there's nothing to handle. I was on the pier writing and got cold. I came back up here to get a jacket. Look, this is my van—I'll show you." The owner pulled out his keys and punched the remote lock, which opened the door. Then he reached into the rear of the vehicle and pulled out his windbreaker, locking the doors again. "See," he repeated. "It was all a joke, I thought my friend had seen my van and me walking toward it and decided to block me in—playing around. I thought I would just scare him so I—"

"Alright, alright, I believe what you are saying but aren't you a little old for practical jokes?" the young man asked.

"I may be," the chagrined jokester replied, pulling his windbreaker over his chilled shoulders. "I'm sorry about this one—really sorry."

As the black Lexus pulled into Ullman Street, Patie looked at the other side of the trunk. It was a Lexus-300.

CHAPTER TWELVE

Walking briskly back to his writing spot on the pier, Patie wasn't exactly ashamed of himself, but he wasn't pleased with himself either. His emotions had depreciated to a mild embarrassment, a characteristic not endemic to his gregarious nature. Primarily, though, he was disappointed that confrontation with his two foreign antagonists had not finally occurred. He wanted witnesses when it did and he had witnesses back there, an entire yard full of witnesses. It would have been a good place to face them, those two Asians, who had inserted such confusion into his life— and his plans, not that the competitor solicited confrontation, he didn't. But he knew this one had to come. He questioned whether or not he had been afraid when he ran to the front of the car and peered in—decided that he had—admitting it to himself. Then he asked himself why. He had endured conflict before. Everything that happened on a football field was contentious, a confluence of desire, anger, and a determination to hurt the other person before he could hurt you, three creeks flowing together producing one great river of physical violence. He had fought—on the football field, in bars, on the street, not a lot, but some. Had he been afraid then? He didn't remember fear. Maybe anger diluted it, or even covered it, like a wet blanket thrown over a Boy Scout campfire. Or maybe he had not been afraid then. Maybe fear comes with old age— a part of maturity. Age produces experience and experience produces wisdom. A young man should fear danger more than a fifty-six year old, wouldn't you think? He has more to lose—more years, more pleasure—more love—more, more—.

"Wait, Meathead, why are you contemplating death?" Corbin murmured out loud, as he sat back down on the bench, his notebook and all his other paraphernalia exactly where he left them. Could his affair with Marti really produce a threat of bodily harm, perhaps death? As much as he resisted acknowledging the possibility, the middle-aged party-boy knew it could happen, and he had to admit that he feared it. He shook his bare head in solemn amazement again that he had allowed Buddy and Jack to talk him into this, finding some comfort in the fact that Buddy encouraged him to bail out if things got out of hand. But he couldn't do that. He couldn't spend the rest of his life knowing he cut and ran in the face of danger. Well, at least his children and grandchildren were taken care of financially, due not to his "illustrious" business ability, but to their inheritances from Mattie. She had been very careful and very diligent in establishing the trust funds, sparing the old pro that worry. All of them were financially secure, and they had never been forced to depend upon Patie for it. He had added little money to their trusts, a fact from which he gained no pride.

"It's time I did SOMETHING to help SOME-BODY," he whispered louder than he intended. Two old fishermen walking down the pier, poles and tackle in hand unnoticed by the "contemplator" who was in deep, consuming thought, happened to be near him when the words exploded from his mouth. One of them glanced at Patie, smiled, and exclaimed, "I agree. You want to bait our hooks for us?"

Corbin jerked his head up toward the two men. "What? Oh! You caught me talking to myself," he laughed. "No thanks. Appreciate the offer though." They laughed and moved on toward their fishing spots. Patie tried to refocus his mind onto his writing.

Two young lovers, as oblivious of Patie as he was of them walked past him, looking as though they had somehow been fused together, and stopped in the gazebo just past the one in which he was writing.

The air was cool, still, and the sun's rays felt good against his windbreaker and bare legs, but the beginning writer did not like the glare of the sun upon his writing material, which was nothing more than lined white note-book paper. Even with sunglasses, the dazzle was very bright. He glanced at his watch. One forty-five—still slightly more than three hours to write and he could do a lot in three hours—if he could steal his thoughts away from the embarrassment of a few minutes earlier, a certain liberal Mississippi State democrat, a black Lexus, two Chinese-looking men and two old Ole Miss teammates who had talked him into doing something stupid.

Okay, okay, Meathead, he reflected all over again, you're in it now—stop crying. You're not gonna' quit. Start writing. You DID come down here for that purpose too, remember?

It WAS a good writing day and twenty minutes later, he had broken into the writing zone, although the mode itself prohibited the novice writer from recognizing it, so lost was he in his work.

On those days, he had better be prepared to write, because they came rarely, maybe one or two a week, and sometimes in the middle of the night. Strange! At those times, his mind seemed to be possessed by a different spirit and he would write as long as physically possible, often until his hand grew so tired he could no longer grip his pen nor hold his weighty eye lids apart.

Other writers, published writers, had told him the same thing, men and women whom he met during book signings at Square Books in Oxford, at Lemuria in Jackson, or various Books-a-Million stores scattered throughout the south. "When those times come," they all declared, in different words, "you'd better be ready to write. Never to be recaptured is a writing day lost."

Today was a good writing day and soon Patie recognized neither the passing of time nor the desire for water, nor the sensation to visit the bathroom. Three incognizant hours later a familiar voice shook the engrossed writer back into a state of consciousness.

"Hello, Reb."

Corbin had not heard her approaching footsteps, nor had he seen her coming. The sound of her voice lifted his head as though she had looped a rope under his chin and pulled. When he twisted his neck to the right and looked, she stood only five feet behind him, slightly to one side. Surprise, acting like air pressure inside him accelerated the volume of his greeting.

"HI!! What the heck—how are you? How did you know I was here? How did you slip up on me?"

"Expected me, huh?"

"No, I didn't expect—. No, but I'm glad to see you. How did you know I was here, Loverly?"

"I saw your van and you told me you sometimes wrote on the pier. I decided to walk the hundred yards out here and watch you work a little. You were really getting with it, Reb, writing hard."

"Yeah," he concurred, "good writing day. Sit down for a minute." Asking Marti to sit made Patie realize that he had completely lost track of the time. Squinting at his watch, which he had taken off and placed in his briefcase, he exclaimed "Gosh, it's almost five. What are you going to do?"

"Well," she answered, "I'm going home, put on my shorts and jog—over to your condo if you still want me to."

"Of course I do—been looking forward to it all day. But that's only about a mile, and you usually run five miles, don't you?"

"I'll run five," she explained, "I'll finish at your house."

"What time do you think you'll get there, to my condo?"

"A little after six. I run about twelve minute miles. I'm gonna' run the streets today."

Patie stood. "Great. That'll give me time to work out on my Healthrider." He started gathering all of his writing supplies, folding the table, preparing to leave.

"You want me to carry some of this stuff to your van, Reb?"

Patie almost said yes, but then he remembered he shouldn't be seen with Marti in broad daylight, almost in the middle in Bay St. Louis. "No, I'll get it, you go ahead. See you in about an hour."

"Okay, Ole Miss," she smiled moving down the pier, her expression indicating that she had read his mind perfectly. "But I'm not ashamed of you."

"I'm not ashamed of you either, Loverly," he called after her, now some twenty yards away, "But I can't run fast enough anymore to dodge moving bullets."

By the time the would-be author gathered all of his writing material and folded the card table, Marti was in her car, pulling away from the pier. The two lovers in the other gazebo still looked stuck together. The two fishermen on the end of the pier were putting their tackle back into their tackle boxes. They had fished all afternoon. Each of them carried a large string of fish. Must have been a good fishing day, too.

* * * * *

The sweating, puffing exerciser, lifted the towel from the floor next to the Healthrider, removed his glasses and wipped his face. "Damn good workout," he assessed, standing straddle the machine, "good thirty minute workout." He had completed twelve hundred revolutions with his feet on the upper pedals and the fatigue in his legs, stomach muscles and arms proved it. The large round clock on the wall said it was five-fifty, still time for him to do his hundred sit-ups, although he didn't have to be finished by the time Marti arrived but he would like to be—didn't want to waste time with her today exercising. He spread a towel on the floor, placed his two bare feet on the loveseat, taking the bend out of his lower back and quickly finished the hundred sit-ups. The retired athlete, pleased that the workout was over, still lay on the floor, watching the local news on television, and sweating when Marti knocked on his front door.

"Come in," the irritated-acting man yelled. When the jogger opened the door, he complained. "Loverly, you don't have to knock on my door. Just come on in. I thought we were THAT close by now."

Marti stepped into the condo dressed in short yellow jogging pants, a yellow halter, both soaking wet and almost transparent. Through the open door, Patie saw the twilight outside, and wondered if anyone saw her come in. The lovely jogger stood at the door for a moment, looking at her friend still sprawled upon the floor, leaning on one elbow, his perspiring head twisted toward her. She ignored his admonition but couldn't resist commenting, "Fallen and can't get up, huh, Reb?"

Patie smiled. He loved her looks, flawed perhaps by her small breasts, but he appreciated again, for what, the tenth time?—her impetuous personality, her unfettered sense of humor, her rapid, good-natured tongue, attributes which he had already recognized, but which seemed to increase in merit each time he experienced them. If one thing causes me to care for her TOO much, it's gonna' be that irrepressible and playful attitude, the relaxed admirer thought.

"More like fallen and don't want to get up, Loverly. I love the view from here. I can see clearly now, the brown doth show," he sang to the tune of, I can see clearly now, the rain has come.

"What do you mean 'the brown doth show'?" Marti asked, standing halfway between the prostrate man and the front door, both hands on her hips in mocked displeasure.

"Top and bottom, through the sweat"

"A gentleman wouldn't look," she accused.

"No, a gentleman wouldn't grab—an idiot wouldn't look."

Marti took a couple of steps toward him, continuing to stand with her hands on her trim hips, looking down into the eyes of a man with a mind as sharp as her own, smiling up at her, a purposeful, silly grin. "I need some water, Reb, may I get some?"

"Of course."

"May I get you some?" she asked taking several more long strides, toward the kitchen, one of them directly over his head.

By the time his visitor had asked if he wanted water, Patie's quick mind had already conceived an obviously suggestive answer to her question, an answer which he knew she expected. But that kind of retort he usually reserved for initiating a relationship. This one was already moving so he saw no need for it. Anyway, sometimes the prankster liked to do the unexpected! "Please, without ice. But you get ice for yourself out of the fridge if you want it."

"You have an icemaker, Reb?" Marti asked as she disappeared into the kitchen.

Swinging his feet off the loveseat, and standing, the bachelor exclaimed, "No, just some ice trays from Wal-Mart. But I wish I had one. I hate filling up ice trays."

"It is difficult for Ole Miss people," she called from the kitchen. "I'll show you how to do it before I leave today." A moment later she emerged from the kitchen holding her glass of ice water and his glass of water, which she extended toward him.

Patie had spread the towel on the loveseat. "Thanks. Here sit down here for a minute. We both need to cool off—physically," he added, "not emotionally!!"

"You sure you want to sit that close to me, Reb? I'm really sweaty."

"No more than I am. Here, sit down. We need to talk a little. Heard anything else from your husband?" Patie remembered Mac's name but for some strange reason, he didn't want to say it—too personal, I guess, he thought. Probably magnifies what we are doing, what I am doing—intensifies the guilt.

"No."

"What time does he usually get home from work?"

"He drove up as I was jogging out of the yard."

"What did he say to you, anything?"

"No—nothing serious. He said he was going to jog too." Marti knew Patie was having a hard time understanding her relationship with Mac, probably made more difficult by the fact that she still lived with him. She could have divorced him after finding out about Lori, but there was no reason, except vengeance— She had no one else. She told Patie the truth about staying with him because of financial convenience. What she had not told him was that she gained a lot of freedom, too. With his adultery, Mac lost the right to question her about her life, her activities.

"He gonna' jog the beach today?" Corbin inquired.

"I don't know. Sometimes he does. Sometimes he jogs the streets, like I did today."

"You don't think he would jog over here, do you? I'm sure he knows where I live by now, and—"

"Reb. I don't give a damn if he knows I'm over here—and you shouldn't. He already knows about us and he can't do a thing about it, not after what he did, and is probably still doing. He has no leverage—no—authority over me."

"He can divorce you—if he can prove we have had sex."

"How? He did the same thing."

"But you forgave him, Loverly, under Mississippi law. Continuing to live with Mac after finding out about his adultery, the state maintains, you have forgiven him. The marital slate is cleaned. Of course the state assumes that the two of you have engaged in intercourse. Living together as husband and wife presumes legal forgiveness—legal forgiveness implies sex has occurred."

"But it hasn't," she retorted immediately. "We haven't had sex."

"That would be very hard to prove to a judge, though, especially if Mac said you have—"

"That couldn't be right, Reb, it makes no sense. It's not fair."

"No, it probably isn't, but it's the law. Trust me on this one Marti. I may be an idiot in some things, but I'm an expert in divorce law."

"I believe that, Reb," the stunned, newly informed wife laughed. "But are you saying Mac can divorce me now—for what you and I are doing?"

"Yes," the experienced man declared, "IF he can prove adultery, that intercourse has occurred between us. Obviously, the photos, if they exist, could not picture something which hasn't happened. Oh, Mac wouldn't really have to prove intercourse occurred between us. If he could prove you spent the night over here, the judge would declare that to be probable adultery and give him a divorce on the basis of it. By the way, oral sex is considered sex under Mississippi law, you know, like what we did last night—or what YOU did," he smiled.

Marti shifted on the loveseat, moving off the towel, now moist from the sweating exercisers, away from her male companion. Then she turned toward him, reached over and held his left hand in hers, and for a few seconds said nothing. Finally she spoke. Her voice was soft, her tone quiet. A slight smile enshrouded her placid face indicating a strong desire for a conversational change. "Reb," she whispered sensually, looking him directly in the eyes, "all this talk is not only boring—it's depressing. Now—I need a bath and so do my clothes which I'm gonna' have to put back on after I bathe. With your permission I'm going to walk slowly up those stairs—right there," she pointed, "and get in your shower. This is your condo and you, of course, will do what you please. You may come with me, get in your shower with me so we can help bathe each other's sweaty body, OR—you can stay down here and wait for Mac to knock on your front door, which I know he doesn't have the intestinal fortitude—guts, in your vernacular, to do. Which do you think you would be interested in doing, Reb?" Her large brown eyes had not, even for a second, left his, the slight smile still spread across her inquiring face—indicating, within her confident spirit the secure belief that she already knew the answer.

Two factors existed, either one of which might propel Corbin up the stairs, two motivations. Only one would prompt him to stay downstairs. He could follow this forty-one year old beauty whose face and body still looked twenty-eight up to the shower because he has a task to perform and he is committed to doing that job, a patriot in action, serving his country, performing his assigned duty. That would be a noble reason, none more sacred, and who could fault him for that? Well, maybe

Kim, but who else? No one, of course. Having sex with this wife of a possible spy who may be selling secrets to a foreign government, would mean ultimate intimacy and comradeship with her. Maybe then she and Patie could combine to develop a plan whereby they might determine whether or not Claiborne, the man suspected by the government, was actually a Judas. Yes, that would be an honorable endeavor, a noble cause. He had won his air force commission in AFROTC at Ole Miss, but he had never served his country in war—too young for World War II and Korea and exempted from duty in Vietnam because of pro football. But he would have served, had he been called, and he supposed that he would have performed well, though he had no way of proving that, not even to himself. The affliction of his conservative patriotic soul was that he did not know— for certain—he had never known and he probably would never know.

Patie might trail this seductive beauty up his own stairs, to his own bathroom for another reason— because he desires her, desires to see her naked body, to behold it, to touch it. Because his ego craves it! Could he love her? He wondered. Maybe, maybe not. He probably couldn't answer that question until he had sex with her. Could a man love a woman with whom he had never been intimate? Of course, he had to admit, but love would yield sex, like fertile ground yields a good crop. Intercourse would help him focus his emotional eyes—enable him to decide the depth of his desire for her, how much he REALLY cares, HOW he cares. He admitted to himself that the entire affair might be nothing more than fascination, however, something new adding to the excitement of forbidden fruit.

Or the fifty-six year old father and grandfather might exercise the prerogative to decline the personable beauty's invitation and just continue to sit where he now sits, on his settee and wait for her to walk back down the stairs, clean body covered by clean, wet workout clothes. But why would he do that? Morality? Probably not. His sins and vices were by now legion, too many to count. Why would one small act of chastity matter at this point in his ignoble life? When faced with the next temptation, would he respond morally and walk away from it? What value a love act of virtue? Should not many ethical feats be linked together before their essence could be measured for goodness?

Decency? A concern for Marti? Perhaps, yet she wants him to follow her up the stairs. But honesty, a decent deed in itself, admits that she wants him without knowledge, knowledge that his pursuit of her began with a plan to use her, not for sex—for information which she may not even have, not right now. Then too, the comely woman has already admitted her resolution to become involved with a man, maybe NOT just any man, as he once thought, but a man, a man of her choosing. Would purity of conduct insist upon a turning away under those circumstances? Probably not, yet ought one person's flaws form a ladder to another person's pleasures?

Fear maybe! Perhaps fear would anchor him to his seat, keep him out of the shower with an immodest beauty, out of the bedroom, out of the bed! If fear would be that singular trait which weights him to abstinence, what would he be afraid of—being caught by a jealous husband, a lawsuit, something he desperately eschewed, to use a Biblical word? No, the husband, jealous or not, already knew, apparently—if Marti's veracity could be trusted. Fear of disease? Since AIDS, a legitimate concern. Probably not. Again if the adamant charmer's word could be believed, she had done nothing to acquire the horrible sickness. Fear of physical pain? Afraid of physical confrontation? A fight. No, of course not. He had no desire to fight for fight's sake, no illusions of supreme pugilistic achievement—but he would fight if cornered—there's that question about how much power remained in his left hook—childish wonderment. Fear that bathing with her and having sex with her would catapult him headlong and irresistibly into an emotional state from which there would be no easy escape? Fear of an emotional state—fear of an emotional—. Yes, he feared that. Until now, Patie Corbin controlled his own destiny, in this life, at least. Last night had been, could be addictive, tonight might be all-consuming, might be much more than addictive, a joining together of bodies, of lives, so indissoluble neither of them could pry apart again, and yet they would be pried apart. That day of agony would surely come. Emotional anguish might not afflict him if he walks up the stairs, it most assuredly WON'T happen if he stays on the loveseat. THAT, decided the seldom-prudent man now trying to exercise circumspection, is my concern. Therein lies my fear. I'm afraid I might get hurt!!

"I have examined my heart, Loverly, and I see—"

"Your what?" she interrupted.

"HEART, at this particular moment, HEART—
and unaccustomed to this manner of delightful invitation
though I may be, yet I find lodged deeply within my soul,
a yearning to accompany you up my stairs to face—oh,
whatever fate has arranged with honor, as strength is
distributed to me."

"You want to go, huh Reb?"

"Yeah."

"Well, then let's go," she cheered "Hotty Toddy
and the ringing of a cowbell."

"I never knew sex could be like that, Patie," Marti
whispered softly, It has been a long time for me, but I
don't remember it ever being that good—not even close."

"Aw, you're just saying that Loverly, trying to
make an old man proud. Been so long, you've forgotten."

The two were lying on Patie's bed, on their backs,
nude, holding hands, having kicked the spread and the
top sheet to the floor, with the ceiling fan above turned
on high. And still the perspiration flowed from both of
them. It had been all they expected and much, much
more, as though the two of them had been wanting one
another and waiting for each other all their lives.

"I had forgotten Reb," she agreed, "forgotten how
much I have missed being desired by a man. This made
me remember how empty sex with Mac had become."

"It was great, Loverly. No one has ever come that
close to washing me completely upon the shore—I mean
the tide came in and then it went out and I had to grab

the bottom sheet, almost."

"Nor have I ever seen a life raft so long and so firm. I mean that canoe just kept on and kept on canoeing. You taking Viagra?"

"Of course not, but even if I were, I wouldn't admit it. I want you to think that was all me, heh, heh. Besides, I wasn't the super-performer—you were, especially after you manned the oars. You know how to paddle, Good-Lookin. How many times did you shift into high gear, six, seven?"

"Well, actually I wasn't counting, Reb, but I would think more like nine or ten."

"WOW. Didn't take long to know you were a multiple Milly, and I love multiple Millys. I'm just glad I could keep floating 'til you reached your dock, wet dock, that is, not dry dock."

"I wish I smoked," the contented lady suddenly exclaimed.

"I thought once or twice you were beginning to—."

"No, No, I don't mean like that—I mean cigarettes."

"Why do you wish you smoked now, Loverly?"

"I don't know, the movies I guess. This just seems like a good time to smoke a cigarette. You ever smoke, Reb?"

"Yeah, for years—Hav-a Tampa Jewels, the little, wooden-tip cigars. Thought I couldn't live without 'em. Kept one in my mouth all the time. You?"

"Not really. I tried cigarettes when I was at State," she added. "I never did really like them."

"Loverly, I don't like bringing up an unpleasant subject or changing the mood, but what time do you need to go home?" The old warrior really didn't want Marti to leave, but it was already dark outside. Thirty more minutes together still must be followed by her leaving, and thirty additional minutes together might cause more unpleasantness when she got home. Patie did not want that, for her sake and his. No need to rub it in Mac's face, he thought.

"You ready for me to go, Reb?"

"NOT ON YOUR LIFE, Loverly. On MINE maybe but not on—just kidding, just kidding," he grinned when she suddenly raised up on one elbow. "Just kidding—promise."

"What time IS it?" she asked, careful to let her companion know she wasn't offended.

"According to my trusty Rolex, its seven o'clock."

"I don't have to be in THAT big of a hurry but I suppose I do need to be going. I told Mac we would eat at home tonight. He wants to talk some more."

"Do you have to cook?"

"We both cook. Actually, he does most of the cooking, when he's home."

"Is he home often?" the volunteer government agent asked, a little ashamed of collecting information on Mac at that particular moment.

"A couple of nights a week, usually—maybe. Since he got involved with Lori, he doesn't come home as early after work. Sometimes he stays out real late."

"Does he ever spend the night away from home?"

"Occasionally he will—Reb, why are you asking

me all these questions about Mac?"

"Oh, I don't know Loverly. I guess being with you today, doing what we did, enjoying it like we both enjoyed it, I just wonder about the crazy rascal, how he could leave this for another woman. He must be nuts."

"I'm probably the one who's nuts, for enduring it."

"No, he's the crazy," Patie disputed. "Trust me, I know. I also know you have to leave. Your jogging things aren't dry, though."

"They would have been wet from sweat anyway, Reb."

"I know," he agreed, "but putting wet clothes back on isn't very comfortable. You want to take another quick shower?"

"No. I don't want to wash you off me—nor out of me—the only way I can take you home with me." Patie could tell—Marti was serious. That pleased him but it also worried him slightly, under the circumstances. Surely she wouldn't try to hurt Mac with the evidence of her promiscuity! Surely she wouldn't do that!

"I love you saying that, Marti, but be careful. He could see a spot on your shorts, or something."

"Oh hell, Ole Miss, quit worrying. Women have ways of handling things like that," she chided.

"Okay, okay. Let's get dressed, and I'll drop you off a couple of blocks from your—"

"I'll jog home," she countered.

"NO! I'll drop you off. You've already run your five miles today. Besides, its chilly out there and you'll have wet clothes on."

"Alright, Patie, but I really don't mind jogging home."

"No, Loverly. I'd feel like hell letting you do that. I'll take you near your house. That's the least I can do for you."

"You mean, after what we did, kind of a payment?" she asked, a solemn tone evident in her voice, no sign of jesting.

"No, not a payment—a joy. Gives me more time with you." Well, at least she's normal, the admirer thought. First friendship, then romance, then sex, then questions "Do you love me?" "How much do I mean to you?" "Is this your way of paying me?" She's absolute woman, the real thing, pure.

"Oh, Patie, you always say just the right thing," she teased. Ah, there it is, he noticed, her sense of humor. It's back and that's good. She doesn't need to get too serious. I'm gonna' try not to—!

Patie swung both legs out of bed, stood, and reached into his closet for a pair of jeans, a T-shirt, and his rubber flip flops. On the other side of the bed the reluctant wife slipped back into her wet clothes, emitting a long "ugg."

"Told you," reminded Corbin. "Uncomfortable, aren't they?"

"Very. Patie?" moving around the bed to him, she whispered.

"Yes, Loverly."

"Patie, I know you don't want to hear this," she spoke, softly, "but I really don't want to leave. Would you get angry if I told you I think I'm falling in love with you?" She had quietly reached for both of his hands and was holding them as she asked the new suitor that question. He figured it would come—but not this quickly.

"No, of course not, Loverly, but I don't think you really LOVE me. You just like me a lot, don't you? Isn't that what it is, don't you think?"

"I don't know—that too, but I really think I'm falling in love with you."

"We need to talk about that, 'Good Lookin'." Had she forgotten so quickly that he came to The Bay to write, that he would be leaving for good in a few months, that he planned to marry Kim, that he had warned her? He had to talk to her about this again, but he couldn't do it tonight. They didn't have time, but they would have to talk.

"When?"

"Maybe tomorrow. You want to walk? We can talk then."

"Yes, but I don't want you to tell me you aren't seeing me again, promise?"

"I'm not going to stop seeing you, Loverly, I promise." Silently, he thought, at least not now. "Come on, I need to get you home."

A few minutes later the lovers drove out of Corbin's driveway in his van. A dark figure in jogging shorts and shirt stepped out from under the ex-athlete's condo, through the thick shrubbery which outlined the elevated building, and watched the van lights disappear around the curve. His arms hung dejectedly by his side, tears glistened in his saddened eyes. His lethargic hands suddenly formed into hardened fists and he swung his right one into one of the large, wooden posts upon which the condo rested. Blood splattered upon his shirt and he screeched with pain. It was Mac.

CHAPTER THIRTEEN

Although the decision seemed to be less than critical when measured against all that happened in the last few days and even now was happening, still delivering Marti to her front door bothered Patie. Yes, Mac knows; yes, he is a weak man; yes, he was certainly incapable of handling the six foot one, two hundred ten pound ex-pro football player physically. But another "yes" always seemed to force its unpleasant presence into Corbin's thinking in situations like this—a .45 caliber pistol provides a fast, complete, and eternal equalizer to such a man. Besides, the experienced womanizer shrunk away from deliberately rubbing salt into the man's fresh, open wound, if in fact he had one. What he and Loverly had done wasn't designed to hurt anyone else, not even a traitor to his country. Mac had it coming, reasoned Patie, but he didn't want to add insult to injury, cruelty upon cruelty—in the unlikely event what Marti and he did DOES bother him, if only because of his ego.

The lady charmer and his emotionally mellow companion had traveled no more than half way to her house when she sighed, "I hate bucket seats. If your van didn't have them, Reb, I'd be sitting gratefully in your lap by now."

"Did you some good tonight, huh?"

"Absolutely! I've heard it said many times that the one thing which a person could get farthest behind on—and caught up on the quickest is sex. I'm not certain I believe that. I'm still not caught up."

"Kinda like the traveling salesman who told his buddy, 'First thing I'm gonna do when I get back home is get me a little—second thing I'm gonna do is set my suitcase down'."

"Yeah, something like that," the serene lady whispered, looking across the console at her lover, her left hand resting upon his right knee.

Changing the subject reluctantly, Patie asked, "Where do you think I should let you out, Loverly?"

"How 'bout in my driveway?"

Patie turned his head slightly toward her, figuring the dim light cast by the instrument panel would illuminate a smile upon her face, indicating the knowledge that he couldn't take her all the way home. He saw none. "I don't want to do that, Loverly."

"I know. It wouldn't be real smart, though I don't think it would matter now. Mac knows everything."

"Not everything," Patie countered, "he doesn't know about tonight—I hope—but you are probably right—it couldn't make THAT much difference. I guess I just kinda' hate smashing him across the face with it, though obviously he deserves it."

"Yes, he does," she agreed," and I suppose I don't really want to smash him in the face with it either, although he sure as hell smashed me in the face with Lori."

By the time the dialog concerning Mac ended, Patie had turned off Beach Boulevard into Marti's sub-division. He pulled the van to the right side of the street, three short blocks from her home, and switched the lights off. "This alright?"

"Yes, although it does seem a little stupid at our ages."

"I know. Maybe soon, we won't—," his voice trailed off.

"Won't what, Reb?"

"Oh, nothing. We'll talk about it another time. I guess you had better go." Then reaching across the console, the apprehensive man drew the amenable woman to himself, both arms locked around her neck, and kissed her deeply. She was still clinging to him when he asked, "Call me tomorrow?"

"Yes," she blurted out as she lowered her window, opened the door, closed it behind her, and leaned upon it her head inside the van, gazing somberly, intently into her companion's face. "I do love you, Patie."

Before the hesitating man could answer, she had pushed away from the van and was jogging toward her house. Ten yards away, she turned her head back toward her silent mate and declared "You don't have to say anything, Reb, I just wanted you to know."

Patie did not hear what she said.

Mac had jogged more than a half-mile when he met Patie going the opposite direction. Well, at least, the saddened man thought, he had the decency to drop Marti off and leave. A few minutes later, he turned into his driveway and stopped, planning, as usual, to walk to his doorstep, sit down and pull his jogging shoes off. Marti would be in the shower now, washing the evidence of the other man from her. He wondered how she would act tonight, how she would respond—no, not respond to him—how she would relate to him. Would she continue to be pleasant, to be jovial. Maybe she would be even more pleasant than usual, now that she had a man in her life. He noticed a slight surge of anger, then fear. Fear of losing Marti. Strange, he pondered, how little he had thought of Lori since finding out about Marti's infidelity. What did that mean?

Before the disconsolate male had time to answer his own question or get to his doorstep, a small man stepped out of the dark shrubbery to Mac's left and whispered, "Mr. Claiborne!"

"Spikes?!"

Marti had indeed, as her lamenting husband imagined, taken a shower, and for the reason he speculated. She did not want to wash Patie from her body but she knew she must. An adulterer, she considered, had an adulterer's nose, and he might be able to smell the evidence of her indiscretion. But her shower was quick, and as soon as she finished, she slipped on some clean shorts, a blouse, and a pair of house shoes. Enough to keep me warm she pondered, along with the memory of Patie. Walking into the kitchen, the housewife wondered what she and Mac would eat for supper, then decided she would wait until he got home for his suggestion. Reaching into the refrigerator, the thirsty jogger extracted her customary bottle of water, opened the side door and eased musefully into a rocking chair on the deck, noticing the brilliance of the moon and stars, intensified, she thought, by the act of love which she had just shared with the Rebel. She did not try—but she could not erase the smile from her face. "Surely makes that old saying about a man placing a smile on a woman's face easy to understand," she whispered thoughtfully to herself, "Wow," a shiver, not of cold, but of ecstasy vibrating throughout her body. Then the lighthearted lady propped her feet onto the stool in front of her and gazed introspectively and elatedly toward the surging sea. She could hear the waves rolling into the sand less than fifty yards away and in the quietness which came between the crashing of the waves, she heard a voice— from the front of the house, on the other side, where the driveway meets the street.

"Spikes?" Claiborne repeated, "what are you doing here?"

"Mr. Chun and I want to talk to you, Mr.

Claiborne. You said you would call today and you haven't."

"There is nothing to tell you, Spikes. I was going to call you tonight after I finished exercising."

The little half-breed, eight inches shorter than the scientist, stood only two feet away from him. Through the dim light, Claiborne could see the distorted face, his features part Chinese, part American, and he could hear exasperation in the spy's voice. Mac knew Marti was inside the house, not more than twenty feet away. He did not want her to hear this conversation and hoped Spikes didn't either, but he could tell that the part American was very agitated. Claiborne noticed his hands making gestures, and could see that he held nothing in them, offering a degree of relief. But he wasn't as confident about the small man's pockets. The uneasy traitor felt a cold chill tinge the muscles of his back, and a thin line of nervous sweat formed, as it had done last night, across his upper lip.

"You believe," Spikes exclaimed with a raised voice, "that your exercise is more important than your obligation to us? We have been waiting all day for you to call us. Are you avoiding us, Mr. Claiborne?"

"No!" the chemist assured the spy, fear momentarily assuming control of the volume of the husband's voice. "I'm not avoiding you. I was going to call you tonight. I wanted to talk to you."

Marti heard clearly Mac's raised voice. She stood and moved quietly to the part of the screened-in porch nearest the front of the house. From there, she was still unable to see the men, but she could hear them better, in spite of the noise of the sea. She listened intently, wishing the ocean would quieten down.

"From where were you going to call us, Mr. Claiborne? From inside your house, in front of your wife?"

"No, not in front of my wife, Spikes," countered Claiborne, desperation again elevating the tone of his voice. "Marti knows nothing about this—please don't bring her into this. She knows nothing—nothing about it."

Marti, her ear pressed hard against the front screen, heard her name spoken by her fearful husband between the crashing waves of the sea. Quickly she turned away from the screen and quietly opened the door into the living room, grateful that she had turned only the kitchen light on. Bending low, the curious wife moved slowly over to the living room window which opened toward the spot where the two men stood, and dropped down to her knees. Then she eased her right eye past the drapery and looked through the open cottage blind. In the dimness, she recognized her husband. She could not identify the other man, but she could easily see that he was much shorter than Mac—and thin. The attentive woman could not hear what the two were saying, only a muffled sound, but she could see the flailing of the small man's arms. She realized the conversation was very serious and the worried teacher knew immediately that she must call Patie. On her hands and knees she crawled through the living room. Standing in the hallway she ran to the telephone in her bedroom— "Please, Patie, be there—please be there," she spoke softly as she dialed the phone.

"Hello."

Marti's heart leaped with joy, not primarily because of her love for Patie, but out of desperation. She wanted to know what to do, aware of the fact that she had absolutely no experience in these kinds of affairs. "Patie! Thank God you're there! Listen, Mac is out in the driveway talking to a man," she spoke, too swiftly for the listener to hear.

"Whoa, whoa, Loverly. Slow down. I'm not able to follow you. Start over."

Disciplining her voice, Marti said again, "Mac is in our driveway talking to a little man. I couldn't hear all they said but I did hear the other fellow mention my name. It sounds very serious. I'm a little scared."

"Are they still there?"

"Yes,"

"Do you think you could get close enough to hear them without being seen?" Corbin asked.

"I couldn't hear from the screened porch. It was on the other side of the house and the roar of the water—"

"Could you slip out the back door, around the porch, up to the front corner of the house?" Patie interrupted. "Don't you have a large flower bed there, shrubbery you could hide behind?"

"I think so. I'm willing to try it."

"Be careful, Marti. I'll be there in three minutes, if that damn train doesn't catch me. I'll park two streets behind your house and go through your neighbors' back yards. I'll meet you at the front corner of your house."

Patie had pulled his clothes off, and was brushing his teeth when Marti called. He quickly rinsed his mouth and slipped back into a pair of shorts, a dark blue tee-shirt, and his good pair of Nikes. Thirty seconds later, he was backing his van out of his driveway.

Marti slipped her house shoes off and quietly opened her back door. At the identical moment Patie started for her house, the self-appointed investigator was moving into position within hearing distance of the men.

Spikes' mention of Marti brought her suddenly and fully into Mac's mind. My God, he thought, surely they don't believe I have told her anything. They ought to know I'm not that stupid, that I would never involve her. She would have nothing to do with this—might, in fact, even turn me in to the authorities. I would never tell Marti—they must believe that.

"We are not certain about that, Mr. Claiborne. We do not know that for a fact."

"You really must believe me, Spikes. My wife would never be a party to this sort of thing, I promise you. If I told her, she would probably go to the authorities and this whole procedure would be uncovered by now. That in itself proves she knows nothing. Please believe me."

"Mr. Claiborne, we cannot afford to believe you. This entire operation depends upon your discretion— and we still do not have the information. We want it now or we want to know what has caused the problem. If you cannot deliver the formula to us, then we must find someone else to do it."

"What do you mean 'find someone else to do it'? What are you saying?"

"Mr. Chun will answer all those questions tonight—he wants to see you. You will have to go with me."

"Right now? I told him all I know last night. What purpose can be served by talking again tonight?"

"Pleasing Mr. Chun, Mac," retorted the irritated spy, who was still animatedly waving his small arms. "You must do so because Mr. Chun requires it."

Claiborne suddenly realized that Spikes, for the first time, called him Mac, rather than Mr. Claiborne. He thought about the significance of that and questioned whether or not it meant that he had fallen from their favor, if they had in fact given up on him. If so, what would they do with me?, he wondered. Would they indeed kill me? Maybe he could convince Chun tonight that Marti wasn't involved and that he continued to work on finding out why the experiment had been slowed. I'll remind Chun that he gave me another week, just last night.

For the next few minutes the two men argued and discussed the situation, and the circumstances affecting Claiborne's visit with Chun tonight. That conversation gave Patie a little more time to get to the Claiborne home.

Corbin parked two blocks from Marti's house, got out of the van and forgot to lock it. Remembering, on the other side of the street, he would be forced to do it with the remote door lock which blew the horn. I'd like to get my hands around the idiot who invented that, the irritated athlete had often complained. Tells everybody you have left your vehicle.

To get to Marti's home, Patie would have to jog, something he didn't want to do, through two yards, across a street, and through the yard of the house directly behind the Claiborne's. It should take him no more than a minute. The night was still young and the air was cool, not cold. People might be sitting outside or walking. He would need to be cautious, and the careful amateur detective made it through the first two lots and to the next street without being seen. Standing behind a large live oak tree between the sidewalk and the curb, he looked both ways before dashing across the street. From where he stood, he could see the lights in the Claiborne home, no more than one hundred and fifty feet away. Peeping around the oak, he saw a black car parked about two hundred feet down the street. Probably the damn Lexus, he thought, considered jogging on across the street, then decided to walk. No need in alerting anyone who might be sitting in it. Having cleared the street, though, the halfback jogged to the rear of Marti's house, crouched down and eased toward the front corner, around the deck, to the spot where he hoped to find his companion. When he got to within six feet of the observing woman, she heard him, quickly turning her head. He held his fingers up to his lips and stopped. She moved slowly toward him. He could hear the two men talking, both of them sounded very excited.

Cupping her hands around her mouth and Patie's left ear, Marti quietly whispered all that she had heard—whether or not Marti knew anything about their involvement, getting someone else to do the job, and if Mac was to talk to a Mr. Chun tonight.

"What does all that mean?" she whispered, her hands still cupping her mouth and Patie's ear.

Corbin pulled her head back away from her hands, turned her face away from him, cupped his hands and whispered into her ear, as she had done him. "I don't know, but we'll sure as hell find out. You go back into the house and turn the T.V. or the radio on—not real loud, but loud enough for them to hear it's on—and be real quiet getting back into the house. I'll handle it from here—okay?"

Whispering in his ear again she asked, "What are you going to do?"

He replied, "I don't know—I'll think of something. Go on, now, please? And be very quiet, especially closing the door."

The worried woman, made silent by the mysterious conditions facing the two of them, nodded her head and slipped around the deck toward the back of the house. A few seconds later Patie heard music coming from the living room. Marti had put a disc in their expensive CD player.

Now, the old Rebel thought, that ought to tell them that Marti doesn't know they are out here—should relax them a little and that will give me a slight advantage, I hope. He had already decided to face the two, made that decision on the way over here, if his memory of Marti's yard and the commons area between her house and the ocean was accurate. He wanted to approach the pair slowly if possible. If not, he would have to sprint again. Wish I had taken time to put on my brace, he fumed.

A low three foot high hedge bordered that side of Marti's yard, just right for crouching down behind. The would-be soldier quickly formulated his battle plan.

Moving slowly and quietly, Patie eased back around the screened deck, to near the rear of the house. Then he walked, bending over, into the commons area and behind the hedge on the Claiborne's property line all the way to the sidewalk, which ran down the front of their property, past the two men, who were still mired down in an abyss of heated debate. The old battler's heart was beating rapidly as he raised up and strode out onto the sidewalk without as yet being seen. George Patton's words, when the general gazed out over a smoldering battle field, marked by a thousand dead soldiers, popped into Patie's frenzied mind, 'My God how I love it.' Corbin could not say he loved what he was about to do but he was damn ready to do it. He would run the little bastard down and catch him if it blew out both his knees and his heart!

"Hi, Mac, how are you?" Patie had gotten to within twenty feet or so of the pair before they saw him in the dimness of the yard. As soon as he saw their heads swing toward him, he spoke, "I'm your new neighbor, Brad Jennings, out for a walk and I haven't met you yet." Now within a few feet of both of them, he extended his hand, not certain which man would grasp it, but assuming the taller one would.

He did, and at that exact moment Spikes recognized him, emitted a shrill "damn", and turned to run.

But it was too late. Patie grabbed the little spy from behind, locking both his arms around him, picked him up and slammed him to the sea-shell covered ground on his back. Then the athlete fell upon him with a knee planted in the pit of his stomach and all the air exploded from Spike's lungs. But that wasn't enough for the old incensed pro, whose secrecy had been discovered and whose condo and van had been compromised. Rage replaced reason. He drew his left fist back and landed it squarely upon the spy's face. Blood splattered upon Corbin's right leg, and he felt it, warm, sticky, delightful. Spikes had stopped squirming beneath Patie's right knee and the fighter knew the semi-conscious spy would be going nowhere soon, so he lifted himself off the stricken man, leaving him twisting and groaning upon the shell driveway. Then Corbin turned toward Mac, who had backed considerably away and toward the front door of his house.

"Hold it, Claiborne. Don't go in the house. I want to talk to you." Corbin was angry beyond belief, almost out of control. Like a great white shark smelling the blood of a human, he had finally tasted the delicacies of vengeance and he wasn't about to stop now. He wanted answers and he was determined to get them. "Who is that bag of crap lying on the ground over there bleeding like hell on your driveway? Huh? Who is he?"

Mac stopped moving, stood still, looked at this maniac who had just destroyed Spikes—may have killed him. The frightened chemist tried to keep his wits. He could not tell this man whom he recognized, Patie Corbin, about Spikes, but he knew he had to tell him something. The man was wild and he had no desire for a physical confrontation with him.

"Before I answer your question, would you answer one for me?" Claiborne quickly murmured.

"Go ahead, ask it," blurted Corbin, the wrath hardening his voice.

"Are you Patie Corbin?"

The violent man faced a decision. He now knew for certain that Claiborne was a traitor—the conversation which Marti heard proved it. But Patie could not arrest Mac, and even if he could, he didn't have proof. He wasn't even convinced yet that Marti would tell the CIA or NASA what Mac had said. If he accused Mac of selling information to a foreign government, probably through the small man lying on the ground and the other one, everyone would know, including Marti, why he was mixed up in all of this. All the CIA and NASA wanted to know was WHO—who was the traitor? They could take it from there. Mac is the traitor—that's certain—but Mac doesn't have to know that I know, quickly concluded the writer. I'll wait to hear what he as to say.

"Yes, I'm Patie Corbin, but you already knew that. Why do you even bother to ask? You've had me followed, haven't you?"

Patie could feel the anger reducing inside of him. His pulse rate was subsiding, the knot loosening in his stomach. He knew why. Pity. He felt sorry for the man, whose wife he was—he was having sex with. As guilty as the man is, and as evil, still the womanizer felt sympathy for him.

"Yes, I had you followed, Patie. I wanted to know

if my wife was unfaithful."

Patie knew, of course, that Mac was lying, but he had no option other than to act as though he believed him. He would play along, for now, with the private investigator story.

"After what you've done to her, how could you have the gall to hire private investigators?"

"I'm a man, Patie. Even adulterous men don't want their wives making love to someone else."

The front door of the house slowly opened and Marti peeped around it toward the two men. Patie and Mac looked at her and she spoke both their names, "Patie—Mac—is everything alright out here?" The husband glanced toward Patie and then dropped his head. In the dimness of the night, Corbin knew Mac was conceding to him the right to respond to her.

"Everything's alright, Loverly, except the little private investigator bleeding on your sea-shells. He has a stomach ache, and a headache," glancing at him, Patie affirmed, looking at the demure beauty, whose nervousness reflected from her voice. "But I think you, Mac and I need to talk."

"Should I come out?"

"No, stay inside, if you will. We'll be in, in a minute or two. I have a little unfinished business with Micky Spillane over there."

Suddenly, Patie heard a rustling sound in the direction of the bleeding spy, some fifteen feet away. He was scrambling to his feet. By the time Corbin reached him, he had made it back to the thick shrubbery from which he had stepped to confront Mac a few minutes earlier.

"Where the hell do you think you're going, pis-
sant?" the old running back yelled, as he yanked the
small man out of the vegetation back into the yard. "We
have a few more things to talk about."

Patie heard the sound before he felt the pain, and
the world started trying to slide from under him. He was
back in old Kezar Stadium, San Francisco, a halfback
volunteering to cover a kickoff. He and the kick return-
er slammed into each other going full speed and the
world went away, spinning and spinning and spinning
into eternity. That day he wore a helmet. Tonight, he
wore only inch long hair. He thought he heard a
woman's voice crying out for him, but he wasn't sure—
and then the world went away again, like in Kezar.

CHAPTER FOURTEEN

The voice drifted up from a deep resonant well. "PATIE! PATIE! PATIE! CAN YOU HEAR ME? PATIE!" Throughout the retired athlete's once active life he had heard it many times—on the football field in Laurel—then on the practice field at Ole Miss and in Old Hemingway Stadium—and at LSU—oh, at LSU. All decent opposing running backs heard the voice at LSU. That was where he took his worst lick—LSU— a concussion which sent him to the hospital for two days and onto the bench for two weeks. Probably ought to have laid out for a month—or is it lain out? Hell, I don't know—what difference could it make? The voice yelling in his ear isn't the English teacher's voice anyway. He was a man, like the football trainers and coaches who yelled from the well. This voice was different. It was a girl's voice. Who the hell is SHE?

Patie opened his eyes. It was dark and he wondered if he was blind and he was lying down, he knew
that finally—he was lying down. And he was moving,
moving, his right shoulder. Why was his right shoulder
shaking? He didn't like it and he tried to swing his right
arm up to stop it but he didn't know if his arm moved
much. And then—he heard the voice again—louder this
time and less resonant, like the person had climbed part
way out of the well. "PATIE! CAN YOU HEAR ME
PATIE?" The voice sounded frantic, he thought, like
something was wrong, and something must be wrong
because I can't see.

The semi-conscious man tried to say "What?" He
thought "What?" and he formed "What?" in his mind. He
opened his mouth and he sent "What?" out of it. He was
answering the voice. He said "What?" he was certain.

"Ummh, ummh," he groaned, the word "What?"
dissolving into a weak moan.

"PATIE—PATIE—ARE YOU ALRIGHT? CAN
YOU HEAR ME? ARE YOU ALRIGHT?"

Why does the woman's voice keep saying that? I
answered her! Why does she keep saying that? He felt
his shoulder moving violently again.

"Quit," he grumbled. "Quit yelling! Quit shaking
me!"

"Thank God," Marti whispered. "Thank you,
God," forgetting that she had not uttered God's name
positively for many years. "Thank you—thank you."

"Patie, can you hear me?" Marti was kneeling on
the seashell driveway next to the prostrate writer's right

shoulder. "Are you alright? Can you hear me?" she asked, her body hovering directly over him, her face six inches from his.

"Yes, I can hear you. Quit yelling," he groaned. "What happened? Why is it dark? Where am I?"

"It's night, Patie," the worried woman whispered, "and you're lying in my driveway."

"I don't think I can see. What happened?"

Marti moved back from him a little, revealing a half-moon which was just then glowing against the darkened Gulf Coast sky, creeping above the out-stretched limbs of the huge live oak tree immediately behind her house. "Look, Patie, the moon. Can you see the moon?"

"Where?"

"Look, right there," she coaxed as she gently pulled his chin toward her and pointed. "Right there, see it?"

"I see it. I see three moons. What happened?" he asked, trying to sit up.

"Don't move, Patie. You're bleeding and I'm—"

"Where am I bleeding?"

"The side of your head. Will you lie there for a minute? And let me get a wet towel from the house?"

"I can get up. I'll go inside," he grimaced softly.

"No, please, Patie, just lie here for a minute, please. I can be back in thirty seconds. Please?"

"Okay." He quietly yielded. "Okay."

"Promise? You promise me you won't try to get up? Promise?"

"What happened to me?" he sighed. "Will you tell me what happened?" The old combatant's mind had almost completely returned. But his body had not. That was the way it always worked when he had been knocked out. First came his mind and later his body. He knew she was right—he needed to lie there for a while. He needed to let his body catch up with his mind. His body was still sluggish, his muscles wouldn't obey him and he knew from experience that they needed a little time—then they would catch up.

"Yes, I'll tell you what happened, Patie. But first, promise. You'll not move until I can get a wet—"

"Marti, is that you?" asked the voice softly, as a light from a flashlight shone directly upon her. So engrossed was she in her stricken lover that she had not heard her neighbor walk up behind her.

"Yes," she almost yelled, nervously, surprised by the man's presence. "That you, Tommy?"

"Yes. What happened?" the neighbor asked, bending over the prone man and dimly seeing the blood running down his face and neck. "Can I help you?"

"A little accident. This is a friend. He fell and hit his head. Would you mind staying with him a second or two? I'm going to run into the house for a wet towel."

"Should you call 911?"

"I'm going to do that too, while I'm in there."

"NO! Marti, NO! Don't call 911. I don't need 911. Don't call them." The old pro seemed frantic. Marti could easily discern the determination in his voice.

"You need help, Patie. You may be hurt worse than you think—"

"NO!" the injured man repeated, softly but resolutely. The concerned female was surprised at his tenacious response to her desire to call for help. It made no sense to her. Surely he wasn't worried about trying to keep their relationship a secret, and surely it wasn't the expense. He must have insurance and even if he doesn't, I have some money, she considered. We need to know he isn't hurt badly, a concussion, or worse.

"But Patie, the smart thing to do would be to—"

"NO! Look Marti, I've been knocked out many times," the fallen competitor asserted, lifting himself upon his elbow trying to focus his eyes. "I know when I'm really hurt and when I've just been knocked out. Ten minutes from now my mind will be perfectly clear. In about thirty minutes, I'll be able to function. I'll have my body back. Look," he contended, "if it doesn't work out that way, then you can call 911 or take me to the hospital. Okay?—Marti—okay?"

Marti hesitated. She knew Patie should see a doctor. She felt responsible for what Mac's friends had done to him on her property. She didn't know why they struck Patie but one thing she did know—Mac could have interceded and he did not. She would find out why!

"Okay, Marti?"

"Okay, Patie, if you will promise me two things. Lie here until I can get a wet towel and until I think you are ready to get up. Then if you are still shaky in thirty minutes you'll let me get you to a doctor or get a doctor to you. You promise me that?"

Patie hesitated. "Yes, I promise," reluctantly he agreed.

"Okay, I'm going after the towel. This is Tommy

Williams, my next door neighbor. He'll stay with you until I get back."

"I don't need anyone to stay with me—"

"I don't mind," the neighbor interrupted.

Marti rose and hurried into the house. A few minutes later she reappeared with two towels, a wet one and a dry one. Kneeling again beside her wounded friend, she folded one towel and gently raised Corbin's bruised head, placing the towel under it. Then she looked at Williams, who continued to stand nearby, "Tommy, could I borrow that flashlight for a minute?"

With the light in her hand, the teacher, who had attended to many student's cuts and bruises when she taught junior high and high school, gently pushed Patie's head to the left. Blood had flowed furiously from the wound earlier but had now slowed to a trickle.

"This may hurt, Patie," she cautioned. I'm going to wipe the blood away so I can see the cut—but I would be very surprised if you don't need stitches. You have bled a great deal."

"Is it still bleeding?" Patie asked.

"Not as much as earlier, I don't think," she answered softly, dabbing the blood from the old footballer's slightly graying hair, above his right ear. "At least it hasn't dripped on the towel under your head."

The neighbor, bending over Marti's back looking at the wound offered, "The cut doesn't look that bad, Marti, but it sure did bleed a lot. He may need a couple of stitches. What did he hit his head on?"

"I don't know," the attending 'nurse' responded, "the ground, I guess."

274

"Gosh, I don't understand how the ground could do this," Williams responded. "It doesn't look that hard. Why did he fall?"

Marti tried to hide her annoyance. She had not invited Tommy out there and she did not need a bystander's observations nor comments, although she knew his interest and his insights were honest, intended to help. He was a good neighbor and a close friend—and his wife Mary Catherine and Marti were close friends. The hurt wife had told Mary Cath, as she was called, all about her marital problems. Marti doubted that her lady friend had told her husband. She and Mary Cath were much too close, but she certainly didn't know that for a fact. Right now she could only hope Mary Cath had not told him and the fuming lady suddenly realized that her female friend had not appeared. She must be away tonight, Marti thought, realizing she had to answer Tommy's questions. Not to do so would create suspicion, as unbelievable as the answer might seem.

"I guess the ground is harder than it looks. And he has a problem with vertigo. He had mentioned being dizzy—and he had been drinking a little. I'm sure that didn't help." Marti continued to hold the wet towel against Patie's head.

Corbin patiently listened to the two discuss his plight and he didn't like it. They talked as though he weren't even there, or unable to hear them, or incapable of answering the questions, which were none of this stranger's business anyway. He didn't know what had happened to him but his mind was clearing and soon he would be able to get up and start getting some of his questions answered. He already remembered a few things, Marti calling him to come over. Why? Yes, because someone was talking to her husband Mac—yes, out in the front yard. Why were they talking? Why were they talking? Mac was talking to a man—Yeah, I remember now, one of the men who had been following him—the small man. But how did I end up like this—on the ground? What happened? "Look I appreciate what the two of you are trying to do for me, but I'm not dead—not yet. I can handle this! Don't worry about it!"

Corbin having raised up on one elbow earlier and lain back down, pushed himself up to a sitting position in defiance of his two medical advisors. His head ached like hell, and he was still dizzy, but lying there, the three moons had decreased to two and then to one. He was recovering, and quickly.

"You aren't going to try to stand up, are you, Patie?" his excited lover bemoaned. "You aren't ready to do that, are you?"

"Look, I'm alright. There's no need for you two fluttering over me. Give me another minute or two and I'll be good as new, okay?" Patie didn't resent Marti being there, in fact he was glad. But he disliked the neighbor's presence. He wanted no other person involved in all of this and his mind was quickly clearing. Soon he would be able to—wait a minute, he remembered suddenly. I had put the little Chinaman on the ground. He started to run. I was talking to Mac—I grabbed him—Mac—that son-of-a-bitch—Mac—he hit me. Then gazing up through the dim light at the neighbor, Patie asked, "Could you help me get to the doorstep?" Corbin thought he might make it without help but he wanted to ask the man for a favor and then he wanted to get rid of him before he became aware of anything.

"Certainly," Tommy replied.

The old football player leaned over to his right, placed his right hand on the ground and bent his right knee, his good knee, upon the ground. Reaching toward Williams, who grabbed his left hand, Tommy lifted the stricken man to his wobbly feet. Corbin's injured head swam and he stood there for a full minute waiting for that to stop.

"Patie," Marti implored disapprovingly, "do you really think you ought to do this?"

"Just help me to the doorstep, please. I need to sit and lean back against something. I'll be alright. I'm just a little dizzy, still."

Ten or twelve unsteady steps later, supported on each side by Marti and Tommy, the faltering man sat heavily upon the front doorstep and leaned against the screen door. He was weak and he sensed it vividly while he was walking, but he felt a little better now. The pain had subsided greatly and his whirling brain would settle down in a few minutes. He suffered a little nausea when he stood, but he knew from experience that it too would soon vanish. He touched the right side of his head and his fingers moved gently over the cut, which he could clearly feel.

"Thank you, Tommy. I'll be okay now."

"You sure?" the questioning neighbor asked.

Marti heard in Tommy what she thought to be

277

honest concern. She appreciated his help but she knew Patie wanted her neighbor to leave now, and so did she. Before long, her tough paramour would be asking questions and expecting answers, maybe even demanding them. She would tell him the truth and then hope he wouldn't try to do anything—not tonight. She answered Tommy before Patie could.

"I believe the old boy will be okay now, Tommy. Thank you so much for your help and concern. I think we can take it from here."

"Yeah," Patie quickly added. "I have a hard head. I'll be alright."

"Marti, call me if you need me, okay? I can be back over here in less than a minute."

Marti watched her neighbor disappear through the darkness back toward his house. A few moments later she saw his front door open and watched him step into his lighted living room. Then she turned back toward Corbin, who had rested his cut head backward upon the door and as best she could tell, in the absence of light, sat with his eyes closed.

"Reb, you alright?"

"I will be in a minute or two, Loverly. What poor bastard hit me? Mac? Did you see it?"

"Yes, I saw it. You sure you want to talk about it now, Patie? Wouldn't you like to wait 'till your head clears?" Marti distinctly heard the anger in Reb's voice and she knew he would not rest until she told him all that had occurred in her dark front yard. She was sorry she had seen everything, but she had. And she believed she knew what he would do with the information once given it.

"No, I don't want to wait. Who hit me?"

"Reb, we need to put some ice on your head. Would you let me get some ice first?" Marti asked, stalling for a little more time. "I have an ice bag and it won't take more than a minute or two, then we'll talk, okay?"

"Okay, Loverly, get your ice, but be prepared to give me a name when you get back. Some son-of-a-bitch is in deep trouble." The lacerated warrior heard venom in the tone of his own voice. He wasn't angry at Loverly but he WAS angry. Some gutless animal had slipped up on him from behind and dropped him with a cowardly lick to the side of his head. Didn't have enough courage to do it from the front. If it wasn't Mac, who was it? The other person from the Lexus? Who? He wanted to know and he wanted to know now.

"You mad at me, Reb?"

Patie softened his voice and looked toward the sound of Loverly's question. The moon and the distant street light cast a vague glow upon her face and although Corbin could not see her clearly, he knew she was worried about him and he knew the apprehension probably showed on her face. He could not afford to alienate her. He wanted a name, but he did not want to provoke Marti in getting it. He would need to exercise care. He knew why he was attacked—she probably didn't, unless she had discovered the reason while he was unconscious. He had to trust her truthfulness. "No, of course not, Loverly, I didn't mean to sound like—"

"I'll get the ice," the woman avowed, satisfaction

reflecting in her voice.

Several minutes later Marti opened the screen door, moving Patie forward just enough for her to slide through it. She sat down beside him, an ice bag in her hand. "You want me to hold this against your head, Patie?"

"No, I'll do it," he replied gently, taking the bag from her and placing it against his cut. "Thank you, Loverly, now will you tell me—"

"Mac didn't hit you, Reb, but he didn't do a damn thing to prevent it either. He just stood there, in fact he backed away—the coward."

"Who did?"

"Somebody else—there was a third person. I heard you hit the man who was talking to Mac and then I heard you talking to Mac. I had come back outside the house and was standing just out of sight around the corner. I couldn't see very clearly but I could hear everything that you all said. The man who was lying on the ground jumped up and ran, and you grabbed him. I think the third man was standing on the other side of the hedge. Then I heard a loud thud like something might sound hitting someone's head."

"Did you see what he hit me with?"

"No, but I certainly heard it—and I heard you falling to the ground. Patie, I thought," her voice cracked,—"I thought he had killed you. That's when I screamed."

"You screamed?"

"Yes, of course I screamed—and ran toward you, and--"

"What happened? I mean, what did the coward do then?" he interrupted.

"The coward? Which one? Mac?"

"No, the one who hit me. What did he do?"

"He yelled at the other man—something about screwing up. Then he told him to go to the car. What he told Mac to do really bothers me, though, Reb."

"What was that?"

"He told Mac to get in the car, too. Why would he do that. I mean if Mac hired them to spy on us? The two men should be working for Mac but it sounded to me like they were in control."

"What did Mac do?" Patie needed to be careful. He could not utter even a hint of why he was attacked—not now, if ever. He hoped all of this would end without Marti ever knowing the part he played in it. An impossibility, perhaps, but this certainly wasn't the time for her to know. He would try to dance around it. Maybe he could indirectly suggest the true reason—let her come to the conclusion that Mac was involved in illegal covert activity on her own.

"Well, I think we can eliminate the CIA or any of the other government agencies checking me out" Corbin exclaimed. If the authorities thought I was trying to get secrets from Mac, they would investigate him until they had proof and then they would serve him with a warrant at the office, probably. And I would be in jail by now. They certainly wouldn't conduct business in the front yard of your home—at night, no less."

"What could it be, then?"

"I don't know, Loverly," the old pretender lied,

"but I think we can eliminate two possibilities. They are not private investigators hired by Mac, nor are they agents of the US government."

"Who could they be, then?" she asked, desperation and disgust lacing her voice.

"I don't know, but you said that Mac worked on highly classified projects, didn't you."

"Yes, that's what HE said."

"Then maybe, it has something to do with that. Where is Mac now?"

"He went with the two men—well, not with them. He followed them in his car."

"Do you know where they went?"

"No, just to some motel in Gulfport. When you fell, I ran to check on you, yelling at all three of the men to get away. The one who hit you told Mac to get in the car. Mac wouldn't—he told the man he would come in his own car. By that time I was trying to find out how badly you were hurt and listen to them too. I asked Mac which motel. All he would say was that it was in Gulfport. Then he got in his car and backed out of the driveway. He stopped when he got to us and said, 'I'm sorry about your boyfriend. I hope he's alright, but he got what he deserved'."

"Did you say anything?"

"I asked him 'Why did he deserve it—because he had guts enough to take something you didn't want anymore?' Then he backed on out of the driveway and squealed his tires, as though I give a damn about his ego, the coward."

"Marti, I want to stand up."

"Do you think you're ready? You want me to call Tommy?"

"No," the recovering man asserted. "He doesn't need to be here. I want to go inside—lie down for a minute. Will you help me?"

"Of course, Reb. How do you want to do this?"

"I'm gonna' stand up and hold onto the post here. You open the door for me. My legs are waking up a little, I think. We'll know shortly." Strange—how a perfectly healthy brain, when bruised a little, loses the ability to move the legs. Both of the old pro's legs were still sluggish, but more responsive than a few minutes earlier when he was helped to the doorsteps. He would be back to normal soon, he surmised, just needed a little more time, but he wanted to lie down, this time under his own strength.

A minute later, Corbin sprawled out on the settee, his left leg lying upon it, his right foot dangling on the floor. Marti quickly slipped his Nikes off and placed both of his feet upon the couch. He was still holding the cold bag firmly to the side of his head, when Marti turned the table lamp on and gently pulled at his right hand. "Here, let me have a look at that, Reb," she implored, dropping the bag onto one of her antique rugs.

"Doesn't look too bad," she observed. "But I think we had better doctor it." She walked toward the bathroom and a few minutes later returned with a tube of Neosporin. "My mother says this is the best medicine for cuts in the world. She uses it by the pound. Says if you could squeeze enough of it into hell, it would turn

Hades into heaven and Satan into an angel. You want to rub it on or do you want me to do it?" she softly asked.

"I'll do it." Taking the tube from Marti, Patie squeezed a large amount onto his right forefinger and gently rubbed it into his torn scalp. "I didn't make it bleed again, did I, Loverly?"

"No, put the ice bag back on it though," she answered after examining it and handing the bag back to him.

"How long was I out, Loverly?"

"I don't think you were ever out completely, Reb. After you fell, you got back up to one knee, cursed, and took a wild swing with your right fist. Then you fell back to the ground. That's when I turned you over. You never stopped squirming. I yelled at you to wake up for at least a minute, maybe two, before you answered. I was really scared, Patie."

Corbin didn't answer. He knew she had been afraid. He could still hear it in her voice, see it in her dark eyes, sense it in her attention to him. He didn't deserve it, but he was glad she cared. In spite of what he was doing to her, he cared deeply about her, too, and therein lay his dilemma. Could he commit his emotions to a person whom he was using? Could he commit his life to a woman whom he would walk away from—and to another woman?" I'm going to get the cowardly son-of-a-bitch, Loverly."

"I wish you wouldn't, Reb. I wish you would let me call the police. Will you?"

"NO, I don't need the police. If the three idiots had killed me, then you should call the police. I'll settle this—but you might as well know something—it's not going to be pleasant for Mac."

"For Mac?" she whispered.

"For Mac," he repeated. "You know, I felt sorry for Mac—for what I was doing to him, even though the pitiful bastard deserved it—and I guess because you loved him once. But I don't pity him anymore. Whatever he's gotten himself into, he's drawn me into it and he's my only link to the two Asians. I may not know where they live yet, but I sure as hell know where Mac lives. He can expect to see me every day until I get some of my questions answered. How comfortable are you going to be with that?"

"I can't blame you, Reb, but I hope you won't hurt him."

Patie jerked the ice bag away from his head and sat up abruptly, looking sternly into the lovely face of the woman with whom he had gained such a close comradeship. "Won't hurt him? Why in hell would you care if I hurt him after what he's done? I thought you loved me!"

"I do love you, Reb. I don't care what happens to Mac, especially after what happened tonight. I don't want you to end up in jail."

"I'm not going to kill the sorry bastard, Loverly. But he will tell me what I want to know about those two men. And he's going to visit them—with me. If he'll cooperate, I won't lay a hand on his worthless hide."

"What if he won't cooperate?"

"Then it's simple. I'll lay a hand on his worthless hide. By the way, you think he'll be back tonight?"

"I don't know, Reb. He'll have to go to work tomorrow so he'll have to change clothes. He's still wearing his jogging outfit."

Patie, already sitting, stood to his feet. Marti lurched to her feet and to his side, grabbing his arm. "Patie," she exclaimed excitedly, "what do you think you're doing?"

"Checking the vehicle out," he retorted. "I'm going to walk around your living room a little—test the old wheels while you fix me a drink—a strong Canadian Club and Sprite. Your living room offers plenty of make-shift crutches for me to hold onto."

"Two fingers enough? Marti asked as she hugged her lover, making certain he could stand without her help. He could, she discovered, and she turned him loose to mix the drink.

"No, four, Loverly. Since when were two fingers enough for you?"

"This drink is for you, Reb, not me. But I'm glad your sense of humor has returned, I think."

Corbin smiled at his companion and took his first unsupported step, reaching for the back of the large chair. His legs were strengthening moment by moment and he worked his unsteady way around the living room, moving from one piece of furniture to another. By the time Marti had mixed his drink he was taking careful steps without support. Taking the drink from his friend's hand, he slowly sat back down on the settee. "This drink ought to bring me back to life, totally," he declared. "You having one?"

"No, I think not. Doctors shouldn't drink while

they are on duty. By the way—Patie?"

"Yes, Loverly," responded Corbin as he sipped his drink. He could detect seriousness, a continuation of her anxiety for him, he thought.

"I want you to understand, Patie, before I say this, my concern is for you, not Mac, okay?"

"I know you, Loverly. I trust what you say. Go ahead and say it."

"Okay," she continued slowly, doubtfully, "if you get physical with Mac, he will file charges against you. I'm almost certain he will call the police. He won't fight you. He's a pacifist."

"He won't call the police," Patie countered. The hopeful author had already considered that possibility, even in his dazed state, and decided that Claiborne did not want the police to investigate anyone connected to him, particularly Corbin. Anyway, Patie had no intentions of getting physical with the traitor unless he refused to name the two spies. In that case, all bets were off. He could tell Marti none of that, of course.

"Why not?" she asked.

"Think about it, Loverly—what I said earlier. The two men aren't private detectives hired to catch us. They aren't government agents sent to investigate me. You heard part of the conversation between Mac and the other man before you called me. I think you need to be prepared to—"

"To what," Marti exclaimed defensively, "to discover I'm married to a man who's selling secrets to another country?"

"I didn't say that, Loverly."

"No, maybe not but you believe it, don't you?"

"Well, I wonder about it," admitted Corbin as he drained the final drop of Canadian Club and Sprite from his glass and set it down on the table. "I think you ought to be prepared to hear it, that's all. Just be prepared."

"How do you prepare for something like that?"

Corbin shrugged, "Acclimate your mind to the possibility, I guess, Loverly—I feel a lot better now," he commented, changing the subject. The dizziness was gone, the strength had for the most part returned to the old athlete's body. His knees weren't shaky anymore and above all, he needed to call Buddy. In order to do that he had to leave by himself and he knew Marti would oppose any attempt to do THAT. Patie, however, knew he had no choice. "Would you drive me to my van?"

"YOU"RE NOT LEAVING?!?"

"I can't stay here, Loverly. I need to get home—get in bed. I'll be a new man in the morning. Besides, Mac may come back and I don't want another confrontation so soon."

"I'll follow you—stay with you tonight."

"NO!" he rebutted vigorously, "I mean—you can't. I need you to be here, in case Mac comes home, or calls. I want to know everything that's happening."

Marti didn't understand, but then, she conceded silently, she could not understand a lot about men's thinking—so wildly influenced by male ego and testosterone—and Patie stood at the front of the testosterone line. He should allow me to follow him home, she thought, but he won't. Well, it's not that far. We'll talk on the phone after he gets there. "Alright, alright, Mr. He-Man. I'll take you to your car. But be careful, okay? And call me when you get home?"

Patie preceded Marti to her car, walking more quickly than he wanted to, but he knew she was closely observing him. He breathed a sigh of relief when he arrived at her vehicle without stumbling, and she seemed satisfied that he could drive safely. A minute later she let him out of her car at his van, parked in the street beside his vehicle, and got out too, following him to his car door. The uneasy teacher threw her arms around his neck and kissed him. Then she leaned back slightly so her eyes could focus on his and whispered, "I love you, Reb. Call me when you get to your condo, okay? And please drive very slowly and carefully." Kissing him lightly again, she walked around to the driver's side of her car. Patie watched her intently and when she turned back toward him, he spoke softly, "Marti, thank you—for everything you did tonight— especially—for caring." The tough old womanizer's voice broke and Marti heard it. She smiled. "I'll pick up your shirt and shorts tomorrow and try to get the blood out of them—I love you, Patie." The lady eased into her car and drove slowly down the street and disappeared around the corner, carrying with her a new surge of elation.

Corbin turned back toward his van and punched the automatic door opener. "Damn," he exclaimed. "I forgot I left my van unlocked."

CHAPTER FIFTEEN

Beach Boulevard was deserted when the battered ex-professional football player turned his van into it. Funny, he thought, that not many people are on the street tonight. Wonder what time it is?—suddenly conscious of the fact that he did not know, unusual for him—but this had been an unusual night. He punched a dial on his radio which instantly lit up AM 1180, the local oldies and goodies radio station. He punched it again and it blazed 10:38. "Gosh," he blurted out, "I had no idea it was that late. I need to get to a pay phone in a hurry. Ol' Buddy may be climbing into bed about now."

Patie noticed a little dizziness, exacerbated, he speculated, by the movement of the van. Damn, he suddenly thought, I have to go to my condo first and call

Marti, else she'll be over there in about forty-five seconds—she may be anyway. Oh, Lord I'll bet Kim has been calling. Man!!— I don't need another problem tonight—I'll call her before I leave the condo. No, I can't do that—I need to call Buddy now.

Folks were still celebrating at the Fire Dog Saloon, the driver noticed, as he drove slowly by. Cars were parked on both sides of the Boulevard. But so lost was the man in arranging his telephone priorities that he did not see the police car parked a few feet down Main Street, which formed a "T" where it dead-ended into Beach Boulevard. Nor did he notice it pull out into the Boulevard behind him until the blue lights shocked him back into an awareness of his immediate surroundings. Instinctively Patie looked at his speedometer. He was traveling only fifteen miles per hour in a twenty mile per hour zone, made slow because it was in the center of Old Bay St. Louis, where all the restaurants and gift shops were located. "Damn," he wheezed out loud, "They can't be after me." But the police car made no attempt to pass him, maybe because the street is narrow here, with cars parallel-parked on both sides, the perplexed driver thought. To be safe, though, he turned his right signal on, indicating to the police, he assumed, that he would turn into the first available parking space. Must have a taillight out!

Whatever else a conservative Republican might claim, one thing was absolute. Patie Corbin and the police were on the same side. He did not break the law, he often boasted to himself and to friends, other than occasionally speeding, but that's about all—well, sometimes he drove with a drink in his hand. But he had always done that—it was a part of Southern Culture, enjoying a drink at home before going out to dinner, then mixing one for the road. He—and his friends, too—some of them did it—for pleasure, not to defy the law. They had always done it! The law changed, not me, he persuaded himself and then argued with others. Liberal bleeding hearts always try to change a culture, build a straw man to knock down, so they can gain a big following and command large gifts. Just like the Rebel flag, he often debated, especially after a few drinks. "I shed my blood, had bones broken, teeth knocked out of my head, concussions, under the Rebel flag, but along comes a group of social misfits who want to abolish it at Ole Miss and who may succeed, it appears. Then they'll try to take it out of the state flag. I have relatives buried at Vicksburg who gave their lives for that flag. What about them? Anyway, I've suffered more under the Rebel flag than anyone living, other than a few other Ole Miss football players. If pain is to be the criteria by which the symbols of a culture are established, what about my pain? Besides, those people can't be satisfied. After the flag is gone, the next symbol they will attack is the Confederate Statue in front of the courthouse." By the time the drinking orator arrived at that verbal position of statesmanship, he usually lost part of his audience. The discussion often ended completely when an inebriated friend yelled "PATIE CORBIN for GOVERNOR—or SENATOR—or PRESIDENT."

There's one at the pier, recognized the injured motorist, and he eased his vehicle carefully over to the side of the street. Cutting his lights and engine, he pulled his billfold from his back pocket. When the policeman knocked on his window, Patie lowered it and immediately two other police cars pulled in front of his van and stopped.

"Good evening, sir. May I see your driver's license?" the officer calmly and respectfully asked.

"Yes, Sir, Officer, Could you tell me what I was doing wrong?" Patie asked, extending his wallet with his license visible through a plastic window toward the patrolman.

The officer refused to take the billfold. "Would you remove the license and give it to me, please?"

"Yes, Sir."

While Patie was removing the driver's license from its pouch, the officer shone the light through the windows into the back seat. Another officer moved to the right side of the vehicle and shone his light into the van. Then turning the light onto Patie's license, the courteous officer asked, "Are you Mr. Reginald P. Corbin?"

"Yes, Sir, but people call me by a shortening of my middle name, Patie, for Patrick." The old pro was certain at least one of the officers would know him, but he still could not understand what he had done wrong. "Officer, could you tell me what—"

"Mr. Corbin, I smell alcohol on your breath. Have you been drinking?"

"No, Sir. Well," he reconsidered, "I had one drink, a small one. You see, officer, I had a little accident and I—"

"Do you have any alcohol in your van, **Mr.** Corbin?"

"No, Sir. I had only one small drink at a friend's—"

"Then, how do you explain these five empty beer bottles and one looking to be about half full behind your seat?"

Corbin, still sitting in his van, wheeled to his right and leaned over the console which sat between the two front seats. Both officers were shining their lights on the beer, one from each side of the van. The empty beer bottles and the half-empty one, resting in the back drink-holder of his console, were clearly visible.

"Officer, that's not my beer," the new Bay resident exclaimed. "I swear to you!"

"Mr. Corbin, do you have any illegal drugs in your van?"

"Absolutely not!"

"Would you step out of your vehicle, please?"

Corbin disconnected the seat belt, opened the door slowly and stepped out of his van. When he stood, his head swam, and he felt a little nauseated, like he might vomit. Everything seemed imagined. He must be dreaming! He didn't remember leaving the beer in the van—when could he have done that? Why hadn't he heard the bottles rattling around? Drugs? Who the hell do they think he is, some illiterate drug dealer living in a shabby house trailer out on the bayou? "Officer, I don't understand why you stopped me?"

"Would you face your vehicle, Mr. Corbin? Now step back and lean on it please." Patie wanted to yell,

Officer don't you realize I'm a law abiding citizen, not a criminal and I'm on your side? We're on the same side, you and I. Surely you can see the sticker on my back bumper—SUPPORT YOUR LOCAL POLICE! The confounded motorist noticed two other police cars stop on the other side of the street. Five cars, two policemen each—that's ten officers!! What's going on here, he screamed within himself.

The officer who looked at Corbin's license ran his hands all over Patie's upper body, up and down his legs, his ankles, through his crotch. This can't be happening to me, he whimpered to himself, this CANNOT be happening. "Officer, will you tell me why you pulled me over?—and why so many officers are here? What have I done?"

"Where did the blood on your clothes come from, Mr. Corbin?"

Patie looked around, searching for the other policemen. They had left the head lights of their cars on, shining in the general direction of the van, and all of them shone their flashlights directly on him, a blinding evil which increased his dizziness. The fifty-six year old Mississippian had never experienced such a conflict with the law. Highway patrolmen had stopped him for speeding three or four times but only one had given him a ticket, the other officers warning him and then talking football. Highway patrolmen, sheriffs, and policemen were his friends and he was their friend. This can't be happening to me, he moaned under his breath, yet with paralyzing dismay.

"I fell on a friend's driveway a little while ago. I

was driving home to get in bed."

"Would you be willing to take a little test, Mr. Corbin?" asked the same officer, the only one with whom he had talked.

"What kind of a test, Officer?"

"A walking test. Are you willing to take it?"

"Certainly." Patie tried to sound confident, as though he had nothing to worry about. He had always believed he could walk a white line even though drunk, and he certainly wasn't drunk.

"Let's step to the front of your vehicle, Mr. Corbin. Now, what I want you to do is walk directly away from the left front light of your van. I want you to walk heel to toe to heel—like this." The officer demonstrated, placing his left heel directly in front of his right toe and then his right heel directly in front of his left toe. "Do you understand, Mr. Corbin?"

"Yes, Sir."

"Then please proceed."

Patie stood unsteadily against his left headlight. Car lights and flashlights shone in his face. Another wave of dizziness swept over him and his nausea increased. Doubt crept into him and suddenly he realized that the test might be harder than he first thought. But he could do it—after all, it was a sport, an athletic challenge, a physical act, and he was Patie Corbin. Cautiously, the wobbly athlete picked his left foot up and slowly placed it in front of his right one. He staggered—immediately thrusting both arms up for balance like a tight wire walker. Then to keep from falling, he quickly jerked his right foot up and attempted to place it directly in front of his left toe but a sensation of whirling caused him to miss the spot. He would have fallen, had he not hurriedly spread his legs and leaned his body forward with his hands on his knees, a winded football player having just finished running his tenth wind sprint, a three hundred pound tackle following five minutes of grass drills. "Damn," he wheezed, "damn it to hell."

"Mr. Corbin, would you step back to the side of your vehicle and face it, please?" The officer's voice was still soft, his manner respectful.

Patie obeyed. His head swam and something was still playing volleyball inside his stomach.

"Now, Mr. Corbin, would you put your hands behind your back, please?"

The law-abiding citizen felt the tug on his arms and heard the metallic snap at the same time. If visited by disbelief before, he was consumed by it now. "HAND-CUFFS?" Officer, why are you handcuffing me?"

"You failed the test."

"That doesn't mean anything, officer. I'm dizzy from falling—the lick on my head."

"We'll have a doctor examine that later, Mr. Corbin. But you may take another test, if you desire."

"What other test?"

"A breathalyzer test—breathe into a machine which will register your alcohol consumption, how much alcohol is in you. Are you willing to do that?'

The wary man almost said yes. He doubted that he had drunk enough Canadian Club to register him—register him what? Through his confusion, Patie suddenly realized he was totally ignorant of Mississippi law. What is it anyway?—A little alcohol makes you what— driving under the influence, DUI?—A lot makes you DWI, driving while intoxicated. What if you have a trace?—is that driving while, what? What? Impaired! Yes, driving while impaired. Is that against the law? Hell, I don't know enough to make a decision, he thought. How much is four fingers of Canadian Club in a tall glass? Did I drink anything before going to Marti's—Marti—what's Marti going to do when I don't call? She'll call and I won't answer—then she'll go to my condo. Will she drive the Boulevard or take the back street shortcut? Maybe she can make the police—"

"Mr. Corbin, will you take the breath test?"

"No, Officer."

"Then you will have to come with me."

"Where are we going?"

"To my car. I need to get some information from you."

The officer, leading Patie by the arm, turned to walk toward his patrol car, parked directly behind the van. He nodded toward the other officers. Four of them got back into the two cars and left. The other five opened the four passenger doors of Patie's van and the tailgate. Upon seeing that, Patie pulled his arm away from the officer and turned back toward his van. "What the hell are they doing, officer?"

"Don't pull away from me, Mr. Corbin," the policeman commanded, reaching for Patie's arm which he without resistance relinquished back to the officer. He continued to lead the dazed writer toward the patrol car.

Patie, forcing humility into the pitch of his voice, asked again, "What are they doing to my van?" He respected authority and the police were exercising it. There had been a misunderstanding and it would be corrected soon. Of that, the cuffed man was certain—absolutely certain.

"They are going to search it," the officer answered, placing Corbin in the back seat of the patrol car, its blue lights and the blue lights of the other two cars still flashing, reflecting off the bay water, creating almost a carnival atmosphere.

"Search it? For what? Don't you need a warrant to search my van, Officer?"

"No, not under the circumstances, Mr. Corbin. We have sufficient reason to believe you are transporting drugs," the officer avowed, looking down at the shocked, handcuffed man through the open door.

"TRANSPORTING DRUGS?" Corbin exclaimed. The door slammed in his horrified face and the captured man watched the policeman walk around the front of his patrol car and open the front door. "Officer, there are no drugs in my van. I would never do that. I have never been in trouble with the law—I'm 56 years old—Can I call someone?" he blurted out while the officer was sitting down.

"You'll be given a chance to make a phone call later, Mr. Corbin. I need to get some information from you. Are you willing to answer some questions?"

"Of course I am officer. I have nothing to hide."

For the next four or five minutes, the Bay St. Louis policeman recorded information about Patie Corbin onto a large form—full name, birthplace, birthdate, profession, Social Security number and much more. The officer had just asked Patie to explain his purpose for moving to the coast, when one of the other policemen moved from the passenger's side of the van past the front of the patrol car in which Patie was sitting, the headlights and blue lights illuminating him like an actor performing a monologue upon a stage. He stopped next to the officer who was writing, holding four small bags, two in each hand.

"What is it?" asked the officer sitting in the car with Corbin.

"Two coke—two weed."

"What's that?" The old reveler loudly inquired, though he knew,—cocaine and marijuana? "That's not mine. I have never taken that in my life. What the hell—!" A sickness surpassing by far that caused by the blow to his head suddenly encompassed the good American citizen, the man who prided himself in being a patriot, in having never been in trouble with the law. Who could have done this to me, he asked, his mind dancing a pirouette inside his skull. Who could have—NO! Those sons-of-bitches. A rage unlike any he had ever known swept over him and a thought of kill instantly occupied all of his emotionally distraught being.

"I know who put this stuff in my van, Officer—I know him—I can take you to his house—I know him—listen to me, please!!"

"Frank?" The young officer turned his head away

300

from Patie, toward the open window. A large muscular officer was bending over, looking in.

"Yes, Jay."

"Frank, a lady just drove up. She wants to talk to the officer in charge. She says she knows Mr. Corbin, and would like to see him. She asked if he was alright."

"Where is she?"

"In that red sports car on the other side of the street," Jay pointed.

"Tell her I'll be there in a minute."

"Yes, Sir," the large policeman answered.

Then the officer named Frank turned back toward Patie. "Who is the woman, Mr. Corbin?—a girl-friend?"

"A very good friend, Officer. She can vouch for me."

"Vouching for you isn't the issue right now, Mr. Corbin. You are in possession of illegal substances. We are going to take you in and book you. Me talking to her can't change any of that." The officer continued to write.

"Can I talk to her?"

"No," the officer bluntly answered.

"You told that big policeman you would talk to her. She can tell you how I was hurt."

Frank turned toward Patie, looked at him for a moment, opened his car door, and stepped out of it. He walked the twenty or so yards to where Marti sat in her automobile. Patie twisted in the back seat and tried to watch. The headlights of another patrol car blinded him and he could not see Marti. He longed fervently to see her and to talk to her, to warn her. Please God, please he silently prayed. Please have her tell the officers I fell. If she tells them the truth, they will believe drugs caused the fight. The prisoner, humbled by his situation, knew he was asking God to make Marti lie, and he whispered out loud, "God, I'm sorry."

Well at least now, he reflected disheartedly, someone knows what is happening to me—that I'm being arrested—but what good does that do? Marti doesn't know anyone who can help me and I can't tell her about Buddy—or Jack. "God, I can't believe this," he whispered out loud, feeling the beginning of tears developing in the inner recesses of his eyes. He pushed them back and the officer opened the door of the car and sat where he had been before. He said nothing and began writing again.

"Did you talk to her, Officer?'

"Yes." He continued writing.

"Did she tell you how I got hurt?"

"She said two men attacked you in her front yard."

Damn, he muttered to himself. The extrovert had never lost his spirit—his sense of humor—his enthusiasm—but he was losing it all now. He wanted to believe that Jack would rescue him from the predicament which very quickly seemed to be plunging him into desperate hopelessness. From the time Corbin arrived at Marti's, everything that occurred had happened to him for the first time. He had no experience in dealing with these kinds of problems—getting knocked out by a foreign agent—drugs found in his car—humiliated with an arrest—handcuffed—and now probably jailed. He tried futilely to keep himself from spiraling into depression. He could not see Marti turn around and drive slowly back toward her house.

In the midst of Corbin's despondent thoughts, another vehicle with flashing lights stopped adjacent to his van. The patrol car which first stopped in front of Patie's vehicle backed out into the street, and the wrecker, which Patie could now see clearly backed into the space. In the thick of everything else, he had not considered what the police would do with his vehicle.

"What are they doing with my van, Officer?" Patie yelped, seeing the wrecker back directly up to the front of it.

"Towing it."

"Towing it? Where are they taking it?"

"To the holding area," the officer quietly answered, continuing to write, his head never wavering.

"I have money in there, Officer—and some important papers. Can I get them out?"

"No, they'll be taken care of."

Patie was about to plead with the policeman about his valuables when a white van with POLICE written across the side stopped next to the patrol car. Officer Frank met the driver at the rear door of the vehicle in which Patie sat and opened it. "Mr. Corbin, please get into the police van."

Patie sat quietly for a moment. Morbidity exceeding that which he already felt smothered him and he wondered where they would take him. Silently he squirmed from the car, his left shoulder, injured in a football game with the Cardinals many years ago, testifying to the strength of the shackles which bound his hands together behind his back. Dignity seemed to be flowing from him faster than either his personal pride or the weak optimistic belief that his ordeal would soon end, could re-supply it. Dejectedly, he finally stood upright, his head drooping a little in spite of his effort to raise it. Standing there, he saw his van, its front wheels lifted now upon the wrecker, fade out of sight. The driver of the white wagon opened the left rear door. A sickening stench of vomit and urine drifted from it.

"Please step up into the van, Mr. Corbin."

Patie turned toward the policeman and asked, "Can you take the handcuffs off, Officer?"

"No. Regulations," he sharply retorted. "I'll help you get in."

Patie stepped up on the small platform with his right leg. The policeman balanced him and pushed. The athlete bent over and slid into the small, dark windowless cubicle and the officer slammed the door behind him. When his eyes adjusted to the darkness, the confused and bewildered prisoner saw that the bench upon which he sat ran, on the outside wall, the length of the van, from the front wall behind the driver, a three feet by seven feet area, forcing him to face inward. Another wall extended down the middle of the van dividing one side from the other. A man, whom Corbin could not at first clearly see, sat sullenly a few feet to his left, his hands also cuffed behind his back. Beyond the vomit and urine, Patie could smell the man's body odor. Neither spoke.

The vehicle started and the AFROTC graduate tried to discern by its turning which direction they were heading. He could not. Five minutes later, the van stopped. Patie heard voices outside and the rear door opened. A large handcuffed, sweaty man was pushed into the back with the other two prisoners. Before the policeman slammed the door, they lifted a small dirty, blonde-haired woman, wearing extremely brief shorts and a flimsy top into the van on the other side of the partition. "I didn't know women were over there," the cuffed athlete muttered to no one in particular.

"Yeah," the man with the body odor sneered, "I don't know how the pig bastards think we can screw with our hands cuffed?"

"Screw?" a female voice returned though the divider. "I'll screw—you go a twenty?"

"Yeah, I got a twenty," the man claimed. "But ain't no whore bitch gonna' take it offen' me."

"You son-of-a-bitch, who you calling a whore bitch, you bastard—I'll cut you when I get these damn irons off me—you bastard."

The man didn't reply.

Ten silent minutes later the paddy wagon stopped again. The door opened and a long-haired hippie-looking male was lifted into it. He wore only a pair of cut-off jeans—no shoes—no shirt. The large man moved toward Patie and their bodies touched causing more disconsolation to the meticulous ex-professional football player. Lord what have I gotten myself into? Is this my punishment for what I have done? Why, O God, why? Dizziness had returned and the side of his head ached and he was beginning to get more nauseous. Twenty minutes later, the van stopped again. The back two doors opened and a gruff voice commanded, "Everybody out." The four men from the male side of the vehicle and two women from the other side stepped down, their eyes squinting from the light. The van had stopped under a covered area connected to a building. The handcuffed writer wondered what time it was but he could not see a clock. Two policemen sat at two desks outside the building, near glass doors which opened into a large room. The sick writer could see several uniformed women standing behind a large counter in the middle of the room.

"Men line up at that desk," a policeman who seemed to be in charge pointed, "Women at that one." Several other officers stood to one side of the desks their hands on their pistols. One by one the prisoners had their handcuffs removed and were told to empty their pockets into a clear plastic bag. When Patie's hands were freed, he looked at his watch, which had been taken from his wrist and placed into his front pocket. It said 12:20 a.m., and he thought, even though I get one phone call it's too late to call Buddy. No—this is critical. I'll just have to wake him up.

After placing all his valuables into the bag, the demoralized man was taken into an ante-room, off the main lighted area. Eight prisoners sat stoically on benches, staring sightlessly at the floor, their chins resting on their hands, or into the space of a limited ceiling. Two others sprawled upon the floor. A smell of sweat, body odor and beer permeated the air. The sick but observant patriot watched the woman being taken into an adjacent room. At that moment Patie tried to face the fact that he was a common dehumanized jailbird, unimpressive, unknown, unimportant to anyone there. No one cared who he was, whether or not he was innocent, whether or not he ever got out of that place. He was a job for somebody. Because of him and the other prisoners, drunks, thieves, rapists, drug dealers, a large group of people worked. He was a statistic—no longer a human—no longer a celebrity—an empty man, suddenly without rights. He might be proven innocent later in a courtroom but right there, right now he WAS nothing, he HAD nothing, he could ASK for nothing, part of the rejected herd. For the first time in his life, there was no one beneath him on the social ladder. The only ones to whom he could speak even horizontally were those seated around him. He was part of the dregs of society looking up at the rest of the world, and his only friends sat dejectedly with him—waiting—and waiting, until finally, one by one, their names were called on the loudspeaker and they were told to stand. A uniformed worker then entered the room, repeated the prisoner's name and led him out of the room.

"Mr. Corbin," blasted the intercom, "please stand." Patie glanced at the large wall clock. It read 1:36 a.m. He had been there more than an hour. "Mr. Corbin," the polite worker asked, "will you follow me, please." The sick malefactor was surprised at the young man's manners. Patie followed him out of the male waiting area, across the lighted main floor, and through a door on the other side of the room, which read "TOILET

AND SHOWER." The policeman, his voice still somewhat compassionate, handed him a large plastic bag and
commanded, "Mr. Corbin, place your clothes, including
your shoes and socks in this bag and get into the shower."
He pointed toward one of several small cubicles with
swinging half-doors. "Please bathe with this medicinal
soap," he ordered, handing a small wrapped bar of soap
to the wide-eyed prisoner.

"Medicinal soap? Did you say medicinal soap,
Officer?"

"Yes."

"What's the medicinal soap for?"

"Lice."

"LICE!?" The word disabled the tough old football player momentarily and thoughts of disgust rico-
cheted through his bruised brain. Lice! Lice! Here you
stand, Patie Corbin, All-American—All-Pro, resident of
a five-thousand dollar a month flat in Manhattan, a five
hundred thousand dollar home in Germantown, a three
hundred and fifty thousand dollar home in Vicksburg to
THIS—LICE. They are making me bathe to kill the lice.
He stood passively in the shower, his head drooping,
struggling to discover enough motivation to turn the
water on, disheartened beyond description.

"Please hurry, Mr. Corbin, and wash your hair."

Wash your hair? Wash your hair? He thinks I
have head lice? disconcertedly brooded the fashion conscious celebrity. God, how could I be here?—how could
I have gotten into this mess? Damn you Buddy—damn
you Jack. He stood dejectedly in the shower, the water
splashing on the top of his despondent head, running

down his drooped shoulders, dripping from his statue-like body. Ashamed of cursing two of his best friends, even subjectively, he muttered, water running over his moving lips into his mouth, "No, I didn't mean that," and then, as though repetition might completely catheterize from him the negativism, he repeated it." "I didn't mean that."

"Mr. Corbin, here is your towel and please put these clothes on."

Patie reached for the towel over the swinging half-door and dried off, unable to prevent self-condemning thoughts from invading his crestfallen mind—from the showers of some of the most luxuriant dressing rooms in the world to the shower in a jail using medicated soap to kill the lice. Oh, God, is this really happening to me?, he cried silently.

"Please put these clothes on, Mr. Corbin, and follow me."

The famous athlete looked at the uniform thrown upon the shower door. His heart, the minute part which had not yet been mutilated by the overwhelming events of the night, sank, and the tears which had lingered so close to the surface sprang free and he turned his head so that the policeman could not see them. A long-sleeved canvas pull-over shirt—a pair of beltless, slip-on canvas pants, both colored with wide black and white stripes, and a pair of soft, brown, cloth slippers. The officer gave him no underwear neither let him wear his own.

"Please hurry, Mr. Corbin."

Patie clothed in the uniform, stepped out of the shower stall, his hair wet and uncombed, the injury on the right side of his head irritated by the soap and the pressure-driven water, was bleeding again and throbbed, a wound of remembrance, forcing the events into surrealism. The proud man, intimidated now, beaten down, followed the young policeman out of the washroom, a cowed lamb led to the slaughter, through the lighted main room, where another prisoner and another policeman joined them. Moving on through the room, the four men, two officers and two prisoners, turned toward a long, well-lighted hallway. The older officer called "Halt" to the two inmates and pointed to a sign overhead. It read "PRISONERS WALK TO THE RIGHT OF THE LINE". Patie saw a line painted on the floor three feet from the right wall. "That's the line," the officer barked. "Walk to the right of it."

The prisoners solemnly obeyed and a few minutes later, the officer called "Halt" again, immediately outside a double door. Reaching into his pocket, the policeman extracted a key and opened one of them. "Go through the door," he commanded.

The room into which they entered was the heart of the justice complex, an open area with a male and a female cop sitting inside a four sided counter directly in the center of the open space. Jail cells, two floors of them, occupied three sides of the large chamber. Ten or twelve empty straight-back chairs sat forlornly twenty feet from the counter, where the two policemen worked. Neither of them bothered to look at the prisoners, who had been herded to the chairs and ordered to sit. The two officers who had brought Patie and the other prisoner into the cell area walked to the counter and handed the man and women paper work, ostensibly regarding the two inmates, Corbin thought.

The exalted football player, now humiliated, glanced around the room. The other prisoner sat two seats away, a long-haired, unshaven middle aged man, dressed, too, in the uniform of the condemned. He sat stoically, as though gazing at everything directly in front of him, yet seeing nothing, his eyes glazed either by drugs, alcohol, hopelessness, or stupidity. A big coffee pot sat forlornly on a small table in the far right corner of the large room, surrounded by four green Krispy Kreme doughnut boxes. Six jail cells occupied three sides of the chamber—on the first floor—eighteen, and eighteen more sat upon them, for a total of thirty-six cells in all.

"My God," the tough old pro suddenly remembered to himself—"My children and grandchildren—my children and grandchildren."

Patie must have made some kind of unconscious noise. The man seated only two seats away turned his hairy face and grunted "Whut!"

"What?" Corbin repeated looking at him. "Oh! Nothing, guess I was thinking of my family." My God, I can't let my family hear about this! Surely the papers won't carry it—will they? Do they print arrests? Yes, they do—they publish arrests—I've seen it in the paper on a special page—a legal page. The nausea intensified within the man who, as a boy, had grown up attending church. "Oh, God, please, please, don't let my family hear—please, please!" he whispered louder than he intended, but not caring.

The man seated nearby cut his eyes disgustingly toward Corbin again and wheezed with contempt, "God ain't gonna' hep you 'ner me. He just heps the rich bastards so they can give more money to th' church."

I don't believe that, Patie murmured to himself. God can help me. I'm not going to grow cynical like that man. Please help, me, God. I am not going to let this destroy me. I haven't broken the law. I'm not guilty. This won't whip me—Patie, gut it out, he challenged himself silently. Gut it out. You're not a quitter—suck it up—don't cow down to this—get tough—damn it, get tough. Remember who you are, you meathead—remember what you've done. It took guts to do what you've done—and hard work. Get your damn chin off your belly-button—summon up the strength which gave you the power to do all that you've done. When you're proven innocent, your children and grandchildren will understand, and so will everybody else. IF the papers run articles on this, sue the hell out of them. Everyone else is suing—Marti is probably making phone calls right—making phone calls—Marti. I've got to get word to Marti—and to Buddy—don't I get a phone call? I thought I got one phone call. Do I get one phone call?

Patie sprang from his chair. "Officer."

"SIT DOWN, MR. CORBIN."

Patie sat down. "Officer, don't I get a phone call?"

Suddenly a yell echoed from one of the cells to Patie's left "PHONE CALL—PHONE CALL." Then one by one, the other prisoners picked up the chant, "PHONE CALL, PHONE CALL, PHONE CALL" until all were shouting and the deafening sound reverberated through the small barred windows of each cell out into the chamber, making hearing anything else difficult. The prisoner who sat near Corbin ignored it.

The four officers gazed angrily toward the cells and then toward Patie. The man, searching for courage, felt insecurity seeping back into him, and uncertainty, which tonight for the first time he had endured. No, he argued with himself, I'm not going to be intimidated again, not even by people I respect. I haven't done anything wrong.

The young officer who had brought Corbin into the room walked briskly toward him. "Mr. Corbin, you will sit in your chair and wait. You will NOT open your mouth again until your paperwork is finished. Then you can ask me questions."

"Don't I get to make a phone call?"

"Mr. Corbin, I told you—"

"Officer, I'm not trying to be a wise ass. I didn't intentionally start this," Patie waved his hand toward the cells, "but I thought I could make one phone call—by law."

"You can, Mr. Corbin, but do you want to make it tonight?" the officer questioned sternly. "You won't be able to get a bail bondsman to come in the middle of the night—and probably not an attorney."

"Officer, I know I have no rights except one and that's a phone call. Don't I get to make my own decision about IT?"

The policeman looked acridly at the prisoner sitting in front of him, a proud man desperately trying to recapture at least a touch of self-worth and dignity. He looked the officer directly in the eye and suddenly realized that the other prisoners had stopped shouting. But he knew they were watching through the small barred windows.

"Who do you want to call, Mr. Corbin, Johnny Vaught?" the officer asked.

YES—YES, the old athlete screamed silently, I'm alive! They do know who I am. YES! They know I'm not a common criminal. YES!

"No, Officer," Patie smiled confidently. "I wouldn't want him to know I'm in here. I'm old, but not too old for him to kick my tail."

"Come with me," the gendarme softly commanded. As the two walked toward a small room off the chamber, the other prisoners began to shout again. "PHONE CALL—PHONE CALL—PHONE CALL." Patie looked around the room and with the other three policemen watching, he summoned enough daring to raise his right arm, tightening his hand into a fist then jerking it sharply down to his chest—three times—a motion of victory which the inmates understood. They were still cheering when Patie, the officer leading, stepped into the little room, a room which contained only a small table, a straight back chair and a telephone.

"You are making a local call, aren't you, Mr. Corbin?"

"No, it's long distance."

"Sorry. You can't make a long distance call on that phone."

"Not even a collect call, Officer?" Patie asked.

"Yes, you can call collect. I'll be waiting outside the door. Hold your conversation to five minutes. The phone will cut off after that."

"Thank you, Officer."

Buddy's phone rang several times before the anxious caller heard an operator say, "You have a collect phone call from"—Patie supplied his own name—"will you pay for the call?"

"Buddy?"

"Patie, what in the world is happening?"

"Buddy, I'm in big trouble."

"I know, I got a—"

"YOU KNOW? HOW?"

"That's what I was about to say, I got a call a couple of hours ago from Marti Claiborne."

"FROM MARTI? How did she get your name?— not from me, Buddy."

"No, not from you—from your carelessness maybe. She knows the owner of your condo complex and she talked him into letting her in. Found my name and address. She got my phone number from the operator."

"Damn, Buddy, I'm sorry, I think! I need to get out of here."

"Why were you arrested, old friend?"

"I don't have time to tell you now. I was framed. I just need to get out. Can you do anything—I mean without jeopardizing—"

"Don't talk. Yes! An attorney will be there at eight o'clock in the morning. I had already arranged that before you called."

"I'm grateful of course, but can't you get me out tonight?"

"No. They can keep you overnight legally. We—ah—I can't do anything—"

"Okay," Patie quickly interrupted, "Hell, I can make it through anything for one night."

"Hang in there, Patie. I know it's tough. I'll be in touch."

The officer motioned for Patie to follow him. When they reached the counter, both prisoners were given a toothbrush and tooth paste and told to follow the male policeman. The three policemen, one in front and two behind walked the two prisoners up the stairs. The officer in front opened the door to an empty cell, measuring no more than eight feet by twelve feet, waved Patie and his roommate into the small cell and slammed the door behind them. Patie stood immediately inside the small area feeling more hope than an hour before, and surveyed the room. The walls were concrete block and on the right one stood a double decked, solid steel bed—no mattresses, no sheets, no pillows, and thick, rough canvas coverings, one per bed. A lavatory and a commode sat openly in the corner to Patie's left, a roll of toilet paper resting on the floor. A thick oak board, twenty-four inches long protruded twelve inches out of the left wall near the back corner, forming a desk. A steel chair, bolted to the back wall, sat in front of it.

Corbin's cellmate quickly fell into the bottom bunk, closed his eyes, and either went to sleep or pretended he did. Patie brushed his teeth, wishing for dental floss, and climbed easily to the top bunk. For a few minutes, he sat with his feet dangling from the bed, and remembered they had not let him see a doctor. Then he folded his canvas quilt, making it into a pillow and lay down. The recessed ceiling light still shown brightly above him, illuminating the room as bright as the noon day sun. "Do they ever turn the damn light off," he fumed, talking to himself as much as to the lawbreaker sleeping beneath him.

Patie's roomie said nothing. A few minutes later the long-haired man was snoring deeply. "That's all I need to make this wonderful day complete," the tired man exclaimed, loud enough for the snorer to hear. Apparently he didn't.

CHAPTER SIXTEEN

Patie could not sleep. The bed was hard, a shelf of stainless steel, no mattress, no pillow except the folded canvas covering, his conscience, a snoring roommate who would have shaken pictures on the wall had there been any, and that damn light!! They never turned it off! How can a person sleep with a bright six foot fluorescent sun burning only four feet from his head all night—pushing its powerful unwanted and unrelenting rays through his squinched eyelids? Even pulling the prisoner's shirt over his head failed to block the reprehensible brilliance. Why would a prison—oh, Corbin thought sarcastically—not a prison—a retention center, leave the cell lights on all night? Well, the fretting inmate pondered, the night won't last very long and it will give me a little time to think, something I need to do anyway.

Reconciled finally with his fate, Patie's mind, like a down hill skier, raced to Marti. She must be worried beyond belief, not knowing why he was jailed or when he might be released—or even if—thinking, probably, that Mac and his two friends provoked his arrest. She, too, would be lying in bed, eyes wide open, mind racing—wondering what she could do—waiting for daylight which more than likely seemed as distant to her as it did to the wide-awake prisoner. Would she leave her light on all night? Would Mac come home? Would she call an attorney friend in the morning?—Or perhaps even tonight? What would she say to Mac if he comes home? Maybe she's at the police station right now arguing with them, trying to make them understand what happened. "I sure hope she hasn't done that," the uneasy man whispered, the discomforting thought making him squirm a little. "A couple of hours ago, I wanted her to validate my innocence. I didn't know then I would be getting out of here at eight o'clock in the morning, though," he remembered. What a difference THAT makes—hell—I can take ANYTHING for six hours. I've endured six hours of hard two-a-days many times."

Wonder who Buddy's sending down here to get me out? Surely he wouldn't send a local attorney unless NASA or the CIA has one on staff here. No, the man's probably flying into New Orleans tonight, or he may already be there. What am I going to do when I get released? Write on my book? Yeah, right, Meathead—like you're going to be able to focus your pea-sized brain on THAT. Run away? NO, not on your life—I'll run toward the three who put me here—if I can find them. Maybe Buddy has found out by now where they are staying. Will he tell me? Probably not—he'd better not, not if he wants me to avoid them. They are DEAD, the sons-of-bitches!! No, I can't do that—think, Corbin think. You can't do that. How did they do this—plant the beer and drugs and then call the cops? Anonymously? Of course—they wouldn't give their names. Why would the police believe an anonymous call? Can they stop and search a car on that kind of tip? What does the law say? Hell, I don't know—but I'll sure as hell find out—tomorrow—the policemen are going to be in trouble if they searched my van illegally. Wait, Meathead, you're on the same side as the police! Yes, I am—I am—unless they searched it illegally.

Marti looked at the clock beside her bed—three o'clock—reached for a tissue and wiped other tears from her face. Mac had not come home. She wished that she had gotten more information from him, like the motel where he went, the identity of the men who attacked Patie, what her husband was involved in. She knew he wouldn't have told her much, but that didn't stop her from wishing she had tried, especially since the police had jailed Patie. She was glad she had called Buddy. He seemed like a very nice man and his assurances to her that he would handle the situation comforted her. He and Patie were close friends and former teammates and several other teammates were attorneys, two of them practicing law on the coast. If Buddy had not asked her to let him handle it, she would have called an attorney by now. Anyway, Buddy had assured her that Reb would be out of jail by noon tomorrow and that was encouraging. She reached for another Kleenex and swabbed a few more tears. "Quit crying, Loverly," she chastened herself and smiled when she realized she had called herself "Loverly". "Now listen," she counseled herself, "the Reb would say 'Gut it out'. Go wash your face and get your tail to bed, like he would want you to do." Several minutes later she turned her light off and tried to sleep. She knew it would be difficult—but Buddy had promised he would get Patie released. How could he be so certain of that? How could he?

* * * * *

Mac drove to the White Sands Hotel parking garage in Gulfport. He found a space on the second floor and pulled his automobile into it. Locking his car, he got out, feeling for the key to Chun's room which Spikes had given him. He considered spending a little time in the hotel casino but decided against it—not knowing how long it would take Chun and Spikes to get there, not understanding why they told him to go ahead and "they would follow later". The traitor wasn't happy about the night's events. Everything was coming apart and now Corbin would probably call the police. It was time for the chemist to bail out of this cataclysm. He could not find out why research on Bryostatin had been delayed. He wondered if NASA suspected him. His bosses had not indicated that but now, Corbin AND

Marti must suspect him. He would give Chun the money back—somehow. Yes, it was time to quit—it was definitely time to quit.

The scientist had been in the suite about forty-five minutes, grateful no one had seen him, a drink mixed from Chun's bar in his hand, the television on, when he heard the door lock turning. Chun and Spikes entered the room. Claiborne stood and lifted his glass, "Hope you didn't mind me mixing a drink, Mr. Chun."

The large Chinaman looked at Mac for a moment, smiled and replied, "No, 'course not Mr. Claiborne. We have not eaten, have you?"

"No. I haven't had a chance. Spikes—ah—Mr. Spikes was waiting for me when I got home."

"We need to talk again, Mr. Claiborne and we can do that over food."

Claiborne was still wearing his jogging clothes and he looked down at himself. "It will need to an informal place. I'm not very well dressed."

"It will be," responded the spy. "Did you park in the garage?"

"Yes. Second floor."

"Good. Spikes and I like the Oyster Pearl. Why do not the two of you go in your car, Mr. Claiborne. I need to make phone calls. I'll meet you there."

"The Oyster Pearl? That little raw oyster place just off 90 in Pass Christian?" asked Claiborne.

"Yes," answered Spikes. "That's the place. Mr. Chun has come to love our raw oysters and po'boys." Turning toward his partner, he offered, "You want me to order for you, Mr. Chun?"

"Yes, why do you not. Order dozen raw oysters, po'boy and pitcher of German beer."

"Sure you don't want Bud Lite?" teased Spikes.

"No," quickly responded the large man. "Cannot understand American's obsession with Bud Lite. Tastes like water. Order German beer."

"I was joking, Mr. Chun," quickly explained the smaller man.

"Understand—understand—but still want German beer."

"Yes, Sir."

"Mr. Chun, what happened after I left?" inquired Claiborne, as Spikes reached for the door. Chun was sitting near the telephone when Mac asked the question. "I mean, I was here almost an hour before you and Mr. Spikes got here. Did anything else happen?"

"Not much," answered Chun as he continued to sit. "We talk about it when I get to Oyster Pearl. We took care of American footballer Corbin."

"Took care of him. What do you mean?"

Chunn looked at the man whom he had paid to steal secrets. "We not kill him, Mr. Claiborne. Police have him. We talk about it when I get there. Get table outside, where we talk—away from other people."

Claiborne was worried and impatient. He expected Chun and Spikes to be angry but both seemed to be in an unusually good mood considering the unnerving incidents of the past couple of hours. He did not relish angering Chun or Spikes but he wanted to ask another question. "Would you answer one more question, Mr. Chun—well, actually, two questions?"

"Certainly, Mr. Claiborne."

"How did you get the police involved with Corbin?—and—what do we do if he tells them about me? I mean—we don't know how much of our conversation he overheard. What do we do?"

"We talk about first question later. Corbin not tell police if he came to spy on you," asserted the Chinaman.

"Why not?"

"He not want police involved. He works for U.S. Government, not local police."

Mac knew he couldn't stretch the conversation but he desperately wanted the information—and he needed to know what the two men were thinking. They didn't seem to be upset at him—practically the opposite, so he ventured another question.

"What if he wasn't sent here to investigate me, Mr. Chun? Won't he talk to the police in that case?"

"No, I think not. He will protect your wife— either way he not talk to the police. Now, go. We talk about that later."

Spikes slowly opened the door, looked both ways, then motioned for Claiborne to follow. The two of them walked quickly to the stairway and down the four flights of stairs to the second floor of the parking garage. Other than three young couples casually moving toward the casino, they had not been noticed. Neither man spoke, not wanting to attract attention. Mac opened the door to his car, got into it and reached across the front seat to open the passenger door for Spikes, who slid quickly into the front seat. As soon as Spikes closed his door,

Claiborne looked at him. "Mr. Chun seems in a good mood in view of all that has occurred tonight. I thought the two of you would be upset."

"Mr. Chun is usually a very jovial fellow, Mr. Claiborne. He's under a lot of stress which I'm sure you can understand. He has talked to his embassy and they have taken some of the pressure off him."

"Is that who he's calling?"

"Probably. We need to go. He said he'd only be on the phone five minutes or so."

"How did they take the pressure off?" asked Claiborne as he started the car, relieved at the notion that he might therefore have some pressure removed from him, too.

"I'm not certain, Mr. Claiborne. He tells me nothing about his dealings with the embassy. That is between his country and him."

Claiborne backed his car out of the parking space, slowly drove down to the first level of the parking garage and out to Highway 90. He stopped at a light, his confidence growing at the attitude of his friends, and asked, "Spikes, are you alright? You were hit pretty—"

"I'm okay," interrupted the small man. "Patie Corbin will pay for what he did to me—if not at the police station then later. His time will come."

Mac turned his car west on Highway 90, easing over into the right lane. More secure now in his new relationship with the two spies, he asked, "How did you and Mr. Chun get the police to arrest Corbin?"

"Planted a little coke and weed. Amazing what a little seed will do when planted in fertile ground. Grows up into all kinds of nice harvests. I hope they lock the bastard up and throw the key away."

Claiborne glanced over at his slight companion, who seemed suddenly to be rather uncomfortable, shifting his position on the seat as though he were tucking his shirt tail into his trousers. "Spikes, I'm not certain where to turn. Tell me when we get there."

Spikes quickly brought his right hand from behind his back. Claiborne saw the gesture, saw Spikes' hand move to his side, but he did not see the black metal in the small spy's hands. He did not see it but he felt it, a sharp pain at the mid-point of his right rib cage—as though the little man was trying to push something into his body. He looked down at a pistol bearing a large glob of metal on the end of the barrel.

Spikes sneered, "We're not turning, Mr. Claiborne, not to the Oyster Pearl."

Though his companion, now turned assailant, could not see it in the darkness, the blood drained immediately from the scientist's face and a knot of horror exploded in his tightened chest. He looked at Spikes, who had moved to the middle of the seat. Their eyes met and Claiborne, seeing dimly, neither saw nor heard compassion. "My God, Spikes, you can't do this. Why are you doing this—please—for God's sake—please don't—don't do this—I'm—" wept Claiborne, lifting his right foot from the accelerator.

"Shut up and drive, Mr. Claiborne, or I'll squeeze the trigger right here."

"Please, Spikes, please—"

"SHUT UP, Claiborne, SHUT UP—DRIVE."

"Where are we going?—Oh, God—where are we going?—God, please, please, don't—."

Spikes quickly looked behind him and saw no other cars. He pulled the pistol upward and closely to the front of Claiborne's face and pulled the trigger. The window shattered, spraying glass out into the street and into the panic-stricken man's lap. Mac screamed, and pulled both knees up to his chest, covering his head with both hands. Spikes shifted the pistol to his left hand and grasped the steering wheel with his right hand, guiding the car down the middle of the two lanes.

"Claiborne, I'll kill you right here. Drive this damn car or die—do you understand?"

The driver groaned. He said nothing.

"DO YOU UNDERSTAND?"

"Yes—please—please don't do this—please don't—"

Spikes looked behind, and to the front. No one was behind him though several cars were coming toward him in the two lanes on the other side of the grassy median which separated the west-bound traffic from the two east-bound lanes, but they were a distance away. He glanced at the speedometer and the automobile was coasting less than twenty miles an hour. He looked quickly to his right and saw several streets leading off Highway 90. With his left hand he raised the firearm to the right side of Claiborne's head, which the chemist tried to shield with his right hand, and pulled the trigger. The bullet penetrated Claiborne's hand between his third and fourth knuckle and entered his head a little above and in front of his temple. He jerked and moaned and slumped to his left, toward the door of the car. Spikes, who already held the steering wheel, pulled the car to the right into a side street and coasted to a stop. The blood from Claiborne's head wound had not splattered, his hand preventing it, and the murderer was grateful. Won't have to clean it off me, he thought. He got out of the car, walked calmly around to the driver's side, opened the door and caught Claiborne's body before it tumbled out. Then the little spy pushed the body, letting it sink to the floor on the passenger's side of the car. Easing into the driver's seat, he rolled down what was left of the shattered window, and drove the car to the nearest residential driveway. He turned around, re-entered Highway 90, and headed west toward the bridge and Bay St. Louis. At that point, he reached for his cell phone to call Chun, something the two spies had originally decided not to do—talk "business" on cell phones, but for tonight they had worked out a code. Spikes was to call when Claiborne was dead, unless he was still alive at the bridge. In that case he would call when he got there.

"Hello," answered Chun.

"I see water."

"Good. Any problems?"

"None."

"Proceed, then, with great care. Understand?"

"I understand."

Spikes traveled west on Highway 90 well under the speed limit, across the bridge, through Bay St. Louis, conscious of the traffic, looking for policemen. When he arrived within one and one half miles of state

Highway 603 he turned right onto a shortcut, figuring fewer street lights and less traffic equated less danger. Two minutes later, he turned north on 603, constantly glancing into his rear view mirror to make certain no one followed him.

The American hated this part of the dirty business—but at least his contact with Claiborne had not been in a lighted area, like the New Orleans airport. He had no choice. Chun ordered it to be done. The authorities suspect Claiborne, else they would have told him why the project had been delayed. Or they might have told Claiborne and he lied about it. Either way, he could no longer be trusted and because he knew so much, he must be eradicated. Besides, Chun reasoned, someone else working on the project could be found, of that they held no concern. They might have to raise the price some. But that would not be a problem either.

A mile up 603, the spy turned west onto a small blacktop road which meandered through chaparral bushes and live oak trees enveloped with Spanish moss. Only one car had been close enough to see his headlights when he turned and it was too far up 603 for the occupants to identify Claiborne's car. Spikes glanced at his clock on the dash. It was 10:40. So far, so good. He was certain no one had discovered his camouflaged bicycle, but he still worried about it. Three-quarters of a mile later, he slowed the car and turned quietly across a shallow ditch into a narrow dirt lane which led to the edge of a bayou. Turning his lights off, he eased down the road until he saw the murky waters immediately in front of him. Sometimes lovers parked on the shadowy road but usually not as far down as the water and the driver was relieved that no one was parked there tonight. Had someone been there, he would have moved to plan B, another wide pathway farther on down the blacktop road. When the killer neared the bayou, he turned the car sharply to the right and crept about fifty yards parallel to the water. Then he turned ninety degrees right again, easing over and through chaparral which sprang back up after the car had passed, taking care not to run the tires over the trunks of the bushes. At the right moment he pushed the accelerator slightly harder and plunged the automobile through low-hanging live oak limbs which were covered with moss, up to the giant trunk of the tree. He opened his door, pushing hard to displace low limbs which pressed against it, and got out of the car. Most of the limbs had sprung back into place—a couple had not and Spikes pulled on them until they rebounded, completely covering the vehicle.

It was a good place to hide a small car—and a body. The killer had known about the site for some time, where fishermen sometimes put their boats into the murky waters of the bayou. He had walked the area that afternoon and determined that from there, fishermen could not see the car. And it certainly could not be seen from the air. Maybe, but likely not from a fishing boat directly adjacent to the oak tree. Yes, it was a good place to hide a car—and a body.

The little spy pulled his handkerchief from his rear pocket and wiped every area of the car which he might have touched inside and out—the dash, both door handles, the doors themselves and the steering wheel.

Then he checked his front pockets, determing that nothing had fallen out. Leaving the key in the ignition, he
locked the doors from the inside, his hand covered by
the handkerchief, and quietly closed the driver's door.
Standing very still for a minute or so, he listened. In the
darkness, he could hear the sounds of tree frogs, and the
occasional bass voice of a bull-frog from the water's
edge—and from a distance, a whip-poor-will. Satisfied
that no human had heard him, he crept to the other side
of the oak tree. Hidden under the low-hanging limbs
and moss, he saw, through the dim moon and star light,
his bicycle. Quietly walking it from under the oak and
through the thick underbrush, Spikes noticed that the
car had broken several chaparral limbs from the bushes. Others had not sprung back up completely. He
threw the broken limbs out of sight in the direction of
Claiborne's vehicle and pulled on the others until he was
satisfied that they would recover no farther. Then he
mounted his bicycle and pedaled slowly back down the
small dirt road out to the blacktop. Stopping there, for
a moment to look, the nervous spy rode quickly toward
Highway 603. When he was able to make out the highway through the shadowy light, he stopped some thirty
yards away and melted into the dense vegetation which
hugged the small hard-surfaced road. Several cars
passed on 603, heading south, each drawing his attention. I don't know why Chun couldn't have picked me up
where I left Claiborne, fumed the jittery man, no one
uses this road this time of the night except boys and girls,
and they sure as hell don't have their minds on us. Well,
at least he's more cautious now. Guess killing someone

ought to make us more careful though he was reckless as hell at Buccaneer and the airport, he thought. It occurred to Spikes, as he sat upon his bicycle seat, one foot resting on the ground, that only he could be connected to Claiborne and only he could incriminate Chun. The Chinaman needed him now, but would he later, after he acquired the rest of the information? Spikes would be very careful then.

The spy was thinking about that when he saw the lights of another car moving south. It slowed, turned into the road where Spikes sat hidden on the bicycle, stopped and flashed its bright lights off and on four times. The little killer pedaled toward the car which moved toward him and farther away from 603, and rode quickly into the lights so Chun could identify him. By the time he reached the Lexus, the Chinaman had released the latch to the trunk of the car. Swiftly the spy dismounted from the bike, lifted it into the trunk, slammed it shut and climbed rapidly into the car.

"Did anyone see you?" asked the large man.

"No. Worked like a clock."

"You kill him before you get here?"

"Yes. He panicked. He would not drive the car."

"And no one else see you?"

"No," answered the small American again.

Less than ten minutes later, the two spies approached the west end of the Bay bridge. Several cars were in front of them and one pulled from Beach Boulevard onto Highway 90 immediately behind them.

"It's going to be difficult crossing this bridge when no one else is on it," declared Spikes.

"Yes, but we keep driving until we are alone," answered the big Chinaman. "We must not be seen."

"I know. It's getting late. Surely after a while—" Spikes' voice trailed off.

A quarter of the mile past the east end of the bridge, the hefty driver pulled into a side street, backed up, and moved west again. Other cars were on the bridge, so Chun continued driving. When he reached Bay St. Louis, he pulled into North Second Street, three hundred yards from the end of the bridge, and turned around again. The spies repeated the process four times. Finally, on the fifth try, the bridge was deserted. Chun stopped the Lexus at about the half-way point and punched the button which opened the trunk. Spikes sprang out of the car, raised the trunk lid and extracted the bicycle. Quickly he stepped up on the narrow sidewalk which spanned the length of the bridge and dropped the bicycle into the salty waters twenty feet below. Then he reached into the back waistline of his trousers for the .38 caliber pistol and threw it too into the bay. Darting back into the Lexus, he slammed the door behind him and nervously exclaimed, "Let's get out of here." He failed to notice Chun silently glaring with contempt.

* * * * *

Patie had never realized how completely he lived his life by the clock—until he had none. He finally dozed off, hours after he had been placed in the cell, in spite of his thundering cellmate, who slept the sleep of either a man accustomed to his surroundings, or one so governed by alcohol—or perhaps drugs—that he could have collapsed in sweet bliss anywhere. When the new inmate opened his eyes, he had no notion about the time—no clock, either external or internal, no window by which he could gauge sunlight. He didn't know whether it was night or day, and he had a terrible taste in his mouth. His right side ached from the stainless steel bed, from his stiff neck to his ankle bone. His head hurt from the blow and in order to rest at all, he had lain on his home-made pillow so that it would not touch the cut. Lying there, he was wondering about these things, especially the time, when he heard unusual activity in the large area below. Easing down from the bunk, taking care not to step on the man below, he gingerly walked to the door and peered through the small barred window. Breakfast was being served—it must be daylight, maybe seven o'clock. He quickly used the toilet and brushed his teeth, wanting to get both of those personal duties out of the way before the other man got out of bed.

"What's goin' on?"

Patie, a mouth full of toothpaste, turned toward the lower bunk, then back to the small lavatory, spit, and rinsed his mouth out. Looking back at his roomie he replied, "I think they are serving breakfast."

"Probably S.O.S.," the long-haired man wheezed angrily, prone still upon his bed, one arm draped over his eyes.

"Been in the army, huh?" Patie asked.

"Yeah." He said nothing else and seemed to go

back to sleep.

Patie watched the policemen, two of them, delivering the breakfast to every cell. Finally the lock to his door turned and one of the men thrust two plastic trays toward the retired football player, who had stepped back a couple of feet from the doorway. He looked at the unappetizing meal; a plastic bowl of corn flakes, a hard, cold biscuit, a cup of semi-warm coffee, a half-pint of skim milk and one packet of sugar. Talking mostly to himself, he complained, "Wish it had been S.O.S. Think it would taste better." His mate did not reply.

Corbin was still looking at the disaster called breakfast when he heard the door lock turn again. A policeman stepped inside the room and asked, "Mr. Corbin."

"Yes."

"Would you collect your belongings and follow me, please?"

Sarcasm dictated that the old pro ask, what belongings? But wisdom rightly rejected the notion. He grabbed his toothbrush and toothpaste and followed the policeman down the stairs, through the large room, down the hall, making certain he walked behind the line of degradation, to the desk where he had first been registered for his stay of legal and moral condemnation. Neither spoke.

"Mr. Corbin?" One of the policewomen behind the counter asked.

"Yes, ma'm." He noticed the wall clock. It was eight fifteen.

The lady reached under the counter and extracted the large plastic bag into which Patie's clothes had been placed the night before and handed it to him. She pointed toward a nearby door and said, "You can change in there."

"Ma'm, can I ask you a question?" Patie didn't feel like smiling but almost did. Marti would have corrected him—may I ask you a question?

"Yes."

"Am I getting out?"

"Yes."

"How? I mean who is getting me out?"

"An attorney is waiting for you in the interrogation room. He paid your bond."

"Thank you." Patie's dispirited heart lept with joy. "What do you want me to do with these stripes, Ma'm?" he asked enthusiastically.

"There's a dirty clothes bin in the room."

"Thank you, Ma'm."

Patie's dirty clothes felt good to him and he put them on quickly. Then he dumped his prison clothes in the bin and walked briskly out of the room back to the desk. In the mind-numbing affair of the last few hours he had forgotten about his valuables but by the time he reached the counter again, the police lady had spread all of them out—his billfold, his money clip with money, fingernail clippers, toothpick holder, and loose change. The invoice of the items signed last night lay beside the items. Everything checked out. When he had replaced everything into his pockets, the woman officer pointed toward another door and said, "Your attorney friend is waiting for you in there."

Patie started toward the room, infinitely more light-hearted and light footed than he had been the last time he had walked across that floor. Half-way to the room, he remembered his van—and the fact that he had not been given the keys to it. He stopped, turned around, and with less regard for his surroundings than before, he called loudly back to the lady. "Ma'm, what about my car?"

"What about it?"

"Where is it?"

"It was impounded, Mr. Corbin."

"Am I going to get it back?" he asked, noticing a little cynicism in his own voice. It surprised him.

"Of course. Your attorney has all the information."

Patie turned back toward the office, and the attorney. He did not say thank you—nor did he knock on the office door. He had not been told to, and with the certainty of release came an intensification of resolve—and boldness.

The attorney was seated in the office alone, reading legal papers. When Corbin entered the room, he stood, smiled and offered his hand. "Patie, I'm Floyd McKaskel. I've been sent to help you out a little."

Floyd McKaskel was a nice looking man, appearing to be perhaps fifty years old, about six feet tall, slim build. He wore a dark brown suit, white shirt and conservative tie. The attorney looked Patie directly in the eye when he extended his hand and the confident expression on his face indicated a total understanding of the situation. That alone welcomed the old self-condemning ex-professional football player back into society—and into the human race.

"You look like an angel to me, Floyd," asserted the inmate, "or maybe even a fast, 280 pound guard leading me around end. Either way you look good as hell—"

McKaskel smiled. "I expect I do. I'm sorry you had to go through this, but it's over now. Let's get out of here."

"Let's do!" agreed the ex-prisoner.

The sun felt good to the newly released man, a heat lamp which warmed his soul as certainly as it did his body. The walk to Floyd's car was a short one, and somewhere between the retention center and the parking lot, Corbin realized he did not know where he was. He had arrived there in a windowless paddy wagon long after dark. He asked, "Where are we?"

"Do you mean what town?"

"No—I know the town—I just don't know the location of the jail."

"I'm not certain," admitted McKaskel. "The police gave me the directions on the telephone and I'm not very familiar with the area."

"You're not from here?" Patie asked, as they neared Floyd's car.

"No. I have a license to practice in Mississippi, too, but my office is in New Orleans—here's my car."

"Looks like a heavenly chariot." It was a Lincoln—new—long—black. "Great looking car."

"Thanks, Patie," the attorney answered, opening both front doors. When the two were seated and the car was moving out of the parking lot, the writer asked, "Floyd, an officer said you know where my car is—"

"I have an address. You want to get it now or do you want to go by your condo first?"

"I would like to go by my condo, but I can't get in. My condo key is on my car-key ring—which I just realized—damn! We'll have to get my van. You say you have the address?"

"Yes. Want to see it?" Floyd pulled a piece of paper from his shirt pocket and handed it to the grateful new friend, slowing his vehicle and pulling into a parking lot.

Patie looked at the address. "Damn," he exclaimed, "it's in Gulfport out by I-10, I think, judging from the high address numbers. We would probably be better off to go the interstate."

"How do we get there from here?"

"Highway 603. You know where it is? I'm still a little turned around."

"I know where it is—I came in that way."

Several turns later, the two men were heading north on state highway 603. Not known to them, of course, they drove within one half mile of where Mac Claiborne lay dead in his own car, hidden by live oak tree limbs and chaparral bushes,—and Patie was finally able to discern the location of the jail. He had lived behind a blindfold for the last twelve hours and he had tried to make mental notes of where he had been taken. Someday, when cleared of all this, he would revisit the place—someday—not any day soon.

"Floyd, do you know my situation? What I'm

doing?" They had almost reached the I-10 entrance.

"Yes. Jack explained everything to me. I do turn east on 10, don't I?"

"Yeah—go east on 10. Gulfport's about twenty miles."

"YOU work for Jack, Floyd?"

"I worked with him for twenty-five years. Great guy!"

"Damn good football player, too."

"Yeah, apparently. I never saw either of you play, although I've seen you on television, of course. Jack was as proud of having played with you as having played, period. Still has your pictures hanging all over his office wall."

"Well, right now," the old pro protested, "I'm not very proud of knowing Jack OR Buddy. Last night about two hours after that cell door slammed shut, I could have killed both of them—not to mention earlier when I got slapped on the head with a lead pipe, or pistol, or whatever it was and then handcuffed."

Floyd laughed, then quickly recanted, "It's not funny, Patie, but Jack said you would be pissed—said for me to calm you down before they saw you. They both knew you would be an unhappy camper."

Traffic was heavy on Interstate 10, which bothered Corbin today far less than usual. Floyd was driving in the right lane, moving in consort with other cars, people going to work, and a myriad of eighteen-wheelers.

"Bad traffic day," commented the writer. Then changing the subject, "I'll tell you something, Floyd—I may never say it again to anybody—but I learned something last night. I had done nothing wrong except maybe that one drink at Marti's—damn—Marti. Floyd, I need to call Marti. Do you have a cell phone?"

"Marti?" McKaskel asked. "Is she Claiborne's wife?"

"Yes. I really need to call her."

"Patie," Floyd glanced over at him, hearing the stress in his voice, interpreting the intensity, "don't you think it would be unwise to use the cell phone? Will you let me stop at a pay phone?"

"You're probably right. We'll be off 10 in a few minutes," Corbin agreed, a little reluctantly. "I can wait."

"You said you learned something last night?" the lawyer asked, hoping to take Patie's mind off Marti for a little while. He needed to collect information about the night's activities, especially concerning the two spies, so he redirected the conversation.

"Yeah. I learned what it meant to be de-humanized, Floyd." The tough middle-aged, experienced man softly yet emotionally recounted. "I had no rights. No one looked at me—nor listened to me—nor cared about me. I was less than nothing, a piece of trash, the offscowering of the world, as the apostle Paul said about himself, a living body of sewage. THAT was my prison— being a non-entity, possessing absolutely no importance, no worth to anyone around me, including the other prisoners. And you know something?—it might have been good for me. I had never experienced that,—I had always—"

"Patie," Floyd interrupted.

Corbin stopped talking, wondering why McKaskel had broken into his monologue, not pleased. What he was saying may not be the most important thing in the world in the overall scheme of things, but it was important to him. With a little displeasure, the old competitor glanced silently at the driver.

"Patie," McKaskel repeated, "I think we're being followed. A black Lexus picked us up on 603 and has been two hundred yards behind us ever since. I'm turning off the next exit."

Floyd flipped his signal light on a quarter of a mile from the next exit and when he turned off the interstate, he neither increased nor decreased his speed. The road led south back toward the gulf, but not in a straight line, turning through mobile home parks and an industrial area. The lawyer, reaching the street, accelerated, sped around a curve, found a driveway, turned into it, and backed quickly out of it, heading back toward the interstate. When he and Patie rounded the curve going in the opposite direction, they met the Lexus. Visible clearly through the windshield, sat the two spies, evident expressions of surprise upon their faces. Before the cars even met, the large Chinaman pushed his accelerator to the floor, squealing his tires, disappearing through burning rubber smoke around the curve.

"TURN AROUND—TURN AROUND, FLOYD. FOLLOW THEM." Patie had twisted around in the seat, watching with dismay the Lexus fade out of sight. If he had wanted to get his strong hands around the two men's insidious necks before last night, his desire had quadrupled now. He looked quickly at McKaskel, who continued to drive back toward I-10, his wide combative eyes assailing his attorney. "TURN AROUND, DAMN IT,—I said turn around."

"Patie, listen to me for—"

"TURN AROUND." The old gladiator reached for the steering wheel. McKaskel quickly removed his foot from the accelerator and touched the brake. The Lincoln stopped. Patie thought the attorney was going to turn the car around and give chase—he expected it— he demanded it, but to his misgiving, Floyd did not pursue. Patie looked at him with disdain, silently.

"Patie, please listen to me for a second." The lawyer talked hurriedly, authoritatively, compassionately. He understood Patie's nature, knew what he had been through, felt great sympathy for him, but he could not follow the spies. He needed to convince Corbin and he needed to do it quickly. He looked the football player directly in the eyes. "They have the advantage right now. The local police don't know anything. If we were to chase them, they could claim we were trying to rob them or kill them. They have guns, we don't. They can't get away. We know who they are and we'll capture the bastards but we have to do it our way. Please trust me in this. Jack will give you a chance at them, I promise, but we can't break the law in doing it. Let's wait until we have the advantage, okay?"

Patie said nothing. He stared straight ahead through the front windshield, past I-10, beyond common sense, past reason.

"You understand, Patie? Let's wait until we have the advantage. That day will come and it won't be long—I promise. Okay? Besides, we probably couldn't have caught them anyway. They had too much of a lead."

The battler knew McKaskel was right—with his mind—but not his heart, not his flesh. He continued to glare unrelentingly through the windshield, said nothing.

"Patie, I'm going on after your van now, okay?" Without waiting for an answer, McKaskel took his foot off the brake and drove on toward the interstate. A minute later they were moving again toward Highway 49 and Gulfport. Still concerned, Floyd asked, "Patie are you alright?"

Corbin hesitated, then responded, "I'm okay. I know you are right. I know you are."

"Thank you. I don't want to be your enemy—I saw that look in your eyes. Now I know why those defensive backs got out of your way."

The halfback smiled, just slightly.

"Patie, tell me exactly what happened last night, if you will, from the time you got to Claiborne's house until the police took you in."

The disquieted "good citizen" started with Marti's phone call and explained, as Floyd requested, the details of the night. When he finished, the attorney was exiting I-10 onto Highway 49 South. Floyd heard the agony in the old athlete's voice, and sensed the depth of his pain.

"You'll have to direct me from here, Patie."

"Turn left at the first light. Go straight until I tell you to turn. Wait, there's a pay phone."

Floyd quickly pulled his Lincoln near the telephone so Patie could call sitting in the car.

The old pro dialed Marti's number. Her answering machine picked up the call. Patie, in welcome defiance of Mac, had already decided to leave a message if she failed to answer.

"Loverly, it's your jailbird. It's 8:55 and I'm in Gulfport getting my van. I'll be leaving here in about thirty minutes, I think, if I don't get arrested again, so I ought to be back at my condo around 10:00. Mac, you son-of-a-bitch, if you hear this message, I would love for you to be there too, or you two Chinese-looking bastards, or even better, all three of you.

"Bye, Loverly. I hope you are teaching today, but I bet you aren't. Hope to see you very soon."

"Patie, I don't like counseling you, but do you think that was smart—telling them where you would be and when?" asked the attorney.

"Hell no, it was stupid," snarled Corbin, "but it damn sure was satisfying."

Floyd laughed. "Be careful, okay?"

"I will be."

"We know the spies planted the beer and drugs in your van, Patie, and then called the police. They may not know for certain that you're working for us, but they want you out of the picture. You are too close to Claiborne. Like you, Jack and Buddy discussed, things might get rough and they did last night. But they may get even rougher. This thing is about to come to a head. Jack and Buddy are on the way down here. As soon as they arrive, they want you to get together with them.

Patie sighed. "I need to go back to my condo

first. I gotta' get out of these bloody clothes and shave and bathe—and clean my teeth. Where will Buddy and Jack be?"

"They are getting a room at Beau Rivage."

"What time are they getting there?"

"By noon. Here, take this." McKaskel handed Patie a small piece of paper. "That's the name they are registering in. When you get cleaned up, call them and find out their room number. Don't go by the registration desk, and remember, use a pay phone, Okay? Look over your shoulder, the men may show up at your condo."

"Got it,—turn right here. This is the street. We ought to be close. Don't worry, I'll be watching for them."

A few minutes later, the two men walked into the impound office, and presented the papers along with one hundred dollars to an officer. Patie took the keys without speaking to the man. He and Floyd walked to Patie's vehicle, opened it and Corbin got in. He checked to see if his papers and cash were still there and they were. Rolling his window down, he asked the attorney, "Will I see you again?"

"No, not unless this thing goes to court."

The thankful and still slightly chagrined man got out of the van. He extended his hand. "Floyd, I can't begin to find either the amount of words or the proper words to express my gratitude to you. I hope to see you again—but not in a courtroom."

"Thank you, Patie. It was my pleasure to help a little." As the attorney turned to walk away, he suddenly wheeled back toward the retired football player. "I don't think you would have made it to the corner of the end zone either."

Patie smiled, and opened the door to his van. "Thanks, Counselor." God, how I needed to hear that, he whispered under his breath, as he turned the key to the ignition and heard the blissful sound of the engine purring, finally—the unmistakable sound of freedom— and rehumanization.

CHAPTER SEVENTEEN

Marti finally crawled out of bed—well before daylight. She had known when she turned the light off a few hours earlier that she would be unable to sleep, and other than three or four cat naps, she was right. No alarm clock chimes louder in the dark of the night than a grieving spirit—or a pulsating conscience she thought, as she stumbled toward the bathroom. She glanced at the clock and saw that it was only 5:15, not especially an early hour for her had she gotten a good night's sleep—she often got up that early to jog on days when she could not exercise in the afternoon. But today she would not jog, nor teach, and she would be made to wait until 7:00 a.m. before canceling her classes. The troubled woman brushed her teeth and scurried nude into the kitchen to start coffee. Then she re-visited the bathroom. Twenty minutes later she emerged to dress, and ambled past Mac's bedroom glancing through its open door to his made bed. She already knew he had not come home last night but seeing his un-slept-in bed made her pause for a moment. "Well, you weak bastard," she murmured, wishing he were there to hear, "I guess you spent the night with your whore—or were you just so gutless you couldn't face me?"

Moving into the kitchen, the distracted wife poured a cup of coffee and sauntered onto the chilly deck, dropping down into the rocker not only to plan her bizarre day, careful to remember her inherent compulsiveness which often drove her to action before thinking—she also wanted to watch the sun come up. The sunrise had become an important part of the day for Marti. It meant things often looked different, kind of like Easter and Christmas—everything made new. Yesterday was gone, with its trials and hurts and disappointments. A new day had come, filled with hope and opportunity. She smiled when she thought of her dad and how he had described his daughter's delight in facing a new day. "She's just like a goose—wakes up in a new world every morning."

"Daddy," she asked him when she was twelve, "Will you buy me a goose?" He did. Unlike her many school mates, most of whom owned dogs—or cats— although one boy in her class did own a pet goat, she owned a goose. It followed her every step until she got old enough to date, then like so many of a child's toys, Miss Waddler was relegated to the "attic" of a small pen in the backyard where she eventually died. By then

Marti was a senior at Mississippi State. Her dad, jokingly, had ascribed Miss Waddler's death to a broken heart. The college student wondered if it might have been true.

The sky suddenly blazed into a bright red, impregnating the many small, fluffy clouds with the same shade of scarlet. When the cherry colored clouds and sky finally faded into its permanent glow of blue and white brightness, the teacher glanced down at her watch—6:50. Pushing her body forcefully from her chair, she poured another cup of coffee and walked swiftly into her bedroom to retrieve her shoes. Then she sat guardedly on her bed, which she had made earlier, picked up the phone and dialed Patie. After four rings, the answering machine clicked on—so the anxious paramour dropped the phone upon the receiver, found the number in the phone book, picked the phone up again and dialed the retention center.

"Ma'm, my name is Marti Claiborne. I'm calling about a man who was arrested last night, Patie Corbin."

"What do you want to know?"

"If he's still there—or has he been released?"

"Ms. Claiborne, I'm sorry, but we cannot give that information out."

"You can't even tell me if he's still there?"

"No, Ma'm."

"Can I see him?"

"No, Ma'm."

"How can I check on him?" Marti asked, trying to manage the growing frustration which she knew must be evident in her voice.

"You might contact his attorney, if he has one,—or his bail bondsman."

"That's the only way?"

"Yes, Ma'm. I'm sorry."

"Can you give me those names?"

"No, Ma'm. I don't have the names."

"Do you know where I might get them?"

"No, Ma'm," the lady answered brusquely.

Marti slammed the phone down. "Servants of the people, my ass," the appalled woman screamed, her face contorted with frustration. "More like the slaves of indifference—the—the —."

The exasperated lady picked up the phone again and dialed the education department of her school. Marti softened her voice, lending it a fevered pitch.

"Evelyn, this is Marti."

"Good morning, Marti. Gosh, you sound like you are under the weather."

"I am," she whispered. "I'm not going to make my classes today. Would you post it for me?"

"Of course. What do you have?"

"I don't know yet. I'll find out at the doctor's, I guess."

"You take care of yourself, Marti."

"I will. Thank you, Evelyn."

Marti shook her head. What could she do for Patie? She had to do something, she couldn't just sit and wait. "I know, Dad," she murmured out loud, "I'm impulsive but I got it from you. I can't just sit here so what should I do? What would you do?"

Three minutes later the impatient beauty was in

351

her car heading for the West Gulf Coast Detention Center. She pulled into the parking lot at the front of the large jail, locked her car and entered the building. A uniformed lady sat behind a counter in a small room. A sign saying "Receptionist" sat upon the top of the counter. Marti wondered if the woman was the same one with whom she had talked earlier. Ten straight back chairs lined two walls. A male policeman stood near the lady. He and the woman were talking. At the sound of Marti opening the door both officers jerked their heads toward her.

"Can I help you?" the lady behind the counter asked.

"Yes. I'm here to check on a friend who was arrested last night. His name is Patie Corbin," answered Marti, as she walked briskly to the three-sided desk where the female officer sat.

"I'm sorry, Ma'm. He cannot see visitors yet."

"Can you tell me what his legal status is—I mean, what does he have to do to get out of here?" She had not forgotten that Buddy promised he would take care of the situation, but she couldn't just wait at home—she had to do something. Talking to the police where they held Patie made her feel closer to him and it eased her conscience—it was doing something. She looked implacably at the woman.

The young man standing nearby intervened, "Ma'm, what is your relationship to Mr. Corbin?" His voice was friendly, compassionate.

"I'm a friend. He had been at my home a few minutes before he was arrested."

"May I see your driver's license?"

"You arresting me too, officer?"

The policeman laughed. "Of course not, Ms—?"

"Marti Claiborne," she answered.

"Ms. Claiborne. May I see your license."

Marti extracted her driver's license from her purse and thrust it toward the officer.

"Marti—short for Martina?" he asked.

"Yes."

"Ms. Claiborne, we would like to help you but we can't—not until disposition of the prisoner, but I can tell you this. Mr. Corbin will probably post a bond and get out this morning. You may be able to see him yourself after that, so why don't you just—"

"Can you tell me if a doctor saw him last night?"

Both policemen looked surprised. "Ma'm?" the man asked.

"Did he see a doctor? He was hurt at my house and I feel very badly about it. Could you tell me if a doctor saw him?"

"No Ma'm, but you may be certain we will check on it," the policeman answered. "If he needs a doctor, he WILL see one."

"Thank you for your help officer—officer," Marti nodded to both of them. "When Mr. Corbin is released, will he come through this door?"

"No—but we can't give you that information, either."

"Thank you," the partially requited woman said. She turned and walked confidently back outside. Well, she thought, if he doesn't come out that door, then he must come out another one. Getting back into her car, she drove to the far edge of the parking lot and looked toward the rear of the building. She saw an extension of the structure, forming what looked to her at that distance through the chain-link fence and over the tops of several cars, to be a covered driveway. The determined teacher was getting out of her car for a closer look when she saw the heads of two men moving from under the covering toward the parking lot. She jumped from her car and ran to the fence for a closer view. "Damn," she exclaimed, "it's Patie."

"PATIE, PATIE," she yelled, "PATIE." An emotion like she had never experienced ravished her spirit and she screamed again—"PATIE, PATIE." The frenzied female jogger climbed part way up the fence to get a clearer look and she called out again. But Patie and his friend had apparently gotten into a vehicle and she could not locate him. Frantically, she jumped back into her automobile and drove to the opposite end of the parking lot, hoping to intercept Patie and the man at a gate. There was no gate there either but there must be an exit from the rear parking lot somewhere! She drove back out into the street looking for a side road which might take her to the rear of the jail. A half-mile away she turned left, then left again and saw a large gate. When she reached it, a policeman stepped from a small cubicle and raised both hands. Marti stopped and rolled her window down.

"Sir," she impassionately asked, "did two men just leave through this gate?"

"Ma'm, men and women leave through this gate

all the time. Several cars just left through here. There were two men in a couple of them."

"Thank you, officer." Marti quickly backed her vehicle into a parking space and turned around. A few minutes later she sat in front of Patie's condo. He wasn't there. "Well, hell," she moaned, and then smiled when she remembered the "Well, hell" football story Patie had told her. Anyway, HE thought it was funny.

"They could have been here, by now," she pondered out loud, "and they aren't. They may have gone someplace else first, maybe an attorney's office." Knowing nothing else to do, she decided to wait awhile. Twenty minutes later she gave up and drove back to her house. Mac's Cavalier was not there. The moment she closed her car door she heard the telephone ringing, and when she burst into her kitchen she heard Patie's voice on her answering machine. Sprinting to her bed-room, she snatched the phone up and cried, "Patie, Patie." He had already hung up. Disappointment covering her apprehensive face, the hopeful lady punched the play button and heard his message. Her heart raced with excitement when she heard that in one hour she would see the Rebel—in one-long-hour.

The first "thing" Patie wanted to see when he arrived at his condo was Marti. He wanted to hold her, talk to her, find out what had been happening since last night—what Mac had said, if he had come home, how much she knew.

The restless writer, anxious to get home quickly,

rather than dropping down to Highway 90 which ran along the coast but through four towns, traveled I-10. It was eight miles farther but he could drive faster, and think more easily. He had a lot to do. For one thing, he had to call Kim, who would be mad as hell about now.

Patie saw Marti's red car when he got to within a block of the condo. She was sitting on the doorstep looking in the direction from which he would come and by the time he cut his engine, the eager lady was grasping the van door handle. She could not have looked more beautiful to the man whose life had taken such grotesque turns since last he saw her.

Neither said anything as he stepped from his van. Each grabbed the other, and for fully a minute, they embraced, smiles on both their faces, tears washing down hers. The old pro leaned backward so he could see her face, "Hello, Loverly." He could not keep his voice from breaking.

The crying beauty pushed her face back into Patie's bloody shirt and squeezed even harder. Her lover knew he had to say something to bring them back to where they had so beautifully lived, to take them past the apprehension which had totally dominated their lives the past twelve hours. "Glad to see me, huh, Loverly?"

She squealed, "YES," pushing her body away from his, a giant smile mellowing her face, imbedding joy into every tear, looking deeply into his unshaven face. "God, I'm glad to see you. I love you. Are you alright? What did they do to you? Why did they arrest you? How did you—"

"Wait, Speedo, slow down. You're talking so fast I can barely tell what you're asking," Corbin interrupted. "We'll talk about all that, but I have to do a couple of things first—now that I've seen you." Patie placed his right hand softly upon Marti's left cheek. "Wait just a minute." Then he pushed through the shrubbery which surrounded the condo, to underneath it. Marti followed hesitantly. The inexorable athlete grasped the small box with the antenna and ripped it from its mooring, not caring if he damaged his own telephone line in the process.

Marti looked questioningly at the man whom she loved walking defiantly toward her, holding the small apparatus. "What's that, Reb?"

Suddenly the determined man realized that he would have to explain the device to Marti, and explain how he knew about it and why he had not told her about it. "A bug. They couldn't plant one under my van so they planted one under my house."

"How long has it been there?"

"I found it yesterday."

"Why didn't you tell me?"

"I didn't want to worry you, and too, I thought you might confront Mac about it and I—"

"What would be wrong about that? He needs confronting."

"I know he does, but I planned to set a trap—talk to you about us meeting and be waiting for him or the other two men to get there."

"Without me knowing?"

"No, not without you knowing, Loverly. I would have told you first." Patie had inadvertently painted himself into a psychological corner, a rarity for him. Standing there, beneath his condo facing the woman who meant so much to him—who was beginning to doubt him, he knew he had to think quickly and clearly. He could not let her catch him in a lie. He knew perfectly the acute sharpness of Marti's mind. Within minutes, she would ask about last night, about his using a compromised phone to invite her to his condo, knowing Mac would hear the conversation. Pointing upward, he explained, "I didn't tell you last night, Loverly, because we met here. I knew the idiots wouldn't invade my turf—and they didn't. The confrontation occurred at your house. I would not have met you anywhere, other than here, without you knowing."

Patie hated lying to Marti but he had no choice, it was academic. She could not confirm an indefinite action. He had rather her doubt his veracity than to know for certain he had lied. *I just hope her love for me is strong enough to keep her from discerning the truth,* he thought.

Marti hesitated. She looked down, then up into his face and said nothing. Patie could almost hear the gears of her highly intellectual mind turning. It was time to say it. Besides he wouldn't be lying.

The experienced admirer reached for both Marti's hands. He looked longingly into her large, tear-moistened eyes, and he waited in that posture for a moment before he spoke. Softening his voice he whispered, "Loverly, I spent a miserable night in jail last night. What I might have done right and what I HAVE done wrong in all of this suddenly became of no importance to me, and my priorities were rearranged quite apart from any attempt by me to do so. When that jail door slammed, only the things which mattered to me remained with me. Everything else stayed outside the cell."

The pretender choked a little, whether from remembering the experience which he was describing to Marti or love for her, he did not know, nor did he debate the issue. He breathed deeply, giving himself the opportunity to study his lover's discerning face. The student of human emotions saw trust in Marti and he knew she wanted to believe him.

"The one thing which mattered the most, when the sound of the door slamming was still in the air, was you, Marti—not Kim, not the disgracing of my name, not the physical inconvenience of jail—YOU. I found myself thinking about you—concerned about you—worried—! The police wouldn't let me talk to you and my heart died. The thought of you gave me hope where there was none, and joy, knowing I had not lost you. I remember our bargain. I would provide you with sex— and you would give me companionship, and we would not become emotionally involved. But the jail door changed all that. My body was imprisoned, but my mind and soul and spirit weren't—they remained free to love you. I love you, Marti. I didn't mean to—I fought to stop it, but prison brought my love for you to the surface and made me admit it. I love you, and I'm not fighting it anymore. I pray that doesn't drive you away but whether it does or not, I won't lie about it, not to myself nor to you, not any longer."

Marti said nothing. She continued to gaze at the confessor, an expression somewhere between disbelief and hope spread across her lovely face, her body immobile, her eyes locked into his as though waiting for the joke which she feared might come.

"Loverly, you there?"

Still, she said nothing. Her mind worked feverishly to absorb and disseminate everything she had just heard. Could it be true? Could he really love me? What about Kim?—what will she do about this? And Mac? How does all this fit together? Is it possible that my first romantic venture after giving up on Mac could actually flourish into a loving relationship? Is Patie telling me the truth?

Patie dropped Marti's left hand and with his right middle knuckle he knocked lightly upon her furrowed brow. "Hey, anyone in there?"

"Not really," she finally answered. "She just got blown away."

"Did you hear what I said, Loverly? I said I love you."

"I heard, Patie. Why now? Why so soon?"

"So soon?!" The old deceiver directed a touch of exasperation into the pitch of his voice, an act requiring no great effort—it was as natural for him as breathing—give hope and suggest, with a trace of mock irritation, that it might be taken away. That was the method of interrogation the Chinese communists in Korea used against American POWs—give hope and take it away—give hope and take it away—You'll be home by Thanksgiving—No you won't—You'll be home by

360

Christmas—No you won't. It was a form of mind control and it forced prisoners to look upon their captors as gods, certainly the progenitors of hope—and freedom. Once the communists had gained that kind of mind control, they slapped a piece of paper onto a table in front of the captives and commanded, "sign". Many did and in the act unwittingly condemned their country.

"So soon?" Patie repeated, softening his voice. "You said you loved ME two days ago! Why does it seem strange that I should love you, Loverly? Do you deem yourself unworthy of my love while at the same time insisting that I am worthy of yours? Isn't that a backdoor version of image problem, at least in relation to me? Listen to me—I love you. It took jail to make me realize it and seeing you again to make me admit it, even to myself. I love you. Now—you're going to have to decide what to do with that, though not this instant necessarily—but at some point."

The stunned look slowly faded from the teacher's face. A smile, her smile, her patented smile replaced it. She threw both arms around her lover's neck and squeezed as hard as she had strength to squeeze and she whispered in his ear, "Oh, Patie, I love you. I never expected to hear you say it to me. I'm shocked. Please forgive me for doubting you—I'll never do that again— please forgive me—will you forgive me?"

"Of course I forgive you, Loverly. I love you. Just believe me, okay?" Then leaning backward again, he locked his eyes into her's. "Believe me, okay?"

"I believe you, Patie, I believe you."

They kissed, deeply, passionately, a long slow,

exciting, intense kiss and when it ended, the woman looked ardently at her man. "I love you, Reb, I love you. I've been worried sick about you. How is your head? Is it still hurting? Let me see it."

Corbin turned the right side of his head toward his "nurse". "It throbs a little, still. It's alright."

"It looks alright, but I'm not a doctor. Have you seen one?"

"No. It's okay. I've been cut worse on the practice field and never missed a down.

"Loverly, I need to go in, take a bath, and brush my teeth. Will you go with me?"

"Of course, Reb. I'm not leaving you now."

"What did you do about your classes today?"

"Cancelled them."

Before Patie led Marti from under the condo, he slowly pushed his head through the shrubbery and looked up and down Beach Boulevard. Then he took her hand and moved to the steps, but before he walked up them, he punched the automatic lock on his key case. The Chrysler's horn honked, signifying it locked.

"Let's get inside," he cautioned, "those idiots might drive by."

The light on Corbin's recorder was blinking. Nodding toward it, Patie remarked "Damn thing's going crazy."

"Several of them are mine," said Marti.

"I imagine some of them are from Kim, too. Look, Loverly, I have to listen to them, and I need to call her back, but I don't mind you hearing. We had planned to meet this weekend and I—".

"You don't have to tell me anything, Reb."

"I want to tell you. I want you to know. We had planned to meet in New Orleans this weekend but I don't want to go now. I want to be with you, but I should tell her I can't go, okay?"

"I don't want to hear. I'll go outside."

"Why don't you make us a pot of coffee. I'll turn the sound down. When I call her, you can sit on the back deck. Agreed?"

"Agreed," the beauty smiled.

Patie turned the volume on the recorder down. Four calls were from Marti. There were five hang-ups, and Kim had left three messages. She was angry. She accused him of everything her active mind could imagine. He dreaded calling her back, but he knew he must.

When the coffee was ready, Marti fixed both of them a cup. She handed him his mug and started toward the back deck.

"Loverly, you don't have to go."

Marti turned back toward the man whom last night she feared she might have lost and whom just ten minutes ago heard say "I love you." She smiled. "Patie, I don't want to listen, but thank you for offering it to me."

Corbin nodded, and smiled. As Marti opened the sliding glass door to the rear deck, the tough old running back breathed deeply and reached for the phone. "Damn, I hate this," he murmured.

"Gorgeous?"

Silence

"Gorgeous, I know you are on the phone. Please

say something."

"Something!"

"Gorgeous, you are too intellectual for that kind of answer. That's the response a meathead might make."

"You are THAT, Meathead. What in hell is going on down there?"

"You are right about that, Gorgeous."

"I'm right about what?"

"Hell. That's where I spent last night."

"No, that's where you're going when you die. Do you remember where you were last night, all night I might add, or you were too drunk or involved to answer your phone. Where were you?"

"Jail."

"JAIL! Visiting whom? One of your girlfriends? All night?"

"I was there all night, alright, but I wasn't visiting anyone. I was jailed—by the Bay St. Louis police."

Silence, continued.

"Gorgeous?"

"Are you telling me the truth, Patie?"

"Yes." Patie kept his voice solemn. He wanted her to believe him so he could end the conversation. But many times he had acted serious before admitting he was only joking.

"What were you arrested for?"

"I had too much to drink, I guess. When they stopped me, I had a beer opened. That's against the law." Handling the embarrassment of him being arrested for drunkenness would be difficult for Kim—she would be unable to manage drugs.

"Did they give you a breathalyzer test?"

Patie hesitated. Surely she wouldn't verify his story. He would make his explanation bad, but not as bad as drugs. "Yes. I failed it. They said I was driving while impaired. It wasn't DWI or DUI, so it wasn't as bad as it could be," he lied.

"Does anybody know about this, Patie?"

"My lawyer. You haven't met him, he's a high school friend from Laurel. He came down this morning and paid my bail. He's going to handle it for me."

"Does anybody else know?"

"I don't guess, but it may come out in the paper. Sorry, Gorgeous. I didn't do it on purpose."

"That's just wonderful, Patie, That's going to make it much less embarrassing. Do you realize how many people on the coast know us?"

"Lots of people, Gorgeous."

"Well, you just delayed our getting back together, you know that, don't you?"

"How so, Gorgeous?"

"Hell, I'm not going to go any farther with this until it's cleared up and—and dies down!"

"Up and down, huh, Gorgeous? Well, I guess this weekend is off, then!"

"Yes, it's off. I'll cancel everything. Well, one more time you've screwed up a great weekend for me. When will I ever learn—when?"

"I'm sorry, Gorgeous. I'll call you back in a few days. Will you forgive me? Will you, huh, huh, will you?" he teased.

Kim hung up the phone without answering.

"Well, she must not be REAL mad," speculated the former husband, "she didn't slam-dunk it."

Patie pushed the sliding door open. "I've done my unpleasant duty, Loverly. Want to go with me to the shower, or do you want to stay down here and wait for Mac, whom I know doesn't have the guts to come."

"Hey, Reb, do I look like I'm worried about that? I'll race you up the stairs."

Patie stripped his bloody clothes from his stiff and sleep-deprived body, letting them fall in a heap on the floor. Marti took her seat upon the white porcelain toilet. The hot water felt good to the man's battered flesh. The cut forced him to turn the right side of his head away from the pressurized water and he stood that way for at least five minutes, directing the warm fluid all the way down his exhausted body.

"You can't stand the water hitting your sore head, can you, Reb?" Marti asked through the shower curtain.

"No, but it feels great to all my other old bones." Patie changed the subject. "Loverly, while I'm showering, we need to talk. What happened last night after I left your house?"

"Not much. When you didn't answer your phone, I went looking for you. Then I saw the blue lights surrounding your van, and I thought there had been a wreck. My heart almost stopped. Why did they arrest you?"

"Answer one question for me first. Did Mac come home last night?"

"No."

"Have you seen or heard from him?" Corbin

asked.

"No."

"That's strange, isn't it?"

"Very. He must not have worked today," Marti answered.

"Why don't you call and find out? You can use my phone now, it's safe. Then I'll tell you about my thrilling jailhouse experience."

A minute later Marti sat back down on the toilet seat. Patie was still in the shower, gently rubbing soap into the hair around his wound.

"Reb, he's not at work and they haven't heard from him. They asked me if I knew where he was. I told them 'No'."

"More than likely that means he's still with his friends."

"Patie," the college professor declared, concern lacing her voice, "I don't understand why those men became so violent with you, I mean, you have nothing to do with all of that—for lack of a better word—intrigue."

Patie thought for a second or two. His answer had to be a good one. "Two possible reasons, Loverly. Apparently you and I became involved at the same time all of this was coming down and they likely saw me as a threat. Then, too, I was about to beat some answers out of that small guy or Mac. They could not allow that."

Patie turned the water off, slid the shower curtain back, and reached for a towel. Marti sat reflectively, her chin in both hands. "Yeah, I suppose so, but something just seems to be missing. Tell me why the police stopped you."

"They found an open beer bottle half full, cocaine and marijuana in my car. It was put there while I was recovering at your house. I'll give you all the details in a little while, but first—," the freshly bathed man, drying himself, leaned down and kissed the woman whom he had just professed to love. Then he raised back up and spoke gently, "Loverly, we need to get the hell out of Dodge. You willing to go somewhere for a few days?"

"Yes, of course," without hesitation, she answered. "Where?"

"Haven't decided yet. We'll talk about that, too." Patie went into the bedroom and removed a nice pair of Bermuda shorts and a matching sport shirt from his closet, lobbing his bloody clothes into his dirty clothes hamper. Marti followed. Slipping the shorts, shirt, a clean pair of athletic socks and his good Nikes on, he took hold of his engaging lover's hand and said, "My teeth and I need about ten or fifteen exciting minutes together—and I haven't eaten anything since noon yesterday. Would you mind stirring up something in my kitchen? I'm starving."

"You have any eggs, Reb?"

"No, I don't think so."

"Give me some money. I can go to the Jitney and be back with eggs, cheese, and biscuits in ten minutes. I'll make us an omelet."

"Great! I already have the fig preserves. We'll talk about everything over food."

"Fig preserves? Ugg," Marti, walking down the stairs, a ten dollar bill in her hand laughingly gagged. "I'll get some grape jelly, too."

Patie knocked lightly on the door. Almost instantly it was opened and Jack bellowed, "Get your ass in here, you old Meathead." As soon as the halfback stepped inside the room, the CIA agent threw his thick arms around him and bear-hugged him almost to the ceiling. "Damn, it's good to see you, Pate. I've been worried as hell about you," the former college teammate declared, dropping him back to the floor. "I knew there would be SOME danger in this, but the idiots are crazier than I thought."

Buddy stepped around Jack, took Patie by the hand and then they hugged, three old athletes, who, every time they saw each other, renewed a deep friendship which began thirty years ago, as though it was still the mid-sixties and they had just won another football game—a friendship which grew through the years and could endure anything, even verbal condemnation.

"If you two Neanderthals had been standing in front of me about twelve hours ago and someone had shoved a .45 in my hand, we would be making funeral arrangements about now."

"Hell, 'Pootie', if I hadn't blocked all those big tackles, you wouldn't even be alive to pull the trigger," retorted Buddy. "And just think of all the snatch you would have missed!"

The three old friends were still standing in a triangle, their arms and hands resting on the other's shoulders. They laughed, and Patie looked each of them in the eye, one to the other, back and forth. "You two apes can't imagine how glad I am to see you today—for more than one reason."

"Patie, I'll mix you a drink—let's sit down and talk about all this," Jack suggested. "Your head alright?"

"Yeah, it's okay."

Corbin glanced at the bar. Bourbon, vodka, and gin were visible. A small refrigerator sat at the end of the bar. "Got any orange juice, 007?"

"Yep—and beer."

"I'll have a screwdriver."

Thirty furious, discussion laden minutes later, Jack concluded, "Patie, we have enough information now for a conviction—if we can find the bastards. I think you ought to get out of Bay St. Louis for a few days. While they're looking for you, we'll be looking for them. Our path will soon cross theirs."

"We'll?" Corbin asked. "Who else is down here, Jack, besides you and your new recruit—here," nodding toward Buddy.

"Reluctant recruit, Patie," Buddy admitted, smiling.

"We have six agents scattered between here and Waveland and we have alerted selected policemen. We ought to have around twenty men in the hunt. We'll find them soon. Plus," Jack added, "we have alerted agents nationwide, especially international airports."

Corbin nodded. "I had already decided to leave town."

"Where are you going, Vicksburg?" asked Buddy.

"No. Kim's pissed—big time—about my arrest. I think I'm going to take Marti to—"

"MARTI?" exclaimed Jack. "Mrs. Claiborne?"

"That's her."

"Patie, are you certain about this?" asked Jack. "They are after her, too. The two of you will be more visible than just one, and make a much bigger target."

"Jack, you remember my one ultimatum when we met to plan this? I told you I would do everything exactly like you wanted it done except—WHAT?—What did I refuse to let you dictate to me?"

"You mean dick-tote, don't you, Pate," Jack laughed, "Yes, I remember."

"What? I want to hear you say it."

"I promised I would not tell you how to romance Mrs. Claiborne—Marti."

"And—?"

"And that I would not tell you where you could go with her!"

"And—?"

"Hell—and what you could do with her!"

"That's right, old friend. Now, do you want to know where we are going?"

"Yes. I would really like to know that."

"I'll give you a hint. The three of us have been there with a former red-shirted enemy whose initials are V.V."

"Red-shirted enemy?" Buddy asked instantly, "you mean football player?"

Patie nodded.

"Well, he would have to be from Arkansas, Georgia, or Alabama. And initials V.V.?"

"Yep."

"Hell, I don't know," admitted Buddy.

Jack shook his head. "I don't either."

"Damn, you two old farts are really sharp. And you are going to protect me?"

"VIPER," yelled Buddy. "Viper Ventress. You're going to the Flora-Bama, to Perdido."

"Well, listen to that," teased Patie, "And they say dead brains can't re-live."

"You going to stay at Eagle's condo?" asked Jack, amused.

"Yes, the Eagle's Nest. I have already called him."

"From a pay phone, I hope?"

"No, from—Oh, that reminds me. I jerked that bug out from under my condo, so I used my own phone."

"Well, I guess under the circumstances, it doesn't matter," declared Jack. "Everybody knows just about everything now."

"I gotta' go," exclaimed Corbin, looking at his watch. "We're leaving the Bay in an hour."

"Patie, please be careful. And stay in touch, okay?" asked Jack, as the old womanizer stood.

Standing with him, Buddy took his hand, "Please jerk your horny eyes off Marti and look over your shoulder every now and then."

Patie walked to the door, turned and faced his two blood-brothers. "My eyes may be more than just horny, this time, old Pulling Guard."

"Oh no, not again," Buddy clamored, as his teammate and friend walked out the door.

Patie smiled.

CHAPTER EIGHTEEN

When Patie left his two team-mates, he went straight to his condo, elated that Jack and Buddy were on the coast assuming control of the affair, although he was surprised that Buddy had gotten off from work long enough to do it. After all, he had been the connecting link between Jack and me, thought the retired athlete, not a full-time government employee. I guess he feels badly about all that I've gone through.

The expectant romantic was even more excited about getting away with Marti. "If I'm capable of loving ANYONE, I love her," he clamored out loud," and I believe I can love! Surely I can!"

Corbin drove past his condo, turned around in a driveway a half mile down Beach Boulevard and sat in his van for a couple of minutes. Then he drove slowly back, looking down each side street. The gutless wonders won't show their perverse faces around here again, he thought, as he stopped his van in front of the condo and went in. He bounced up the stairs to the bathroom, at first wondering where the energy was coming from, then remembering with a smile—Marti, of course. Picking up his hand mirror from the top of the cabinet, the old pro leaned toward the wall mirror and saw, for the first time, his wound. "Hell," he exclaimed, "I've played entire football games with worse cuts than that." Smiling, he remembered a teammate once declaring, "If you want to hurt Corbin, you gotta' hit him somewhere other than his head, his jewels, maybe."

He may have been right, thought the Halfback, recalling all the times he had been hit there. Each time, he swore to the trainer he was dying.

Patie quickly threw three changes of clothing, including walking shorts, shirt, knee brace, and his old Nikes, along with all his toiletries into a bag. When he walked back downstairs, he opened the "junk-closet" door and lifted his 12 gauge Browning automatic shotgun with a poly-choke on the end of the barrel from the corner behind empty cardboard boxes. Then he picked up two boxes of shotgun shells, seven and a half size shot with which he hunted quail and doves, and six shot, for squirrel. "Wish I had some double 0, damn it," he complained, "but I don't." He set the box of six shot on the floor by his traveling bag and seized the poly-choke on the end of the barrel, moving the setting from "full" to "improved-modified". He wasn't as good a shot as his dad had been, but he had grown up with a gun in his hand and he still loved to hunt. If he had to use it, the setting would spread the six-shot out some, better to hit a moving target. Placing his bag, shotgun and shells by the front door, he reached for the telephone.

"Hey, Loverly, I'm back, packed, and ready to go. See you in five minutes. Heard from Mac yet?"

"No, and I don't expect to—I'm packed, Reb—ready to go. You carrying your swim suit?"

"Yes, but I forgot to pack it. Thanks for reminding me. See you in seven minutes."

Before Patie stopped at Marti's house, he circled the block and saw no one. A few minutes later, he had loaded her two bags into his van. As they locked her door, he asked, "Got all your make-up, medicine, and vitamins?"

"I think so. Wow, you DO know women, don't you, Reb?"

"Sometimes I wonder. But I do know how they love their make-up. Medicine and vitamins are important, but make-up is vital—critical—life giving—essential," grinned the elated boyfriend, putting his arm around Marti's shoulder, squeezing her, leading her to the passenger's side of the van. He reached to open the door, changed his mind and threw both arms around her neck and kissed her. A few delirious moments later, a slight smile embraced her face and she whispered, "What about my neighbors, Reb. Aren't you afraid they might see?"

Patie grinned. He knew Marti was recalling his own words, but he also knew she was doing it in jest.

"No, and I never have been," he lied, opening the door for her. She smiled at him through the window.

"I find it hard to believe that you have never been to the Flora-Bama, Loverly," Patie commented, cranking the van, backing out of Marti's driveway.

"Why?"

"I don't know. You like to party and it's a shore-nuff, o'l timey, beer drinkin' party place."

"I have missed a few partying places, Reb. I haven't hit them all," his companion retorted.

"I know—but Flora-Bama is special. Every one needs to go at least one time."

Patie turned his van north on 603, then east on I-10.

"How long will it take us to get there?" Marti asked, when they reached the interstate.

"About three hours."

"I'm as excited about spending three hours all alone with you in the van as I am anything else," Marti sighed. "I can't believe I'm getting to do this."

"I love you, Loverly."

Marti placed her left hand on her man's right thigh and squeezed. He could not see the small tear of joy which formed in her eye.

* * * * *

"Well, Loverly, there it is, Perdido Beach. We ought to be at the condo in ten minutes." The old pro had been there many times. Today he had driven I-10 east to Pensacola, meandered through the town and crossed the bridge over Perdido Bay to the beach, and headed back west on Florida highway 292. On their left lay the ocean and beach lined with giant condominiums, one almost touching the other, beautifully built towers, outlined by flower gardens and swimming pools. Perdido Beach was a long narrow peninsula of land, from two hundred to five hundred yards wide, stretching from Pensacola to the Alabama line. Although the ocean side of the road was filled with residential buildings, retail commercial businesses were notably absent, whether by covenant or some other reason, Corbin did not know. It was a great place to disappear. The most famous night spot on the beach was the Flora-Bama, which sat almost on the Florida-Alabama border.

"It's beautiful," observed Marti. "Is this beach as beautiful as the one at the Bay?"

"Yes—and minus two Chinese and a husband. Only one problem with the beach here though," Patie smiled.

"What's that?"

"It doesn't have a big, black drainage pipe."

"The hell, you say," declared the beauty. "Terrible, isn't it?"

"We'll find a substitute."

The man and woman were still considering that titillating thought, when Patie turned into the Sunrise-Sunset Condominium driveway. He followed it past the front door where he would normally unload the baggage to the four-storey parking garage, located on the west side of the building. The condo structure was a twenty-storey pale yellow stucco tower, constructed between the highway and the ocean. An extensive Hawaiian flower garden adorned the front of the building and two beautifully designed and decorated swimming pools lay invitingly between the structure and the beach, as did fifty yards of beautiful white sand. The condo units offered two fine restaurants, one outside in consort with the larger swimming pool, and one inside on the east end of the second floor. Each condo unit featured large balconies which overlooked the ocean.

The elated driver turned into the parking garage and immediately found a parking space, a surprise. He had been there many times when the garage was full.

Patie handed Marti her smaller bag and he grabbed the other two. "The elevator is right over here," he directed. The two got into it, and he punched the button—17.

"You're going to love this condo, Loverly, especially the view—and the decor."

"I can't wait to see it," she mused. "And I can't wait to live with you even if only for a few days."

"Maybe longer than that, Loverly," Patie answered just as the elevator stopped. They stepped out on the glass enclosed walkway which ran the length of the building. He stopped in front of a door marked 1706.

"You have a key, Patie?"

"The door is supposed to be open and the key on the dining table," he answered as he twisted the knob. It was unlocked and Patie held it for Marti. The door opened into a short hallway with bedrooms on both sides, then emptied into a large living, dining, kitchen area. A third and larger bedroom lay to the right of that room. The condo was exquisitely decorated in bright beach colors, and expensive furniture. A sliding glass door ran the length of the beach-side wall, covered by loosely woven linen draperies. Patie set the luggage down and pulled the drapes, revealing a beautiful picturesque view of the beach and ocean.

"Let me show you our bedroom, Loverly." Holding her hand, he escorted her through the door into a room decorated around a king-sized four-poster bed, covered with a yellow silk coverlet and like the living area its ocean-ward wall was sliding glass. Patie pulled that drape, revealing the same romantic view as the living room and a small private balcony with a coffee service, two chairs and a table. A door on the opposite side of the room opened into a large private bath, complete with sauna.

"Oh, Patie, this is beautiful. It's more than I imagined, much more."

"And this isn't all. Follow me, Loverly."

Patie took Marti by the hand again and led her into the kitchen-bar. He opened the refrigerator. It was packed with every imaginable food and hors d'ouevre, milk, Cokes, beer, and wine. Then he turned her toward the bar and showed her a completely full cabinet of bourbon, vodka, gin and assorted other alcoholic beverages.

"All of this is marvelous, Loverly, but do you know what looks best to me?"

"Yes, I do."

"What?"

"That king-sized four-poster bed."

"You're right. I got very little sleep last night and absolutely no—ah—no—"

"Fulfilling, satisfying, and stimulating physical relationship with an attractive member of the opposite sex?"

"Unh—hunh!"

"Well, then let's do something about that," she whispered sensually, taking his hand this time and leading him toward the bed with the four posts.

It was dark when Patie woke up. He eased from the bed and looked at the clock in the bathroom. "Damn," he exclaimed louder than he had intended, "it's eight-thirty." By the time he got back to the bed, Marti had raised up onto one elbow. "What is it, Reb?"

"It's eight-thirty, Loverly. I had planned for us to be at the Flora-Bama by now."

"Well, let's get with it then. I can be ready by nine. How far is it?"

"Two miles. We can eat there."

The parking lot on the Flora-Bama side of the street was full, so Patie pulled his van into a gravel parking lot a block down the highway and across it. Holding Marti's hand, Patie led her across the road to the front door of the famous night spot. Several policemen stood around the entrance, pistols strapped to their sides, mingling with and talking to customers, who were standing outside, perhaps thirty or so.

Patie stopped directly in front of the club and with a wide sweeping gesture of his left hand, he said, "Marti, my love, may I present to you—Flora-Bama."

Marti looked at the nightclub, a slight smile on her face, awe drifting from her eyes.

The old beachside roadhouse's parking lot, building, and the strip of beach behind were almost level with Hwy 292. Weathered gray board structures tacked onto one another and a palisade fence sprawled and lurched across the beach as if they had grown out of the sand, complete with every beer sign Marti had ever seen and some she hadn't. Passing through the liquor store, the first room in the compound, loud music of several varieties formed a wall of noise. Off to the right in what was designated as a "lounge" was a busy bar, a good band, and a packed dance floor the size of a small house-trailer bedroom. Splintery uneven open decks on two levels overlooked a covered stage and a dance floor made of— sand. Booths on the deck sold one food item—each— Daiquiris, beer, chips. Crowds of people of all ages filled the different areas, dressed in an amazing range of clothing with tee shirts predominating, sprinkled with motorcyclists in leathers who might have been accountants or other professionals in weekend fun clothes and stick-on decals saying "Born To Kill", and several younger women in full battle dress—very short, tight, black dresses and spike heels, and all of them appeared to be having a great time.

"Ice cold beer tastes mighty good on the top deck, Loverly, and we can get food there, too," said Patie in a voice loud enough to be heard above the crowd noise and music. Marti smiled assent.

Turning his solid frame sideways to the crowd, Patie, as in his halfback days when his hard-charging style opened holes in defensive lines, confidently cleared a path for Marti up the wide wooden stairs to an upstairs deck looking over walkways to the ocean. They settled side by side on stools at the rail over-looking the beach.

"Coors Light with a glass for me, and your usual white wine, Marti?"

The waiter returned quickly with the Coors and a small bottle of screw top white wine which made Marti's mouth pucker at the first sip. Corbin's eyes widened and he inquired innocently, "Great vintage, Loverly?"

"Right, Reb. Bottled last week."

Marti observed that all which had at first seemed totally random and hap-hazard was really organized chaos, with everything working smoothly to keep the crowd, the drinks, and the food flowing. At frequent intervals stood a number of large, strong looking young men in yellow Flora-Bama tee shirts with walkie-talkies on their belts and, she thought, the outline of brass knucks in the pocket of one security guy, quite unnecessary since he looked a solid three hundred pounds of buffed muscle with shoulders that started just below his ears.

To the left of the Flora-Bama compound stretched a line of upscale beach houses occupied, Marti thought, by very tolerant fun and music loving or profoundly deaf people. Behind them was Hwy. 292 and in front of them was the Gulf slapping the sand rhythmically while blowing off a pleasant breeze on this mild spring night. On the right loomed a huge still under construction concrete high rise garage, likely much appreciated by the occupants of the hotels, condos, and houses that stretched down the beach in that direction. On the sand at the water's edge a small light scurried in a continuous erratic pattern. Marti and Patie watched and wondered what they were seeing, and both laughed when they realized someone had a flashlight and was crabbing on the beach.

"You sure are purty, Ma'm. Leave this Ole Miss meathead and come with me and I'll show you a real Alabama fun night," a gravelly voice behind Marti and Patie said as strong hands gripped their shoulders. Marti turned to see an apparition in narrow denim jeans and shirt, both well broken in, hanging with ease upon a lithe frame that looked as if it could still twist and weave its elusive way through a beefy defensive line with the long right arm cocked and ready to fire a football downfield with the speed and deadly aim of a longbow. His sharp world-weary eyes raked Marti, a laser like look that sized her up instantly, while she took in a face that was a roadmap of every joint on the coast surrounded by a five inch fringe of gray hair, thick on top and hanging below his collar in a pony-tail.

"You've always been a great passer, Viper, but do you have to make a pass at my girl?" Patie mildly inquired, the two old enemies hugging the hug of—glad as hell to see you.

"Hell, Corbin, I've never had to make passes at women. I just open my door, stand there, and watch them pile out of cars. The cars don't drive up as often, but still all the Ol' Vipe can handle."

The old Saturday's heroes joshed in this vein for a while, both enjoying talking to someone who understood the pain that went with the glory and catching up on a few mutual friends. Soon the Viper went on his way through the Flora-Bama crowd, talking to many in the place like the regular he was, working the crowd like a politician at the Neshoba County Fair.

Their senses heightened by their excitement at finding each other and the Oceanside setting of the raffish old hangout, Marti and Patie talked over recent events. She knew he was making light of the danger, but her mind rebelled at the thought of any harm coming to him.

"Ain't he the cutest, though," the tough looking girl in the graffiti covered plywood toilet stall next to Marti said loudly. "If he'd just lay down, I'd screw him right on the dance floor."

"I bet you would," said her buddy through a blue cloud of smoke off the cigarette hanging from her lip. "On the sand floor, at that."

Recounting this exchange to Patie on her return from the bathroom, they laughed and did one of those "what are kids coming to" things. In that spirit, there was some discussion about the effects of eating raw oysters, which they had ordered, and a decision to switch to daiquiris on the grounds that they couldn't be more lethal than the wine. The mellow mood lingered as Marti sat back and observed and listened to Corbin. He was a wonderful conversationalist—humorous and widely read, well traveled, and with an amazing range of acquaintances and interests gained through a hectic life.

"Guess you've figured out I tell it all, Marti, good and bad, truth and fiction," the semi-truth teller lied. "All except there's no lie about me being with the most exciting, beautiful and interesting woman on this coast or any other—and one I love." Corbin was a very physical man and this quality showed as he held Marti's hand and slipped a thumb under her belt at the back of her waist. He bent near her, allowing her to inhale a slight scent of his clean healthy body and an elusive masculine aftershave he always wore and she couldn't quite identify.

"You always say the right thing, Reb," grinned Marti, giving him in return, irony for exaggerated compliment. He grinned back, then launched into a funny tale about a French fighter pilot named Jean Claude who thought of himself as "The World's Greatest Lovaír Who Went Down In Flames". He told the tale with a teasing sparkle in his eyes and the very faint rasp in his voice that made Marti want to hear him say lover's words. His eyes shone with intelligence and humor, and as his mood shifted, the fleeting expressions across his mobile face made Marti's heart give a sudden squeeze.

"Dammit, dammit, dammit," Marti muttered under her breath as she watched him walk away toward the bar for refills with the brisk sure-footed gait so characteristic of him. I've fallen for him so hard it's a bodily pain and I'm flying at the same time. Maybe that's what I need—time out! Setting out to find the fulfillment and the affirmation of her womanhood that Mac had coldly withheld from her was supposed to be a rational decision that would bring an addendum to her life, not this consuming whirlwind that was turning her feelings and maybe her life upside down. Had her impetuousness completely overruled her usually sound thinking? Maybe. Would she give him up, change things, go back to square one? Hell, no, she thought. I'm not going to hold back a damn thing—I'm going to roll it all on this one. I'll either have the relationship I've always dreamed of or I'll be as empty and hollow as I was those last years with Mac, only with the painful knowledge of how good it could be.

When he reseated himself, Patie teased, "Loverly, I know your strict Baptist upbringing didn't give you much chance to learn the evil art of dancing—I know some Baptists who say it's just sex standing up—but a trip to Flora-Bama isn't complete without a trip around the floor, or sandpit, as the case may be. How about it?"

"You mean how about a trip around whatever, Reb?" Marti joked. "Well, shall we dance on your toes or mine?"

The band, much improved by the beer, wine, daiquiris and good company, launched into Patsy Cline's "Crazy" just as they reached the sand.

"That song pretty much says it all about anybody who'd risk dancing with me," announced Marti, opening her arms to Patie. She was swept into a close embrace, their cheeks together, her body bent slightly backward, and after a few faltering steps, they fell into each others' rhythms. The warm sand underfoot, the plaintive country song and their undeniable attraction made one unit of them as he expertly guided her in a weaving easy pattern that caught both of them up in a surrender to the music and to each other.

"Wal, Ma'm," not quite releasing her and leaning back, Patie said, "I'm gonna' have to do something I hate to do, and that's call a lady a liar. I do believe you've been kicking up sand at the Flora-Bama for years."

Laughing with relief at having successfully negotiated at least one hurdle, Patie's good-natured ribbing made Marti feel almost adequate in the dance department. Leaning back against the railing and totally absorbed in each other, a gleam of light shone on dark metal in the hand of a small man who had pressed to the edge of the crowd. The shining tube with the bulbous tip came up in the man's hand and pointed toward Marti, who heard no report from the silenced weapon, just a high velocity rush of air past her ear which fanned her back. "Look out, Patie!" she gasped. "He's got a gun!" Corbin whirled, but the small man had already melted back into the crowd of bodies gyrating to the nasal tones of George Jones hit:

"He stopped loving her today
They placed a wreath upon his door,
They just carried him away,
He stopped loving her today."

Several other whirling couples had seen the same sideshow which Marti had seen. Some of them screamed—some fell silently to the floor. Patie looked around—saw that no one appeared to be hit, grabbed his still wide-eyed companion by the arm and commanded, "Stay, here, Loverly."

"No, Patie, no," she begged in vain, as he pressed his way through the unsuspecting crowd, hampered by the same party mood which he had brought Marti to become part of. A few minutes later, he made his slow way back to where he had left her. Two of the policemen who had been standing out front were talking to customers. Oblivious of the excitement, the band continued to play—the dancers continued to dance. A policeman had already talked to Marti by the time Patie returned. She volunteered a worried look, but had told them nothing. The joy of seeing him was evident and she threw her arms around his neck. "This is a great place, Reb, but I think we need to go."

"I agree, Good-looking—you alright?"

"Just a little scared. How did they know—?" her voice trailed off.

The embattled fighter found himself growing angry again, but he knew he could not succumb to the emotion, not with Marti present. Nor could he explain anything to the policemen without divulging his role in all this—why he moved to the Bay—why and how he had met Marti. But neither could he carelessly risk her safety. "Loverly, it's a long way from the front door to the parking lot," he cautioned as they moved slowly through the packed crowd of revelers toward the front exit. "I'm going after my van and I want you to wait just inside the door of the liquor store. I'll pick you up there. He won't try anything out front, if the police are still outside."

"Please be careful, Patie? It's dark in that parking lot."

"I'll be careful. Be looking for me."

Patie saw only one policeman out front when he opened the front door. He saw nothing suspicious, then walked quickly to his van, rotating his head in every direction like an owl searching for a quail at evening-time. The wary driver unlocked the van before he reached it, quickly got into the back seat and retrieved his shotgun and shells. He double checked the gun, making certain a shell was in the barrel, ready to fire, and that two more were in the magazine. Then he placed the weapon and extra shells on the floorboard immediately behind the front seats, an easy reach when he was driving. A few seconds later, he wheeled to a stop in front of the Flora-Bama and Marti darted out the door and into the van. The moment she sat down, she touched Patie's right arm. "Reb, if they knew we were here, then they may know where we are staying, do you suppose?"

"They may. We have to assume they do," agreed the old pro, as he moved his van back onto 292. "We're going to be careful—very careful. I want you to climb over into the back of the van and stay down."

"Patie, I'm not going to—"

"Please, Loverly, don't argue with me. Two people are easier to hit than one. Besides, we don't know whether they are after me, you, or both of us."

"Both of us, I imagine," Marti gasped fearfully as she stepped over the console, onto the shotgun, which she had not seen.

"Reb, you have a gun," she exclaimed, both surprise and disapproval evident in her voice.

"And I know how to use it, too, Loverly. You

Mississippi State farmers aren't the only ones who hunt, you know." Patie's attempt at levity did little to alleviate his lover's concern.

"Patie, I don't like this—I'm afraid that—"

Corbin interrupted her again. "Don't get TOO liberal on me, Marti. If words could solve our problem I'd be talking a blue streak right now. I love you—and these men are trying to kill us. I'm going to protect you, and I'll do it with that shotgun if necessary."

"Then, let's call the police, Patie."

"I'm going to—as soon as we get inside the condo," he lied, intending rather to call Jack, "but we have to get there first. It's only two miles. Look behind us. Make certain a car doesn't slip up from the rear. He may have his lights off. I'll watch to the front and each side. Keep your head down as much as possible. Okay?—You with me?"

Marti swallowed hard. Damn Mac, damn him for getting me into this kind of fix—and Patie. Patie! Thank God for Patie, she thought, as she gazed intently over the rear seat through darkened glass to the stretch of highway behind her. "Okay," she blurted quickly, "I'm with you."

Two minutes later, the driver turned abruptly into the Sunrise-Sunset parking lot. "We're almost home, Loverly. Be looking for that black Lexus or any-one who looks suspicious."

Neither of the hunted saw a black Lexus, nor any other car moving. Patie turned into the well-lighted garage. More cars were parked there than earlier, vaca-tioners arriving late, he thought. He pulled into one of the few parking spaces remaining on the first floor, turned his lights and engine off, considerably farther from the elevator than earlier when he had stopped near it. He saw no black Lexus in the garage.

"Stay down, Loverly. I want to look around," cautioned Patie, grasping a handful of shotgun shells which he crammed into his front pocket. He considered getting out of the vehicle with his shotgun in his hand, but then decided against it. What if a regular guest suddenly drove into the garage?

Patie slowly stood. No one can slip up on me in here, he speculated confidently—too much light. Then he remembered—there had been light at Flora-Bama—and people too. The cautious driver walked slowly to the rear of his vehicle. He stopped there and studied every automobile parked against the opposite wall. He saw no one. In order to inspect the vehicles parked on his side of the garage, though, he would be forced to step out into the center area. He took four careful steps.

Out of the corner of his eye, the athlete saw sudden movement to his left, a head thrusting up between two cars four or five parking spaces away. He twisted his upper body toward the head and he saw the pistol brought up from between the cars, held in both of the man's hands. And then everything reduced to slow motion—the resting of the firearm on the roof of the car—Patie beginning to turn away—the flash of light from the barrel of the weapon—the slow, mushy noise of an explosion—the stinging pain as the bullet tore into flesh—the excruciatingly slow dive onto the concrete floor—and the silence—when it seemed to the stricken football player that it took forever for the back of the sound to catch up with the front of it.

CHAPTER NINETEEN

Patie would have sworn it took a minute to fall and it seemed as though he would never reach the security of a flattened, prone position. The pain had not yet caught up with his wounding. He knew he had been hit—on the left side. He looked at the left side of his shirt, under his arm, and he saw the hole in his shirt and he saw blood, and felt blood, warm, sticky. He fell to the floor of the garage moving—moving back between the cars—moving toward his shotgun. The sound of another shot filled the resonant air of the garage. The bullet glanced off the floor six inches from the halfback's left ear. The sound of the shot and the ricocheting of the projectile echoed a dozen times in the hollow building and would have confused the location of its source had the target not already known.

"Patie—Patie," the muffled sound came from the enclosed van.

"Stay down, Marti," Patie yelled, scrambling on hands and knees to the sliding rear door which gave access to the shotgun. Opening the door quickly, he grabbed the weapon and whispered to the frightened woman again, "Stay down—stay down."

"You're bleeding."

"I'm alright—stay down," he commanded as he eased the sliding door shut. Falling to the floor again, the gun clutched firmly in his right hand, he looked under his van toward the spot from which the shots came, hoping to see two legs. He did not and he lay still for a few seconds surveying the situation. The shooter might be standing behind tires, or he may have gotten back into his car. Patie was surprised that the assailant had not sprinted to him after the first shot. It would be over with by now—I would be dead, he thought. He had to devise a plan, but first—but first—.

In the moment of lull, the pain had finally worked its way through the emotional turmoil into the old scrapper's nerve system. He glanced down at the wound again. Lying on his right side, he tugged his shirt-tail out of his Bermuda shorts and raised it. He couldn't see the bullet hole so he reluctantly probed it. The slug had penetrated the muscle immediately under his left arm and exited, it felt like, maybe two inches away. Hell, he thought, I've been hurt worse in tackling drills, but the pain was intensifying and the old bird hunter knew he had to change positions. The assailant could not walk upon him without Patie spotting him—under the vehicles, but he could not lie there all night, either. The only point from which Corbin could see between the cars where the attacker crouched was on the other side of the garage, between the vehicles parked on the opposite wall. But he could not get there without exposing himself. Could the attacker hit a running man at twenty to thirty yards? How fast can I run? Damn knee—I can't run fast—maybe fast enough, though. Is there just one man, or are both of them there?

"Lord, please, let me make it to the other side. That's our only chance, Lord." Patie peeked under the cars again. He quietly raised to one knee and positioned himself behind his own back tires in the event would-be assassin looked under the cars, took a deep breath, "Lord, please," and bending over at the waist, lunged from behind his van. Halfway across the open area, Corbin heard the shot and heard the bullet hiss by his head. He glanced in the direction of the shooter. His wild dash had pulled the man from his hiding place. He was standing upright two feet out in the open, drawing a bead on the sprinter. At the same instant the Chinese American squeezed off the fourth round, the sprinter dove into the concrete, ripping the skin off his elbows, rolled over twice and from a prone position leveled the barrel of his twelve gauge shotgun squarely on the man's mid-section and squeezed the trigger.

It was as though the hunter, who had become the hunted, and now became the hunter again could follow each of the handful of six-shot straight into the small man's chest, guiding them with his eyes, a laser upon which they rode straight to the target. Some of the shot glanced off the pistol, knocking it from his hand onto the roof of the car from behind which he had first fired, and it clamored, slid off, and crashed to the concrete. Some of the shot entered the man's hands and arms, elevating them far above his head, a fruit grower picking apples from a high limb, a charismatic preacher trying to touch heaven with outstretched arms. But most of the small lead pellets struck the killer in the lower chest and upper stomach, lifting his little torso six inches off the floor, slamming him against the trunk of a car, depositing him on the unforgiving concrete. He groaned once, then again. As the life drained from his body so did blood and urine, surrounding his stilled body with a strange mixture of red and yellow.

The tough old competitor lay still for a moment, making certain that the little man was dead and had been alone. Then he gently laid his shotgun down, rubbed his bruised and bloody elbows, and dropped his head onto the back of his crossed hands which rested on the garage floor. In the quiet aftermath, Patie heard sirens and immediately a set of squealing tires. The Buick spun into the garage and stopped at the far end, thirty yards away. The injured man lifted himself to one knee but before he could identify the occupants of the car, Marti flung the side-sliding door of the van open. "Patie, are you alright?" she screamed, stepping guardedly from the vehicle. Before he could answer, he heard a familiar male voice from the window of the stopped car. "Patie, are you alright?"

"Yes, I'm alright."

The Buick drove close to Corbin and stopped.

The same moment Patie got to his feet, Marti ran to him, throwing her arms around his neck. Her face was still embedded in his bloody shirt, whimpering, when Jack and Buddy stepped from the automobile. Before anyone had a chance to say anything else, two police cars cut their sirens and pulled into the garage behind the Buick.

Jack and Buddy waited a few seconds patiently, then Jack touched Marti's arms, which were still clamped around her lover's neck. "Pardon me, ma'm. Can we take a look at Patie's wound?"

Marti, tears flowing down her face, removed her arms from the Rebel's neck and grabbed his right hand. Jack lifted his shirt at the wound. "Well, I'll be damned, Meathead, the bullet went clean through the muscle, and I don't believe it even hit a rib. Just two little holes, no more than three inches apart. We need to stop the bleeding though—and you'll need to see a doctor."

Marti stood silently to one side, still holding Patie's right hand, a bewildered look on her face surfacing through the tears. The policemen had walked over to the dead man, felt his pulse, determined that he was dead, and surrounded him as though they were protecting him from wild animals or maybe someone who might destroy evidence. Buddy had placed his hand on the back of Patie's neck, expressing with the touch of a life-long friend his love and concern and compassion. The confounded woman looked from one face to the other and back again, finally to the Reb. "Patie, who are these people?"

The trickster felt the blood drain from his face, emotional fear mixing with physical pain. He knew the time had come when he could no longer conceal his purpose for knowing her, the woman whom he had come to love. He sure as hell had not meant to love her, but he did—and now she would be told the truth about him. She was proud, this beautiful college professor, jogger, housewife, great lover, wife of a traitor. Patie turned toward her and spoke gently. "Marti, I love you, please remember that, I love you."

Her voice was soft, but it was insistent and Patie could hear the doubt in it when she asked again, "Who are these men?"

Patie knew he would have to introduce Marti to them. He was not one to break the rules of common courtesy but he did not want to start the process of explanation. Once it started, it could not be stopped.

"Marti, I love you."

Jack and Buddy knew the dilemma which Patie faced—because of them. They wanted to give him an opportunity to justify his actions to her, but Jack knew the procedure must begin. A man lay dead no more than seventy feet away.

"Ms. Claiborne, my name is Jack—"

Patie swallowed and held up his right hand. "No, Jack, I'll tell her." His mind swirled. Could he lie to her?—Say he had called two old teammates as bodyguards—one with whom she had already talked?—Would she believe that?—Maybe for a while, unless these things made the newspapers—then she would know he lied and that would make matters worse. He needed to ask Jack about that. If Jack could keep this out of the papers, if she did not have to be interviewed by the CIA, then he wouldn't be required to tell her the truth—but how could he ask Jack? No, he had to tell Marti the truth and it had to start right now.

Marti stiffened. "Tell me what, Patie?"

Before he could answer, Jack interrupted again. "Patie, you need to see a doctor—now. Why don't you let Buddy take you to the emergency room? I'll go with Ms. Claiborne up to the condo and tell her the story? We'll wait for you and Buddy there."

Patie thought for a moment, then turned toward Marti. "Loverly, this is Jack Burkes and Buddy Fisher. They are Ole Miss teammates and close friends. Will you go with Jack?"

"I want to go to the hospital with you."

"This is no more than a scratch. I really wish you would do this—for me."

Marti hesitated. Then she nodded. "Okay, if it's important to do it that way."

Patie put his right arm around her and she threw both of hers around his waist, ignoring the blood which continued to drip slowly down his side. "Please remember I love you."

"I love you, too, Patie," but the words seemed to falter in the lovely woman's throat as though they were afraid to move out into such an uncertain world. Her eyes dropped.

Patie turned again toward Jack, who had just picked the shotgun up from the garage floor. "Jack—be gentle."

The trained agent knew what his old friend was demanding. Patie wanted Burkes to grant every conceivable justification to him, to hone down the sharp condemning edge of their arrangement. The veteran CIA officer knew it could not be done. The truth would flow beyond compassion, but he would try.

Jack nodded, then asserted, "Patie, you, Buddy and I will have to talk to the police soon. You get that wound tended to—I'll work that out with them. I'll have a representative of the police department meet you at the hospital to verify your relationship with us.

Patie reached into his pocket and handed Jack the key to the apartment. As he and Buddy turned toward the Buick, the sound of another siren filled the air and an ambulance drove slowly into the garage through the exit, directed there by one of the policemen. Patie opened the car door and hesitated, to look at Marti, who, with Jack, was walking to the elevator.

"Loverly."

Marti stopped and looked over her shoulder at her wounded paramour. She said nothing. Patie could see sharp apprehension lining her face and he knew she feared what she was about to hear—and he feared it, too, perhaps more than she.

"I love you."

She smiled, nodded, and turned back toward the elevator. Patie got into Buddy's car and they drove slowly around the ambulance. Two medics were lifting Spikes' body.

At 1:15 a.m., two hours later, Patie and Buddy arrived at the condo. The emergency room doctor had medicated the wound and sewn the two small holes back together. He gave Patie some Percoset for pain, joked about not getting addicted to it, gave Patie a list of do's and don'ts, got the old athlete's autograph, and sent him on his way. When he and Buddy entered the living and kitchen area, Jack held a mixed drink in one hand, the open refrigerator door handle in the other, and was bending over looking intently into it. He raised up and asked, "Get it sewed, Patie?"

"Yes, finally," Corbin answered, looking around for Marti.

"Did you cry?" Jack teased.

"Wanted to—where's Marti?"

"On the deck." Jack nodded, and Patie took a couple of steps toward the sliding glass door. The agent caught his arm. "Ol' friend, we need to talk before you go out there. Won't take but a minute or two. Fix yourself a drink and we'll—"

Patie stopped and turned back toward his old teammate. "What did you tell her, Jack?"

"Everything. I had to tell her the truth, Patie. I softened it as much as I could without lying. I told her I had known you for a long time and that I believe you care deeply for her."

"Care deeply?" Patie exclaimed. "Not love?"

"Hell, Pate, I don't know your heart. You'll have to tell her that."

The halfback turned again to walk toward Marti. Jack caught him by the arm a second time. "There's one other thing you need to know before you talk to her."

Patie stopped, turned back toward the old end,

said nothing.

"Mac's body was found in his car near a bayou earlier tonight. He was shot—in the head."

"WHAT? WHERE?"

"Off 603, between Waveland and the interstate."

"Did you tell Marti?"

"Yes."

"How did she take it?"

"Not well—she cried. She was already crying when I told her THAT."

"Do you know who killed him?"

"Not yet. Probably Spikes, that man whom you—that is, who tried to kill you tonight."

"I can take it, Jack. I killed him. I'm not sorry. I had no choice."

Facing Buddy, who had mixed a drink and was sitting on a barstool sipping it, Jack asked, "Did you tell Patie why we came down here?"

Buddy nodded. "I told him we followed him. We figured the spies would, and that we had arrested the Chinaman at his motel earlier."

"Patie, Jack asked me not to tell you about Mac. He wanted to do that," the pulling guard explained.

Jack nodded agreement. "Marti has been through a lot tonight, Pate. She was shot at; she watched you get shot; she saw a man die; she feared for her own life; she learned why you are involved with her; hears that her husband is a spy—and that he's dead. I'm not a counselor and even if I were, I wouldn't try to counsel you, but if I were you, I would not push her tonight. She's in shock, justifiably. Her mind cannot function properly just now."

Patie stared at his old friend.

"I know you don't want to lose her," Jack continued, "and she may say some pretty tough things. Don't
let them get to you, okay? She may change tomorrow."

The rugged football player nodded at his close
friend, said nothing, and walked to the sliding glass
door, grasped the handle—and stopped. Because of the
light in the condo, he could not see through it, but he
knew she could. Was she looking? Could she see the
remorse in him? Did his regret show on his face? Could
she tell by his hesitancy that he loved her? Was she
angry—or hurt—or both? Should he stand there a little
longer? Would that make her respect him more or less?
A woman must respect a man to want him, to give herself
to him. Surely she could understand his love for her
AND his love for his country. She might even agree with
what he did—hurt a little, true—but knowing he loves
her—surely she sees that.

The man whose intestinal fortitude had never
been doubted pulled the handle with trepidation.

"Loverly?"

The devastated woman was leaning forward, her
hands grasping the rail which surrounded the deck. Her
back was turned toward the glass door, her head was
lowered and she seemed to be watching the dark waves
crashing into the sand seventeen stories below. She did-
n't answer.

Patie slowly linked his arms around her waist,
burying his face in her shoulder length auburn hair, half
expecting her to pull away. He felt warm drops of mois-

ture fall upon his hands, and he waited.

Marti's body stiffened, but she did not pull away, and then she spoke. Her voice was hoarse, her vocal cords raspy as though the waves far below had washed across her throat, depositing a great salty residue there. "How could you have done that to me?"

"When I agreed to do it, Loverly, I didn't know you."

"Please don't call me THAT—ever again?"

"I didn't know you then, Marti. Didn't Jack tell you that he and Buddy were concerned because I had fallen in love with you? Didn't he?"

"He would have told me that whether it's true or not—for you."

"It's true, Marti—I do love you."

"You deceived me."

"I love you."

"If deception is a part of your kind of love, I want none of it." The "petite amie" grasped Patie's forearm with each hand and pulled them apart, something she could not have done if the strong middle-aged man had not permitted her to do so. She wheeled her body around and gently yet firmly pushed him away—an arm's length. The light from inside the condo illumined her face like a thousand spotlights. The sparkle of life had left her eyes and they were swollen and almost closed, squinting with the stare of extreme pain. Tears continued to stream down her face and her once-proud shoulders slouched downward, lending to the hopelessness festering inside of her. The man who professed to love her saw lines across her brow which he had not seen before and he knew he had placed them there as surely as if he were a plastic surgeon and had carved them into her skin.

"You are a deceiver, Patie, and you can't help it and don't even realize it. You're a pretender, the "great pretender" in that damned old song you hum and sing all the time. Your entire life is false. You are a fake—a fake," Marti lamented, her voice rising in anger—" and I don't want to see you again—ever. I was a fool, a damn fool." Marti quieted for a second, then whimpered, "Maybe you were right—maybe Bulldogs are stupid. This one certainly was." She twisted away from Patie and faced the ocean once more, her body heaving with deep agonizing sobs.

"Marti, Bulldogs aren't stupid and neither are you. I'm the one who's stupid. Please forgive me for what I have done to you."

For a minute or two Marti did not answer. When she did, her words tore into Patie's heart like the six-shot had torn into Spikes body. "I want to go home, Patie—tonight."

"Tonight! Please, Marti, not tonight. It's late. Stay here tonight. I'll take you home tomorrow. I'll sleep in another bedroom, I promise."

"I want to go home tonight. Take me to the bus station."

"Not tonight, Marti, please."

Marti turned to walk back into the condo. "Then I'll ask Jack to take me."

"No," conceded the debater, blocking her way. "I'll talk to Jack and Buddy." She halted. Corbin slid the glass door open and went back into the condo. A few minutes later he reopened the door and stepped back onto the deck. Marti was waiting, her arms crossed in front of her body as though she expected them to somehow control the lurching in her stomach.

"I talked to Buddy, and he will drive you back to The Bay tonight. Won't you reconsider—?"

"Thank you. I'll gather my stuff."

"I would take you, but Jack and I have to talk to the police tomorrow."

Marti said nothing. She walked determinedly through the open door, a woman who had decided, through the living room and disappeared into the bedroom. A few minutes later she emerged carrying her two bags which Patie, moving briskly to her side, took. She reluctantly gave them to him. Buddy set his drink on the bar and reached for the bags but Patie held onto them and offered, "I'll walk down with y'all."

Without looking at him, Marti spoke. "I don't want you to do that."

Patie quietly deposited the bags in front of Buddy, reached into his pocket and handed him the key to his condo. "Thank you for taking Marti home, Buddy. I owe you, big-time."

"We'll meet you at Patie's condo tomorrow afternoon around five. Be careful driving tonight—don't fall asleep," declared Jack.

Marti was already at the door waiting for Buddy. Patie followed and when he opened the door to let the two of them out, he looked at the heartbroken woman moving past him. "I love you, Marti." She said nothing.

Patie shut the door behind them, a hollow sound thundering through his soul like another explosion of the twelve-gauge automatic shotgun with a poly choke on the end of the barrel.

* * * * *

It was 4:00 o'clock the next day when Patie and Jack arrived at Patie's condo. They had spent the night at the Eagle's Nest, although neither slept much, called Buddy around 10:00 a.m. to make sure he and Marti had arrived safely, and turned the condo key back in to the office. By noon they had talked to the police. The two old teammates ate vegetables at Cracker Barrel and headed back to the Bay.

Patie was tired and his wounds were hurting, all four of them—his side, his head, and both elbows, so he had taken a couple of Percosets, too close together, most likely, he figured. Buddy was watching the golf channel when they walked into the condo. After greeting one another, Corbin asked with impatient concern, "Was Marti still adamant about not seeing me when you got here last night, Buddy?"

"Yeah, pretty much, Pate. She didn't talk a lot. Asked about my family and Jack's family—things like that."

"She didn't talk about me—about us?"

"No, but that doesn't mean anything, you know how women are."

Patie reached for the phone. He dialed the woman with whom he had discovered such a rapport, such companionship as he had never expected to find, a perfect fit for an imperfect man. He prayed that she would answer.

The phone rang once, then twice, then three times. On the fourth ring he heard the blessed sound of her voice. It was subdued but not pressed down beyond recognition. "Hello."

Patie choked. For the first time in his life he felt quivers of nervousness at the thought of talking to a woman. "Marti?"

She did not answer.

"Marti?"

"Please, Patie, I told you I never want to talk to you again. Please have the decency and class to honor that, please. Don't you understand, I have lost everything. Please don't call me again," she pleaded, as if she were about to cry. The woman's man, unaccustomed to female rejection, never-the-less recognized unqualified finality in the voice of the one whom he loved. He had always won these kinds of skirmishes—turned on the matchless charm, flashed the heart-warming smile, swamped the woman with lofty compliments. But he could not impose those scintillating pressures upon Marti. He loved her too much—it would be sacrilegious, profane. And he knew he had to honor her wish, not because he wanted to, but because he had no choice. He had never tasted rejection—it would be for him very hard to endure.

"I love you, Marti."

"I loved you too, Patie, with my whole being. Please don't ever call me again." And then there was the click—and then there was the silence and then the old womanizer knew, for the first time he knew, a woman had decided she wanted no more of Patie Corbin before he decided he wanted no more of her. Should it be so cruel, he thought, as to be the woman whom he had loved the most?

Patie knew immediately he would leave the Bay and he would leave now, today. Buddy and Jack had listened to him on the phone, had heard him choke, had seen his nervousness. A man in whom they had never known "timid", turned now to them for help.

"I want the two of you to do something for me. I can't stay here," his voice broke. "Will you help me load my van—now."

"Of course we will," answered Jack. Buddy nodded in agreement. "But why don't you wait—think about—"

"NO, I can't wait. Will you help me load now? And will you close the apartment for me?"

"Yes, of course we will, Patie, if that's what you want. Tell us what to do."

The old pro found himself about to cry and his two friends could see it. They looked at each other in disbelief. Patie Corbin? Both thought, this can't be happening, not to Patie Corbin!

"Patie," Jack asked, "are you certain about this. Stay here another day or two—give it a little time."

"I'm certain. I have to do this."

"Where are you going?"

"I don't know. I'm going to Mom's in Laurel right now, I guess. I may stay at my place in Banner Elk for a while and finish the book. I don't really know."

"Patie, I have a proposition for you and for Buddy. I've already talked to him about it. I'd like to bounce it off you, if you feel like listening."

"Hell, Jack, I don't know. I don't know what I want. I'll listen—because it's you, of course—but I don't know."

Jack explained, "I know you don't think this business has worked out well, and it hasn't for you, but for us, for the government, it worked beautifully."

Patie breathed deeply, and raised his eyebrows. "That's putting it mildly."

"I know," agreed Jack, "but let me explain. My superiors have asked me to talk to you. We need somebody like you, with your name, experience, and—well—abilities. Hell, Patie, let me be honest, you can snow a woman, just about any woman. I can think of at least five or six situations in my files right now where we need to plant someone to do precisely what you've done down here—"

"Wait," interposed Corbin in disbelief, "are you telling me that you are willing to hire me full-time to make out with other wives of suspected—"

"Patie, we already have women on our payroll doing the same thing. The culture has changed. Men and women act about the same now. Hell, women pursue men faster than men pursue women. We can use you!"

"Yeah, and help me get my tail shot off? I don't know, Jack. To be honest, I'm so miserable right now, all I can think about is getting out of here. I'll be at

Mom's for the next couple of months, maybe more. Call me there.

"You going to do it, Buddy?" asked Corbin.

"Thinking about it, but you are the key. I'm only the connecting link. If you'd like, we'll get together, play a little golf and talk about it."

"Call me sometime, we'll do that."

An hour and a half later, Patie's van was packed and he was ready to go, physically if not psychologically. Buddy and Jack had agreed to close the condo for him: pay the rent and tell the office he was gone; disconnect the phone, electricity, and cable; get the water and gas turned off; and have the furniture rental come pick up everything. Corbin didn't want to leave but he knew he could not stay in The Bay and fulfill his vow to Marti. This way was painful but it was the only way. Maybe the pain would end when he was gone—maybe—for Marti— not likely for him.

The old football players walked out to the van together, three old friends who had just been through a little corner of hell. Patie knew he was about to cry. He did not know how strong his friends heart's were but he had better not test them, he smiled to himself, and if they saw tears on his cheeks, their entire cardiovascular systems might collapse. Hugging both of them, he babbled louder than necessary, words designed to cover the ache in his heart. "Thank you for helping me get out of here tonight. You old bastards take care,—and call me."

"We'll be in touch, Patie. How does your side feel?" Jack asked, as the old pro swung the van door open and sat down under the steering wheel. "Loading your stuff hurt it?"

"Naw, it's okay. Throbs a little. My hard head does too, but the Percoset will help, I think."

"Take care of yourself, Old Friend," smiled Buddy. Patie hesitated, cranked the van, hesitated again. Then looking away from his two friends, he backed up and turned south on Beach Boulevard.

Where Beach Boulevard intersects Highway 90, the heavy-hearted man pulled his van to the side of the street and stopped. He sat there watching the traffic speed by him, two lanes going east across the bridge— two lanes moving west toward 603, Waveland, New Orleans. A few minutes later, after gathering his emotions, he saw an opening and darted across 90 in the direction of Old Town and the Beach. His affairs with the police returned vividly to him when he passed the spot where he was arrested and he turned his head to look at the pier. Then he was through Old Town and past Saint Stanislaus, where Doc Blanchard played high school football. And there it was, the beach. Tears rolled down the cheeks of the tough old Don Juan, football player, writer, inmate.

"There IS a parking lot on this beach," he called out to no one, the tears streaming down his face, flowing into his mouth, down his chin. "St. Charles St., huh? I guess a touch of New Orleans—and look," he yelled, as he lowered his window, "They're tearing the sand up again. WHY ARE YOU DESTROYING THE BEACH? And look, there's the big black pipe. It drains water under the, under the, under—" The driver slammed on brakes, threw his door open and stood up on the interior running board of the van.

The beautiful woman sat stoically near the end of the pipe, one leg on one side of it, the other leg on the other side of it, her back toward the street, gazing out to sea. She did not move, for the entire time Patie looked at her—not when the other cars squealed their brakes—not when they blew their horns. Her eyes and her heart were fixed upon the sea.

Her old paramour slowly sat back down and almost reverently closed the door of his van and through the open window he spoke the words out into the mild Bay St. Louis air, knowing somehow the ocean wind should deliver them to her. "I love you, Marti."

Then Patie Corbin turned off Beach Boulevard onto the street which would take him to the road which would take him to the interstate which would take him away.

Thank you
Becky and Gene Dallas
Daisy Yarbrough
Joynelle Pearson

An excerpt from *An Academy Called Pain...*

THE CONFLICTS WITH COWS

THE RUNAWAY

Not every Poole birthed with the ability to play football at Ole Miss did so. James Swepson "Sonny Boy" Poole, born on the banks of Brushy Creek two years before I came into the world, signed a football scholarship with the Rebels in the Fall of 1951, and reported to Wobble Davidson for practice. My cousin stood 6 feet 2 inches tall, and weighed a very muscular 215 lbs. Had he remained on the training table, he could have comfortably carried 250 lbs., which would have made him one of the largest and fastest linemen in America for his playing years. He would have been a great athlete for Ole Miss.

Sonny Boy chose instead to, as the old-timers phrase it in South Mississippi, "make a doctor." He quit football, entered pre-med, and for more than forty years, practiced medicine in Centreville, less than 20 miles from Homochitto, the Poole enclave and place of his birth, a mile down the dusty gravel road from Mama Poole's, where Buster, Ray, Barney and I grew up. He became the resident Poole family doctor until his recent retirement and few weeks passed in all those years when he wasn't attending to one of our relatives, either in his

I

clinic or at Field Memorial Hospital nearby.

Sonny Boy's entrance into medicine presented all my other relatives, and me, with an interesting problem. I grew up with him; swam naked with him and all the other Poole boys in the cold, clear, spring-fed waters of Brushy Creek; went to Crosby High with him; and played all three sports with him. To me he's Sonny Boy – then - now - and always. How do you call a Doctor of Medicine, Sonny Boy, especially before other people?

Upon periodically seeing him again, my greeting usually trailed along these lines as I extended my hand. "Hi, Sonny, oh, er, oh, Doc, ah, oh — what the hell, I can't do it. How are you?" I couldn't call him Doctor – he was family! I didn't want to call him Sonny Boy – he was a doctor. In Homochitto, preachers and doctors were practically gods and certainly elevated beyond first-name status. Now that he's retired, I think my con-science will allow me to call him Sonny Boy again. I tried it last Father's Day at Mt. Vernon Methodist Church and it seemed to fit.

Growing up at Homochitto, Sonny Boy's intellec-tual and academic abilities weren't always recognized, however, not even by the closest of relatives, including his Dad, J. C.

J. C. Poole was one of the few older relatives who gained a college education. After earning his degree, he returned to his home community to become principal, teacher, and coach at Homochitto High (the school long ago consolidated with Crosby High, which in the early sixties, consolidated with arch-rival Gloster High). The lay leader of Mt. Vernon Church, he was a tall, stately, serious minded and highly respected man. By the time Sonny Boy and I entered high school at Crosby, Cud'n J. C. had retired from teaching and was involved almost totally in farming and raising cattle. His was one of the few families in our community who owned horses.

Like the rest of us, Sonny Boy usually caught the "picture-show" bus which circulated through the community freely picking up passengers for the Saturday night western movie at the theatre in Crosby. And like the rest of us, he sometimes pretended to be Gene Autry, Roy Rogers, Lash Larue, Randolph Scott, or Johnnie Mack Brown – but with more authenticity – he owned a horse – and a saddle, something no other Poole boy could claim. Sonny Boy loved to ride his horse, which he did as often as Cud'n J. C. would release him from the corn field.

One hot July afternoon in about 1947 or 1948, J. C. had taken several cows to the sale in Liberty. A prized milk-cow tore out of the pasture and headed up the gravel road toward the Robertson's place. Sonny Boy Autry, then about 14 or 15 years old, quickly saddled his cow-roping pony and pursued the fleeing animal. He and his trusty companion caught up with the renegade on the Brushy Creek bridge, an arched, wooden span with banisters, from which we all jumped into the cold water, some ten feet below, after a hot day's work. The courageous cowboy had a rope but decided not to use it. Instead, like the bull-dogging westerners on the silver screen at Crosby, he "dove" off his sprinting charger, aiming for the runaway cow's head. At that precise moment, the milk-producer, obviously realizing she had been overcome, decided to stop, turn around, and go back home. Sonny Boy missed bossy and bull-dogged the Brushy Creek bridge.

By the time J. C. returned from the cattle sale, the catapulting cowboy had been taken to Dr. David in Crosby, who had sewn up his numerous cuts, treated his multiple bruises, and encased his broken arm in plaster-of-paris. He was lying upon his bed, his left arm, stiffened by the cast, extending upward into the hot air of a house not yet blessed by the advent of air-conditioning, when his disconcerted Dad walked into the room. For a full minute, the two males faced each other without speaking a word – the suffering son and the dumfounded dad. J. C. looked at his offspring's skinned feet, bare when he dismounted his mount, bandaged in white gauze, and his knees, both which clearly displayed several stitches. The father gradually moved his eyes up his son's midsection, now covered with tape and punctuated with stitches. He slid his gaze out to Sonny Boy's broken arm, slowly following it all the way to his finger-tips which protruded from the white cement. Then he retraced his visual steps back down his son's arm, across his battered chest up to his expressionless face which, like the rest of his bruised body, was covered with cuts. Finally, the tall, dignified, and mystified parent, looking directly into his elder son's blank face, quietly and reflectively broke the apprehensive silence.

"I DO believe I have SIRED an IDIOT."

THE RAM

Sonny Boy wasn't the only Poole who appeared to be an idiot because of a cow. I did too, although obviously my last name disqualifies me from claiming pure-Poole rights. It happened in the Summer of 1949. I was 14 years old and already a starter on the Crosby High football team, big for my age back then, a svelte 170 lbs.

Like Sonny Boy's situation, our best milk cow tore out of the pasture, too. Unlike Sonny Boy's situation, she was our ONLY milk cow. We sent word to all our relatives and neighbors throughout the community that the cow had gotten out and asked that they be on the lookout for her. About noon the mail-rider, sitting in his car at our mailbox, honked his horn.

Normally the mail-rider honking his horn offered good news – probably a package too big for the mailbox, so I sprinted barefoot the 30 yards from our front porch to his car.

"Paige!"

"Yes, Sir."

"Mr. Hollis waved me down and asked me to tell you that a cow had gotten into his pasture. He thought it may be y'alls."

"Yes, Sir, it probably is. I'll tell Mama Poole."

Mr. Hollis Seale was a strange man, at least to

me, a mystical figure, seldom seen off his own farm, one of the few neighbors who never came to Mt. Vernon Methodist Church. Mama said the Seales were members of another church off somewhere which added to the mystery. Only rich folks could travel a distance to church.

Mr. Hollis differed from the rest of the Homochitto families another way too. He raised sheep, the only farmer in the community to do so. And he owned a ram, a big, mean-looking ram – with curved horns. I had seen the impressive creature many times from the school bus window, snorting, pawing the ground, chasing the ewes.

That's a mean animal," some school kid would comment almost every morning, as the bus rolled down the gravel road which circumvented Mr. Hollis' sheep pasture.

From Mama Poole's, the gravel road to Gloster and Crosby ran directly into the front of Mr. Hollis' house one mile away, where it then turned 90 degrees left, dropped down a hill for 200 yards, and turned 90 degrees right. The sheep pasture lay between the Seale home and the gravel road, which bordered the field on two sides. I hoped our cow had broken into one of Mr. Hollis' other fields and not the one containing the ram.

"Got your rope?" Mother called from the front porch as I started running toward the Seale's, wearing only a pair of UMAA athletic shorts, and barefoot. I turned my head back toward her and raised the rope, which I had coiled around my arm, above my head so she could see it. She waved and I kept jogging.

The mid-summer, high-noon sun splashed upon my thinly clad and darkened body like dirty dish water thrown from the kitchen door upon the bare ground. The few cumulus clouds were small patches of cotton pinned to a blue sheet, still, lifeless, anchored by stubborn air which refused to move. Like a great uncle blowing smoke rings from his corn-cob pipe, puffs of dust sprang from beneath my moving feet, and rocks on the gravel road challenged, uselessly, their hardened soles. Less than 10 sweaty minutes later I stood in front of Mr. Hollis.

I had never actually talked to Mr. Hollis alone, having seldom seen him that close. He was a large man dressed in over'hauls, as we Southerners often refer to them, about a two day's growth of beard upon his surprisingly friendly-looking face. He wore no shirt beneath the over'haul suspenders and an old felt hat, riddled with cut-out air vents, crouched upon his greying head. An encouraging twinkle brightened his eyes. Even so, I was a little apprehensive.

"How d'you do, Mr. Hollis?"

"Fine, son, how are you?"

"Fine. Mail-rider said our cow might be in your pasture."

"She might be. Walk right over here and you can see her, right down yonder," he pointed.

"Down yonder, Mr. Hollis? – down yonder in your sheep pasture?"

"Yeah – see her? – right yonder?" the old man pointed again.

"Yes, Sir, I see her. That's our cow alright. She in there with the ram?"

"Yeah, the ram's in there somewhere, maybe over on the backside."

"I've heard folks say that ram might be mean, Mr. Hollis," I pleaded, "reckon I oughta' go in there?"

"That ram won't bother you boy, he's a sheep. Sheep ain't mean. Now if he was a bull, you might want to worry 'bout him – but a ram? Naw, he won't bother you. Je'st go on in there and get your cow – that ram won't be no problem."

Mr. Hollis' eyes were still twinkling.

Fourteen year old Southern boys in 1949 neither argued with, nor doubted older men, not verbally, unless they were kin and prone to joking. If my uncles Buster and Ray, or great uncle Boss or Toad had told me what Mr. Hollis had just told me, I could be forgiven for wondering - but a stranger? A neighbor? I had no choice but to retrieve my cow. I could not call Mr. Hollis a liar.

"You can go through that gate right yonder, son. And after you get your cow, you can come back out the same way. The other gate is way down at the bottom of the hill."

"Yes, Sir."

I opened the gate and walked slowly down the inclined pasture toward my cow, who was grazing peacefully about two hundred yards away. Mr. Hollis leaned against the gate watching me. I couldn't see the ram although I did spot some ewes standing near a clump of trees about a hundred yards past ol' Shelly. I wanted to get a rope around the animal's neck as quietly as possible and get out of the pasture as quickly as possible. Although Mr. Hollis had convinced me the ram wasn't dangerous, I didn't want to test him. Maybe our primary source of milk will lend me a little cooperation, I hoped.

She didn't.

When I got within about 25 yards of my object, she jerked her head up, looked at me for a moment, lowed, turned and started trotting away.

I ran to her left, circled around her and turned her back toward the gate uphill. Mr. Hollis continued to watch – intently, still standing 30 degrees above me, 200 yards away.

Shelly started running again, and so did I – to head her off – several times. Each time I sprinted to get in front of her, I reduced the distance between us, until finally I dropped the noose around her neck. I had captured my prey and turned to lead her toward the gate where Mr. Hollis continued to stand, and watch.

Two important events occurred during my commotion with the cow. I became oblivious of everything except capturing her. And apparently the fuss attracted the attention of the ram, who must have been weathering the heat of the day in the clump of trees.

The sudden and intense pull upon the rope indicated quickly that all was not well. The intensifying sound of "clompity, clompity, clompity" provided the second clue. I turned my head toward the unnerving noise, yet confident in the assurances of the ram's owner, at the same moment my cow, who lacked my conviction, decided to desert me. "The approaching beast," I thought, "advanced only to inspect the invasion of his private domain." Running at half-speed he certainly seemed less than hostile, if not docile. My cow however, violently disagreed, and I suddenly found myself in a volcanic contest with a 400 lb. terrified animal. She had been too hard to capture to let her easily go. Stumbling but holding onto the rope, I focused all my attention onto her, assuming she offered my only REAL problem.

Shelly ripped the rough rope from my burning hands and I regained my balance just in time to realize that the clompity clomps had gotten much louder and with far less interval between them. I wheeled toward the charging brute, now no more than 10 yards away. He dropped his head and kept coming. Balanced upon the precipice of indecision and doubt, I stood there, still believing in the innocence of his intentions.

The raging ram hit me just about my knees!

I gained neither psychological nor physical preparedness for the contact. All I had time to do was jump and I elevated my bare feet 6 inches off the ground before impact. The snorting ram ran directly under me. By the time his steel-plated head and rock-hard body cleared the spot where once I stood, my feet and head had exchanged positions – perfectly. I crumpled upon the heat soaked grassy ground like a country boy falling from a broken tree limb. I caught myself on my hands, rolled on my back through a pile of fresh cow manure, and scrambled to my feet in time to see the mad sheep stop, turn, snort, paw the ground, and from only 5 yards away charge again.

He hit me a second time.

The same things happened to me.

Mr. Hollis, leaning now upon the gate laughed deeply and profusely.

He hit me a third time.

The same things happened to me.

That old man, bending over, laughed more deeply and profusely, his body shaking with the glee of rural entertainment.

He hit me a fourth time.

The same things happened to me.

That idiot on the hill, now on his knees, was losing his breath.

I was too easy. By the time I extricated myself from the ground, my new and formidable foe would be upon me again. Should I run? No, I can't outrun a ram.

Should I drop a shoulder and take him on–? That was stupid. Should I side-step him? – jump to one side? Maybe. Surely when he lowers his head he can't see me. I need something to hit him with, a baseball bat – a two-by-four – a shotgun!

Twenty yards away, an old corn crib, or perhaps hay crib had fallen, a pool of clear water upon an arid desert, an armored car. Maybe I could run in increments to it, find a weapon and at last offer token defense, if not offense. The maneuver would have to be accomplished in several small moves. I couldn't get there in one sprint. I wouldn't have time. The ram would hit me from behind.

He hit me a fifth time.

I got off the ground and dashed five yards, turned and partially evaded my adversary, jumping to my left. He caught part of my right leg and flipped me again. I quickly arose from the turf and ran another five yards and repeated the tactic – and then another five yards – and then another five yards. On one knee and looking at the now fully-incensed creature, I groped behind me for the weapon. My fingers encircled a piece of wood, a two-by-four, about 3 feet long. I sprang to my feet, drew my bat back like Joe Dimaggio and when the speeding fast-ball got within 3 feet of me, I "swung" – from the ground. The two-by-four against the enemy's horns cracked like the sound of a whip. It accomplished nothing.

The battering ram hit me again.

Now smeared with the oil of pain and dangling from a rope of hopelessness, I knew I had to find SOME way to end the agony. Maybe, just maybe, instead of swinging a two-by-four into cyclops' head, I could swing my right arm under his neck and bull-dog him, like Sonny Boy intended to bull-dog his runaway cow. We weighed about the same!

Yeah! It might work, especially if I could flip him onto his side and then fall on top of him. Running backs who crushed your helmet when hit head-on often went down easily when tackled from the side.

I got ready.

So did Bronko Nagurski. He snorted, pawed the ground and charged again.

I assumed my tackling stance, dropping my right hand to the ground, a fool about to attack a train – head on! Two yards away, the Cannonball Express dropped his head. I quickly stepped to my left and swung my right arm under the beast's neck and at the same time drove my right shoulder into his right side. Then I charged with all my strength, digging my bare toes into the grass covered ground. The attacker crashed to earth under my weight and I fell on top of him, a wrestler who finally threw his opponent, a defensive back who had been smeared for three and a half quarters, but managed a knock-out blow upon the fullback in the final minute of play, a tortoise who outran the hare.

My fallen antagonist struggled to rise against the force of my body, whimpered and lay still in defeat. But

I wasn't satisfied. I locked my hands under the ram's neck, dug my knees into his side with all my weight upon them, and pulled with all my strength, wanting only to hear the sound of breaking bone.

The helpless assailant rolled his eyes and emitted a loud, shrill cry.

So did the frantic farmer, who by now had lost his glee and with rope in hand, dashed madly toward me. "PAIGE, PAIGE, DON'T KILL MY RAM – PAIGE, DON'T KILL MY RAM!"

Vengeance, soaked by fear, wrapped in anger, knows no compassion.

I felt two arms slip around my body. "Paige, don't kill my ram. I've got a rope. I'll get him off of you."

"I'm gonna kill him, Mr. Hollis," I screamed, "besides, he ain't on me. I'm on him."

"I'll take care of him – just let him go – please."

I kept pulling.

"You get that rope around his neck, Mr. Hollis and I'll let him go, but I ain't gonna let him go 'til you do."

I felt the old man's arms loosen. Then he quickly tied the rope around his prize animal's head. I turned the ram loose, reluctantly, and stood to my feet. The whipped charger lay there, breathing heavily.

"You may have broken his neck, Paige."

"I hope I did break the son-of-a-bit – ah – gun's neck, Mr. Hollis," I retorted, as I brushed the grass and dirt off my sweaty body, "but I don't think I did. Did you see where my cow went?"

"Yes," he grunted and pointed. "She's right over there by the fence."

Indeed Shelly stood quietly by the fence, some 300 yards away, the rope still dangling from her brown neck, gazing mournfully in my direction. I walked slowly to her, reached down and grabbed the rope. She offered no resistance. "Um huh," I said. "You saw me whip that ram you were so afraid of, didn't you. Don't want none of ME, do you girl?"

Shelly's big brown eyes didn't reply.

A few minutes later, I unlatched the gate, led my troublemaker through it, and latched it again behind me. Only then did I glance toward the dynamic duo. The ram stood shakily on his feet and his relieved landlord seemed to be soothing the whipped animal's furrowed curved horn brow.

"Thank you, Mr. Hollis," I yelled and waved.

"You're welcome, son."

Twenty minutes later I led Shelly into our barnyard and took the rope off her neck. My mother, standing in the back yard, watched me move toward the well where I planned to draw some water and bathe.

"What happened to you, Son? And why is that cow manure all over your back?"

"Let me wash off some, Mother, and I'll tell you," I answered, "but you ain't gonna believe it."

"Don't say ain't, Son."

I told her the story. She believed it – just like I REALLY knew she would. Mothers always do.

Within a week or two, so did everyone else in the community.

Eight years later I pulled a Los Angeles Ram's helmet down hard upon my head and jogged proudly out upon their practice field for the first time. A thought suddenly coursed through my mind. "I'll bet I know better than all the rest of you why someone named a pro football team the Rams.